YASMINE

GALENORN

OAK &
THORNS

A WILD HUNT
NOVEL

BOOK 2

A Nightqueen Enterprises LLC Publication

Published by Yasmine Galenorn
PO Box 2037, Kirkland WA 98083-2037
OAK & THORNS
A Wild Hunt Novel
Copyright © 2018 by Yasmine Galenorn
First Electronic Printing: 2018 Nightqueen Enterprises LLC
First Print Edition: 2018 Nightqueen Enterprises
Cover Art & Design: Ravven
Art Copyright: Yasmine Galenorn
Editor: Elizabeth Flynn

A Nightqueen Enterprises LLC Publication
Published in the United States of America

Acknowledgments

Welcome to the world of the Wild Hunt. This is one of those series that has been haunting me for a while, and now, it's time to put pen to paper (fingers to keyboard) and let the stories out. And boy, do they want loose.

Thanks to my usual crew: Samwise, my husband, Andria and Jennifer—without their help, I'd be swamped. To the women who have helped me find my way in indie, you're all great, and to the Wild Hunt, which runs deep in my magick, as well as in my fiction.

Also, my love to my furbles, who keep me happy. And most reverent devotion to Mielikki, Tapio, Ukko, Rauni, and Brighid, my spiritual guardians and guides.

If you wish to reach me, you can find me through my website at Galenorn.com and be sure to sign up for my newsletter to keep updated on all my latest releases!

Brightest Blessings,
~The Painted Panther~
~Yasmine Galenorn~

Welcome to Oak and Thorns

Life isn't easy when you bear the mark of the Silver Stag.

I glanced up. Stalactites dripped down from the ceiling, sparkling with crystals of quartz. They flickered, illuminated from within. As we fully entered the chamber, the entire ceiling blazed to life, a brilliant light spreading throughout the network of crystals.

I blinked, momentarily blinded. As my eyesight adjusted, I found myself staring at a giant throne in the center of the room. It too appeared to be formed of roots and branches, twigs and limbs all knotting together in a woven tangle to create a giant chair. It, too, had sparkling crystals peeking out from crevices and nooks that hid between the branches.

Seated on the massive throne was an equally massive man.

His muscles rippled, his olive skin gleaming, showing every shadow and highlight of his muscles. His biceps and chest were bare, a topographical map chiseled in flesh. His hair was long, hanging in multiple braids that draped over his thighs. He wore a bearskin cloak and his face was illuminated by the crystals shining from both throne and ceiling.

Cernunnos's eyes were wide set, tilted like a cat's, and they flickered with gold and green lights, reminding me of faceted gems. His lips were full, and I saw where Herne got his good looks, but the Hunt Master's smile held the slightest hint of cruelty, although I didn't feel any sense of malice coming from him. But I knew that to cross him would be dangerous—deadly, no doubt. He stood as we approached.

I stared at him, stopping in my tracks when I realized he was wearing a pair of camo pants. I blinked, trying to take in the juxtaposition in his dress.

Herne led me up to the throne, where he went down on one knee, bowing his head. Since I wasn't wearing a dress, I felt odd curtseying, so I followed suit, lowering myself to one knee beside Herne.

Cernunnos towered over us, he was at least seven feet tall. He stared down at us for a moment and, as I snuck a peek, he caught my gaze and the haughty smile widened into a grin.

"Well met, Ms. Ember Kearney. So, I finally get to speak to the woman who has stolen my son's heart."

Oak & Thorns: Book 2 of the Wild Hunt Series

Chapter 1

I LEANED BACK in my seat, feet propped up on the desk, suspiciously eyeing the sunlight that gleamed through the blinds. It had been a chilly spring, with only sporadic sunshine, but now the weather seemed to be making up for lost time and the days were soaring into the seventies. I was grateful for the break from the rain and cool temperatures, but I wished I had time to get outside and enjoy it. The Wild Hunt had been swamped lately, and none of us had been able to take a day off for over three weeks.

Angel peeked around the door. "Got a minute?"

"For you? Any time." I waved her in. Angel was my best friend and roommate. She was also the receptionist for the agency.

"Guess what?" She entered the office and dropped a file folder on my desk. "Yet another new case."

"Oh, lovely." I stared at the folder for a moment, then grunted and lowered my feet to the floor. When I picked up the file and was about to drop it on another stack of folders sitting in my inbox, she stopped me.

"Not so fast. Take that file back *out* of the basket and read it. This one goes to the head of the pack." She slumped in the chair next to my desk, looking as tired as I felt.

"Another priority case?" I closed my eyes, wondering what miscreants we were going to have to corral this time, and whether they'd be Light or Dark Fae. Not that it mattered. Both sides of my bloodline were batshit crazy and I had ceased caring which side of the fence our targets hearkened from. "Who called us in on this one? Cernunnos or Morgana?"

Angel shook her head. "Neither. This is a private case."

I blinked. Herne was taking on a private case, *now*? The agency had been mired knee-deep in crap going down between the Dark and Light Courts to the point of where we should have advertised a two-for-one special. Apparently the feud between Névé and Saílle had been jammed full speed ahead, given how many fires we had been called on to extinguish. Some of them literally. A week ago, the Dark Court had taken potshots at a warehouse owned by Navane and they had burned it down.

I hadn't been the only one wishing business would slow down. We *all* needed some breathing time. But I still had four open cases sitting on my desk, although they were all private. Stamping out *collateral damage* cases—or CDs, as we called them—always took priority.

Five cases, I corrected myself, now that Angel had added another to the mix. I retrieved the file from the wire basket and squinted at it as I read the label.

FOAM BORN POD—WHIDBEY ISLAND

"So, what's this?" I ruffled through the intake pages, frowning.

"As I said, it's a private case. Herne wants you to sit in on the conference with the new client."

"When?"

"Now." Angel reached in her pocket and tossed me a candy bar. "Eat up."

I groaned. Angel and I had made plans to go out to lunch at Joe's Burgers, but this shot that idea to hell. My stomach rumbled at the sight of the chocolate, and I peeled open the wrapper. "I love chocolate, but it's not a good stand-in for a sandwich."

She grinned. "Take heart. I'm going to run out and get some fish and chips for our lunch. I should be back by the time your meeting's over. I imagine Herne will call an agency meeting if he decides to take this case, so we'll just eat here."

"What's the case about?" I skimmed the form until I came to the line regarding the client's reason for approaching the Wild Hunt Agency. It looked like she—I assumed it was a she, given her name was Rhiannon—wanted us to look into a murder. *Great.* Another dead body. At least the case wasn't a CD case.

"The only thing I know is that it's an unsolved murder case. A cold case, no less." Angel shrugged. "The Foam Born Pod are a group of hippocampi who live up on Whidbey Island."

"Hippocampus? I didn't know we had any of those around here."

Not many people knew who the hippocampi were. Fewer still understood the nature of the water-horse shifters. While in the water, a hippocampus took the form of an actual water horse— but not the cute little seahorse creatures bobbing around in the ocean.

No, a hippocampus had the front half of a horse, with the tail of the fish. And they were huge. As they rose out of the water onto the shore, they could turn into startlingly beautiful white horses, or into human form. When a pod of them emerged together, it was astounding to watch as the elegant white horses came racing out of the sea foam. Poseidon hired some of them as his steeds in the depths of the ocean. They were as elegant in their water-horse form as they were on land.

"I had never heard of them, so after she filled out the form, I took the opportunity to do a search. It's amazing what you can find on the Net." Angel giggled, rolling her eyes. "Never search on 'horse people' with safe-search off."

"I can imagine." I pushed myself to my feet. "I'd better get in there before Herne comes looking for me."

"Somehow I don't think you'd object to that," Angel said, a knowing smile on her face.

I snorted, glaring at her, but she knew I didn't

4

mean it.

Herne and I had been dating for three months, and I was just settling into the idea that I was in an actual relationship again. So far, so good. We hit it off, and our chemistry was like flash powder—igniting at the slightest touch. Add to that, we enjoyed each other's company. I just hadn't quite come to terms with the fact that I was dating the son of a god.

I TAPPED ON Herne's office door, waited a moment, then quietly opened it. Peeking in, I caught his attention. He waved for me to take a seat by the desk.

Herne's office was a veritable jungle of plants, with walls the color of robin's-egg blue, and a white ceiling that was suggestive of clouds. A huge rack of antlers was mounted on the wall, polished and glowing. They were a nod to his father—Cernunnos, the Lord of the Forest. Beneath them sat Herne's desk, old walnut, dark and gleaming, and he sat in a leather chair behind the massive desk.

The room held two pairs of wingback chairs, one set by the desk, the other guarding an end table. Against the wall near the chairs and end table stood a locked glass case, holding several crossbows, a number of daggers, a sword, and various other weapons. A daybed in the corner, complete with comforter and pillow, provided him with a place to catch a nap when he was working late on a case. All in all, the office felt like old money, luxurious but not indulgent.

An elegant woman was sitting in one of the chairs by his desk. Her pale skin had a faint tinge of blue to it, and her hair was plaited back into a long braid, creamy white and looking as soft as spun silk. In comparison, her features were chiseled, angular to the point of rigid. She had rich brown eyes, and she was dressed in a cerulean linen pantsuit.

Herne stood as I approached the desk. Close to six feet tall, his shoulder-length hair was swept back in a neat ponytail, and his beard was well trimmed. He was lean and muscled, with piercing blue eyes that shimmered with a magical light. Every time I looked at him, my pulse raced. I knew every inch of his body by now. Beneath those tight black jeans and that hunter green V-neck sweater, Herne truly had the body of a god.

"Rhiannon of the Foam Born, I'd like to present Ember Kearney, one of our investigators. I asked her to sit in on our meeting since this is a complicated case."

Etiquette in the world of Fae demanded that I allow her to dictate whether we shook hands. I gave Rhiannon a gracious nod, and she gently held out one hand, so I accepted with a firm shake.

"How do you do?" I sat in the chair next to Herne's desk.

"Pleased to meet you, Ember." She gave me an appraising look, one that I was well acquainted with. Anybody connected with the Fae could usually pinpoint my heritage.

"So the rumors are true. You are one of the…" She stopped, her cheeks flaming, come to life from their delicate porcelain. "Forgive me," she stammered. "I didn't mean—"

"I understand. There really isn't a good term for my heritage." I knew what she had been about to say, and it wasn't a word that I'd expect out of such a pretty mouth. Technically, in the common Fae tongue, I was what was known as *tralaeth*, or *tainted blood*.

I was half Light Fae, half Dark Fae, and I was anathema to both sides. Neither court accepted me. In fact, I was considered an insult to the race, even though they pretended my kind couldn't possibly exist. My parents had been murdered because of their love, and if I had been home at the time, I would have been killed as well.

"I truly didn't mean any insult," Rhiannon said, casting her gaze at the floor.

She sounded so sincere that I believed her. I wasn't one to hold a grudge if somebody made an honest mistake.

"Why don't we start over? I'm Ember Kearney, and you're Rhiannon of the Foam Born, and here we are."

Herne took it from there. "Now that the introductions are over, Rhiannon, why don't you tell us what the problem is. I wanted Ember to be here, because when I looked over your intake chart, it's obvious that this case will require our entire agency's focus. *If* we accept the job, that is. And it's always helpful to have a second set of ears present during the initial meeting. Do you mind if I record our conversation?" He held up a digital recorder. "It helps me focus on what you're saying rather than me having to take notes."

I pulled out a notebook. "I prefer pen and paper." I winked at her.

"I don't mind." She took a deep breath, and her smile faded.

Herne clicked on his recorder, recited the date and the case number, and then asked Rhiannon again if she agreed to the conversation being recorded.

"That's fine."

"Please state your name for the record."

"I'm Rhiannon, the Matriarch of the Foam Born Encampment."

"And why are you here today?"

She cleared her throat. "I'm here because a little over a year ago, my cousin Jona disappeared. He was missing for over a week."

"What was he doing when he vanished?" Herne asked.

"He was on his way to a meeting over at the grange."

"Grange?" I knew the word "grange" meant farmhouse in the UK, but I wasn't familiar with any other use for the term. "You mean your house?"

"No. On Whidbey Island, the SubCult still has a grange." She paused, then realizing I really *didn't* understand, added, "The grange is a farmers' organization. A number of the Foam Born are small farmers. My cousin raises blueberries. It may seem an outdated custom, but the S-C Grange—the

SubCult Grange—offers our community a chance to talk over issues that human farmers don't have. And trust me, there are plenty."

"Thank you," I said as I jotted down the reference.

"Anyway, Jona was headed for a meeting over at the grange and he never showed up. Nobody there thought anything was wrong when he didn't show, because Marilyn had recently had a baby. That's Jona's wife. The other farmers thought he stayed home to help her. It wasn't until Jona didn't come home after the meeting that anybody realized anything was wrong. Marilyn started to worry around ten P.M., the usual time Jona returned from the meetings. But sometimes they can run late, so she waited until near midnight before texting him. When he didn't answer, she called him and was sent right to voicemail. That's when she contacted the sheriff."

Herne chewed on his lip. "What day did he vanish?"

"May thirty-first. So it's been a little over a year."

"Do you remember what the weather was like?" I wasn't sure if it would be pertinent, but it made sense to gather every scrap of information we could.

"It was raining. We had a big thunderstorm that afternoon. After the thunder and lightning passed, the rain came down the rest of the day. It didn't let up for a week." Rhiannon stared at the floor. "Before the police arrived, Marilyn called me and I hurried over to their place. His parents are still over near Greece. They stayed behind under the water when we decided to immigrate to the land, so Marilyn turned to me. You see, Jona and I grew up together. He was my best friend."

"How did Jona and Marilyn get along? Were they happy?"

I wasn't sure how he managed it, but Herne had the ability to ask discerning questions like that without insulting the client. Somehow, he inserted just the right inflection into his tone to avoid sounding like a jerk. It was a skill I admired, but hadn't been able to emulate.

"Marilyn and Jona adored each other. They were married for about three years. They wanted to start a family right away, and they were thrilled when she got pregnant. There was a scare with the baby, but it only brought them closer together."

"What kind of scare?" I asked.

Rhiannon's eyes misted over. "Ryan almost died during his birth. Marilyn's labor came on so fast that she didn't have time to get down to the shore. Our people must be born beneath the water or they'll suffocate. It was touch and go whether she'd make it to the water before he came out, but luckily a neighbor had a swimming pool. He offered it to her for a birthing pool and everything worked out. Anyway, I don't think I've ever seen anybody as much in love as they were. When Jona died, it devastated Marilyn. I think that Ryan is the only reason she managed as well as she did."

"Walk us through what happened. What did the sheriff do?"

"She asked a lot of the same questions you are. Both the sheriff and her deputy are Fae. I think

Light Fae. They followed the path Jona took to the grange. Even though it was raining, he decided to walk. My people aren't shy about water. But they didn't find anything out of the ordinary. The next morning, a search party went out the moment dawn broke. They combed the area but the only thing they found was his phone, which was under a bush. It looked like there might have been a scuffle in the mud. It was difficult to tell, though, given how hard it was raining." Rhiannon shook her head. "We *all* went searching for him, but it was as though he had just vanished from the face of the earth. At least, until a week later, when they found his body."

"Would you like a glass of water?" I asked. She looked far too pale for comfort, even though I knew that was her natural pallor. Herne flashed me a silent thank-you.

Over the past couple of months I had learned to break the tension by offering to fetch water or coffee or anything else that would give our clients a chance to gather their thoughts. It gave them time to breathe when they were talking about painful subjects, and it tended to prevent breakdowns in the office.

"Yes, thank you," she said. "I still can't believe he's gone. It's been a year and I *still* expect him to come dashing around the corner, laughing and saying it was a bad joke." The tears were thick in her throat, but she maintained her composure, only her eyes exposing the sorrow in her heart.

I poured her a glass of water from the jug on the sideboard. Herne waited for a moment before he asked the next question.

"Where did they find his body?"

She flinched, closing her eyes briefly. Then, taking a deep breath, she answered.

"At the bottom of the ravine, near the shore. The police didn't let us know until the next day. I'm not sure why they waited so long, except they probably didn't want us mucking up the crime scene. Jona...his body had been mangled. He had over a hundred puncture wounds on him, but the coroner couldn't tell us what caused them. Apparently, his throat was so scratched up inside that it looked like someone had taken a giant razor blade and shoved it down his throat, scraping it round and round. There was no blood left in his body."

The tension rose in the room and I could tell she was trying to keep control. I waited a beat, then asked, "Vampire?"

In cases of exsanguination, that was always my first thought.

"That's what the police thought. Or at least, what they told us. Any of those punctures on his body could have been from a fang, they said. But what kind of vampire bites their victim all over their body? And how the hell did they rip up his throat from the inside? We asked a lot of questions, and got a whole lot of nothing for an answer."

"They wouldn't tell you anything else?"

"Well, one of the deputies made the mistake of telling us that Jona had been alive as recently as the day before, but the sheriff barked at him and he clammed up. So whoever had him kept him alive for a while." Again, she closed her eyes. We all knew what that meant.

"Were all the wounds made at the same time? The coroner would be able to figure that out."

"I have no clue. We asked, but as I said, nobody ever got back to us."

Herne was frowning. "Did they say anything else? Anything at all?"

She thought for a moment, then shook her head. "A few days later, the cops told us they would probably never be able to find the killer because 'vampires move around too much.' The case is still unsolved, even though they stamped 'vampire kill' on it. But since we don't know exactly who killed him, it's considered a cold case. And everybody knows that once you label a death as a vampire kill, you might as well kiss any further investigation good-bye."

The look on her face told us what she thought of the way the police had handled the case.

"Did anybody ever come forward? Were there any witnesses?" I was finding myself pulled in.

She shrugged. "I don't know. The police shut us down. All they would say was that we needed to let it go and move on. It's been a year, but after the first two weeks, I don't think they lifted a finger on the case."

"Why did you wait until now to come to us?"

It was never easy to fathom why our clients came to us when they did, especially with older cases like this, but we always asked. Usually there was some sort of trigger that sparked off the sudden desire to find a resolution.

Rhiannon worried her lip for a moment.

"Marilyn has tried to make a life for herself and her son. As she should. Three weeks ago, she confided in me that she was going on her first date since Jona died. She said that she owed it to her son to move on. I guess..."

"You aren't ready to move on," I said softly.

She nodded. "It feels like everybody has forgotten Jona. I suppose I'm angry. Oh, I didn't say anything, because I wouldn't hurt her for the world, and I know she's doing what she needs to. But Jona was brutally murdered and everybody's acting as though he just moved away. I want closure, damn it. I want to know who murdered him. Every time I go to the police—and I've been there several times throughout the past year—they've told me go home and talk to a therapist. They say there's no way they can ever figure out who killed him. But I know full well that it wasn't a vampire."

And there it was, her reason for sitting here in our office, asking us to help.

"Playing devil's advocate for just a moment," Herne said, "*why* don't you think a vampire killed him? I'm just trying to get a feel for what strikes the wrong chord for you."

Marilyn hesitated, then said, "I've become acquainted with some of the local vampires. Every single one of them told me that it couldn't be a vampire kill. They keep close tabs on their community. One of the vampires—his name is Rayne—told me to look into the history of the island. I'm not sure why, but that's all he would say. So I decided to come to you. I chose you because I've heard of the work you do, and you aren't on the island. I didn't want anybody who might be..."

"Paid off by the authorities?" Herne asked, a faint smile on his face.

She nodded. "Yes. Exactly."

He tapped his fingers on the desk. "You do realize this will be an expensive investigation? We'll have to drive up to Whidbey Island and stay for a few days, at the very least. And we can't guarantee any results, although we will do our very best."

Rhiannon waved off his comments. "I'm the Matriarch of the Foam Born Encampment. With that title comes the keys to the treasure chest. I can afford your fees."

"All right." Herne began jotting down a string of numbers and I realized he was putting together an estimate of the retainer.

Without skipping a beat, she pulled out her checkbook. "Just name the figure and I'll write you a check right now."

Herne looked at me. "What do you think? Should we take this on? We've had a busy season and I know everybody's tired."

It sounded like a difficult case, but I wanted to take it. There was something behind this—something that wasn't right. "Hey, for a chance to get away to Whidbey Island? Even though we'll be on a case, I can use some time out of the city, and I think the rest of us can, as well." The thought of getting away to the relatively unpopulated island where we could breathe clean air and saltwater appealed to me.

"All right," he said, nodding. He turned back to Rhiannon. "How about if we drive up to Whidbey

Island for a few days? We'll see what we can find out. If it looks like the case is going to hit a brick wall, we'll call it quits. I don't want to drain your bank account. If we *do* find anything, then you can make a decision whether you want us to continue." He pulled out a retainer form and jotted a few notes on it. "Take this form to Angel at the front desk. You can pay her and she'll give you a receipt. We have to wrap up some things here in the city, but we can start in a couple of days. Will that work?"

Rhiannon breathed a long sigh of relief and nodded. "Thank you. Just knowing that you're going to even take a stab at it gives me some hope. And right now hope is all I've got." She stood, shaking our hands. Then, clutching the form that Herne had given her, she exited the office, closing the door softly behind her.

Chapter 2

"WHAT DO YOU think?" I asked, turning to Herne after she left.

He slipped from behind the desk, stopping by my side. As he slid his arm around my waist and pulled me to him, I caught my breath. His very touch set me on fire. This had been the first time in a while that I had been able to sustain a relationship without something deadly happening to one of my boyfriends.

"What I think," he said softly, "is that you should give me a kiss."

He kissed my nose, then tilted my chin up with one finger as he bent down, pressing his lips against mine. They were warm against my own, yet his kiss was demanding as he pressed himself close. It was one of those kisses that said, *"You belong to me."*

I moaned. I wanted to rip my clothes off right

here in his office, but I had more self-restraint than that. Although more than once I had thought seriously about doing just that. But Herne and I did our best to keep it professional at work, limiting ourselves to stolen kisses. It wasn't that everybody didn't know we were knocking boots. We just didn't want them to be too uncomfortable, given how loud we could both be.

"That's better," he said. "I missed you last night. And the night before. And the night before that."

Angel and I had been attending a week-long series of evening seminars. Given the time we spent there, plus our workload, it had been several days since Herne and I had had a chance to get in a good fuck-fest. And right now, standing so close to him, that was all I could think about.

I pressed my hand against his chest, feeling his heartbeat. Even the gods had hearts. "You were the one who suggested Angel and I take a course on police investigation for the layman."

"It made sense at the time," he whispered, taking my hand and kissing each finger in turn.

Even though I had been a freelance investigator, I haven't dealt much with the police. And Angel had steered clear of them as much as she could. The course was giving us insight into how investigations were run, although the teacher conveniently sidestepped the fact that the Fae heavily influenced the police. Just like the vampires stacked the deck at Wall Street, the Fae manipulated the puppet strings of the police. There wasn't much anybody could do about either situation, so most people ignored it and went on as usual.

"I've missed you too. It's been almost a week," I said, thinking that I actually had *missed* him. While I enjoyed my time with Herne, probably more than I wanted to admit, I still needed my privacy and time spent with my friends. Although, to be honest, I didn't have many friends beyond Angel. She and I had been BFFs since childhood, but otherwise I had been a loner until I came to work for the Wild Hunt.

"Trust me, I'm feeling the lack." The way he said it made me stare at him for a moment. He sounded hungry. Very, very hungry. I could see it in his eyes.

"Dude, remember, I'm not immortal, even though I am Fae. I bruise." But I winked, and he laughed.

"I promise, I'll take it easy on you. So, are you busy tonight?"

Reluctantly, I nodded. "It's the last night of the seminar and I don't want to miss it. You were right, I think this is going to be a big help to us. Angel and I are learning a lot. And given how busy we've been the past few days, I'm already dead tired. So, changing the subject, when do we leave for Whidbey Island?"

"Day after tomorrow, I figure. And changing the subject right back, what about a rain check? To-morrow night?" He wiggled his eyebrows, making me laugh.

I conceded, planting a kiss on his cheek. "Sounds good. Do you want to call a staff meeting this afternoon?"

"I think we'd better. We have some research to

do before we leave. Go ahead and alert the others. We'll meet in half an hour. That will give people time to order in lunch. Meanwhile, as delightful as you are, I have a few calls I have to return." He kissed me again, then let go of me. "Remember— half an hour." As he waved me out, turning back to his desk, I shut the door behind me.

Angel was waiting at her desk.

"You were right. Meeting in half an hour." I sniffed the air, the smell of fish and chips hanging heavy, and my salivary glands went into overdrive. "That smells so good. Please tell me you bought enough for me?"

"I bought enough for *both* of us." She held up a sack that read ANTON'S FISH SHACK on it. "Why don't you go ahead and tell the others about the meeting? I'll meet you outside on the stoop. We might as well catch a little sunshine while we can."

I nodded, heading back to the other offices.

DOWNTOWN SEATTLE WAS a jumble of stately old brick and modern chrome and glass. The streets showed signs of neglect, with too many potholes and crumbling patches of asphalt, but all in all, the city was beautiful. At night, when the neon was blaring, and during the long rains, Seattle could feel gritty and cold. But right now with the sun shining, and the *streeps*—the people who lived in the back alleys, and the homeless shelters—blasting out their music as they danced on the sidewalks, it was a welcoming place.

The Wild Hunt Agency was on First Avenue, in a five-story brick walkup. We had the entire fourth floor to ourselves. At least the building superintendent had finally fixed the elevator. The fifth floor was empty, but a low-income urgent care clinic had taken over the bottom floor, a daycare and preschool had control of the second, and the third floor belonged to a combination yoga and dance studio. I was grateful they weren't on the floor above us, because every time we passed by when dance class was in session, the noise was overwhelming.

I joined Angel on the stoop. She had claimed a place on one of the wide stone railings. It was seventy-two degrees, with barely a cloud in the sky, and I sucked in a lungful of the air, coughing as a cloud of exhaust hit me from a passing car.

Across the street, a series of fetish brothels with darkened windows waited for evening to entice their customers. On one side of our building, the smells of sandwiches and pizza wafted out from Nigel's Deli. On the other side, old men shuffled near the entrance of the Spank-o-Rama, another fetish shop.

The kinky boutiques were everywhere, but they brought in good tax revenue for the city and were well-regulated, keeping out the world of pimps who desperately tried to eke out a living by trading flesh for dollars. Legalized prostitution was pushing them out of business, even as it kept the hookers and sex workers safe, and forced them to have regular checkups.

Angel handed me a white cardboard carton. "Here. Never say I don't love you."

I opened it, finding two servings of fish and chips. "Bless you." My stomach protested that it had waited far too long, thank you, and would I feed it *now*.

"I wish I could eat like you do," she said. "Then again, I'd be broke." Angel was human, which meant her appetite wasn't as big as mine. The Fae ate a lot.

The sun glowed against her skin, which was a beautiful golden brown. Angel could have been a model, she was so striking. At five foot ten, she had a dancer's body. Her tightly crimped curls were caught back in a neat ponytail, and she was wearing a pair of black leggings with a blue tunic that acted like a mini dress.

I rested my container on the railing between us and hopped up on the wide stone slab.

In contrast to Angel, I was five-seven, and one hundred and fifty pounds of boobs, muscle, and contrariness. My hair was wavy, though not as curly as hers, and it reached the middle of my back. I usually kept it back in a braid, but today it was hanging loose, falling over my shoulders. I was wearing a pair of torn jeans, my knees poking out, and a snuggly fitted tank top that was vivid blue, which contrasted against my pale skin. We had been so busy that I hadn't had a chance to do laundry for over a week and was wearing my clean but ragbag-destined clothes.

I bit into the fish, letting out a contented sigh as the flavors of salt and fat and cod trickled down my throat. "We get to go to Whidbey Island," I said after swallowing.

"Want to make a bet I have to stay here to man the desk? I could sure use a couple days away." She picked at her french fries, holding one up. "Limp. Figures." With a sigh, she added, "I suppose I shouldn't complain. I got to see DJ last month, even though we were so busy that I wasn't sure Herne would let me have the time off."

DJ was Angel's brother, or rather, her half-brother. Ten years old, he was Wulfine—half wolf shifter. Angel had taken care of him after their mother died and did her best to make a good life for him, but working for the Wild Hunt could put DJ's life in danger, and so Herne convinced Angel to let a shifter family take care of him. It'd been a difficult adjustment for them both, but being able to visit him regularly made a world of difference.

"I doubt he'll make you stay behind. We all need a rest. Even though this isn't going to be a vacation, just getting out of the city sounds so freaking good."

"I like that idea," she said. "So, ready for our last night of the seminar?"

"More than ready. It's interesting, but honestly, I'm exhausted. I even turned down a date with Herne after class because I'm so tired."

At that moment, a car pulled up across from the building. It looked familiar, but I couldn't place it until the door opened and a man stepped out. It was Ray Fontaine, my ex-boyfriend who had gone from friend to stalker with a startling rapidity.

"Oh fucking hell. Just what I need." I stood up,

staring at him without a smile. What the hell did he want this time? Besides for me to take him back, that is.

"Should we just go inside?" Angel touched my elbow, watching Ray with a wary look as he crossed the street toward us.

I shook my head. "It wouldn't do any good. He'd just follow us up to the office."

I had dated Ray briefly, ending our relationship months ago. We hadn't even slept together. I called it quits when I realized that I was going to put him in danger. Since he was human, he didn't stand much of a chance against my lifestyle. Most of my other boyfriends had ended up seriously injured or dead and after thinking about it, I had decided to shut down that side of my life.

Until I came to work for the Wild Hunt, I had been a freelance investigator, and I had encountered more than my share of nasty creatures. Unfortunately, humans bruised easier than members of the SubCult. Ray had a nasty scar on his body to prove it. So I broke it off before one of my adversaries ended up taking him out for good.

Everything had been fine until he called me to look over a break-in at his bakery, and it was then that his obsessive nature had presented itself. Ever since then, he had phoned me, texted me all the time, although I never responded, sent me bouquet after bouquet of flowers, and parked outside my condo building more than once, waiting for me to get home. I had repeatedly told him to stop, and had refused every gift that he sent me, but he refused to listen.

I folded my arms, saying nothing as he approached. Angel stood beside me, looking as stoic as I felt.

"I called you ten times last week. Why won't you answer? Why won't you call me back?"

I shook my head. "I told you to leave me alone. I'll tell you once again: Ray, I don't want to talk to you, I don't want your gifts, and I don't want you around. What's so hard to understand?"

His expression shifted from determined to petulant. "You *owe* me. You owe me an explanation, and an apology."

I was quickly losing my patience. "I owe you *nothing*. How dense are you? We've been over for a long time. Go away. Leave me alone."

"No, we're not over! You still love me. I know it, because I still love you. Ember, you can't just walk away from me. I won't let you go. We're meant to be together."

For a man who made the best doughnuts in the city, he was distressingly divorced from reality. But if there was one thing I had learned during the past year, it was that you didn't have to be dysfunctional in *every* part of your life to be a nut job.

"I'm done. Keep bothering me and I'll call the police." It was an empty threat—oh, I'd call them, but they wouldn't do anything. But it sounded good. I turned to head up the stairs but before I could take another step, Ray grabbed me from behind. He managed to get hold of my wrist and tried to drag me down to the sidewalk.

"Please, just talk to me. I know you'll change your mind if you just talk to me."

Startled, I almost tripped over the steps. Immediately, I began to pull away. Ray was strong, but I was stronger. I shook him off, but as I started to back up on the stairs, my boot heel caught on a crack and I fell backward, landing hard against the concrete stoop.

"Leave her alone," Angel said, hurrying down to my side.

"Stay out of this, it's none of your business." Ray shot her a nasty look.

I took the opportunity to push myself to my feet, and before he could grab me again, I shoved him away. We were three steps from the sidewalk and he went tumbling down to the concrete, landing on his ass. He jumped up, his eyes flashing dangerously.

"You shouldn't have done that, Ember."

I turned to Angel. "Get on in, he's off his rocker."

I reached for the dagger strapped to my thigh. If Ray wanted to play rough, I'd play rough. I kept my eye on him as I began to back up the stairs, one cautious step at a time. Ray would reach me before I made the top, but I didn't want to turn around to run. Never give your opponent the edge, and presenting my back would give him an edge.

"You fucking women. You treat us like dirt, you lead us on, you make promises and then you break them, and we're supposed to turn around and run away with our tails tucked between our legs. Not anymore."

I held up my dagger. "I will use this if you push it. I told you to go away and leave me alone. I told you we're done. I told you I'm never going to start up with you again. What more do I have to say to get you to believe me? Do I have to fucking beat the crap out of you?"

Apparently, that was a challenge. He snorted, then began to bound up the stairs toward me. But two steps in, he froze, staring beyond me, an uncertain light in his eyes.

From behind me, a voice boomed out. "Think twice before making another move."

Oh shit. *Herne.* I froze. If Ray knew what was good for him, he'd turn around and run right now.

"Ember, what's going on?" Herne appeared by my side, never taking his eyes off of Ray.

"Once again, I was trying to convince Ray to leave me alone." I hadn't told Herne much about what Ray had been pulling, more for Ray's sake than anything else. I had been hoping that he would quietly withdraw. Calling the cops wouldn't do any good—it never did in situations like this, unless you either had money or your stalker managed to hurt you first. But Herne...he could do some serious damage to Ray, and I knew he would if I said the word.

"How long has this been going on?" Once again, Herne kept his focus on Ray.

"For several months," Angel spoke up. "I know Ember was hoping he'd stop, but it's time to stop covering for him."

Herne stepped in front of me and started down the steps toward Ray. "When a woman tells you to leave her alone, you *leave her alone.* What's so difficult to understand about that?"

I wasn't sure just how much Ray knew about

Herne, but I doubted that he knew Herne was the son of a god.

"Don't interfere, man. Ember just needs to realize how much I mean to her." But there was a flicker of hesitation in his voice, one that made me question just how much Ray actually *believed* what he had been saying to me.

At that moment, Angel tugged on my elbow, motioning for me to join her a few steps higher. "He's not crazy," she whispered. "He knows full well what is going on. He's just trying to fuck with your head."

"You mean he's just been harassing me because he's a jerk?"

It was bad enough thinking Ray had asked for a divorce from reality, but if he really was just harassing me to make my life miserable, then as far as I was concerned, Herne could twist him in knots. Angel was an empath, and she had the ability to sense when people were lying. If she said that he was fully cognizant of the situation, I believed her.

"Oh, yeah. This is the first time I've been close enough to him to feel out the situation. I can tell you right now, he knows exactly how to push your buttons. He doesn't think you love him. I don't even think he loves you. He's just being an ass-hole."

I hadn't caught what else Herne had said to Ray while I had been talking to Angel, but at that moment Ray puffed up and pointed to the sidewalk.

"Seriously? I'd think twice over challenging me." Herne flexed his fingers.

I groaned. The thought of two men fighting over me wasn't a scenario I had ever longed for. I wasn't into drama, but I resisted the impulse to race down and intervene. Ray had set the stage for this, he needed to take the fall.

"Prove it, pretty boy. Put up or shut up," Ray said.

By that point, the two men were on the sidewalk. Ray was blustering, and I wondered why I had ever found him attractive. But the Ray I had first met had conveniently hid his contempt for women, his controlling nature, and his lack of impulse control.

At that moment, Ray gave Herne a little shove on one shoulder. I leaned against the wide railing, glancing at Angel, who rolled her eyes and shook her head. As we watched, Herne picked up Ray and, in one smooth move, threw him halfway across the street. He crossed his arms, waiting, as Ray flopped around, then managed to pick himself up.

The look on Ray's face made me break out in nervous giggles. He looked stunned. He obviously hadn't expected that response. For a moment, he fidgeted, still standing in the middle of the street, until a car headed directly toward him. Ray darted back to his own car, shooting laser-sharp glances toward Herne. Then, he slammed himself into the driver's seat and screeched out of his parking spot.

Herne let out a loud sigh. "Are you all right?" He jogged back up the steps to my side.

I nodded. "Thank you. I don't know why he's intent on trying to make me miserable, but something set him off a few months ago."

"You need to be careful. He's not crazy, he's just pissed out of his mind. Crazy, we can deal with. But that sort of deep-seated anger can be deadly." Herne wrapped his arm around my waist as we headed for the elevator, followed by Angel.

I wasn't sure how, but I needed to defuse the situation, and defuse it quickly.

AS WE GATHERED around the table in the break room, Angel prepared a fresh pot of coffee. She had settled into her job quickly, and seemed content. In fact, both of us had become far more comfortable over the past few months, and it didn't hurt that we were making more money than we ever had before. Oh, we weren't rich, but we could actually make ends meet and still have some left over at the end of the month. Shopping was no longer confined to the thrift shops and garage sales.

Without missing a beat, Herne slid into his chair and turned to Talia, our resident researcher. A harpy who had lost most of her powers, Talia was an older woman with long silver hair, kept out of her face by small braids on either side, caught back by a butterfly barrette. She was neatly dressed, wearing a pair of tan culottes, and a black linen tank top. A narrow gold belt encircled her wasp waist, and as usual, she looked perfectly pulled together.

"I want you to look up Ray Fontaine. He owns

the bakery over on the Eastside—A Touch of Honey, I believe it is. Find out everything you can on him." Herne glanced at me. "He's been harassing Ember, and it's going to stop. I want you to dig up every skeleton in his closet."

For a moment, I felt guilty, then shook it off. That's what friends were for. They helped you bury the bodies and hide the shovel.

"Second, and more important at this point, we're starting a new case day after tomorrow. It's on Whidbey Island, and it's private."

Yutani frowned, glancing over at him. "Are we driving there every single day? That's a long haul."

"Yes, it is, which is why we're going to stay there for a few days." Herne flipped open his file. "We should plan on being there at least three or four days. It may take longer, depending on whether we find enough evidence to warrant taking the case any further."

He ran down what Rhiannon had told us, hitting the high points.

"Tomorrow, I want Talia and Yutani to find out whatever you can about Jona—Rhiannon's cousin. Also find out whatever you can about his murder. I'll make a couple phone calls and dig up any dirt I can through official channels. Since Cernunnos and Morgana aren't behind this, we may find it harder going. But a few people owe me favors, so I'll see what I can find out."

"The hippocampi, what are they like?" Viktor asked, crossing to the refrigerator to poke around inside. Viktor was half-ogre, startlingly tall and brawny, with a smooth bald head that he kept well oiled. He was also brilliant, and one hell of an investigator. Viktor had his sensitive side, though, and all around, I liked him.

"They're water horses, at least while they're in the water. On land they can take either horse or human shape. They're relatives of the Fae, but they don't consider themselves part of the Fae community. They tend to hold themselves above and beyond. They are a proud people, but not snobbish. At least, that's my takeaway from the interactions I've had with them," Herne said.

"Why do you think the cops wouldn't look into the murder?" Yutani asked.

"I don't know. That's one thing we need to find out. I don't think Rhiannon was holding anything back about her cousin, and it sounds like he was happy. But if this had been a run-of-the-mill homicide, you'd think the cops would have done their best to find the murderer." Herne leaned back in his chair, tapping the table with a pencil. "Something has been bothering me about this case since we talked to Rhiannon, but I don't know what. I just feel like there's more here than meets the eye, so if anything triggers an alarm, be sure to mention it."

"When she filled out the intake form, I can tell you that Rhiannon was really upset. I think she really loved her cousin." Having Angel as the receptionist meant that we were able to use her empathic sense as a first impression. Herne had been one smart cookie to hire her.

Herne nodded. "Okay. We'll meet tomorrow at noon to compare notes. Yutani and Talia, use the rest of the day for research. Viktor, go through the armory and decide what we might need. It's hard to say until we know what we're up against, but we'll want to take an assortment of weaponry."

"What should I do?" I asked.

"If you could update the paperwork on all of the cases we've closed in the past couple weeks, that would be great. I doubt if you can finish all of the notes, but do what you can. Angel, find a hotel for us on Whidbey Island near the hippocampi encampment. A moderately priced one. Make reservations." Herne consulted his tablet. "We'll check in on Thursday. Also, find out when the ferry sails, and plan our itinerary in order for us to make check-in time. Give us some leeway, considering traffic."

"How many reservations should I make? Who's going?"

He grinned. "Everybody. We'll close up shop for a couple days. I know how hard all of you have been working lately. While this is no vacation, it wouldn't hurt for any of us to get away. As far as rooms, I'm assuming you and Ember, Yutani and Viktor, and then Talia and I will each have a room. So, four."

He gave me a quick look, and I smiled. I wasn't offended that he expected me to share a room with Angel. As he said, this wasn't a vacation, and we were on the job.

"Any preferences on whether there should be a restaurant in the hotel?"

"Find one with restaurant and room service. We don't want to spend an arm and a leg, especially since this will come out of the hippocampi's pockets, but we're not going to skimp either." He frowned, then glanced at his phone when it chimed. "Excuse me. I have to take a phone call." He stood, and without further comment, left the room.

"How often do you guys get cases outside of Seattle?" I asked.

Viktor swallowed the rest of the sandwich that he had made. "Not all that often. Oh, sometimes we end up over on the Eastside, or a little farther. But usually not far enough away that we have to rent a hotel. I won't be sorry to be out of the city, though. I feel like I haven't had a day off in weeks."

"That's because we haven't," Yutani said. "I wonder how they feel about coyotes up on Whidbey Island. I haven't had a chance to go running for a while."

Yutani wasn't talking about jogging. He was a coyote shifter without a pack. He had been ousted from the small town he used to live in because Great Coyote dogged his heels, so to speak. And anybody that Coyote chose to take under his paw, well, by the end of things, they usually didn't have many friends left. Yutani often found himself at the mercy of Coyote's sense of humor. Or at best, at the butt end of the joke. Sometimes, it was better to be somebody's enemy than their friend.

"Why don't you look up their ordinances while we're doing our research?" Talia said. She glanced over the dossier. "There's something fishy about this murder. The cops usually don't ignore homicides unless there's a reason."

"Maybe it's really as simple as a vampire kill. Sometimes, when there isn't an easy answer, people don't want to face the fact that they're not going to get the closure they want." Viktor shrugged. "I don't care whether or not she talked to the vampires on the island. Most vamps aren't going to own up if they think one of their own killed somebody. Especially not with the treaty in place. The United Coalition has been both a blessing and a curse in that sense."

"So you'd rather see humans making all the laws without the rest of our input?" Talia shook her head. "No thank you."

"Don't put words in my mouth. I didn't say that." Viktor twisted his lips into a frown. "I think all the major races have to be represented in the United Coalition. However, that doesn't change the fact that politics can be problematic, especially with creatures like vampires. The Vampire Nation has a vested interest in protecting its reputation, given the past, *and* given the fact that they have managed to finagle their way into most of the economic markets in the world."

"It's not like the Fae Courts don't do the same thing, though." I decided to jump into the argument. "They influence the authorities—especially law enforcement—heavily. Hell, they practically run the police stations in most major cities. I think the *only* group in the United Coalition that hasn't tried to pull strings is the Shifter Alliance."

Yutani snorted. "Think that if you like, but I wouldn't place bets on you being right."

I stared at him. "What are you talking about?

I have never heard a single complaint that the Shifter Alliance has tried to influence politics, other than laws relating to their lives."

The United Coalition was composed of four groups that ran the country. Most nations followed a similar formation. In the United States, the UC was composed of the Shifter Alliance, the Vampire Nation, the Fae Courts, and the Human League. A set number of legislators from each group joined to form the governing councils of both the nation, and the varying states. By law, there had to be a proportionate number of lawmakers in each government body as there were members of that particular population. It didn't ensure that justice was fair, but it was a long cry from the gerrymandering that had gone on in the past.

Yutani leaned forward, resting his elbows on the table. His hair spilled over his shoulders in a silken cloud. "Just because the Fae come on like sledgehammers, and the vampires sneak in with their money, doesn't mean that the shifters don't look for ways to influence society and the laws. Take a long look at the school boards and PTAs. Education is a good venue from which to change society."

I frowned, biting the inside of my lip. I had never really thought about the matter, nor did I take any notice about who was in the PTA or on school boards, given I didn't have children and I wasn't really that interested. But if Yutani was right, it might actually be something to pay attention to. Especially since the shifters didn't care much for the Fae, and they sure as hell didn't like vampires.

"Save the political discussions for later, children," Talia said with a dry laugh. "While you were busy arguing, I took a quick look at the shifter ordinances up on Whidbey Island. There is a large park where you can go running safely, Yutani. But pay attention to the hours. The big cat shifters and canine shifters are kept separate. And prey-shifter types have their own times as well. You can be fined heavily if you break the rules."

Most shifters were able to interact without a problem in their human form, but there had been several cases where their animal instincts took over when they were in-shift. The unfortunate death wasn't unheard of. Rather than murder, those homicides were usually tried as manslaughter.

At that moment, Herne returned. He glanced at me, a worried look on his face, then turned to Angel. "Change of immediate plans, at least for the moment. I got a call from Cooper. DJ is having a lot of trouble right now. Apparently, it's the anniversary of your mother's death?"

Angel bit her lip and stared at the table, nodding. "Tomorrow. It's still so fresh, especially for DJ..."

She was trying to be strong. When Mama J. had died, it devastated both Angel and her brother. Mama J. had been the light of their lives. She had been a bright light in my life as well.

"I've made arrangements for Cooper to bring DJ up here to see you. Tomorrow, you and Ember can spend the afternoon with him. Come in during the morning, but you can leave at noon to spend the afternoon with him. We still need to leave Thursday morning, but this will give you some time to help him through this."

"Thanks, Herne," Angel said, ducking her head as a tear trailed down her cheek.

He let out a soft sigh. "It's never easy. But we're here, and we'll do our best to help you and your brother, whatever the case." With a look around the table, he added, "Everybody know what they need to do?"

Everyone nodded.

"Then let's get busy. We've got a lot to do in a short amount of time." And with that, we were excused.

Chapter 3

I WAITED AS everyone else filed out of the break room. Herne closed the door so that we had some privacy. He turned to me, a worried look on his face.

"I didn't realize that we were so close to such a painful anniversary. I know it affects you, too. Are you all right? Coming on the heels of Ray's unfortunate outburst, today can't be described as the best day for you." He sat on the table, waiting for me to speak.

I had never been in a relationship like this before. Herne treated me like both friend and girlfriend. At times it felt disconcerting, switching between the two. But I was getting used to it, and I realized that I actually preferred it. I didn't want him to treat me any differently during work hours than he did the others. I didn't want the potential for any misunderstandings, or hurt feelings, because I actually liked my coworkers.

In the three months that Angel and I had been working for the Wild Hunt, I had come to realize that I was happier than any other time in my life. And it wasn't just that I was canoodling with the hot, handsome, son of a god. This was the first time that I felt comfortable interacting with anybody else besides Angel. Talia, Yutani, and Viktor had all become friends. And I wasn't used to having friends, other than Angel.

I pulled out a chair and sat down again. "I loved Mama J. as much as I loved my own mother. Well, that's probably not true. But Mama J. was special. She was like the community grandmother for the entire neighborhood. Every time I went over there, she made me feel special. When my own parents were killed, I didn't even have to ask if I could stay with her. She gathered me up, and took me home with her and Angel, and without a single question, I became part of their family. So yeah, it still hurts. But I have to be honest, and I feel horrible about admitting it. Until Angel mentioned it yesterday to me, I had forgotten that it was the anniversary of her death."

There was no way that I could lie to Angel, either. When she had mentioned it the day before, and I realized that I had forgotten, the look on her face kicked me in the gut. It was as though I had deliberately tried to hurt her. I couldn't cover it up with a lie, either, because she could sense the truth. So I had just apologized, without qualification, and Angel—being Angel—accepted my apology, without question.

"I wish I could have met her. Between what you and Angel have said, she sounds like she was a remarkable woman."

"She *was* a remarkable woman. She was an excellent card reader, and she was one hell of a chef. Her diner was so popular that it was always full. But every Wednesday evening, like clockwork, she shut down to the public and opened it as a soup kitchen. She paid for everything out of her own pocket, in fact, although people donated money and time to help her keep it open." I paused, then glanced at Herne. "So, DJ's having a rough time? Do you think he's doing okay with Cooper and his family?"

"Oh, I think he's fine with Cooper. In fact, his grades are holding steady—straight As, no less. His teachers are giving him props for adjusting to the new school. But anniversaries like this are meant to be spent with those who understand. That's why I thought you might want to spend some time with Angel and DJ. Unless you think they want to be alone?"

I bit my lip, pondering the question. I didn't like intruding on people's grief, but it might help both of them if I were there to take the edge off the rawness. "I'll ask Angel tonight. If she wants to be alone with DJ tomorrow, I'll just stay at work."

"Whatever you think is best." He stood, picking up his files and his tablet. "And you don't mind rooming with Angel at the hotel? I just thought it might seem odd if we shared a room while we were out on a case."

"That's not a problem," I said. "When we're at

work, business is business. But I like the idea that you have a room to yourself." I flashed him a wicked grin. "After all, there's nothing to say that after hours we can't spend a little bit of time together."

His face crinkled into a sly smile, and he swatted my ass with a file folder. "Get along with you, wench. We have work to do."

And with that, we got on with the day.

THE STACK OF paperwork that Herne wanted me to take care of was over an inch thick. Most of it just needed to be filed. While that would normally be Angel's job, there were some notations that I needed to make, and the closed cases still needed to be signed off on.

I opened the blinds, letting the sun pour into my office as I stared down at the alley below. My office was against the back of the building, and when I looked straight across the alley, I was facing the back of another building, though more modernized than ours. Whoever had the office opposite mine usually kept his blinds closed. But that building was only three stories high, so I had a bit of a view over the top, and it didn't block the afternoon sun. The alley itself was wide enough for one car. The dumpsters for our building were directly below my window, and even though they were four stories down, I had learned the hard way not to open the window on the morning before garbage collection.

I settled in at my desk, typing in my password.

As I ruffled through the papers, I realized that I really didn't miss my old life. It was so much easier having a job than scouting for clients. While the freedom of working for myself had been appealing in theory, in reality, it'd been damned hard and far too frugal at times.

As I began typing notes into the computer, and filing papers away in their respective folders, the sun passed behind an approaching cloud. I glanced out, realizing we were in for a summer shower.

About an hour had passed when someone tapped on the door. I glanced up to see Angel peeking in.

"Have you got a minute?"

"For you? Always. What's up?" I pushed the remaining stack of papers to the side, grateful for the interruption. I had made my way through about a third of them, and I needed a break.

"I wanted to make sure you were planning to visit DJ with me tomorrow. I know what Herne said, but I also know you. You're family." The tremor in her voice told me she was nervous.

I cocked my head, giving her a sideways smile. "I was going to ask if you wanted me there, or if you wanted to be alone with your brother. I'm happy to help, either way." I still felt bad about having forgotten the anniversary of Mama J.'s death.

"I think DJ would like you there, too. I'm a little worried, Ember."

"What's wrong?"

"He's changing. Maybe it's that he's living with other shifters now. Or maybe, he's just getting used to his life. I can't put my finger on it, but he's

43

different. Or maybe I'm just worried that if we're alone tomorrow, it would be too easy for us to fall into a spiraling depression." She gave me a little shrug. "Maybe I'm paranoid."

"Where are we meeting him? Did Herne say?"

Angel and DJ weren't allowed to be alone together without outside supervision. Once Angel had turned him over to foster care within the shifter community, even if they were left alone to talk, Cooper was always near enough to prevent them from sneaking off together. It seemed a little on the drastic side to me, but then again, agreements made within the Wild Hunt were binding and far-reaching.

"Yes, there's a sanctuary house not far from here, on East Spruce Street, off of Boren Avenue. We'll meet DJ there at noon for lunch." She paused, rubbing her temples. "I know this is a better life for him, but it's still difficult. I miss him. He was my last link to Mama J. But I was always afraid that he'd fall in with the wrong crowd. It's difficult for young boys without a good authority figure. Especially in the SubCult community."

"Do you think it's harder for boys than for girls?"

"In a way. They have all that burgeoning testosterone to deal with. With the Wulfine blood, when he hits puberty he'll be a handful. I've never talked about this much, but I've been nervous about facing his teenage years. So much goes on, and I know nothing about raising a teen shifter, except that they can be volatile and difficult. I don't know if I could handle it on my own. I'm almost relieved about what happened. Does that make me a bad sister?"

I felt for her. Angel not only had to deal with her own loss but she had suddenly become a mother to a ten-year-old, and the combo had wreaked havoc on her life. She had taken a job that she hated just to put food on the table. At least now, she liked her work.

"You're a wonderful sister. DJ's lucky he has you. And now, at least we know he has a good role model. I know things are difficult right now, but over the months and years it will become easier."

"Yeah, there is that. And Cooper treats DJ like his own son."

I nodded to the stack of papers on my desk. "We'd better get back to work. Did you make reservations yet?"

She smiled then. "I found us a nice hotel. I'm so glad Herne is letting me come. I need some time away. And I know you do, too. You're the one who's been out in the field investigating. At least I get to sit inside where it's safe."

"Somehow, I doubt any of us are in safe positions."

I glanced down at the tattoo on my arm. Angel bore a matching one. In fact, everybody who worked for the Wild Hunt had the same tattoo—a long dagger with vines twining around it. In the field, it marked us as protected, at least from the Fae. Whether it always worked was up for debate. But both the Light and Dark courts were supposed to respect it and allow us to go about our business without interfering.

As Angel returned to her desk, I went back to my

notes, and the afternoon wore on.

BY THE TIME we finished with the seminar, we were both dragging butt. We were on our way home to my condo in the Spring Beach area when I had the sudden inclination to take a detour.

"Do you mind if we go for a little ride?"

Angel shook her head. "I don't care as long as I don't have to get out of the car, and as long as you're the one driving."

On a whim, I decided to take Emerson over to 36th Avenue, which skirted Discovery Park. We were headed north when all of a sudden I pulled to the side, just past Thurman Street.

"Look, a house for sale." I pointed to the sign. Angel and I had been looking for a house to buy.

It was still light enough to see. I jumped out of the car and walked up to a box holding a stack of flyers. As I pulled out a copy, I glanced over at the house, which was hidden behind a thick tangle of trees. It was cute, although it didn't seem to have a lot of square footage. But it was two-story, and from the outside it looked to be in good repair.

I carried the flyer back to the car, sliding back into the driver seat. Angel turned on the overhead light and we glanced over it. The house was 1600 square feet, two-story, with three bedrooms and two bathrooms. It had a finished basement, and the flyer said the kitchen and baths had been recently upgraded. The best part, it was in my price range.

Angel had moved in with me a few months ago, and my condo wasn't big enough for the both of us. While we loved being roommates again—we had lived together during college, and before that, with her mother—we definitely needed more space in which to spread out. We had been looking for a house for the past few months, but they were either overpriced or run down to the point of being shacks, or they would require a brutal commute. But this looked like a possibility.

"It *is* cute, at least what I can see from here," Angel said, peering out of the window. "And while it's closer to work, it's not directly in the city. And best, Discovery Park is right across the street."

"That's what I was thinking. Not only would we have a relatively private lot, but we'd have the entire park to go running in." I looked at the flyer again. "Wait, this place *isn't* so small. At least the lot isn't. See the empty lot next door, to the left? That belongs to the house. I wonder why it's so inexpensive if it has that much land, and why nobody's grabbed it up yet."

I had long ago learned that if it sounded too good to be true, it was. But it was too tempting not to give it a look-through. I glanced at the car clock. 8:30 P.M. It wasn't really so late, so I decided to call the real estate agency and leave a message. After leaving my name and number, I reluctantly started the car. For some reason, the house beckoned me, and I wanted to just park in the driveway and go inside.

"Well, hopefully we'll hear back tomorrow. I'd

like to at least see it before we leave for Whidbey Island." I put the car into gear and pulled back onto the street. As we headed home to my condo in the Miriam G building, I felt more lighthearted than I had in a while. I wasn't exactly sure what to ascribe it to, but decided I wouldn't question small favors.

MORNING CAME FAR too early for my taste. I still wasn't used to getting up before ten, and I didn't know if I'd ever be. But I rolled out of bed, took a shower, and dressed in jeans and a tank top. It looked like our nice weather was holding, so I shrugged on a light denim jacket and pulled on my ankle boots.

Angel had breakfast ready—she was a fantastic cook, just like her mother had been. As for me? I couldn't cook my way out of a cardboard box. I dug into the sausage and eggs, feeling exceptionally hungry. I had a big appetite anyway, but I had a feeling that the promise of a potential house had spurred it on. We had seen so many places over the past few months that I was getting buyer's fatigue.

"I wanted to pick up something for DJ before we head into work." Angel handed me a latte. She had finally learned to use my espresso machine. She was a tea drinker, whereas I was a devout java freak.

"Didn't you take him a bunch of toys when you saw him last month?"

She shrugged. "Yeah, I know. I just feel like I should have something for him every time I see him."

"You're trying to apologize with gifts. I don't think he needs that, not DJ. Just seeing you is gift enough." I suddenly realized that I might be over-stepping my boundaries. "I'm sorry. Forget what I said."

"No," Angel said, finishing up the last of her own breakfast. "You're right. I'm not going to deny it."

"If anything, find him a picture out of the ones that survived the fire—a picture of you and him and your mom. I bet he'd like that more than any-thing else."

Angel smiled, ducking her head. "Yeah, that's a good idea. I'll just go grab one now, if you wait for me."

"Do you want to ride in together? Or take your own car?" Some days we rode together to work, other times we drove separately, depending on what we had going afterward.

"Now that you mention it, why don't we go sepa-rately? That way, if you have something to do after we see DJ, you can take off. I know you and Herne were planning on getting together tonight."

As she headed into her bedroom—my ex-weap-ons room—to find a picture, my private cell phone rang. I glanced at the number, surprised to see the Maximum Value Real Estate Company calling me back so early.

"Ember Kearney speaking."

"Hi, Rachel Madison here. I'm returning your call from last night. I'd love to show you the house, if you have some time today?"

I wanted to ask why it was so inexpensive for the amount of land that it had, but decided I'd wait until we'd actually met and were looking over the house.

"What about early evening? Four or five?"

"I have an opening in my schedule at four-thirty. If you'd like to meet me at the house, I can show you around." She paused, and I could hear a hesitation in her voice as she added, "Will that work?"

I chewed on my lip for a moment. My inner alarm was ringing, but it wasn't loud enough to totally warn me off. But it was warning me to keep my eyes and ears open.

"Sure. I'll see you then."

When Angel returned, picture in hand, I told her we had an appointment to view the house.

"I have the feeling there's something odd about it, but it wasn't enough to warn me off. Just keep your spidey senses open, so to speak."

She nodded. "I'm guessing that they won't let me see DJ longer than a few hours, so that will work."

And with that, we took off for the office.

THE MORNING PASSED unobtrusively, as we all did what we could to prepare for our trip to Whidbey Island the next day. At quarter to twelve, Angel and I took off for the sanctuary house, stopping at a burger joint along the way to grab lunch for all of us.

Sanctuary houses were safe havens, where anyone who found themselves in danger and a target could go. All members of the United Coalition—the Shifter Alliance, the Vampire Nation, the Fae Courts, and the Human League—had signed treaties agreeing to the stipulation. The person being targeted could stay there until the Grand Council made a decision on their situation. I didn't know how many sanctuary houses there were, and I had only a vague idea of who the Grand Council was. But it was a nationwide network, and it occurred to me it would be a good idea to find out more about it. I decided to ask Herne later on about it. There was so much that I didn't know. My parents had never explained much to me about my heritage before they were killed, and since then I had flown under the radar.

When we arrived at the house on Spruce Street, I wasn't surprised to see bars on the windows and doors. When we knocked on the door, an armed man answered. He glanced at our ID, then at the tattoos on our arms, then motioned for us to walk through a metal detector on the porch. Of course, my underwire set it off, as well as my dagger.

"I'm sorry, but you can't bring the weapon inside. There's a locker by the porch swing. Place your dagger inside, and lock the door. Keep the key and retrieve your blade on the way out."

I complied, without question.

We were escorted into the house, but instead of finding ourselves in the living room, it looked like a reception room. The woman sitting behind the desk looked at our identification again, then motioned to the man who had let us in.

"Room 2E. They have two hours, and no grounds privileges."

"Okay to leave them alone?" he asked.

"Yes, they are okayed for privacy." The receptionist nodded for us to follow him. She didn't seem friendly, but it occurred to me that in a sanctuary house, you could never be too careful. Even though all four members of the United Coalition had agreed on the rules, that didn't mean individuals always abided by them.

He led us up a narrow staircase, to the second floor, and then turned right. It looked like there were five rooms, and he led us to the second door with the number two stenciled on it. After he unlocked it and opened the door, he stood back so that we could enter. Inside, DJ was sitting at a small table.

We entered, and the guard locked the door behind us again. I began to understand what it must be like to be in jail.

The room was spacious with the sofa, an end table, a folding table with four chairs, a water dispenser, and another door to one side. There was motel room art on the walls, and a bookshelf with a few books on it. There was also a TV.

Curious, I walked over to the other door while DJ and Angel were hugging each other, and peeked in. It was a half bath. There were no windows in either room.

"Ember!" DJ ran up and threw his arms around me. "It's good to see you."

I gave him a tight hug. "How you doing, sport?"

He scuffed his foot, shrugging. "Okay."

Angel unpacked our lunch, setting out the burgers and fries and shakes. I gave DJ another squeeze around the shoulders.

"Hungry? We came armed with hamburgers." I wriggled my eyebrows at him, surprised that he had grown a couple inches since last time I saw him. He was still a small boy, solemn beyond his years, and too smart for his own good.

"*Starved.* They gave me some chips, but it wasn't enough." He headed over to the table, sitting in the chair next to Angel. I joined them, still feeling like a third wheel, but if they both wanted me here, I wasn't going to complain.

"So," Angel said after a moment. "Cooper said you were having a hard time? Is that true?"

DJ averted his eyes, stuffing his hamburger into his mouth. After a moment, he swallowed, then gave her a short nod. "Mostly it's okay. It's just... Today..." He struggled with his words, falling silent.

"I know. Today's the day Mama J. died. And it's still too close, and too painful. Anniversaries like this are freaking hard, aren't they?" Angel reached over, running her hand over his closely shorn head. "What happened to all your hair?"

"I asked Cooper to give me a buzz cut. Like his." DJ took a sip of his shake, then wiped his mouth. "I've been dreaming about Mama a lot lately. I miss her." The words came out garbled with tears, but he dashed them away, sniffling as he stared down at what was left of his meal.

As I watched Angel and DJ share their grief, I

wasn't sure what to say, but decided to give it a try. "DJ, it's good you think about her. Mama J. was a wonderful woman. You know she took me in when my own parents were killed."

He glanced up at me. "Angel told me. She said you moved in when you were both teenagers. I'm sorry you lost your parents, too."

"It's never easy. And it never goes away. But as time goes on, it gets a little easier. I hope you don't mind that I came in today. I wanted to say hi." I had been worried that I would say the wrong thing, but both Angel and DJ smiled at me.

"You know, Mama wouldn't want you to be sad. You remember what she was like. What do you think she would tell you?" Angel lifted DJ's chin so that he was staring into her face.

DJ swallowed, then let out a sigh. "She'd tell me to get on with it. She'd say feel it, then let it go. That's what she always told me when I came home upset from school."

"Then I think we both need to take her advice. We want to make her proud, don't we?"

He nodded. "Yeah, and I guess thinking about the past doesn't help much, doesn't it?"

"Good memories always help, but we can't live in the past. Trust me, I've learned that the hard way." Angel pointed to his lunch. "Eat before that gets cold."

"You too," he said, a smile creeping across his face.

We finished lunch, chatting about nothing in particular.

"So how do you like living with Cooper and his

family?" I asked.

"Actually, it's pretty good. It's not that I didn't love living with you," he glanced at his sister. "It's just… It feels good to be with a family again. The kids are really nice, and even though we get into arguments at times, they treat me like I'm part of the family. And I'm learning a lot about how to control my wolf." At that, a broad smile spread across his face. "That's one nice thing—they're all wolf shifters."

"How's school?" Angel asked.

"Pretty good. There are a few bullies in the class, but it doesn't feel as scary as school did here. I'm getting straight As." He launched into telling us about his classes, and his friends, and as he continued, his spirits seemed to rise. Finally, he asked, "Do you really think Mama would be proud of me?"

Angel and I both nodded enthusiastically.

"Mama would say you're doing just great," Angel said. "I think she'd be proud of us both. We both have made a lot of changes over the past few months, and I know it's scary, but we're doing good. Did you know Ember's going to buy a house and I'll live there with her?"

"Will I come and live there, too?"

I glanced at him, not sensing much enthusiasm in his question.

"No, dude. Angel and I are working for a business that can be dangerous for friends and family. You *do* know that's why you had to go away in the first place, right? Angel didn't just arbitrarily send you to live with Cooper and his family."

DJ nodded. "Yeah, Cooper explained it to me. I guess things are better off the way they are. But I do miss you," he said to his sister.

"I miss you too, DJ. At least we get to see each other and talk to each other a lot on the phone."

There was a tap on the door, and the guard peeked in. "Excuse me, but it's time."

I blinked, glancing at the clock on the wall. Sure enough, we had already spent two hours talking.

"I wish we had more time," DJ said. "But Cooper said in the fall, maybe you can come down for the weekend?" He gave Angel a hopeful look.

She nodded. "Yeah, we've talked about that. We'll make it happen. Until then, promise me you'll do your best? At school, and with Cooper and his family. And I know today's hard, but remember, Mama's watching over you. And she watches over me, too. So don't you worry about me, okay?"

"Okay," DJ said, holding her tight around the waist.

The guard led us away, locking the door behind him. I felt bad leaving DJ behind.

"Cooper will come for him soon, won't he? He's not going to be sitting there alone for a long time, will he?"

"He'll be leaving for home before you know it. Don't worry about him, he's going to be fine." The guard's reserve cracked just a little. "The boy will be okay. His guardian is coming for him now."

As I retrieved my dagger and we left, we saw Cooper heading up the sidewalk. We said nothing, as per the rules, but he flashed us a wide smile as he passed us, and a nod of the head that said, *Don't worry, I've got DJ's back.*

BY THE TIME we left, it was a little past three.

"We have a little over an hour until we're supposed to look at the house. Let's go back to the office and tidy up things before we have to leave tomorrow." I glanced at Angel. "Are you okay?"

She nodded, wiping her eyes. "Actually, yes. It's hard to walk away from him, but I know it's for the best. And every time I see Cooper, I feel secure about DJ's future. He's taking care of my brother better than I ever could. I think that's what hurts the most."

She sounded so depressed that I couldn't stand it.

"Stop that. You did your best. You did everything you could. You love DJ, and he knows that. Just because Cooper can offer him a better opportunity doesn't mean you failed at your job. Mama J. would be proud of you. I hope you know that."

"I like to think so," she said.

Back at the office, I cleared my desk and finished inputting the last of the information from the forms. After that, it was time to head out to look at the house.

I stopped to let Herne know where we were headed. "We've got a lead on a house, and I want to see it before we head out to Whidbey Island tomorrow."

He was staring at his phone. When he looked up, he was frowning.

"Okay. Unfortunately, we need another rain check on our date. After you're done looking at the house, I need you to come back to the office. Yutani and Talia have some information for us on the case. It's best if we go over that before we leave rather than on the way."

I rolled my eyes, not exactly irritated but definitely not thrilled either. I really wanted to be alone with him for a while. Well, truth be told, I wanted to get buck naked and jump in bed. But given we had an early start the next day, I was resigning myself to the fact that might not happen.

"Sure, a rain check's fine. But maybe we can make an exception and stay late after the others leave? Nudge, nudge," I said, winking. I wasn't the best flirt in the world, but by now I figured that we had been together long enough for me to be relatively blunt.

He chuckled. "It's been a while since my daybed has gotten any use. I'm willing to break our unwritten rule, if you are." And with that, he blew me a kiss and headed back to his office.

ANGEL AND I decided to just take my car to go see the house, given that we had to return to the office anyway. She seemed in better spirits, and along the way we chatted about what we should keep an eye out for.

"We need to ask her about urban flooding, what the neighborhood's like, mold, and be sure to keep an eye out for anything that might have been done on the cheap. If they flipped it, inexpensive materials are fine, as long as they're sturdy. I'm not expecting high-end upgrades for the price were looking at."

I parked in front of the house, behind a small Subaru. It had a real estate sticker on the window, so I assumed it was Rachel's car. Sure enough, as we got out of the car, a short, petite woman in a linen pantsuit came running over. She was probably around our age, but her hair was piled high on her head in a messy chignon, and she had a slightly frazzled look to her.

"Hi, I'm Rachel Madison," she said, thrusting her hand toward me. "Ember?"

I nodded. "I'm Ember Kearney, and this is my roommate, Angel Jackson."

She gave Angel a quick nod. "So, are you both looking to buy the house?"

I shook my head. "No, I'll be the one buying. Angel would be renting from me."

Rachel led us through the picket fence, opening the gate for us. The walkway was crowded with overgrown rhododendrons, and to one side a tall maple towered over the house. A gate led into the next lot, which was also overgrown, but it looked like someone had at one time attempted a large vegetable garden there.

The sidewalk was cracked and bumpy, and the pavement was broken. Rosebushes stood to either side of the porch, sprawling in a messy disarray. The lawn looked to be more moss than grass, which wasn't uncommon around here.

The house itself was two-story, and was navy with white trim. The porch was weathered, and wide enough for a porch swing, with a spindle railing flanking the sides and front. Overall, the place didn't look too broken-down. As we clattered up the stairs, I realized that I was holding my breath and I wasn't sure why.

Angel gave me a nudge and leaned over to whisper in my ear. "Something happened here. I can feel it. I don't know if it's haunted or not, but there's a cloud over this house."

I decided to get the question out of the way. "Rachel, before we go on, I'd like to ask you something. Why is this house priced so cheaply? I notice it comes with the lot next door."

She paused, then let out a long sigh.

"I was hoping you'd save that question until you've seen the inside, because this is a charming house, and it has so much potential." She looked about to cry, and I got the distinct impression that she'd been trying to unload this house for quite a while.

"What are you talking about?"

"This house has been on the market for 400 days. Over a year. The reason the price is so low is because the family really wants to sell it. By law, I'm required to inform you that this is a murder house. An elderly woman and her granddaughter were killed here about two years ago. They were murdered by the granddaughter's boyfriend." She paused, the key dangling between her fingers. "So, do you still want to see the house?"

Chapter 4

A MURDER HOUSE. Lovely. I glanced beyond her at the house. Was it haunted? Or was the neighborhood really that dangerous? So many questions flew through my mind, and I knew that Angel was probably entertaining most of them as well.

"Before we head inside, tell us about the murder, please." I wasn't ready to throw in the towel just yet. If we didn't find any ghosts hanging around, owning a nefarious house might be worth the stigma, if it was in good condition and given the size of the lot.

Rachel led us over to the porch swing, where she motioned for us to sit down. She leaned against the railing, and I had the feeling she had told the story more than once.

"The granddaughter—I think her name was Aimee—broke up with her boyfriend a few weeks before the murder. He wanted her back, and she didn't want anything to do with him. He was from a troubled family, if I remember the story correctly, and violent. She told him to get lost and he started stalking her. I'm not clear on what happened, but he snapped. Aimee was staying with her grandmother. The guy broke into the house, and took an axe to both of them. It was brutal, and grisly. The neighbor found them the next morning when she went over to borrow some sugar from the grandmother."

"Did they catch the guy?" My first concern was that the murderer might still be out there and for some reason decide to revisit the house.

Rachel shook her head. "He killed himself at the scene."

Well, that was one worry off the table, but it meant there were three violent deaths that had happened in the house.

"Who owns the house now?"

"Aimee's mother. Juliana Tallwood. She can't bear to even come near the house. She's been trying to sell it since shortly after the murder. It was on the market for about six months, without a single nibble, so she delisted it, and had it fully upgraded so it would sell faster. It's been on the market for a total of 400 days. Nobody seems to be willing to live in a place where people were murdered." Rachel glanced at me, and it was apparent from her expression that she expected us to get up and walk out.

I glanced at Angel. "That's probably why I felt an alarm go off. What do you think? Should we have a look inside?" I trusted her judgment.

Angel closed her eyes for a moment, then glanced back at me. "I don't know if it's haunted or not, but there's a lot of *cobwebby* energy around. We'd have to do a thorough cleaning if we take it. And if there are any ghosts, we'll have to have someone exorcise them. I'm not very good at doing things like that."

I thought about it for a moment, then looked back over at Rachel, who was pretending that she wasn't listening to us.

"All right, let's take a look since we're here."

A look of relief spreading over her face, Rachel led us to the door and unlocked it.

THE INSIDE OF the house was a pleasant surprise. The rooms were spacious, and the layout was good. It maximized every square foot of space. The hardwood floors gleamed, and although there weren't as many windows as I would have liked, there was enough light to make it feel airy. The walls were painted a creamy white, and the trim, a rich walnut color. As we entered the foyer, a coat closet to the left offered storage. Straight ahead, an arched opening led into the living room. The room was large, with a long row of built-ins along the opposite wall, with the fireplace being the central focal point. The brick had been painted white. They had done everything in their power to make the house feel clean and new.

We looked around, then Rachel led us back into the hall where the staircase led up to the second floor. We skirted it, passing a half-bath on the left, then an office space on the right, as we headed into the kitchen–dining room. It occurred to me we could blow out the end wall in the living room to create one giant room.

The kitchen was also spacious. The counters were a silvery gray quartz, and the backsplash was composed of long narrow strips of pale blue glass interspersed with dark blue ceramic. The appliances were stainless steel. All in all, it was an inviting room. The energy was heavy, though, and it felt poised, as if waiting, especially in the dining nook where the table was. To the right of the kitchen was a nook with a stackable washer and dryer in it, both new, along with a narrow pole for hanging clothes. The washer and dryer appeared to be included with the house.

"So, where were they murdered?" I glanced over at Rachel.

She paled. "Aimee was sitting at the table. Her grandmother was baking cookies. The kitchen has been upgraded and the floors were replaced."

Even though she didn't say it, I knew it was because of the blood. I remembered the blood on the floor of the kitchen when I found my parents.

Angel was looking around carefully, but if she had anything to say, she kept it to herself.

After that, Rachel took us upstairs where we looked at three bedrooms and two baths. One belonged to the master suite, the other was a Jack-and-Jill between the other two bedrooms.

There was also an open space upstairs that could be used for a sitting room. All of the rooms seemed relatively spacious, given the amount of square footage, and Rachel informed us there was also an attic, accessible through a trap door in the third bedroom, as well as a finished basement. She led us downstairs, opening a door between the kitchen and the hall bath, showing us the stairway leading to the basement. The basement itself felt slightly cramped, but it would work for storage. I looked around for signs of water damage.

"Has this house ever flooded? You know the urban flooding we get in Seattle."

There was a lot of urban flooding in Seattle during the rainy season, which lasted from mid-September till around May.

"I don't think so, but I will check. The owner didn't mention anything about it."

Of course she hadn't. And if the house had ever flooded, that would be one more strike on top of it being a murder house. I glanced over at Angel. "Rachel, can you give Angel and me a moment?"

Rachel nodded, pointing toward the stairs. "I'll be upstairs when you need me. Take your time."

After she left the room, I let out a long sigh and sat down on a built-in banquette.

"Well, what do you think? I suppose we should see the outside first."

Angel shrugged. "It's not a bad house. There's a lot of room, and while I prefer an open concept, for the price, it's going to be hard to beat."

"I suppose we could open up the wall between the kitchen and living room. That would be ideal, though we don't know what the situation is with load-bearing walls. But what do you think about the energy?"

"This is one of those times I wish I could read the cards as well as Mama J.," Angel said. "I don't feel any ghosts, at least not outright. I do know the energy is stagnant and a little creepy, but I think we could take care of any lingering shadows. It's hard to tell if there are ghosts here on such a short visit, and until we cleanse the house, we won't really be able to tell what we're dealing with."

We rejoined Rachel upstairs, where she escorted us onto the deck that wrapped around the house from the living room around the kitchen. It looked to be in good repair, and as I looked closer, I realized it wasn't actually wood, but that wonderful polyresin material that never needed care except for the occasional hosing off.

Rachel led us over to the gate that opened into the second lot. The lot was a tangle of undergrowth, but a rose garden was hiding beneath the overgrowth of tall grass and ferns, and there were some raised beds that indicated someone had indeed raised vegetables at one time. A large apple tree stood in one corner of the lot, and several fir trees in another. The potential was incredible. We could create a magical garden out here. Visions of a water fountain and birdbaths and a gazebo danced in my head.

I turned to Angel, who smiled slowly.

"You love it, don't you?" she asked.

I nodded, barely able to say a word. "Do you realize how beautiful this could be? My mother had beautiful gardens when I was young, and I helped her keep them tidy and neat."

"Let's do it," she said. "I'm pretty sure we can clear out the lingering energy, and while I don't sense any ghosts, even if there are I'm sure we can find a way to make peace with them."

"Are you sure? You wouldn't mind living here? The mortgage would be a lot cheaper than I thought we'd be facing." In fact, with the sale of my condo, I could probably pay off half the house upfront. And I *knew* my condo would sell.

Angel nodded. "It's beautiful. The house is actually nice. I think we could make this a showplace." She paused. "Do you think Viktor can swing a hammer?"

I laughed. "I think Viktor can swing a *sledgehammer* with no problem. Are you thinking of enlisting him and Herne to help us renovate?"

"Isn't that what friends are for?" Angel snickered. "You know, I think my Wulfine friends work in construction."

At that point, Rachel appeared. "Well, what do you think?" She appeared to be prepared for yet another rejection. I looked at Angel, who gave me another nod.

"I think we're interested. I'll need an inspection. And since it *is* a murder house, and since it's been on the market so long, I'm going in with a lower offer." I might as well try to negotiate my way to the best price, given the circumstances.

"I don't foresee that being much of an issue." A smile spread over her face. "The list price is $592,000. If you want to make an offer, I'll need a check for earnest money."

I had enough in savings for that. "All right, but I want a stipulation that if the house inspection shows damage that they are unwilling to fix—other than minor issues—they either lower the price to match the cost of fixing it, or I get my earnest money back. Fifteen thousand okay?"

"That's fine." She motioned toward the house. "Would you like to go in and formalize the offer?"

"Why not? I'll be out of town for a few days starting tomorrow, but you can always text me. Meanwhile, I'll do some research and find a good inspector." I had brought my checkbook just in case.

We trooped into the kitchen, where she spread out her papers on the counter. As she filled out the form, I looked around again. Angel was right. This was a beautiful house, and it could be spectacular with enough work. I suspected that Herne would know plenty of people who could clear out the energy, so I wasn't too worried about it.

"All right, I've added the stipulation about the earnest money. What would you like to offer?" Rachel glanced at me, her pen poised over the contract.

"Given how long it's been on the market, let's go in at $550,000. I know that's low, but if she wants to sell, I'm ready to buy. And there doesn't seem to be any other interested parties right now."

Rachel blinked, and I could tell she wasn't all that thrilled with my offer, but she wrote it up without comment. "Sign here, and here, if you would."

She handed me the forms and I looked them over, reading them carefully before I added my signature. I handed them back.

"You have my phone number. Text me when you know anything. As I said, I'll be out of town for the next few days, so you might let the owner know that as well."

As we left the house, I glanced back at it. In some ways, it already felt like home. I could see the potential of what it could become, and that made me happy. All we had to do was get rid of the residue energy, and evict any ghosts who weren't supposed to be there.

BACK AT THE agency, we told them our news.

"Do you have any recommendations for a good exorcist? I'm not sure if there are any ghosts there attached to the house, but there's definitely some residue energy that feels squirmy. But the house is lovely, and it has so much land."

Herne just shook his head. "Only you would come across a murder house. Yes, I know several talented witches who can exorcise spirits. If you end up buying the place, I'm sure that we can clear it without a problem. Now, can we talk about Whidbey Island?"

We all pulled out our notebooks and tablets, prepared to take notes.

Talia handed around a printout to each of us. "So, I did a background check on Jona. It wasn't squeaky clean, but there wasn't anything problematic that would lead me to believe he was the target of an assassin. He didn't seem to have any enemies, and although he had wracked up a few debts, he was in the process of paying them off on a regular basis. His wife's family liked him. He had plenty of friends, and he was a hard worker."

"What did he do again?" Viktor asked.

"He was an urban farmer. He raised blueberries, and he also sold eggs and honey at the local farmers' market. He had beehives on his property." Talia shrugged, shaking her head. "He had a real talent for farming—a real green thumb. His blueberries received rave reviews from his customers."

"So what's his wife doing now? Is she keeping up with the family business? And his rivals? Or rather, the other farmers? Were there any that seemed to resent him?"

Talia consulted her notes. "There was an insurance policy, so his wife received a payout for $200,000. She sold the hives to another farmer, but she's continuing to raise the blueberries and eggs. She put most of the cash in a trust for their son. She's not wealthy by any means, but she seems to do all right. As far as other farmers, a Mr. Strickland Davis bought the hives. He has a thriving honey business and used Jona's hives to expand it."

"Could Jona have been cutting into his business enough to make him consider murder?" Viktor asked.

Yutani shook his head. "I suppose it's always possible, but I did a little sleuthing into their bank accounts. Don't ask how, you don't want to know. Davis is what you might call a 'gentleman farmer.' Meaning he inherited money from his parents. He's human. I doubt if the hives he bought from Marilyn will actually make much of an improvement. In fact, I get the impression he bought them to help her out. He bought them for more than the going price, from the looks of things. He and Jona were friendly rivals, from what I can tell."

A thought occurred to me, given Ray's recent behavior. "If Davis bought the hives for more than the going price, could he have a thing for Marilyn? If so, could that have led to Jona's demise?"

"Good question," Herne said. He motioned to Talia. "Any ideas? Was Marilyn having an affair? Or were there any signs that she was having trouble with this man?"

Talia shrugged. "That I don't know. I doubt it, given she had just had a baby shortly before Jona died. We've barely scratched the surface on our investigation, so there's not a lot to go on. I did, however, discover that someone warned the editor of the *Whidbey Island Gazette* to back off from sensationalizing the story. I happen to know somebody up on Whidbey Island. Rosetta, my friend, works part-time for the *Gazette*. She's the society reporter. I called her to see if I could find out any dirt on the incident. She told me that shortly after Jona's body was found, somebody called the editor. Rosetta happened to be listening on the line after she transferred them."

I raised my eyebrows. "Small-town life, hmm?"

Talia laughed, shaking her head. "What can I

say? It's not like there's a whole lot of action on the island and Rosetta *is* nosy. But what can you expect from a werecat? Curiosity, etc."

"Rosetta's a cat shifter?" Angel asked.

"Yes, Norwegian Forest cat—like your Mr. Rumblebutt, only he's not a shifter. She's a transplant from Norway. There's a large Scandinavian population in the islands. Anyway, she overheard someone—a man—warning the editor in no uncertain terms that he was not to sensationalize Jona's death, to tamp out the rumor mill as much as possible. Rosetta has no clue who it was, except that his first name was Roland."

"Well, that's an interesting tidbit." Herne cleared his throat, riffling through the papers. "Is there anything else we should know before we hit the island?"

"The hippocampi are a proud people," Yutani said. "They like elegance, they're usually well off, and they don't like being lumped in with the rest of the Fae. They tend to look on both the Light and the Dark courts as their country bumpkin cousins."

"In other words, don't call them Fae to their face?" I grinned at him. "Got it. I don't blame them." I might still be a tad bitter toward both, considering both courts were to blame for my parents' deaths. Add that to the fact that they considered me a pariah, a blight on their names, and there really wasn't much love lost between me and either side of my heritage.

"Where are we staying?" Herne asked.

Angel scanned through her tablet. "I made reservations at the Edgewood Star, near Seacrest Cove.

It's run by a Wulfine family, but they cater to all races. The prices are reasonable, and the rooms look spacious. There's a pool and a weight room. They have an in-house restaurant, and a coffee shop."

"Sounds good. When's check-in?"

"Noon tomorrow, and checkout is eleven A.M. I've booked us for three nights to start, and I asked them if there was a chance we could extend it if necessary. I had to pay them a twenty-dollar deposit per room to hold the rooms for longer, but the fee will be applied to our bill if we end up staying. If not, we'll get half back."

"Sounds good. Now, about transportation. I suggest we take three cars. I'll drive, Yutani—bring your car, and Ember, can you also drive? That way we can split up into teams of two. Be sure to pack what you need for a week, just in case. Don't forget your chargers, your phones, your tablets, laptops if you need them. Viktor will pack the weapons. We can always drive back to Seattle, but that's a long jaunt."

I rubbed my forehead. "Hell, I almost forgot. I need to find someone to take care of Mr. Rumble-butt. If we're going to be gone for more than a couple days, I don't want to leave him alone all that time."

"I have the name of a good pet sitter," Talia said. "I'll call her and ask her to come over to your condo tomorrow morning, if you like."

"Sure, but..." I blinked. This is the first time I'd ever heard that she had a pet. "*You* have a pet?" Realizing how that sounded, I blushed. "I didn't mean—"

"I know what you meant," she said, flashing me a cunning smile. "I know harpies are famous for eating animals, not cozying up to them. Remember, I can't turn into my natural form and haven't been able to for a long, long time. I actually have two dogs, greyhounds. They're both rescues. I like a good steak, but I gave up exotic meats a long time ago."

I laughed, still embarrassed. "I'd like to meet them some time. I've never been around a greyhound."

"They can be skittish creatures, especially when they've been trained for racing. But they're faithful, and they make for good company in the evening. I'll call Ronnie and give her your address and let you know when I've set it up."

I realized I didn't know much about Talia's home life, or really, much about any of them beyond the office, except for Herne. The past few months I had been so focused on him, and on the new job, that I was just starting to feel truly comfortable around the others. Viktor I knew better than Yutani and Talia. We hit it off, the half-ogre and I, and we had been out for drinks several times after a long day's work.

"It's seven now," Herne said. "Why don't you take off for home. Meet back here at seven thirty tomorrow morning. We'll drive up, catch the earliest ferry we can, and we can scope out the island before we check in at the hotel. Get moving, we've got an early morning facing us."

"I'll catch you at home," I told Angel, glancing at

Herne.

She waved at me, then headed out of the room. Talia, Yutani, and Viktor filed out after her. I turned around, leaning against the wall, waiting for Herne to finish gathering his things.

"You still interested?" I gave him my best suggestive look, which I hoped didn't look like I had a stomachache.

He looked me up and down, his eyes glimmering. "*Interested* is an understatement. Meet me in my office. I'll be there in a moment."

I swung out of the room, heading over to his office. Everyone was gone, so I paused at the reception area, locking the elevator so that nobody could enter the waiting room while we were in Herne's office.

HERNE WAS WAITING for me when I opened the door. He was sprawled out on the daybed, naked as a jaybird. I caught my breath, once again struck by how incredibly gorgeous he was. Being the son of Cernunnos and Morgana had its perks, and one of those perks was a face and body to die for.

He slowly stood as I entered the room, rising gracefully as he flashed me a mischievous smile. "I'm ready for you," he whispered.

And he was ready. The thews of his thighs were rippling, sturdy and rock solid. His hair spilled over his shoulder, brushing his shoulder blades.

His chest was broad, and his arms and biceps were muscled without being bulky. His torso narrowed into his waist, and his abs were firm and trim, leading down into a beautifully formed "V" that highlighted his cock. Ready he was, standing at attention, firm and erect.

My knees went weak as I feasted on the sight of him.

He held out his arms to me. "Come here, you."

"How the hell did you end up so beautiful?" I asked, leaning against the door jamb.

"Luck of the draw. But I'm not the one who's beautiful here." His gaze was fastened on me, the words rolling off his tongue like honey.

I slowly edged my way over to him, taking my time, enjoying the sight of his naked body. It'd taken us a month before we actually slept together, even though both of us wanted to jump in bed right away. But we gave it time. We went on dates, went out to dinner, to movies. By the time we were ready, we knew that what we were feeling was real. The chemistry had sizzled, and it still did.

I reached for my tank to pull it off, but he shook his head.

"Let me." His voice was husky, ragged with lust.

I stopped just in front of him, and held up my arms. He took hold of the hem of my tank top, slowly stripping it from my body, the material brushing my skin as he removed it, then tossed it on one of the chairs.

"Turn around," he ordered, and I obeyed.

He unhooked my bra, and my breasts bounced lightly as he slipped it off and tossed it on top of the tank top. The sudden coolness in the air chilled me, and my nipples stiffened.

Still standing behind me, he reached around with both hands, cupping my breasts, his fingers running lightly over my nipples. I moaned as I leaned against him. His erection pressed against my back, hard and thick and demanding.

He squeezed my breasts, almost hard enough to hurt, burying his face in my hair as he nuzzled it aside to kiss my neck. Then his hands slowly slid down to my stomach, coming to rest on my belt. I trembled as he unbuckled it, sliding it out from the belt loops and dropping it on the floor. I tried to stand still, though I wanted to squirm, to turn around and press against him.

"Don't move," he whispered as he began to unzip my jeans. "Not a muscle."

I was shaking with hunger as he pushed the material down my hips, just enough so that he could slide his hand down the front of my stomach, down to the thatch of hair between my legs.

"Don't stop—" I started to say, but he hushed me.

"Be quiet." His voice was firm and commanding.

I fell silent, reveling in the touch of his fingers on my skin. He lowered his hand, sliding it between my legs to slip between the folds of my labia. With one finger, he began rubbing my clit, slowly at first, circling the nub, then harder.

I let out a faint cry as I pressed back against him, against his erection, and he shifted position.

"Spread your legs."

I did as he asked, and the next moment he

slipped his cock deep into me from behind, his girth stretching me wide, filling me so incredibly full that there was no spot inside me that he wasn't touching.

I leaned forward, resting my hands on the arm of the wingback, as he began to pump, thrusting deeply into me, holding my hips as he slid in and out, at first slowly and then speeding up. My breasts bounced with the rhythm of his thrusts, and I reached up to finger my nipples as Herne shifted, changing angles. I groaned again as he hit that perfect spot.

After a few moments, he slowly withdrew, his body sweaty against mine. "On the bed, woman. Ride me." He stretched out on the daybed on his back.

I straddled him, holding his gaze as I growled, feeling feral and wild and on the prowl. Herne was my prey, now, and *I* was the hunter.

He gripped his cock, holding it erect, his eyes glowing.

I lowered myself onto his shaft. As he penetrated me, his girth once again making me gasp, he reached up to squeeze my breasts. I leaned one hand against the wall to brace myself, and with the other, I slowly fingered my clit, dropping my head back as I exposed my throat.

"Ride me," he ordered, his voice hoarse and thick. "Fuck me hard."

And so I rode him, bouncing up and down as he bucked beneath me. He brought his hands to my waist, holding me tight, lifting me up and down on his cock. I was wet, slick from hunger, and I picked up speed, leaning forward so my breasts raked his chest.

"I'm close," I whispered, breathing hard as I tried to focus.

But the edge was near, and all around me I could feel the wild forest. And Herne was the silver stag, Lord of the Forest. Lord of *my* forest. The world spiraled around me, the distant sound of drums echoing with my heartbeat. And then I came, hard and fast and strong, hot tears catching in my throat as the orgasm hit me.

Herne was right behind. He stiffened, holding me still as he thrust one last time, so deep that it felt like he had penetrated every cell of my body. He let out a roar, then thrust again and once more, as I fell across his chest. Finally, we sprawled in a pool of sweat, exhausted and satiated.

"You good?" he whispered after a moment.

"I'm good," I whispered back. And then, he kissed me, deep and loving, with all the tenderness in the world.

Chapter 5

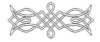

BY THE TIME I got home, Angel was packed. She had started a bag for me, too. She took one look at me as I entered the door and laughed.

"You got lucky tonight." She pointed toward the kitchen. "I already ate, but I left some for you. I made up a quick spaghetti and if there's any left, we can freeze it till we get back."

"You're kidding, right?" The aroma of garlic and meat sauce filled the condo, and my mouth began to water. As much as I had enjoyed my time with Herne, now I was starving. "If there's any left, I'll eat it for breakfast." I loved cold spaghetti for breakfast. Cold pizza, too.

"I started packing for you, but I wasn't sure what you wanted to take. By the way, Talia called. She made arrangements with her pet sitter to swing by tomorrow morning before we leave. So we need to get up by six. I have a good feeling about the woman, just from the way Talia talks about her. So I don't think you'll have to worry about Mr. Rumblebutt." She peeked around the arch into the kitchen, then leaned against the wall. "By the way, thank you."

"For what?" I asked, licking a drop of sauce off my finger as I forked a large serving of spaghetti onto a plate.

"For coming with me to see DJ. To tell you the truth, I was afraid he might be angry at me. Sometimes I think he blames me for Mama J.'s death." She said the latter so softly that I almost didn't register her words.

"What the hell? Of course he doesn't. Mama J. was hit by a drunk driver."

"Yeah, but she wouldn't have been on the road except for me. She wanted me to come over that night, but I didn't have time. I told her I'd meet her at a coffee shop for a few minutes, because I had to work late. She was on the way when the accident happened."

I suddenly began to understand. Angel had never told me this and I realized that she blamed herself.

She shook her head, a strained look on her face. "The last thing she told DJ was that I needed to see her and she'd be back later. There was one point last year, where DJ and I were arguing. I think it was over him hanging out with a kid that I didn't like—the boy was trouble. Anyway, in the heat of the argument, DJ told me point-blank, 'It's your fault Mama's dead. If she hadn't been going to see you, she'd still be alive.' Since then, those words have been running through my mind. I keep wondering, did he really mean it? He apologized later, but sometimes when we blurt out things, that's when our true feelings show."

I wasn't sure what to say. There was no way on earth that anybody could blame Angel for Mama J.'s death. But when you were ten years old and you had lost your mother, it wasn't so clear. On the surface, I doubted DJ meant a word of it. But somewhere inside his broken heart, I could see how he might think that when he was hurting enough.

"DJ loves you, Angel. Whether or not he meant it—and if he did, I'm sure it was only at that moment—DJ loves you. He trusts you, and he knows you've done the best you could for him. Of that much, I'm positive."

She held on to the edge of the counter, gazing at the refrigerator. She was blinking back tears, and I realized that as hard as it had been on DJ, it was just as hard on Angel. I understood. The anniversary of my parents' death was never easy for me, but in some ways I had blurred out as much as I could, and it had been fifteen years ago, compared to only one for Angel and DJ. And as close as my parents and I had been, we were never as tight as Mama J. had been with her children. I wrapped my arms around Angel's shoulders, giving her a tight hug.

"Cry if you need to. It's better out than in."

At that, she turned and wept against my shoulder. I rubbed her back, rocking her gently, until the sobs began to subside. Another moment later, and she stood back, wiping her eyes. She gave me a fragile smile.

"I guess I've needed that for the past couple of days. I've been pushing it away and pushing it away, trying to pretend that I was too busy to pay attention. It's just—her death still feels *so close*." She wrapped her arms around her stomach, leaning back against the counter. "In some ways it feels like it's been a thousand years. It's been tough, taking care of DJ and trying to figure out what to do. And yet, some days, I think it happened just yesterday." She looked up at me. "Do you know what I mean?"

I popped my dish into the microwave to heat up. "Yeah, I do. Sometimes, it feels like it was just yesterday that I opened the door and found my parents. There are images, you know? Ones I'll never forget. Like, I remember there was a little frog sitting on a rock outside the door when I came home. I looked at it, and thought how cute it was, and I remember thinking that I was going to tell my father about it. And then, I opened the door, which—well, it was already open, I just pushed it a little more—but I entered the kitchen. Even though my mother was sprawled out there on the floor, the first thing I remembered seeing was a plate of cookies on the counter. My first thought was over, she made chocolate chip cookies. And the next second, I was screaming, and there was blood, and then the world changed."

I carried my plate to the table after the bell dinged, stopping at the refrigerator for a glass of milk. Angel followed me, a mug of tea in hand.

Every day she used a different mug before bed, or at least it seemed like it. She had picked up new ones after her home had been destroyed, and by now she had at least a dozen. Each one had a cute picture or saying on it. Tonight, she was carrying one that read *Look for the light*.

"I suppose over the years I'll get used to this. I know it will never be easy. But the immediate pain will fade. I just didn't expect it to still be so cutting. Let's talk about something else, okay?" she asked. "How was tonight? You have fun?"

I blushed despite myself. "Sex has never been so good. I mean, a couple of my boyfriends were spot on, but Herne... He's the son of a god and I can *really* tell that when he's inside me."

"So are you Goldilocks? And was he *just* right?" She gave me a nudge and I broke out in a loud guffaw.

"You're lucky I wasn't eating or you might be performing the Heimlich maneuver on me. Yes, trust me, he's *just right*." I finished eating, polishing off the rest of the spaghetti, and we moved on to packing. By ten thirty, we were both exhausted. We took our showers, and then after saying good night, headed to bed. Mr. Rumblebutt came bouncing out of Angel's room, landing on the bottom of my bed. As he crawled onto my side, I curled my arm around him and pulled him close.

"Tomorrow you're going to have a pet sitter. Talia made arrangements for me, so no complaints about a dirty litter box. I want you to behave for her, okay? I'm going to miss you, you goober."

In response, Mr. Rumblebutt reached out and

gave me a long lick on my nose. Then he settled down to washing his paws, purring as I drifted off to sleep.

RONNIE ARCHWOOD SHOWED up right on time, at six thirty. I was bleary-eyed, drinking the quint-shot mocha that Angel had prepared for me. She had also somehow managed to fix toasted sausage-cheese muffins, and I was plowing my way through my second when Ronnie knocked at the door. I let her in, surprised to see that she was Fae. Light Fae, if I didn't miss my guess. I steeled myself, expecting her to give me the usual look that most of my mother's people had over the years. But it didn't come.

"Hi, I'm Ronnie. Talia sent me." Her eyes were clear and the smile on her face seemed genuine.

I shook her hand, smiling graciously. "I'm Ember Kearney. Come on in. Thank you for coming over at such short notice. I didn't realize that I was going to be away for more than a couple of days. Mr. Rumblebutt is fine on his own for a day or two, but I don't want to leave him alone longer than that."

I escorted her into the living room, where we sat on the sofa. Mr. Rumblebutt came running out of my bedroom, down the hall, and bounced on the sofa between us, staring up at Ronnie expectantly. He wasn't usually so excited about visitors.

"Well, he seems to like you. Mr. Rumblebutt

doesn't usually take to people at first meeting." I scratched him between the ears.

"I have a way with animals," Ronnie said. "You know the term 'animal whisperer'? That seems to be my main talent. So I decided to put it to good use and become a pet sitter." She paused, then glanced at me over Mr. Rumblebutt's head. "I might as well get this out of the way. *You* know I'm Light Fae. And *I* know that you are what is crudely known as *tralaeth*, but that doesn't matter to me. I was kicked out of my family a long time ago. I don't circulate within either court. I've been ostracized from my people for quite a while."

I had to give it to her for being blunt—even more than I was. "What happened? If you don't want to answer, that's fine. It's obvious why I'm not welcome in either court."

"I fell in love with a woman."

"But the Fae have no problem with *any* sort of sexuality or gender-identification. At least, I thought so. I really don't know much about either side of my heritage, since my parents didn't talk about it a lot while they were alive."

"It wouldn't be a problem if she were Fae. No, I fell in love with a human. I chose to live in her world, rather than the world of my people. This was over 150 years ago, and Sara is long dead, but I couldn't go back. My mother told me they'd welcome me home if I would admit I had screwed up. But since they wouldn't accept my relationship as valid while Sara was alive, I wasn't about to go back once she was dead and pretend that it was a mistake. I've been living on my own since then."

She ducked her head, shrugging. "What can I say?"

I wasn't sure what to say either, except that I admired her for standing her ground.

"I'm sorry that happened. In an odd way, that gives us some common ground." And that was about all there was to say about that.

"Tell me about your kitty." She scratched him behind the ears and he began to purr, basking in the attention.

"So, this is Mr. Rumblebutt. He gets fed twice a day. Rather, he gets wet food twice a day. He gets free feed kibble. He loves to play with feather toys, and he loves to be snuggled." As if to prove my point, Mr. Rumblebutt decided that he'd climb on her lap. Paws against her chest, he stood, staring her in the face. He licked her nose, then turned around to look at me as if asking, *Why are you still here? Leave me alone with my new friend.* I relaxed, realizing that Talia had been spot on about Ronnie. I could leave Mr. Rumblebutt in her care with no worries.

"How long do you think you'll be gone?"

"At least three or four days. Possibly a week. We have a case taking us to Whidbey Island. I can come back if there's a problem, but I feel safer knowing he's got somebody here just in case I can't get back to town right away."

I pulled out a piece of paper and scribbled my permission for her to take him to the vet in case of emergency, then I wrote down the vet's name and the address and phone number.

"Here you go. I will try to remember to call them later today and let them know that I've given you permission to bring him in, just as an added security measure. Here's a key, and I ask that you don't touch any of the weapons around here. Feel free to make yourself a snack, we've got some food in the refrigerator that will go bad by the time we come back. So eat if you want. Can you check on him twice a day?"

"I'll come in the morning at around eight A.M., and in the evening at about six thirty, and I can stay for about an hour each time. Will that work?" She scratched him behind the ears again, and he purred, then turned around and bounced back into my lap as if he knew I was getting ready to leave.

I gave him a tight squeeze and kissed his head. Mr. Rumblebutt had been my friend for quite a while, ever since I had moved into the condo, and he was the one person—so to speak—besides Angel that I trusted in this world.

"That will work," I said, sliding him off my lap and standing up. "We have to leave now. There's plenty of food in the cupboards for him."

Angel was standing by the table. She had placed our bags on the floor by the door. I joined her, leaving Ronnie to visit for a while with Mr. Rumblebutt. As we left, I realized that I wasn't worried. For once, I actually trusted one of my own.

BY THE TIME we got downtown to the office, everybody else was already there. Morning traffic was a bitch, as usual, and I had to take four detours just to avoid collisions. It was raining, not unusual for Seattle, but apparently a few days of sun had managed to wipe out any common sense about driving on wet pavement.

"Talia, thank you for sending Ronnie over. She's perfect."

"I didn't want to tell you she was Fae until you had a chance to meet her," she said, grinning. "I wasn't sure how you would react."

"Probably a good thing." I knew when to admit my prejudices.

"I'm glad she set your mind at ease. She's never failed me yet."

"Mr. Rumblebutt took to her immediately." I paused as Herne entered the break room.

"Everybody ready?" he asked, casting his gaze around. As he met my eyes, he blew me a kiss. Everybody snickered, but I didn't mind. The sex last night had been too good to just ignore.

I held up my hand. "Okay, enough. Yeah, I'm sleeping with the boss man. We all know it."

"Just so long as you don't get special brownie points for canoodling him," Talia said, but it was obviously a joke. "So I'll ride with Yutani?"

"Sounds good." He turned to me. "I assume Angel's going to ride you?"

I nodded. "Can't break us up, dude."

"That leaves Viktor with me." Herne shouldered his duffel bag, jerking his head toward the door. "Let's get a move on. Traffic's rough. I estimate a good ninety minutes to reach the ferry."

As we filed out of the office, Angel flipped off the lights and locked the elevator from stopping at our floor. It could be overridden in an emergency but only by the building owner or the police or fire department. We headed to our cars in the parking garage. As we split up, Herne and I managed a quick kiss.

"Last night was incredible," he said, rubbing his cheek against mine. "I hope we'll manage some time for a walk on the beach while we're there. We need a little time away together."

I nodded, kissing him again. Our relationship seemed to be moving from casual to more serious, but I wasn't certain yet. I still couldn't trust that this wouldn't implode, but for the first time in a long while, I felt some hope. And even that brief spark of hope scared the hell out of me, because it meant I had something to lose.

THE I-5 FREEWAY stretched from the Canadian border all the way down through California to Mexico. And our section of it was a madhouse at least twice a day. Technically, it was only about twenty-six miles from Seattle to Mukilteo where we would catch the ferry, but traffic was stop and go all the way. We landed right in the thick of the morning rush hour—or hours, rather—and the top speed was zooming along at a steady twenty-five miles per hour when the going was good. At spots, we were sitting in gridlock.

"I'm glad I went to the bathroom before we left." I squinted, pulling the visor down to shield me from the morning sun. We were sitting in bumper-to-bumper traffic, easing along at a speedy five miles an hour.

"Me too." Angel shaded her eyes, then fumbled through her purse for a pair of sunglasses. "So, how long do you think before we'll hear about the house?"

"I'm hoping sometime today. While we're sitting here in traffic, why don't you look up house inspectors? We want one who's licensed, bonded, and approved by the state, I guess. I'd use the one who checked out my condo, except I think he moved to Oregon."

She paused, then said, "In the cold light of day, I have to admit that I'm a little more nervous than I thought I was. It's a murder house. Even if there aren't any ghosts, the energy is pretty thick."

"Getting cold feet?" I asked. "I didn't have much time to talk about it with Herne last night, but I'm sure we'll figure out a way to remove the residue gunk."

"And why is that?" Angel asked with a grin. "A little busy, were we?"

"Oh, shut up." I snorted. "It's the first time in over a week that we've had a chance to play doctor. Give me a break."

Angel paused before she spoke. "You know I'm just jealous. Well, not jealous. Envious, I guess? It's been a long time since I've met anybody I wanted to date. I haven't had a chance to even think about dating since Mama J. died and I took in DJ. I'm not even sure I remember how to flirt."

I managed about three car lengths before we

were stuck again. "What about Yutani? Or Viktor? They're both gorgeous, and they're nice."

"Yes, they *are* both gorgeous. And nice. That doesn't mean I'm interested in dating either one. Neither is my type. And before you ask, Herne isn't my type either. I like him but he kind of scares me. I'm not sure I know what I'm looking for."

I glanced at her. "You never have dated much, have you?"

"There's always been something else or somebody else that needed my help. I've never felt I had much time for it." Angel shook her head. "I suppose I'd like to have a relationship at some point, but the past year I've been so focused on making a life for DJ and myself that I put all of that on the back burner." She paused, looking out the window.

"What about before DJ moved in? Even in college, you didn't go out much."

"For so long I did everything I could to help Mama J. at the diner at night. And I had my own job during the day. Before that, I was focused on college and in high school...well, I just never met anybody who interested me long enough to warrant a second date."

I glanced at her. "I suppose the first thing is for you to figure out if you actually *want* a relationship. That doesn't mean you can't date in the meantime, but do you even want to?" I paused. "I don't know what to think about Herne. I feel like we're getting closer, and that scares the hell out of me in some ways. It was so much easier to go it alone. I wasn't responsible for anybody else, I didn't worry about other people—except you, of course. I had less to lose. I think I kind of miss that, though maybe that's fear talking."

"Ember," Angel said, her voice hesitant. "I think you're searching for a reason to keep him at arm's length."

I frowned, not liking the sound of that. "What do you mean?"

"Just that you've never let anybody new get close to you since your parents were killed. You built a wall around yourself. I was lucky—I was already inside that fortress. But you've found one reason after another to keep people out of your life. And now, that gorgeous hunk of god-spawn has cracked the gate and I think you're terrified about what will happen if he sets up camp inside the barricades."

I pressed my lips together, staring at the road as traffic began to pick up.

"Don't be mad at me. I just think that you've got an idea in your head of what a relationship means, and you're not seeing all the variations of what it can be. You're not afraid of hurting Herne. You're afraid of being hurt. I know you, girl."

"Why would I be afraid of being hurt? I'm the one who's hurt my boyfriends. Or rather, my life-style has." I really didn't like the lines along which this conversation was running, but when Angel got a bug in her cap, she didn't let up.

"You're afraid he'll leave you, like your parents did. You've found one reason after another to keep people out. I think it's all a defense against being abandoned." She shrugged. "Take it for what it's worth."

I stared at the road as I switched lanes, keeping

pace with Yutani and Talia, who were in front of us. I wasn't up for this conversation, especially this early in the day.

"Want to change the subject?" she asked after a moment.

"Yeah. I'm not ready for this much introspection at this time in the morning."

"Fine, but Ember, you're going to have to face this at some point." She shrugged. "How much farther?"

Relieved by the change in subject—Angel could be annoyingly perceptive, and right now I wasn't up for a trip through the landscape of my personal issues—I shook my head.

"I'm not sure. Looks like we're back to stop-and-go traffic." I inched ahead a few feet, about one car length. "Can you check the traffic app to see how long this lasts? Is there a collision up ahead?"

Angel consulted her tablet. "One, up ahead. And there's also plenty of construction. Once we get past the accident, traffic picks up, although it still shows heavy yellow and orange all the way up to Mukilteo. Hopefully, we'll be able to catch the eight-thirty ferry. If not, there's another at nine o'clock. Let me check their alerts and see how far behind they're running."

The ferry system that ran through Puget Sound and the San Juan islands was extensive, and intricate. But certain runs and certain times were constantly backlogged. Sometimes you had to sit through one or more sailings just to board.

"Well, that's a spot of good news. The backlog's cleared up, so we should be able to make whichever ferry we arrive in time for. I haven't been on the ferry in a while." She paused, then glanced at me. "Have you ever met a hippocampus before?"

I blinked. "Well, we met Rhiannon. Why?"

"I guess what I mean is have you dealt with them before? Have you ever worked with any of them? I'm feeling a little intimidated, given what Talia said. I just don't want to make any stupid mistakes that will offend anybody."

I frowned, easing over into the right lane behind Yutani. I waited to answer until we had bypassed the collision. One of the cars looked to be totaled, and the firemen were spraying foam on the engine, which was shooting out flames. The other car appeared to be smashed up as well, but it was obvious who had hit whom. The HOV lane had been cordoned off for emergency vehicles, and an ambulance was speeding off, headed for the next exit into Everett.

As soon as we passed the accident, traffic began to speed up, and we were able to navigate back over to the left lane. We were nearing the turnoff to Highway 526, toward Mukilteo. When we came to 40th Avenue, we would swing a right and follow it to the Mukilteo Speedway. From there, it was a straight shot to the ferry terminal.

"Angel, I've never seen you make a 'stupid mistake' in your life. Why the sudden insecurity?"

She shifted in her seat. "I don't know. Everything's suddenly so different. In my old job, I didn't have to deal with customers much. I did what the boss wanted, and tried to keep my nose clean. He was a jackass, but it was routine and I knew what I was doing. There are so many factors to this job that I'm still getting used to them."

"Are you unhappy?" I glanced at her, worrying.

"No, not at all. Don't get me wrong. I love the job, but I sometimes worry that I'm in a little over my head. Like today, for example. I'm glad I get to go, but what do I do while I'm there? I'm not one of the investigators, and I'm not really one of the researchers. So I don't know what purpose I'm serving."

I started to blow off her worry, but stopped myself. Fear was fear, unfounded or not.

"You'll coordinate everything for us while we're there." I paused, then asked, "Are you interested in being one of the investigators? Or doing research?"

She shook her head. "I wouldn't make a good investigator and I know it. I'm a little too chicken for that. Research, I love. So if they need me to help, I'm glad to. I just don't want to feel like I'm sitting around, riding on anybody's coattails."

"I don't think you have to worry about that. We rely on you to keep everything organized. Your talent for management has really shone through the past few months."

Both Herne and Yutani veered onto the exit ramp up ahead, and I followed suit.

The highway was still tree-lined, but they were sparser and shorter, more like scrub brush. There was a lot of wind up here, and a number of the trees had bent trunks from being caught in the constant flow. Traffic was lighter, and we were going at a good clip, zipping past stores and strip malls. Finally, we were past Boeing and Paine

Field, where we turned right onto 40th Avenue. It curved to the left into 78th Street, then to the right again, then one more bend and it turned into 76th Street. As we drove through the residential area, I thought it might be nice to live up here. There was a different feel about it—even though it was still relatively dense city, it felt more open, with room to breathe. Before long, the road curved onto Highway 525, and from there, we were only a short drive from the ferry terminal.

Mukilteo was a small town of around twenty thousand. Located on Puget Sound, it was home to one of the Washington State ferry terminals. It was also home to a historical lighthouse, which was part of Lighthouse Park and Mukilteo Beach. Right next to the ferry terminal, the site was famous for being the place where a treaty was signed between Governor Stevens and the Native American chiefs from twenty-two Puget Sound tribes. Throughout its evolution, Mukilteo had been a fishing village, a lumber town, home to a cannery, and even the location of a gunpowder factory. Like most of the towns in northwestern Washington state, Mukilteo was heavily wooded, with large swaths of trees running through it.

To the east, the town buttressed Everett, which in turn bumped up against farmland. To the west was Puget Sound. The Mukilteo ferry had one route, and that was over to Clinton on Whidbey Island. Halfway up the shoreline of Whidbey Island was the Keystone ferry landing, crossing over the sound to Port Townsend. And on the upper tip of Whidbey Island, a bridge led across Deception

Pass into the Anacortes area. All and all, the entire area was incredibly beautiful, heavily wooded, and a marine wonderland.

We arrived fifteen minutes before the next ferry was scheduled to load. As we pulled into the terminal and paid our fees at the tollbooth, I glanced at my watch. It was almost 8:40, so we'd be able to catch the nine o'clock ferry. As I pulled into the slip behind Yutani and Talia, I turned off the ignition and stepped out of the car. Within minutes we were all gathered around Herne's car, chatting.

The wind was whipping at a fairly stiff rate, although the rain had died back with glimmers of sunlight breaking through the clouds. It was about sixty degrees, but the breeze made it feel cooler and I was glad I'd brought a jacket.

"Once we get off the ferry, where do we go?" I asked.

Angel consulted her map. "Take Highway 525 until we reach East Bush Point Road. Turn left and follow the road as it curves around the coastline. It will turn into Smugglers Cove Road. We follow that until we're past the South Whidbey State Park. Before we reach Seacrest Cove, we'll see a road to the right—Ruby Lane. That will take us right into the Foam Born Encampment. I'd estimate it's about seventeen miles or so from where we get off the ferry."

"What about the hotel?" Herne turned to Angel. "Where's that located?"

"A few miles further north, in Seacrest Cove. The Edgewood Star is on Oceanside Drive, at the south end of the town. Check-in is at noon." She brushed her hair back from her face and pulled out a tie, catching it back into a ponytail. I thought of doing the same myself, since the wind was whipping so hard that strands of hair were lashing across my face, but I didn't want my ears to get cold.

"How long does it take the ferry to get over to Whidbey Island?" Yutani asked.

"It's a twenty-minute crossing, so once we board, it will take us a little over half an hour to get there. I'm estimating that with a seventeen-mile drive and considering that these are winding roads, we should arrive at our destination at around ten o'clock. That should give us two hours before we can check in. I don't know about the rest of you, but I could use something to eat," Angel said. "I made a good breakfast but it seems to have vanished somewhere along that insane mess on the freeway."

"That idea's fine with me," Herne said. "Once we get over to Seacrest Cove, we'll find a restaurant and eat. I suppose we can poke around the general area, check in at noon, and then go meet Rhiannon at the encampment. Sound good?"

The rest of us nodded. Apparently we were all on the same page.

I glanced at the other waiting cars. The ferry system in Washington State was heavily used, given how many people commuted from the various islands in Puget Sound to Seattle for work and shopping. I hadn't been out on the islands much, although I had been over to Bainbridge a couple times.

I realized that it felt like I had been trapped in

the city most of my life. And it wasn't as though I'd *had* to stay there. I just never got my ass in gear to go exploring. There was so much natural beauty in our area that limiting myself to the city seemed pathetic. I made up my mind that Angel and I would start adventuring around more. I would drag her out of the city, if I had to. Herne, too, if I could get him to come along.

"Hey Viktor," I said.

"Yeah?"

"Sometime, will you take us up to Mount Rainier? I'm not saying that you should take us up to where you lived, I know how you feel about that. But you know the area up there and it would be nice to have a guide."

He looked surprised, but pleasantly so. "I'd love to give you a tour. Anybody who wants to go is welcome. I like getting out in the mountains."

"I think somebody's been bitten by the wanderlust bug," Angel said with a laugh.

Herne's eyes sparkled as he caught mine. "I think we all needed this outing more than we thought. When we're done with this case—hopefully we'll be able to solve it—maybe we should spend an extra day here goofing around at the beach."

The terminal worker gave a signal as the ferry docked and cars began exiting. On that note, we prepared to board. The ferries that crossed Puget Sound were usually huge, two to three stories high, the largest holding close to 150 cars, and almost 1,900 passengers. The bigger ferries had elevators and snack bars, and felt a lot like a luxury yacht.

Angel and I belted ourselves back in the car. I

started the engine as the cars in our lane started to move, driving forward, following the directions of the terminal worker who was flagging us along. As we drove over the metal latchway that connected the ferry to the terminal, another worker motioned for us to turn to the right, driving up onto the second deck, where we parked next to the railing. We were on our way.

Chapter 6

ONCE AGAIN, I turned off the ignition and we got out of the car, walking over to the railing to look down at the water.

Puget Sound was an inlet for the Pacific Ocean, coming off of the Straits of Juan de Fuca and the Salish Sea. The sound stretched well over a hundred miles, all the way down into the Olympia area. All along the stretch of water, tributaries and waterways branched off, and the sound was considered to be the third-largest estuary in the United States. The complex geology that went into creating the watery passage stretched as far back as the Ice Age, and considering that the entire edge of Washington sat on the Cascadia subduction zone, it was an extremely complicated marine environment. The beauty of the sound and its islands was unmatched.

I leaned against the railing, shivering in the

bracing air. But the saltwater scent of the sound pierced my senses, bracing me up. I closed my eyes, taking in a deep breath as the mammoth engines of the ferry started. A voice echoed over the loudspeaker, welcoming us aboard, and giving safety regulations and notifications. I listened vaguely, taking a moment to note where the life-jackets were stored. The ferries were usually quite safe, but now and then an accident occurred. Usually it was some car going off the end into the water, or a ferry hitting into one of the terminal landings and busting it to pieces.

As the ferry chugged out into open water, Herne slipped up beside me.

"Come on, let's go up top." He took me by the hand, and pulled me over to the stairs. We jogged up to the third deck, wending our way through the milling passengers. Some were eating, some scrambling for a seat where they could stare out the window, while others were at the numerous tables, hooking up to the Internet. We passed by them, crossing to the doors that led out onto the observation deck. As we walked out onto the deck at the back of the ferry, we found ourselves staring at the shoreline as it receded into the distance behind us. The water was choppy thanks to the wind, but the ferry rode the waves easily, and the motion calmed me down. I loved the water, and now that I was pledged to Morgana, Fae goddess of the sea, it felt good to be on the open water. I needed to do this more often.

I had been working with my water magic more, trying to recall what my mother had taught me. It was slow going, but starting to come a little quicker. Now and then, Morgana came to me in dreams and whispered in my ears, guiding me as I felt my way through the watery labyrinth of her magic. I was self-conscious. After all, she was Herne's *mother*, but at the end of the day, my relationship with her had nothing to do with him.

I stretched my arms wide as we leaned against the forest-green steel railing. The breeze railed against me, the wind growing brisker as it picked up the scent of the saltwater. I sucked the briny air deep into my lungs, holding it tight before letting it out again.

"This is so beautiful. I don't know why I haven't come out here before." I turned to Herne, feeling giddy, as though a whole new world had opened up around me.

"A lot of people don't think about it. I like to come out on the ferries and go over to the islands, to get away from things. Sometimes Viktor comes with me, sometimes Yutani. But mostly I go by myself." He paused, then added, "Running the agency is a lot of responsibility. My father has high expectations, and so much rides on doing our work correctly."

"Just how long have you been in charge of the Wild Hunt?" I leaned against him and he wrapped his arm around my shoulders as we stared out over the water.

Herne had been running the agency for several hundred years as far as I knew, first over in the UK, and then in the United States for a little over a century. Cernunnos and Morgana had relocated him to the United States when they saw technology starting to advance. Talia had come with him. At the same time, a number of the Fae began retreating across the Great Sea, which linked the Lands of Fire and Ice with this world. Across the Great Sea, massive Fae cities stretched in magnificent glory. TirNaNog and Navane were the Dark and the Light capitals. The two Fae cities on the east side of Lake Washington were named for them, but they paled in comparison to their namesakes in the Fae world.

"Not as long as some of the others. Mielikki's Arrow and Odin's Chase have been running for far longer. But yes, I've been doing this long enough to need a vacation on a regular basis." He leaned down and kissed the top of my head. I noticed he conveniently skirted my question, but decided to skip it for now.

"I had no idea I'd ever end up doing something like this. My mother and father never really seemed to have a vision for me. They left the choice up to me. I had already decided to go into law enforcement—in one way or another—before they were killed. I thought about becoming a lawyer, but I can't stand to be inside that much. So I was thinking investigator, or something along that line. I guess I ended up there anyway, didn't I? First on my own, and now with the Wild Hunt."

"I was born to it," Herne said. "From the very beginning my father and mother brought me up, grooming me for this responsibility."

He didn't talk much about his childhood, and I hadn't asked, feeling like it was too soon to pry.

But now, it seemed like the timing had clicked into place.

"Where were you born? I don't think those of us not from your world understand the nature of the gods. I know I never did. I still don't. I knew my mother was pledged to Morgana, though I had no idea my father had been pledged to Cernunnos. I never really thought much about the gods while I was growing up. I was too focused on keeping my ass out of trouble at school, and on having fun with Angel. She really *is* an angel in disguise."

Herne leaned on the railing, staring out over the water. "The gods exist in a world a step or two away from this one. Some of them live farther out, in different realms. Every pantheon seems to have its own niche. There are gateways leading into the worlds of the gods all over the world. They're usually found in natural places along the ley lines. Sometimes there's nothing overt to mark their existence. Other times, you'll find the opening through a hole in the stone, and in the center of the great stone circles around the world, or over the rainbow bridge, or at the bottom of a deep cavern. Some can be found on top of the mountains, or in the center of an ancient tree trunk."

"Where did you grow up? Do you live over the rainbow?" I flashed him a wide smile, trying to imagine Herne crossing an arc of light.

"No, the realm I grew up in is heavily forested. There are a multitude of rivers and lakes there, and an ocean. I know there's a large city somewhere, but my father is Lord of the Forest, so I didn't grow up around a lot of people. Neither my father nor mother had much to do with the other Fae gods, although my mother interacted with them more. I did grow up knowing Bran and Bloudewedd. I met the Morrígan several times, and Epona. In fact, over the years, I've met a number of the Celtic gods and goddesses. I'm one of the younger ones, you understand. So is Morgana—since she was deified rather than born a goddess."

"I thought that the gods lived here, on earth. They phone you occasionally."

He shrugged. "They have a headquarters here. You might say they have office hours. Most of the time they spend over in their own realm. But every so often they visit. It's just a hop skip and a jump to our compound. I'll take you there sometime. You should really meet my father. You've already met Morgana." He said it so nonchalantly that I almost didn't catch what he said, and then his words sunk in.

"You want me to meet your father?" The words stuck in my throat. I had heard enough about Cernunnos to know that meeting him was a big deal, and not likely to be pleasant. The Lord of the Forest didn't run around in bellbottoms getting stoned and hugging trees, that much I knew.

"Yeah. You and Angel need to anyway. Everybody who works for the Wild Hunt meets him eventually. Trust me, be glad you're meeting my father and not someone like Odin or Mielikki. Or even Artemis. Artemis is one of the most solemn women I've ever met, and she *doesn't* have a sense of humor. At least Mielikki has a sense of humor, but it's dark and a little twisted. Odin, well, he's as imposing as all get out, but he can tell a good story."

My head was reeling. The thought of meeting any of the gods left me numb, and once again, the realization that I was dating a god, albeit a young one, hit home. Herne seemed so unassuming, but the truth was, I had never seen him at his full power and I didn't know what he could do. Now curious, I debated the best way of asking the questions running through my mind.

"Okay, here's the deal. You're a god. You're the *son* of a god, but you're still a god."

"Technically, I'm a demigod. My mother isn't fully divine." A smirk began to creep across his face.

"Quit laughing at me. You know what I mean. Anyway, what can you do? I never asked you before because it never fully sank in. But...just what kind of powers do you have? Can you throw a thunderbolt? Cause an earthquake? Grant wishes? Give me a big raise?" I threw the last in to break the tension.

"Oh, Ember." Herne laughed. "I cannot throw lightning bolts. Neither can my father. That's not his domain, nor is it mine. Hell, Morgana can call up a storm faster than either one of us, but only when she's near the water. As far as an earthquake? Not so much."

"Then what is your magic?"

"Think. My father is Lord of the Forest. So my magic is the magic of the trees and animals, especially within a forested realm. I can summon plants and trees to do my bidding. I can speak with the animals—just call me Dr. Doolittle. I can speak with plants and trees. I can turn into the silver stag, that you *have* seen. I have other abilities that I'm not even sure how to explain. I can shoot dead on with a bow and arrow almost every time. I can start fires, and because of my mother's blood I have some connection with the water as well. And I run with the Wild Hunt—the *actual* wild hunt. Not just the agency."

I thought about what he said. He had answered my question, yet he hadn't. In some ways, he was more of an enigma than ever. But I felt like I was slowly beginning to unravel the tangle of knots that made up who Herne actually was. It frightened me to be in a relationship with someone about whom I knew so little, but you don't just pry open the secrets of the gods in a couple months. Hell, there was a lot about myself that I still hadn't told him. I had the feeling he knew some of it, given his powers of investigation, but I had hidden dreams and secrets that I didn't feel comfortable revealing yet.

"Do you feel safe around me?" he asked.

I thought about the question. "That's not easy to answer. I haven't felt safe around anybody except Angel since my parents were killed. And before that, I felt safe only around them and Angel. I learned early not to trust people, and not to trust my heart—or my feelings—with anybody until I knew that they weren't going to hurt me."

I had been taught young that I was different. Most of the humans at school treated me civilly, with the same respect they would treat anybody else. But not the Fae. I could never trust that I wouldn't end up the butt of their jokes, and more than once I found myself tripped by an outstretched foot as I dashed through the hallway, slammed against the lockers as one of them shouldered past me, used as a living dodgeball if I happened to find myself in a ring of them…that sort of thing. I had toughened up and started keeping my feelings to myself. At the most, I only told Angel about what happened. I didn't like the hurt that I saw in my parents' faces when they found out about some of the incidents, so mostly, I never mentioned them.

"Do I feel safe around you? Mostly. I suppose that I always keep a part of myself safe and secure, locked away, protected from anybody and anything. I have to. I never open up that secret vault that contains my core essence. I never give it away, and I seldom expose it. I don't know if anybody or anything can change that. So far, Angel's been my closest friend, but I don't tell her everything either. And I don't expect her to tell me all of her secrets. I don't think it's a good thing to reveal every single thing about yourself to anybody else."

"You're a wise woman," Herne said. "I don't expect you to tell me everything. I don't even *want* to know everything—not just yet. I like that you're a puzzle. I want to get to know you, I want to explore what it's like to be with you. I'm not into info dumps, and I think you're quite right to keep a part of yourself protected. Even among the gods, there's treachery and backstabbing and deceit. Neither my mother nor father are exceptionally extroverted. They tend to keep to themselves a lot. I suppose it rubbed off on me."

A voice suddenly came over the loudspeaker, announcing that we were nearing our destination and would we return to our cars, but not start them yet. Twenty minutes had flown by. I took one last, long, slow breath, and let it out, ending on a gentle sigh.

"Well, I didn't expect an in-depth heart-to-heart, but you know? I'm glad we talked." I looped my arm around his. "We haven't had much time the past couple of weeks to really sit down and do anything but..." I stopped, rolling my eyes at him.

"Knock boots?" He asked.

"Well, if you want to put it that way, yeah. Come on, let's get back to the cars."

Laughing, we clattered down the stairs. Angel and Talia appeared out of the elevator, and Viktor and Yutani were both leaning against the railing, staring over the edge of the water. We split up and went to our respective cars.

AS WE PULLED off of the ferry, we found ourselves on a gently ascending road. We were on Highway 525, which we would need to stay on for some time. The town of Clinton had about a thousand people, although the village served several thousand more in outlying areas.

It didn't take long before we were into what seemed like an unending stretch of road that ran between wide swaths of forest. Here and there, a side road led off into a smaller part of the community. We passed the Magical Winds Sanctuary, a forty-acre private habitat offering nature trails and community ritual, and Blue Azure, a glass and pottery company.

As the miles sped past, we found ourselves zipping through Freeland, and shortly after that, we turned onto Bush Point Road. Angel and I fell into a comfortable silence, me focusing on the road while she looked out the window. That was one of the best things about a good friend—you didn't have to talk all the time if you didn't feel like it. Being able to sit in silence with someone and feel comfortable was my mark of a good friendship.

Bush Point turned into Smugglers Cove Road, and we found ourselves driving up the west side of Whidbey Island. We passed through the South Whidbey State Park, and then a quick jog onto Oceanside Drive brought us to the Edgewood Star.

Herne pulled over into the parking lot, and we followed suit. He texted: WHAT ABOUT EATING AT THE RESTAURANT IN THE HOTEL?

I glanced at Angel. "What you think? Eat at the restaurant here?"

She nodded. "I don't care *where* we eat, as long as we get some food soon."

I texted back that it was okay with us, and apparently Yutani and Talia concurred. We all got out of our cars, stretching after the drive. I looked over at the hotel, surprised that it looked so modern and up-to-date.

The Edgewood Star was a three-story hotel. Most of the rooms on the upper two floors had balconies. It wasn't close enough for a clear view of the water, but the air was crisp and smelled like sun-dried salt, and the sound of gulls echoed overhead. I drank it in, feeling the surge of energy as I connected with the water elementals that were nearby. There must be a lot of them for their energy to reach out this far inland.

The hotel was painted in shades of umber and mustard, with hints of forest green and black in the trim. It had a curved front so that it was convex, and an access road ran directly in front of the doors, giving guests a chance to unload their luggage before driving back to the parking lot. A couple of valets sat by the sides of the doors, waiting for clientele to arrive. The walk from our cars to the front door wasn't far, so I suggested that we shoulder our duffel bags and carry them with us since we'd be checking in shortly after our meal. Making sure everything was locked, we headed for the Edgewood Star.

"You said this hotel caters to members of the SubCult?" Viktor asked.

Angel nodded. "It's run by wolf shifters. I specifically requested an oversized bed for you. So Yutani, you get one, too, since you're rooming with Viktor. Talia, your room is a single."

Talia laughed. "Good enough. I have my suitors, but I left them back home."

Yutani snorted. "If you're calling that numbnut Jack a suitor, then you need an intervention."

"Who's Jack?" I asked.

Talia rolled her eyes at Yutani. "Jack happens to be my handyman. I hire him for a number of odd jobs, but keeping me warm at night isn't one of them. He's a necromancer, or at least he wants to be. I wouldn't trust him to cast a simple directional spell."

"He's human, isn't he?" Angel asked. "Most of the necromancers that I meet tend to be."

I gave her puzzled look. "Since when did you start hanging out with necromancers?"

"I have a wide variety of friends," Angel said. "But those I met at my old job. They're working the day job in hopes of becoming some famous wizard or something after hours. And I stress the 'or something.'"

"Well, Jack isn't human." Talia said, nodding at the doorman who opened the door for us. "To tell the truth, I've never been quite sure *what* he is. And I haven't had the desire or courage to get close enough to ask. But he can swing a hammer like nobody's business, and that's all I care about."

The conversation abruptly ended as we entered the hotel lobby. Angel walked over to the reception desk, whispering to them for a moment. When she returned, she had a wide smile on her face.

"Our rooms are almost ready. They said we can check in if we want after we eat, even if it isn't noon yet. The restaurant is right over there." She nodded across the lobby.

As we crossed the lobby to the restaurant, which was called Smugglers Bay, I could smell eggs and bacon and toast. It felt like it had been hours since breakfast, and actually, I thought as I glanced at the clock on the wall, it *had* been. It was ten fifteen now.

The waitress took us to our table, handing us menus. She took our drink orders, which was pretty much coffee all the way around, except for the tea Talia and Angel ordered. Then she headed back to the kitchen, leaving us to decide what we wanted.

Herne pulled out his cell phone. "I'm going to give Rhiannon a call and let her know we're in town. I'll be right back. If the waitress comes back before I get back, order me a cheeseburger with everything on it, a side of onion rings, a large chocolate shake, and a bowl of clam chowder."

I glanced at the menu, trying to decide between clam chowder and cheese bread, or a personal pizza, which boasted of white sauce, clams, fried shrimp, and smoked salmon. I finally gave up and ordered both.

The waitress didn't seem surprised by our appetites. She just took down our orders and said that she would be back with our food soon.

"Did you remember what I wanted?" Herne asked, returning to the table.

"Yes, O Mighty One," Talia said, wrinkling her nose. "Did you get a hold of Rhiannon?"

"Yes I did, and she and Marilyn will be waiting for us after we check in. I told them we would be there by one o'clock. That gives us some time to unpack. She sounded extremely relieved to hear from me. I know her cousin's death is eating at her."

A few minutes later, the waitress was back with our food. It was hearty, and there was plenty of it, and even better—it tasted fantastic. We set to eating, nobody saying much, and by the time we finished, the plates were practically licked clean. As we headed back to the registration desk to check in, I hoped that the rest of our trip would be as good as the food.

AS SOON AS our luggage was stowed in our rooms, and we had freshened up, we headed out to the Foam Born Encampment. We continued along Oceanside Drive until we reached Salmon Street in the south part of Seacrest Cove. Turning right, we followed the street as it turned and wove its way through side streets, and then we were back on Smugglers Cove Road. From there, we drove south again until we came to Ruby Lane. The private road took us directly into the Foam Born Encampment.

I wasn't sure what to expect, since the word "encampment" conjured up visions of military barracks and training facilities, but the suburb was anything but military in nature. It was a gated community, yes, but the drive was spacious, and the gates reminded me of an old-fashioned estate. A security guard manned the gates and, after asking our business, he opened the gates for us and we drove down the long winding road into the center of the community.

There must have been about thirty homes, along with a general store and a community center. A farmers' market had set up nearby, and a sign next to one of the stalls told us that it was open on Saturdays and Sundays from eight A.M. until eight P.M. From the way they had looped the drive into the farmers' market parking lot, then out again, suggested a great deal of traffic.

"From what Talia said, I'm gathering this farmers' market gets heavily congested on the weekends. Apparently the Foam Born are magicians at growing vegetables and fruit," Angel said. We had brought all three cars with us, just in case we needed to split up.

"So only the Foam Born live around here?" I had gotten the impression they were mixed into the community rather than off to themselves.

Angel shook her head. "I had a glance at the notes while we were on the ferry, and asked Talia about them. While it's true that most of these houses belong to the hippocampi, just beyond here, there's another suburb of houses where humans live, along with a few shifters."

"I thought sure they would live right on the water, given their nature."

"Real estate is expensive on the water, especially out here on Whidbey Island." She paused. "The body was found down by the park near the water line."

She had a good point. It was super expensive to live out on the islands, at least if you were new to the area. If you had inherited a family house or had bought the house before the tech industry boomed in the 1990s, it was probably worth gold now.

We followed Herne's car out of the main neighborhood, veering to the northeast. Ruby Lane ran between thickets of trees, then into another small clearing, where there were more houses, spaced out further. I estimated each house sat on two to five acres.

Herne pulled into the driveway of the third house on the left. We followed suit, and behind us came Yutani and Talia. As we parked, Rhiannon stepped out onto the porch of the beautiful old farmhouse. She was wearing a floral dress, with an intricately woven shawl over her shoulders. Her hair tumbled down, looking for all the world like a halo of soft light.

As Angel and I stepped out of the car, I was struck by how clear the air seemed. I inhaled deeply, filling my lungs. Everything felt clear and clean.

The farmhouse was two-story, with a wide front porch and steps leading down to the slate stone path that ended at the driveway. It looked well kept. The paint was fresh, a pale lemon like whipped egg yolks, and to either side of the porch steps was a row of rose bushes, some of them already in bloom. The roses were beautiful, ranging from deep crimson to a peach with rust tips. A huge oak stood in the front yard, towering over the house, and to one side was the tree line of the thicket of fir and cedars. To the left of the house, and behind it, I could see a large lot of blueberry bushes. They were covered with leaves, though I couldn't tell if they were in flower yet. A swing set sat near the oak, and a picnic table. All in all, the house felt lived in, warm and inviting. It made me want to peek inside.

Rhiannon slowly descended the stairs, smiling as we approached.

"Thank you so much for coming. I'm so happy you were able to make it. Marilyn's inside—I told her to wait there with her son. She'll do her best to tell you whatever she can, but she is still shaken. It's been a year, but trauma like that never fully goes away."

Herne nodded. "We've dealt with a lot of trauma over the years. We'll be discreet and as gentle as we can."

Rhiannon thanked him and turned back to the stairs, motioning for us to follow. As we entered the farmhouse, the scent of cinnamon was overwhelming. Either someone had been baking, or there was a lot of incense around. The living room was tidy, with a modest leather sofa to one side, a rocking chair, a playpen, a television and desk—just about everything you'd expect to find in somebody's living room. The walls were pale blue, and the icy color both calmed and chilled me at the same time. A fireplace abutted one side, the mantel neat and tidy, and it looked like it'd been scrubbed as clean as it could possibly get. I wondered if Marilyn ever used it to actually *burn* anything in.

At that moment, a woman appeared in the doorway from what looked to be the kitchen.

"Welcome," she said. "Please, take a seat. I just have to finish feeding Ryan, and I'll be right in. Rhiannon, will you see if they want any refreshments?"

Rhiannon turned to us and motioned to the sofa.

"Please, sit. Would you like anything? Lemonade, coffee, tea?"

We declined, so Rhiannon joined us. She looked tired. "It's been a long day already," she said. "There was an incident at the Treeline—the local diner—today."

"What kind of incident?"

"Havely, one of our local schoolteachers, found her dog dead this morning." Rhiannon gave us a long look. "The poor thing had been mutilated. Nobody in our community would ever think of doing any such thing. We're not sure what happened, but apparently Havely said that he went missing yesterday."

A dead dog was one thing. A mutilated dog? That spelled trouble. Killing animals sometimes led to killing people. Especially in brutal ways. Herne seemed to be thinking what I was, because he stiffened, narrowing his eyes.

"Have you had any other animal murders around here? Within the past year or two?"

Rhiannon frowned, worrying her lip. "Yes, actually, a few. We always assumed it was just some freak passing through who wanted to mess with us. There are those who still don't appreciate the fact that humans don't run the world without interference."

Talia spoke up. "Want me to jot that down on my list of things to research?"

Herne nodded. "It might be a good idea." He stopped as Marilyn appeared in the door, carrying a toddler. Ryan was a pudgy little kid, with blond hair and sea foam gray eyes. He looked tired, leaning against his mother's shoulder. Marilyn walked over to the playpen, leaning in to lay him in it. She covered him with a light blanket, and he rolled over and fell asleep without a single sound. Once she had raised the railing, Marilyn took a seat in the rocking chair.

"If we talk, will we disturb him?" Angel asked.

Marilyn shook her head. "He's a remarkably easy boy. Surprising, given his start in life. But once he's asleep, he's out. I could blast the Red Hot Chili Peppers in here and he wouldn't wake up. So, Rhiannon tells me that you're going to look into Jona's murder?" A faint hope hung in her voice, but her eyes were impassive.

Herne gave her a long look, then nodded. "We're going to see if there's any cause for us to reopen the case. If we come up with any new leads, we'll check into them and see what we can find. Please understand, though, it's difficult with cold cases."

"The investigation into Jona's murder was dead in the water before it began," Marilyn said. "Apparently the authorities around here didn't deem it worth their time. They chalked it up to some passing vampire, but I know full well it wasn't a vamp execution. I've seen vampire murders before. Their...bodies...looked nothing like Jona's."

"I thought they wouldn't let you see his body after they found him," Talia said.

Marilyn snorted. "I have friends who have friends. They managed to get hold of a few of the crime scene photos." Her expression hardened. "Trust me, Jona wasn't murdered by a vampire. No vamp in his right mind would put that many holes in a body, and they were too large to be fang marks."

That she could sit there and discuss the state of her husband's body surprised me, though I supposed it shouldn't. The hippocampi were a reserved people.

"Before we take this case, I have to ask you something." Herne cleared his throat, looking uncomfortable. "Rhiannon wanted to hire us, but do *you* want us investigating? After all, Jona was *your* husband."

Marilyn shrugged. "I'd like to know what happened to him. I'd like to know who killed him. I'm moving on with my life. I *have* to because of Ryan especially. But that doesn't mean that I've let go of Jona's memory. And it doesn't mean that I've settled his death in my heart."

"Well, then," Herne said. "We'll see what we can find." As he spoke, there was a knock on the door. Rhiannon answered and when she returned, she was followed by one of the sheriff's deputies. He was Fae, and he did not look happy.

Chapter 7

THE DEPUTY LOOKED around the room, stopping short when he came to me. He held my gaze, sneering as he looked at me. I stared straight back at him, challenging him to say something. Whether it was because I held my own, or because I was sitting next to Herne, I didn't know, but he said nothing. Instead, he turned to Herne.

"Lord Herne, well met. We heard you were in town. I've come to ask if you're on any official business we should know about."

Herne returned the officer's look with an unreadable expression.

"I'm investigating a cold case for a client." He waited, confidently silent. The officer looked uncomfortable, tugging on his collar.

"Will you be requiring our assistance for Lord Cernunnos?"

"I'm not on *that* kind of official business. If I

need your help, I'll drop in at the station. Thank you for your concern." Cool as a cucumber, Herne might as well have dropkicked the deputy across the field.

Shifting from one foot to the other, the officer waited, expectantly, but Herne said nothing more. Finally, looking at a loss, the deputy tipped his hat to the room.

"Yes, well. I'll tell my superiors. Feel free to ask for help if you need us." With a disgruntled shrug, he turned and left the room. Rhiannon escorted him out, then pressed her back to the door, suppressing a laugh.

"Well, I can't say I'm surprised he showed up."

"Who is he?"

"Jakovan. He's the sheriff's lapdog. Absolute toady. The sheriff—Astrana—is one of the Light Fae. She's got her fingers in every pie she can. I'm pretty sure that she's the one who told her underlings to warn people to keep their noses out of Jona's murder."

Talia made a note. "Astrana... For some reason that name sounds familiar."

"That's because she was one of Névé's guards for a while. I remember a kerfuffle we had with her about forty years back, when she still lived in Navane," Yutani said. "I didn't realize that she had moved over here. I remember she had a lot of ambition."

Talia snapped her fingers, a light flashing in her eyes. "Oh yes! I remember her. She was a pain in the ass. I'm surprised she's still alive, given how grasping she was."

"Well, she hasn't changed any, then," Rhiannon said. "Nobody really likes her, but she uses her authority to influence as much as she can. You'd think she was looking to take over the island as Queen."

"That's her, all right," Talia said. "Névé dressed her down for overstepping her boundaries. Yutani's right—we met her when we were on a case about forty years ago. Astrana interfered with the investigation in a number of ways. We had to ask Morgana to intervene. That must be when Névé kicked her out, or when she left on her own volition."

"We'll have to walk carefully," Herne said. "If she's anything like she was back then, she delights in causing trouble. So just be cautious, and keep your noses clean. Don't speed, don't do anything that could get yourself in trouble. At least legally. We're bound to clash with her at some point if we find enough to really continue this investigation. In fact—Marilyn? Was Astrana leading the investigation into Jona's murder?"

Marilyn nodded, her face grim. "Yeah, she was. There were several times I wanted to smack her in the face. She's been sheriff here for around thirty-five years, maybe a few more."

"Okay, well at least we know one of the blocks we're up against. Can you tell us about Jona's last night? At least, the last night you saw him."

Marilyn let out a long sigh. She pursed her lips, looking like she was trying to hold back tears. "Jona and I were planning our upcoming anniversary. We were married five years ago, so it would have been our fourth anniversary. We had so much to celebrate. Ryan almost died at birth, I don't know if you know that. But our neighbor saved him by letting me give birth in his pool. As a hippocampus, I have to give birth underwater. Anyway, Jona and I were discussing where to go on our anniversary. We were going to take Ryan with us, given how much fear there was around his birth."

"Rhiannon said that Jona went to a grange meeting. Was it a normal meeting? Or was it a special one—called suddenly? Would other people have known he was going to attend?"

"Oh yes, the meeting flyer was up at the farmers' market. And Jona was a well-known member. It was a normal meeting in every way. Jona always walked to the meetings, even in the rain. He loved to be outside, and he loved the rain. I asked him not to go that night because we had so much to do. But he said there was an important vote. He wanted to be there for it. In some ways, I don't know if I'll ever forgive him for going. I know that's ridiculous. I know it's unfair, but part of me just keeps wondering why he insisted. Why didn't he listen to me?"

"Anger like that is normal," I said. "Do you know what the vote was about?"

She frowned, thinking. Finally, she snapped her fingers. "Yes, I do, now that I think about it. They were voting on whether to expand the farmers' market. The grange had been discussing the possibility of opening it during the week. During the holiday season it's open all week long, because crafters bring out their wares...holiday sales and all. But they had been talking about opening it during the weekdays from June through October, as well as November and December."

"Was your husband in favor of expanding the hours?"

Marilyn nodded. "He thought it would be good for the community if we opened up for at least two more days during the week. The grange was split on the subject. It was a close vote even without him. I think, if I remember right, the members voted fourteen against and eleven for expansion. So Jona's vote wouldn't have made a difference."

I wondered if anybody had thought otherwise. Had someone been looking to cull the vote? But then again, why Jona? And why would they have tortured him? Why wouldn't they have just killed him? Or even just prevented him from making it to the grange meeting to vote? They wouldn't have had to resort to murder to stop him.

"Rhiannon said it was storming that night. Didn't that faze him, or make him think twice about walking to the grange?"

"No," Marilyn said, shaking her head. "Jona loved storms. We come from the water, from the ocean. The storms out there rage like no storms you've ever seen on land. They energize us. Whenever he went out in the rain or in a thunderstorm, Jona felt refreshed. We all do. He left here—a few minutes late because of our argument. Before he left, he gave me a long kiss and told me he'd be home as soon as he could. And then he kissed Ryan, and...and I remember looking out the window as he jogged down the path. That was it. That's the last time I saw him." She fell silent, staring at the rug.

Rhiannon reached over, rubbing Marilyn on her shoulder. "Jona didn't have enemies. Of course there were people who didn't like him—and people he didn't like. But the word 'enemy' would be an overstatement. Whoever killed him, they didn't do it because of the grange vote, or to get control of his beehives."

"Can you show us the path to the grange? How far is it?" Herne asked. "I'd like to drive it first, and then, perhaps, walk the route. How far is it?"

"It's about a ten-minute drive—maybe a twenty-five minute walk—to the grange from here. I can take you," Rhiannon said.

Herne stood, turning to Marilyn. "Do you mind if we ask you more questions later? We'll call before we come over, of course."

"Of course. Let me give you my cell number." She gave us her number, and then escorted us to the door. "I don't expect you to find his killer, but I feel better that you are looking into it. Like Rhiannon, I know that it wasn't any vampire. But there's nothing I can do."

"Was it Astrana who told you to back off?" I asked, remembering the conversation with Rhiannon at the office.

Marilyn's face drained of color. Her hand fluttered to her chest.

"Yes. Astrana told me to back off. But so did someone else. Astrana sent a couple of her goons out. They told me that she strongly suggested that I move on with my life and quit prying. That maybe the vampire was still hanging around, even though they didn't have a hope in hell of finding him, and he might decide to try to shut me up."

Marilyn paused, her eyes darkening. "I also got a phone call suggesting that I keep things quiet. They claimed to be from an insurance company and I was told I would receive a payout if I signed off on the case. I told them to go fuck themselves—I had already cashed Jona's insurance policy. It felt like whoever this was, they were trying to buy me off."

"What else did they say?"

"Not much, though they left me with the impression that if I pushed too hard, they'd cause trouble. They mentioned that I had my son to worry about and might want to focus on him. I don't know who it was, and I'm too afraid to dig any deeper. I do have Ryan to think of, and even if I were to find out who killed Jona, it wouldn't bring him back. I warned Rhiannon that I wasn't sure about this—but she assured me that you'll be discreet. Obviously, though, the cops have eyes all over this town."

"We can stop right now if you're uncomfortable," Herne said. "If we leave now, life will probably go on as usual."

"Not necessary." Marilyn shook her head. "I've already made a decision. And your showing up to investigate has nothing to do with it. I've been thinking about this for a few months, actually."

"Thinking about what?" Rhiannon asked.

"I'm taking Ryan and returning to the sea. Back

to the home pod. Life on land isn't all it's cracked up to be. In fact, I think we'd be happier with our own kind. It will give Ryan a chance to learn about his heritage in a way that no amount of living on land can do."

"Are you sure?" Rhiannon asked, looking stricken. "I don't ever want you to feel like you can't stay here."

"Jona was taken from me. Somebody wanted him dead—whether it was personal or not, it doesn't matter. There's a murderer out there. Whoever it is has already claimed my husband. I won't want to take any chances on losing my son. I've already lost the life that we hoped for here. Even if I move on and marry somebody else, it will never change the past. I think my son and I need a new start. I've been in contact with Jona's parents, and they've encouraged me to come back to the ocean. I have an appointment tomorrow to meet with a real estate agent. I'm putting the house up for sale."

She sounded so resigned that it tugged at my heart. She looked tired, and there was a longing for comfort in her voice. I understood the pull to the water—although I'd never understand it in the way someone who was born to it would. But I understood her longing to go home, to find safety for her and her son.

"If you think that's best," Rhiannon said. "I won't try to stop you. But you have to do whatever you think is best for you and Ryan." Her voice was strained and I could tell she was doing her best to be upbeat and supportive, even though it was obvious that Marilyn's news had hurt her. Angel poked me in the arm, and I glanced at her.

"What?" I mouthed.

Angel pressed her lips together and gave me a quick shake of the head, then motioned for me to follow her out on the porch. We said our good-byes, and headed outside to wait for the others to join us.

"What? What's going on?"

Angel started down the steps, dragging me with her. "Rhiannon was in love with Jona. I can tell you that right now. The stress between her and Marilyn tells me that. And trust me, there *was* stress there, and it was because Marilyn knew that Jona loved Rhiannon as well. There's no way I can prove it, but I know in my gut that I'm right."

Looping her arm through mine, Angel walked me away from the house. "You don't think that Rhiannon had anything to do with this? Could she have gotten furious at Jona for something?"

"What? I don't think so." The idea seemed too far out of possibility. Women killed out of jealousy, but Jona's death hadn't been spur of the moment.

Angel thought about it for a moment, then agreed. "You're right. Rhiannon wouldn't have killed Jona like that. Maybe in a fit of anger, if she lost her temper, but not torture. I don't think Rhiannon could ever torture anybody. But she loved him. That I can tell you."

"You're probably right about that. I don't know how it can help us, but you should tell Herne what you're thinking. Every single piece of information is helpful, that's one thing I've learned on the job."

Just about then, Herne and the others came out of the house. They joined us, Rhiannon with them. I decided that Herne should hear about what Angel had to say before we went much further.

"Herne, I want to ride with you. I have something I need to talk to you about—something I forgot before we left the office. Angel can drive my car and bring Rhiannon with her." I didn't want Rhiannon to think we were talking about her. I wasn't sure how empathic she was, but at least I could stave off any immediate questions.

He gave me a bewildered look, but nodded. "Sure, if you like."

I tossed Angel the keys to my car. "Go ahead and start out. We'll follow. Go slow. We don't want to miss anything."

As we scattered to our respective cars, I glanced across the road. Behind us, about two houses back, I could see one of the sheriff's cars. Apparently, we were under scrutiny.

As we buckled ourselves in, Herne glanced at me. "What's going on?"

"Angel had a flash. I suggest we trust her on this, because she's so damned good."

"Fine. What is it?"

"Rhiannon was in love with Jona. Angel is positive. She picked it up when we were inside. At first she thought maybe Rhiannon had something to do with Jona's murder, but both of us feel that, unless it was a fit of uncharacteristic temper, Rhiannon wouldn't ever hurt him. And it's obvious that his death wasn't spur of the moment."

"I wonder if that affects the case. What do you

think?" Herne started the ignition, following Angel and Rhiannon. "Keep an eye out the window, would you? I have to watch the road, but see if there's anything that you can pick up. Anything that you notice along the way."

I glued my attention to the window, watching as the road ascended in a gentle grade. The asphalt was cracked and broken here and there, but the road was still in relatively decent shape. To either side were homes on large lots. The smallest looked to be set on half an acre, while others I estimated at three to five acres.

But shortly, the homes thinned out as heavy foliage and trees set in on both sides. Unlike the main suburb, the area felt dark and shaded, and an alarm bell began to ring in my head. In fact, it was so insistent that I asked Herne to stop as I texted ahead to Angel and Rhiannon, who stopped a few yards in front of us.

I jumped out of the car, walking over to stare intently at a dark patch of trees and brambles. There was something in there, or something had *been* there. Whatever it was, it was dark and squat and frightening. Goose bumps rose along my arms, and the hair prickled on the back of my neck. I found myself holding my breath, waiting for something to leap out at me.

"What's wrong?" Herne asked, crossing to my side.

I shook my head, unable to tell him. All I knew was that there was something here that put me on full alert, the *danger danger Will Robinson* kind of alert.

"Something...is here. Or was here. I can't tell if anything bad happened here, or if it's just the general malaise of the area. Whatever it is, it feels stunted and tainted. It makes me want to get away from it." I motioned to Angel. "Can you feel what I'm feeling?"

She walked over to me, stopping by my side and holding out her hands. She closed her eyes, and then shivered and let out a gasp.

"What the hell?"

"I don't know. All I know is it makes me want to get away from it. It's squirmy and slimy, and feels like it hides under rocks." I looked over at Herne. "I don't know if something's living in there, or if something just passed through, but whatever it is, it makes me queasy."

Herne stared at the thicket with narrowed eyes. "I'm going in."

"Do you think that's wise? Will that tip off who-ever it is that we're here?" Of course, for all I knew, whoever was hiding in those bushes already knew we were here. In fact, whatever—or whoever—it was might have nothing at all to do with Jona's murder.

"We aren't going to find anything by standing on the side of the road. Do you want to come along?" Herne looked at me.

I *didn't* want to go, but that wasn't going to stop me. While the others went back to their cars to wait, Herne and I started into the woods. Viktor offered to come along, but we asked him to stay with the others as protection. Yutani could take care of himself, but Talia and Angel and Rhiannon might not be quite so adept.

Herne and I slowly made our way into the thicket, stepping over bramble patches that snagged at our jeans. I shook off a spider that raced across my arm, tossing it to the ground. It scuttled away, although for a second it seemed to stop and look back at me.

I must be getting paranoid, I thought, *if I think a spider is spying on me.*

We broke through the front line of brambles, finding ourselves in the thick of the woods. Here, the fir trees towered overhead, thick with moss and lichen. A nurse log lay across our path, a good four feet high. The tree must have been massive in its day, and I imagined that when it hit the ground, it thundered like a quake. I placed my hands on the top, swinging my legs over the side. Herne followed suit.

The undergrowth was growing thicker, and it was hard to see the ground below for all the ferns and skunk cabbage in the way. Trailing vines looped and twined their way through the woods. It smelled *green* here, that green that comes after a long rain, mingled with the scent of decay and pungent soil and mushrooms and the clarity of the chill air that hovered in the forest, even on a warm day.

"Do you still feel it?" Herne asked, lowering his voice.

I stopped, closing my eyes as I reached out.

And there it was, to the left, hiding in a thick layer of mulch. The forest detritus was a mire of matted fir needles, and soggy leaves from the vine maple, and mold, and mushrooms, all compacted together to create a spongy blanket that covered the ground.

I pointed to an area where the energy was most pronounced.

"I think there."

Herne slowly moved toward the area, his hand on his dagger. I flipped the snap on my sheath, unbinding my own dagger, ready to bring it to bear at first notice.

As we pushed through the trees, I wasn't sure what to expect, but it certainly wasn't that we would break through into a clearing.

The semi-circle was surrounded by trees—shrubs, really—that I didn't recognize. In fact, the type didn't look familiar at all. They stood about twelve to fourteen feet tall, and were covered with small green leaves. On one hand, they reminded me of huckleberries. In fact, they were covered with dark blue berries, but they were like no huckleberry bushes I had ever seen. They felt dark and foreboding, and I found myself incredibly uneasy. The trees were covered in branches from the ground to the top, to the point where I could barely see their trunks. The branches twisted out in every direction. As we drew near, I could see long, sharp thorns covering the limbs, wickedly dangerous.

"I wouldn't want to fall into one of those," I whispered, keeping my voice low.

"What the hell are *these* doing here?" Herne asked, his eyes widening. He glanced around, his shoulders stiffening.

"What are they?"

"Blackthorn trees. We had them back in England, but I didn't think they grew over here. At least, not in the Pacific Northwest. Watch out for those spines, they can cause septicemia."

I started to move forward, trying to get a closer look, but he cautioned me to wait.

"There's something here," he said. "I can't quite place it, but something knows we're here, and it's watching us very carefully."

I huddled closer to him. As a hawk shrieked, flying overhead, I jumped, not expecting the sudden cry. I took a step to the left, trying to steady myself, but my foot came down on a rock, unbalancing me. I tripped, landing near one of the blackthorn bushes. As I started to get up, a branch suddenly whipped out, curling around my left wrist, digging in with its thorns.

"Motherfucking hell!" The shooting pain hit me and, instinctively, I tried to pull my arm away but the branch tightened around my wrist, a ring of the thorns digging deep into my skin.

Herne darted to my side, bringing his dagger down against the branch. The branch snapped under the force of his blow, but another one reached out, trying to grab hold of my ankle. I rolled away, even as I realized that the tendril around my arm was still digging in. I tried to loosen it, but it still seemed to be almost alive, and it was only by force that I managed to yank it free from my wrist, the thorns ripping out of the skin, spurting blood everywhere. I threw it to the side, hard. It writhed on the ground, trying to inch toward me, but then stopped. As we watched, it dug itself into the ground, forcing itself deep into the soil.

"Watch out!" Herne yelled, grabbing me by the other arm and dragging me to my feet just as yet another branch snaked out, again heading toward my leg.

We turned, racing away from the thicket. The sound of scuttling followed us, and as we turned, we saw tendrils emerging from all sides of the clearing, stopping a few yards from the trees. They could only go so far, it seemed, but I didn't want to give them a chance to prove me wrong.

"Are they *supposed* to do that?"

"No." Herne shook his head, staring at the bushes. "Wait here."

He stepped forward, back into the clearing, and the bushes scuttled again. In a loud voice, he barked out a string of words that I didn't under-stand. I wasn't even sure if I was hearing them aloud—but the energy rippled through the clear-ing, loud and clear.

I was trying to stanch the blood pouring out of the wounds in my wrist when an answer came thundering back. This time, I knew it wasn't aloud, but I could hear it as well as Herne.

"You are not welcome here. This is not your do-main, son of Cernunnos. You do not claim power over us."

A dangerous light flickered in Herne's eyes, and he seemed to grow taller as he stood there, his shoulders straightening, as he held out his hands. *"I am Lord Herne. You will listen."*

Again, a response echoed through the clearing, as clear as if the words were being shouted through a bullhorn.

"Leave this place, son of Cernunnos, before you anger us. Return only at your own peril."

Herne looked ready to rumble, but then he turned back to me, staring at my arm. The puncture wounds were continuing to bleed, and they burned. He turned back to the clearing.

"I will return, and you will acknowledge who is Lord of the Forest."

And with that, he joined me. "We need to get you to the doctor. Come on," he said, keeping an eye over his shoulder as we left the patch of woods.

I had never been so relieved to see the pavement. "What was that?"

"I don't know. Whatever it was, it was ancient and deadly. Very seldom will you find trees so sentient. Or so mobile. They shouldn't be able to do that. Blackthorn can be a deadly tree and often houses dark creatures, but it seldom takes a life of its own like that."

As we returned to the car, a sinister pall filtered over the area, and it felt like it was following us. I nervously glanced over my shoulder, but could see nothing there.

The others were waiting anxiously, and when I held up my wrist, Talia let out a gasp.

"Do you know of a SubCult doctor nearby? Ember needs to have her wrist looked at immediately," Herne said to Rhiannon.

"Yes, I'll call him immediately."

While she put in the call, we told the rest of them what happened. Viktor, especially, gave a wary shake of the head.

"That's not natural. Not at all."

"You're right, and it brings up a whole lot of questions. Take a good look at the puncture marks on her wrist," Herne said. "I don't think they're as deep, but don't they look like the puncture marks on Jona's body?"

"Crap. Do you think the blackthorn patch killed him? A bunch of trees?"

"It could well have, but there has to be more to it than that. Something had to wake up those trees, and I guarantee you it was no vampire. I'm not sure *what* we're facing, but whatever it is, I want to get to the bottom of it." Herne's look of anger turned to concern as he glanced at me. "How are you feeling?"

In truth, I was shaky, but I wasn't sure whether it was because of the surprise attack, or the puncture wounds. They hurt like hell, but I had been seriously wounded before without feeling faint. "I'm not sure. I don't feel normal, I'll tell you that."

"The doctor's waiting for us," Rhiannon broke in. "He's back at the encampment, so let's head back there." She stared at my wrist, a worried look on her face. I could see she was making the same connections we had.

As we returned to the encampment, I tried not to think about septicemia and sentient plants that were out to kill people. Scenes from *Little Shop of Horrors* flickered through my head, only this wasn't a comedy and I was the one in danger.

The doctor was Wulfine, that much was clear the moment he opened the door. There was a certain look to those who were full Wulfine blood—a ridged brow and angular jaw, though anyone not belonging to the SubCult probably couldn't pick them out of a crowd. He hustled me in, motioning for me to hop up on the examination table.

"Thank you for seeing me." I held out my arm.

He looked at my wrist, frowning. "What happened?"

"I fell into a patch of blackthorn bushes."

Without missing a beat, he shook his head. "You must be mistaken. We don't have any blackthorn bushes around here. It was probably a nasty blackberry bush or something."

"This was no blackberry bush," I said. "I know my brambles."

"Don't be so sure. They can grow terribly large."

I was about to argue the point, but Herne gave me a faint shake of the head.

"These look fairly deep. I'll rinse them out and give you a salve to stave off any infection. You'll need to wrap it up and keep it wrapped up for a couple days." He glanced up at me, clearing his throat. "You're Fae, correct?"

Wondering why he wouldn't admit to the blackthorn bushes, I shrugged. "Yes, Light and Dark mix."

"*Hrmph*," he muttered, but went on with his work.

He rinsed the puncture marks with a solution that stung, then he packed the holes with a runny salve that also stung. Finally, the doctor bandaged my wrist. Afterward, he handed me a packet of bandages and medical tape, and a little bottle filled with the salve.

"Leave the wrap on for twenty-four hours, then remove it, rinse with cool water, and spread the salve around your wrist again. Re-bandage. Continue for four days. This should take care of it. If the wound worsens in the next few days, come back. Or, if you're out of town, find a good SubCult doctor."

I thanked him, staring at the bandage. Herne paid him, then we filed out to the cars again.

"Why do you think—" I started to say, but Herne stopped me.

"Later. Don't ask questions here." He paused, staring at the sky. "Let's get back to the hotel. Tomorrow, we'll head over to the library. There are things I want to check on before we go take a look where Jona's body was found."

As we headed back to the hotel, it occurred to me that Whidbey Island, as pretty as it was, contained dark secrets below the surface.

Chapter 8

BY THE TIME we dropped off Rhiannon and returned to the hotel, my wrist felt like it was on fire. The doctor had also given me a mild pain-killer, so I took that, and then joined the others in the dining room. My stomach was rumbling, and the combination of pain and medication made me queasy. I asked the waitress to bring me a choco-late shake right away, just to get something in my stomach.

"So, why do you think the doctor flat out called me a liar? Not in so many words, of course, but by denying that I fell into a blackthorn patch, he pretty much negated everything I said."

Herne scratched his chin. "I'm not certain. But I felt an urge to drop the subject around him—not a compulsion, but a warning. But the puncture wounds really *do* look like the ones that were on Jona's body. At least according to the photo." He

paused as the waitress returned with my shake and
menus for everyone. She took drink orders, and
I asked for coffee to go along with my shake, and
then she left again.

"There are a lot of things that don't add up.
Rhiannon was right. Those puncture wounds *can't*
be from vampire fangs, unless the vampire is the
size of a giant. I wonder if there's a land wight out
there? But if so, why would the sheriff cover it up?"

"Wights are a form of Fae. Sub-Fae, yes, but they
are still part of the Dark Fae court. Maybe they're
just protecting their own?" Yutani asked.

I shook my head. "That wouldn't make sense.
Astrana is Light Fae. She wouldn't do anything to
help any of the Dark Fae. Even if she was shunted
out of Névé's court, she's still going to be loyal to
them. My guess is, she's trying to work her way up
to return to Névé's good graces."

Just then, Talia's phone rang. She excused herself and stepped off to the side to answer it. The
waitress brought everyone's drinks, and we put in
our orders for food. I was feeling particularly hungry, so I ordered the all-you-can-eat pasta bowl.
Viktor surprised the hell out of me by ordering the
sushi.

"*You* like sushi?" I blinked. Somehow, it had
never occurred to me that an ogre, even half-blood,
would like such delicate fare.

"I like a lot of things," he said with a wry smile.
"I happen to love Japanese food. And the fish here
is fresh."

Talia returned at that moment, sliding back into
her chair. "That was Rosetta. She has some infor-

mation for us and wants to meet us. But she asked to meet in an out-of-the-way place. There's a dive called the Prancing Púca not far from our hotel. I told her we'd meet her there in an hour. I hope that's all right?"

"Any information we can gather would be helpful at this point," Herne said. "Should we all go? Or does she just want to see you?"

"I was thinking we might as well all go. That way, we won't have to run through everything she says afterward. Are you up for it, Ember? I know your wrist is hurting."

I frowned. I ached, but the food would settle me down. The shake already had helped. "I can go. As long as I don't get in another fight tonight."

"We'll try to avoid any brawls," Herne said with a snicker. "Seriously, though, if we are facing a land wight, we have to destroy it. Whatever that thing is, it's far too big, and far too aggressive."

Finally, our food came, and we fell silent, the only sound the clicking of forks on plates and the occasional *yum* from one corner of the table or another.

THE PRANCING PÚCA was a dive, all right. For one thing, the neon sign actually had a depiction of a large rabbit on it. I wondered who ran the joint. It couldn't be an actual Púca or they would have been offended as hell. A number of motorcycles were leaning against the curb. They looked heavy-duty, as though they got real use and weren't just weekend rides. Herne gave them an admiring glance.

"Now *that's* a bike," he said, pointing to the one on the end. It was decked out in chrome and leather to the point of where it looked like it belonged to some BDSM top. "I need one of those."

"Your bike isn't fancy enough, is that it?" Talia said with a laugh.

"She serves her purpose, and she's a faithful old girl, but I think she's reaching the end of her life span." He shrugged. "After a while, machines just wear out."

"If you ride her as hard as you ride me, no wonder she's wearing out," I said under my breath, but apparently my voice wasn't low enough and everybody started to laugh.

"Just be glad you aren't dating my father," Herne said, his eyes glimmering.

Talia let out a cackle. "I imagine your daddy keeps Morgana pretty busy. The Lord of the Hunt is also the lord of sex, wouldn't you say?"

"Well, he's definitely the Lord of the Rut," Yutani said, his serious demeanor cracking under the weight of a broad smile. "Herne has to have inherited some of the family genetics."

"Yeah, maybe Ember needs to take a few yoga classes," Angel said, winking at me.

I blushed, rolling my eyes. It was my own fault, so I took the ribbing good-naturedly. "All right, all right. I know I started it, but make like Elsa and let it go. So, how about this bar?"

As I tried to change the subject, we came to the

front door. I pushed it open, standing back so Talia could go through first. She glanced around the room, then gave a little wave. I followed her gaze, staring at the woman who was waiting in one of the larger booths in the back.

Rosetta looked to be in her mid-fifties, and her hair was streaked with gray. Since she was a shifter, that meant she had to be fairly old. Shifters aged far slower than humans, although not nearly as slowly as the Fae. A stocky woman, she looked well muscled, and was wearing a pair of jeans and a floral tank top. Her hair was pulled back in a utilitarian ponytail, but her face captivated me. Her features were beautiful, reminding me very much of a cat's features, and I couldn't help but wonder what she looked like in her shifter form. Norwegian Forest cats were beautiful, and I suddenly found myself missing Mr. Rumblebutt. I pulled out my phone and quickly texted Ronnie, asking how he was.

We headed over to the booth as Rosetta smiled at Talia. She gave the rest of us a once-over, as though she were trying to gauge whether we were a threat. We scooted in, Talia sitting next to her.

"Thank you for seeing us," Talia said. She introduced the rest of us.

Rosetta looked around the bar, studying the other patrons. Finally, she motioned to the waiter. He hurried over, taking our orders. Yutani and Herne ordered beer, Talia ordered a glass of wine, and the rest of us ordered soda. Once the waiter had brought our drinks, Rosetta let out a long sigh.

"I'm putting my neck on the line, but given the

scuttlebutt that you're investigating Jona's death, I thought you should know. The cops sure won't be a help in this. Hell, they'll probably try to keep you from finding out." She played with her glass, staring at the amber liquid.

"We appreciate anything you can tell us," Herne said.

That seemed to make up her mind.

"You have to understand, I *liked* Jona. He was good man. His wife is a wonderful woman. Hell, I like the hippocampi. They keep their noses clean, they go about their business, they interact with community in a good way...pretty much, they're model citizens. Which is why it pisses me off that nobody actually looked into Jona's death. Oh, the cops say they did, but you can bet they didn't."

"Any idea why?"

Rosetta's gaze flickered around again, then she leaned forward, lowering her voice. "I suggest that you take a look into the back issues of the newspaper, at least two decades' worth. Around May to June for each year, and again in late October, November. Look for missing people, odd murders."

A shiver raced up my spine and I had the feeling we were about to fall far deeper into this case than we had expected to.

"You're saying there have been murders other than Jona's?" Herne asked.

She nodded. "I got curious after I overheard somebody named Roland tell my editor to bury the story about Jona, so I did a little snooping. I'm not sure what I stumbled onto, but you'll know whether it's anything. You'll see the pattern. I haven't had time to look any deeper into what I found, and in fact—I've been too frightened to. But I have a feeling about this."

Herne paused, staring at her for a moment. "How many murders are we talking about?"

Rosetta nodded. "I found suggestions of at least seven or eight. I don't know if there are any more than that. All unresolved as far as I can tell, and all buried under secrecy."

I quickly glanced at Angel, who raised her eyebrows. If this wasn't an isolated case, then we were on the tail of something much bigger than we expected.

"We'll take it from here," Herne said. "Thank you. I know it takes a lot to go against instinct. I imagine that neither your boss nor the sheriff would appreciate you talking to us, so again—thank you for having the courage to step up. We'll do our best to protect you as a source, although we can never guarantee it."

"Well, if I end up having to move abruptly, maybe you can help pack my boxes for me." She laughed, although the look in her eyes told me that she was truly worried.

We chatted a little bit more, then paid the bill and left. We had taken two cars, with Yutani and Herne driving. Viktor and Angel rode with Yutani, while Talia rode with Herne and me. Once we were safely in the car and on the way back to the hotel, Talia told us a little bit about Rosetta.

"I met her about ten years ago at a workshop on researching. We hit it off right away and have kept in touch ever since. We get together about two or three times a year for lunch and an afternoon of shopping. Truthfully, she's probably one of the best friends I have, outside of the agency."

"She's truthful, then?" Herne asked. "I suspect she'd have a hard time lying, just from meeting her."

"She's cagey like a cat, but Rosetta is one of the most hard-working and truthful people I know. She's a busybody and nosy, but I think that's just her nature. Cat shifters tend to be that way. But she's always stood up when she thought something was wrong. This has probably been eating at her conscience ever since she overheard the conversation between her boss and Roland."

By the time we got back to the hotel, I was dragging. We had been up since before six A.M., and it was close to eleven now. The pain medication made me groggy, and the adrenaline rush from the attack had sapped a lot out of me as well. I gave Herne a quick kiss at my door, and whispered that I'd see him the next morning.

Angel and I were both tired, but the first thing we did was check our room and make sure that it was secure. Over the past few months, we had learned to take precautions. There was nobody there and nothing looked out of place, but I still had an odd feeling. I held up one finger as Angel started speaking and motioned toward the hallway again. Reluctantly, she followed me into the hall, where I knocked on Herne's door and crooked my finger, nodding for him to join us.

I motioned for them to follow me down the hallway a ways away from our rooms. Once there, I leaned in and whispered, "I just had a thought. The sheriff doesn't want us here, that much we know. Do you think our rooms could be bugged?"

Herne let out a sigh. "I should have thought of that. Go get Yutani and ask him to join us. Talia and Viktor as well."

Once we were all together we headed over to a seating area near the elevators. There was nobody else there, so we took it over and pulled our chairs close together.

"Ember brought up a good point. The sheriff knows we're here and she doesn't like it. They would have had ample time while we were out today to bug our rooms." Herne glanced at Yutani. "Did you bring any of your surveillance equipment?"

Yutani leaned back in his chair, sliding his thumbs through the belt loops on his jeans. He looked just as tired as the rest of us.

"Actually, yes. I have a bug zapper—it can find bugs and disrupt them, but if we destroy them, anybody listening in will hear it. However," he said with a mischievous grin, "I happen to have a new little goodie that recently came out, and it will disable any camera and/or audio equipment in the room. Which means I need to remove my gear from my room before I use it, and so will the rest of you. It's quick, it only takes a moment, and I can adjust the size of the field based on the room's dimensions. It won't cover a large area, but it should manage a hotel room of the size that we have. I'd better get ready. Ember and Angel, let's do your room first. Take all of your tablets and phones and cameras out of there first. When you go in there, act normally. If you can," he added with a grin.

I stuck my tongue out at him. "Will it tell us if there's anything to worry about?" It seemed pointless to do all the work if there weren't any bugs to begin with.

"Yeah, it should find any—at least any up to this generation of tech. It's a pretty sophisticated piece of equipment. Let's go. The rest of you stay here. It doesn't make sense for us all to traipse around from room to room. I'm going to make a quick sweep of my room first." He stood, and after a quick stop at his room, where he nonchalantly carried out a bag of his gadgets, he swept for bugs.

"Nothing. They aren't worried about me. Let's do your room next."

We waited as he scanned the room. There were three lights on the top of the sandwich-sized black box, green, red, and yellow. Below that were a series of gauges. A moment later, the red light flashed twice. Yutani gave me a quick look, and nodded. Once again, we stepped out into the hallway.

"Let me just check my app." He pulled out his phone, tapping away. He skimmed over the information, frowning. "One camera and two listening devices. Apparently they wanted to make sure to catch whatever you said, as well as get an eyeful."

"Pervs," Angel spat.

"The deputy had to recognize my heritage, which is probably why they bugged our room." I was livid. The idea that they had been watching Angel and me was nauseating.

"Go in there and get all of your electronics. Don't make it obvious. Try to be discreet. The camera appears to be fastened to the television but it doesn't have the ability to swivel. So it's pointed directly at your beds."

"What happens when it stops recording? Won't they know something's up?" Angel asked.

"Actually, the way this works is that they'll continue to see the empty room, just as though the camera is still working. It will throw them off their game for a little while, at least. When they don't hear anything, they might think that you guys spent the night elsewhere."

"Yeah. So either we strip for them or they'll think we're stripping for someone else. Most of my gear is in my purse, although I think I've got an e-reader in my suitcase. You know, we can set them up," I said. "When we go in there, I'll tell you that I'm spending the night with Herne. You can say that Talia asked you to come over to her room to discuss something. Then we can turn off the light and they won't be able to tell whether we come back in or not."

"That works for me," Angel said. "But if Herne's room is bugged and they don't see anybody in there, they'll be suspicious."

I groaned. "Good point." I glanced at Yutani, who blinked at me.

"No, you don't—"

"Dude, they may not know about Herne and me. Your room wasn't bugged to begin with. Deal with it."

"Fine. Let's just get on with it." Yutani gave us

the go-ahead, so we entered the room, yawning.

"I'm going to head over to Yutani's room," I said.

"Talia asked me to drop by for a while. She wants to tell me about some perks of the job." Angel looked a little like she wasn't sure what she was saying, but it worked.

I rummaged through my bag, pulling out a robe and using it to surreptitiously wrap up my e-reader. Angel rummaged through her suitcase, turning it so that the lid hid what she was doing from the camera. A moment later, she flipped off the light as we exited the room.

Yutani slipped inside, keeping himself away from the sight line, as Angel and I backed away from the door. A moment later he returned.

"Let me just check here... Okay, your room is now clean. Go on in. It's safe for your electronics. I'll do Talia's room next, and then Herne's."

Ten minutes later, he was finished. My room and Herne's room had been the only ones with bugs in them. Herne's hadn't even had a camera. Secure in the knowledge that we had our privacy back, we once again bid good night, and headed to bed.

NEXT MORNING, WE decided to go as a team to the library. Before we did anything else regarding Jona's case, we wanted to see if it was the tip of an iceberg like Rosetta had suggested.

The Seacrest Cove library was an extension of the larger Sno-Isle library system. But it had a computer system, and an impressive number of books. We asked the librarian where we could find the back issues of the paper for the past twenty years or so.

"Oh, we don't keep those in print. They're being scanned into the computer system right now, but you can still find all of them on microfiche." She looked almost apologetic.

Yutani blinked. I had the feeling he was almost offended by the ancient technology.

"There are four microfiche readers in room 2A. Which paper did you want? I can get you the film cassettes."

"*The Whidbey Island Gazette,* please." Talia glanced at Herne. "What do you think? Go back thirty years?"

"That should be good, or at least I hope it will be. We need the issues for April through July and October through November for each year."

The librarian jotted down the information, then motioned for us to wait in the microfiche room for her. As we entered the room, I had a flashback to my childhood. There had been microfiche readers in the school library for the first few years, before things were transferred over to a computer system.

"Remind you of anything?" I asked Angel.

She laughed. "I have flashbacks of writing reports using microfiche. It was a pain in the ass."

"Well, at least you did yours. I skipped out on as many as I could."

"Since you and Angel seem to be familiar with these machines, why don't the two of you take those over there. Talia, you and Yutani take the other two. Meanwhile, Viktor and I will poke around the rest of the library. I'm thinking we need to find out what we can about the vampire who talked to Rhiannon as well. She said his name was Rayne. I'll see what I can find out on him."

Herne fell silent as the librarian returned, tapes in hand. She handed them to us, and Angel and I sat down, starting to feed the film through the reader. I began punching the fast-forward button, wishing to hell that it had a search feature on it. Luckily, the paper was small, given the surrounding area, so it wouldn't be too much trouble to look through each issue.

As we got down to work, Herne and Viktor exited the room. I stuck my tongue out at their departing backs, given they were missing out on all the fun of wading through hundreds of yards of film.

About ten minutes later, I paused, staring at a small article on page three of the June issue from 1977. I zoomed in, scanning the story.

The body of Ivan Hinkleman was found last week, on the Cold Step trail in South Whidbey State Park. He was found near the beach, after having gone missing over a week ago. Police suspect foul play, but say they have no leads. Lena Hinkleman, his wife stated her husband went out to buy ice cream at the local Dairy Freeze, but never returned home. A thorough search turned up no signs of Mr. Hinkleman until a jogger found his body.

There was a picture of an elderly gentleman

there, looking almost stately in a three-piece suit. I jotted down notes, then printed out a copy of the story. I looked through the next few issues, searching for any mention of the murder, but saw nothing.

"I found one, I think," I said.

"So did I," Talia said. She was busy printing out a second article. "Two, actually."

Two hours later, we had gathered seventy-two stories, spanning from 1977 through to the present day. Fifty-two were missing persons, while twenty were odd murders that had gotten very little coverage. When we finished, we took our microfiche back to the librarian and then headed over to a table where Herne and Victor were waiting.

"Next step: find out which of the missing persons reports have been closed out. As far as the murders, we need to find out everything we can about the victims. Were any of the cases solved?" Talia placed the sheath of papers in the center of the table. "Notice that every murder and missing-persons article is short—a paragraph or two at best. Very little is said about the murder itself. In every case, we scanned forward through the next few weeks and saw nothing else mentioned about each of the unexplained deaths. For any other murders or deaths during those times, there were follow-up stories. But these twenty or so? It's almost as though they were a blur on the highway."

Yutani pulled out his laptop and begin typing in names, searching through the Net. A few moments later, he paused, then slowly turned the laptop so that all of us could see the screen. He clicked over to an images search, and there was another picture of Mr. Hinkleman. Only Mr. Hinkleman wasn't wearing his three-piece suit. He was naked, on a morgue table, his skin covered with deep puncture wounds. They looked exactly like those on Jona's body.

"Somebody got a hold of one of the morgue pictures and posted it. Let me follow this back..." Yutani tapped away at the keyboard. A moment later he frowned, shaking his head. "All right, the image is part of a private file system, but I can't seem to bring up the webpage it's attached to. I think somebody forgot to set this picture to private. It's part of a locked-down, unlisted website as far as I can tell."

"What do you mean 'unlisted'?"

"Somebody has taken pains to hide a website from view. I'm not sure how they're doing it, I'd have to look into it more, but they forgot to set the privacy settings on the picture. I was able to find it because I did a search on Hinkleman's name."

"What about the others?" I asked.

We waited while Yutani went back to work. Half an hour later, he came up for air. He glanced around, looking to see if anybody was nearby. But apparently the library annex wasn't extensively used on Friday mornings.

"I have the names and addresses of four of the murder victims' families. It appears the other sixteen all moved away shortly after the murders. I also searched on all the missing persons' names. Twelve were reported found—most were just lost or forgot to tell their families they were going out of town. But the other forty? Crickets. Nothing. No reports of them being seen anywhere. I hacked into the nationwide database and none of them were ever listed with the FBI or any other missing persons database."

Herne let out a low whistle. "So, we have twenty murder victims and forty missing people, and all the cases during the months of May and June, and October and November."

"That sort of pattern can't have gone unnoticed by the cops. There's no chance they didn't pick up on it. And yet...nothing has ever been said or done." I leaned back in my chair.

"Serial killer?" Talia asked.

"It seems like it. One with a definite pattern," Herne said. "But if forty people went missing and were never found, then what happened to them? Are we prematurely lumping them into the same case? We can't assume they're part of the pattern, and yet, that's a lot of missing people who were swept under the rug."

"What kind of serial killer has the self-control to keep at it on a steady pattern like this? Don't most of them start to escalate, or spiral out of control?" Angel rested her elbows on the table, leaning her chin on her hands.

"Not all of them. The more organized ones don't." Herne motioned to Yutani. "Anything else you picked up on?"

Yutani scanned his notes. "Each of the murder victims was found in the state park, usually near the water, and most of the missing went missing near the state park. While I've only been able to find references to two of the bodies besides Hinkleman, it seems that they too were indicated as having multiple puncture wounds. Those were two of the early murders. There's very little about any of the ones later on. And I can only find references to the victims online *before* their murders. There's very little mention of them afterward, except in a couple ancestry sites. One person mentions their dead uncle."

"What about the missing persons? Are there any mentions of them?" I asked.

He shook his head. "Not as far as I can see. It's as though once they disappeared—or were killed, in the case of the murder victims—they were promptly forgotten."

"So, four of the murder victims' families still live on the island? I suggest we pay a visit to them. We can do that after lunch." Herne glanced around. "This case makes me uneasy. We have evidence of a serial killer, but nothing's being done about it. Twenty people are dead and forty gone missing, but again, nothing is being done and it's as though they were all just wiped out of existence. We have evidence of a possible land wight, but the doctor denies the possibility. Tell me again, how long has Astrana been sheriff here?"

Talia was quick on the job with that one. "Rhiannon said about thirty-five years. Remember, all that crap went down with her around forty years ago, so she must have left the court of Navane shortly after that."

"So, she started here five years after the first murder. Who was sheriff before her?"

Yutani did a quick search. "An older human—Jack Bingham. He died of a heart attack and Astrana was elected. From what I can see, people thought he wasn't doing his job very well by the end and Astrana promised the community she'd step up and keep a tighter rein on crime."

I could practically see the wheels turning in Herne's head. "Are you thinking she has something to do with this?"

"Not necessarily with the murders themselves, but she's definitely covering them up. She's narcissistic, but she's *not* stupid. She has to see the pattern here. And *that* tells me that she probably has something to lose if word about this gets out." He glanced over at Talia. "Why don't you get to work digging up her background? Find anything you can on her—every piece of dirt. I don't care if it's gossip or not, we want to sift through everything that we can."

"I found out something else," Yutani said.

"There's another piece to the puzzle?" Viktor asked.

"Yeah. I've been doing some more sleuthing while we've been talking. Each of these four families who are still here? Received a sizable stroke of financial luck a few weeks after their loved one was killed. The sixteen who moved away? Not so much."

"Marilyn's moving, and she doesn't seem to have had any big stroke of luck." I straightened in my chair. "I don't think she feels safe here. I wonder if there's something she hasn't told us."

"I think there are a lot of things that a lot of people haven't told us," Herne said, standing. "Let's go back to the hotel and eat lunch, then we'll split up and go talk to the various families. We need to figure out our line of questioning first, though. And if there's any chance they were paid to keep their mouths shut, we're going to have to figure out a way to break through their reserves. Be careful, though. We don't dare run the risk of being accused of harassing them or we could be chased off the island. And when the sun sets, we need to find Rayne—the vampire Rhiannon talked to. I want his take on this."

At that moment, his phone rang. He grimaced as the librarian shot us a dirty look from across the room. "Yes, okay. Really?... Yeah, I can be there. Really? You want me to bring her too? All right. We were going to grab some lunch first—okay, no problem. Be there in a bit." As he slid his phone back into his pocket, he glanced at me. "Cernunnos wants to see me right away. And he said he wanted to meet you too, Ember. You ready to meet my father?"

My mouth went dry as I stared at him. "You've got to be kidding. You want me to meet your father *today*?"

Herne laughed, winking at me. "Don't worry, he doesn't bite. Much."

And with that, he ushered us out of the library, refusing to say anything more.

Chapter 9

MY FIRST THOUGHT was that this had to be an elaborate practical joke. My second thought was that I was scared spitless.

My family pretty much consisted of Angel and Mr. Rumblebutt. I seldom gave any thought to family gatherings, reunions, or the proverbial "meeting the parents" situation.

I tried to remind myself that I had already met Morgana, but even then, I had met her in the context of being swept into her service, not as her son's girlfriend. We had only briefly talked about Herne, and the only warning I got from her was to mind my oath and stick to it. Given my mother had been pledged to Morgana, I wasn't really sweating it. I wasn't sure *what* Morgana had planned for me, and until I found out, I wasn't going to borrow trouble.

But meeting Cernunnos seemed more fraught

with danger. Granted, I'd recently found out my father had been pledged to him, but that didn't necessarily make it any easier.

"Just *where* are we going to meet your father? Is he coming here? To the hotel?" It seemed like a ridiculous question, but given Herne talked to his parents on a cell phone, it seemed just as likely as anything else.

"You'll see." He turned to the others. "This shouldn't take long. I'd rather you didn't start interviewing the families until Ember and I return. Why don't you head back to the hotel, eat lunch, and we'll be back as soon as we finish talking to Cernunnos."

They just mumbled and waved and I handed Angel my keys. Herne escorted me to his car, opening the door for me. I meekly slid into the passenger seat, fastening my seatbelt. What the hell had I gotten myself into? I wondered if I still had time to back out, but given the fact that Cernunnos had asked to meet me, it didn't feel prudent to refuse.

I wasn't sure where we were going, but Herne seemed to know the way. We headed toward the other side of Seacrest Cove until we came to a one-story rambler. It stood on a bluff, overlooking the water, with two gigantic oak trees in the front yard. I blinked. Oaks weren't all that common around the area. Then the thought fluttered past that Cernunnos might own the house, but that was ridiculous. The Lord of the Hunt owning a rambler? Somehow, it just didn't compute.

Herne shifted into park, then turned off the ignition.

"So, does your father live here? On Whidbey Island?" With a glance at the house, I added, "In a rambler?"

He laughed. "No, my father does not live on Whidbey Island, nor is his palace a rambler built in the 1970s. However, the man who lives here is an agent of his. And those two oaks? They guard the portal we're crossing through in order to meet him."

I blinked. "Agent? As in, like we're agents of the Wild Hunt?"

"Not exactly. Most of the gods have an intricate network of spies and agents throughout the world. My father is no different. Come on, let's go."

As I opened the door, a shaft of sunlight broke through the clouds, burning them away. It was still cool, in the low sixties, with a stiff breeze, but the sun felt good on my face as I stepped out of the car. I shaded my eyes as the light splashed across the ground with a dizzying array of color.

At that moment, the door to the rambler opened and a short but sturdy man stepped through. He was muscular, with dark wavy hair that trailed down his back. He was wearing a muscle shirt, and a pair of blue jeans that curved around his butt nicely. A hunting knife was clipped to his belt, and by the look of him, I pegged him as either partial or full Native American. His eyes lit up when he saw Herne.

As we approached, Herne held up his hand and the other man clasped it, in one of those solidarity-type handshakes that men seemed to favor.

"Herne, my man. It's been awhile." The man's

gaze flickered over me. "I don't believe we've met."

"Ember Kearney. She works for the Wild Hunt." Then, to my surprise, Herne added with just a touch of possessiveness in his voice, "She's also my girlfriend. No poaching."

"Excuse me?" I asked, giving him a *what the fuck* look. "In the first place, I may be your girlfriend, but I'm not a fish or a game animal. Nobody can poach me. And second, I make up my own mind. Just remember that, dude."

Herne snorted. "Yes, ma'am." He said it so obsequiously that I smacked him on the arm.

"Behave and introduce your friend to me."

"Yes, ma'am." His eyes twinkled, and I realized he was just baiting me. "Ember, let me introduce John Shelton."

"Pleased to meet you." John inhaled softly. "They were right about you." As if realizing he had just spoken out loud, his cheeks colored, and he dropped his gaze. "I'm sorry, I didn't mean..."

I suddenly realized what he was referring to. "Yes, I'm half Dark and half Light."

He gave me a short nod. "Scuttlebutt gets around the island quickly, I can tell you that. As I said, I didn't mean anything by it. I just didn't realize that it was actually possible."

"The Fae Courts prefer to bandy the rumors that the two sides can't interbreed. It goes against all of their sensibilities. But as you can see, I'm living proof. And you are...a shifter?" It was rude of me to ask, but given my own heritage had just been dissected, I wasn't feeling particularly diplomatic.

John seemed to understand. "I'm part of the

Puget Sound Orca Pod."

I was surprised. It was unusual to meet water shifters on land, and given we were working with the hippocampi, it seemed a little startling to meet a whale shifter. Though technically, he was actually part of the porpoise family. Orcas weren't true whales.

"What can I do for you today?" he asked, returning his attention to Herne.

"Need to use the portal. My father wants to talk to me about something. He also wants to meet Ember."

"Of course. I was just getting ready to go into town to pick up some groceries. Do you need me to stay here and guard your back?"

Herne shook his head. "We'll be fine. I'll make sure to close the portal when we leave."

"Then I'll let you get to it." John turned back to me. "It was nice to meet you, Ember. Have a good trip!" And with that, he headed over to a beautiful vintage white pickup, waving as he pulled out of the driveway.

"He seems nice. How long have you known him?"

Herne led me over toward the oaks. "Fifty, sixty years? Somewhere around there. And you're right, he's extremely nice, and trustworthy. If you ever need help and I'm not around, come to John and ask him to help you."

I nodded, filing away the information for later.

We walked up to the oaks, which had to be sixty feet tall each. They were scarlet oaks, with massive trunks that splintered off into narrower children.

A writhing array of branches littered each section of the trunk. The familiar scalloped edges of the leaves made them easy to identify, as well as the scattered acorns on the ground. But these trees felt different than most of the oaks I had encountered. There was a magnetic resonance between them, a pulse that I could feel from even ten yards away.

"So, how do you activate it? How do we go through?" I looked around for some sort of touch-pad or key, but didn't see anything out of the ordinary. I wasn't exactly attuned to the nature of portals, although once or twice I thought I had been on the verge of entering one. But I knew they existed, and that going through them wasn't ex-actly like just stepping through a door.

Herne wiped his hands on his jeans, then mo-tioned for me to follow him. When we were stand-ing in front of the two oaks, he stretched out his arms, and dropped his head back. A light began to emanate from between his hands, forming a long beam of brilliant green light between his fingers.

He slowly moved his hands until his palms were facing forward, and whispered something that I couldn't quite catch. A few moments later, the earth rumbled, so loud that I wondered if the neighborhood could hear it. The ground beneath my feet began to shake and quiver.

An earthquake? What was going on?

I wanted to ask Herne, but he focused all his at-tention on the light between his palms that shot to-ward the trunks of the oaks. I staved off my panic as best as I could and tried to keep steady on my feet. Another moment, and a ripple formed in the air between the trees. And then the ripple became a swirl, and the swirl began to spin widdershins.

"Take my hand," Herne yelled over the roar of the turbulence. "Whatever you do, don't let go or I might not be able to find you."

I took his hand, holding on for dear life. We began to advance toward the ripple between the trees, the swirl of energy making me dizzy as it echoed out to surround us with a magnetic pull. As we reached the base of the trunks, Herne took a deep breath and lunged through the trees, dragging me with him. I started to say something, but the next moment everything went haywire. I felt like an egg being scrambled, or ice cream being whipped up into a milkshake. Nothing felt stable and the only thing I could see were worlds of brilliant colors. It was like a crazy hallucinogenic trip, I thought. And I'd had my share of those in college.

I wasn't sure how long it lasted. I wasn't sure of anything, to tell the truth. It was as though every nerve ending in my body screamed for attention. It wasn't exactly pain, but more like a series of jolts that just kept on coming—and it wasn't the good kind of jolt like an orgasm, but more like being shocked over and over again by static electricity.

I was starting to get dizzy when my feet hit solid ground again. I opened my eyes and realized that they had been closed the entire time. I was still holding Herne's hand. As I looked around, I saw that we were in the middle of a forest. We were standing in front of a massive grove of giant oaks, and the roots formed a staircase winding around the sides of the trunks, spiraling up to what looked like a palace in the tree canopy.

Everywhere I turned, sparkling lights illuminated the dark forest, dancing and darting like fireflies in the night. Around the base of the massive trunks, people were going about their business. They turned as we appeared. I realized we were standing between another pair of oaks, similar to the ones back on Whidbey Island.

Overhead, the stars whirled. We had gone from day to night. The panorama spread out, a vast array of constellations and galaxies. I had never seen the sky look this way before, and I realized it wasn't just because of the lack of light pollution. There was something different, almost alien to the vista that unfolded above us. It felt cold, and yet incredibly active. As I squinted, staring up, I caught a glimpse of a silver wheel in the stars, and in the center of the wheel, a castle. I truly felt farther away from home than I had ever been.

"Is that a castle?" I asked, scooting closer to Herne, feeling terribly out of place.

"Yes. That's Caer Arianrhod, the silver castle of Arianrhod, goddess of the stars and of the Eternal Wheel." He wrapped his arm around my waist, nuzzling my forehead. "I know this is strange. You're probably feeling a long ways from home, and the truth is, you are. You're in my realm now. But you'll be safe. Everything's all right." He pointed at the palace among the trees. "That's where my father lives."

"Does Morgana live with him?" I wasn't sure if they were actually married or if they had just had a child together.

He shook his head. "No, she has her own palace, a Faerie Barrow. But she comes to visit often, especially when it has to do with the Wild Hunt." He gave me a reassuring hug, then took my hand and started forward. "Come, let's go meet my father."

I followed him, holding tight as the brilliant orbs of light darted around us. One landed on my shoulder and another on my nose, and I got the impression they were actually creatures, not simply magic sparkles.

"What are these? Are they like fireflies?"

"These are true Lightning Flits. Not like the lightning bugs you have over in your world, but these are shards of lightning that have taken on life. They shine through the darkness. They sleep during the day and come out at night. My father caught a bolt of lightning and shattered it in order to spawn enough Flits to light his palace and grounds."

I was about to ask how the hell he had caught a bolt of lightning, but just then we passed a group of people, carrying branches balanced on their shoulders, headed toward the palace. I realized they looked a lot like the Fae, but different.

"Who are they?" I asked.

"These are Elves. You won't find them over in your world, at least not in any great numbers. They live in the realms of the gods. Especially in Valhalla, Asgard, and here, in Annwn."

I had heard of Elves, but I had never met one. They were supposed to be similar to the Fae, only less emotional, and uninterested in anything outside the borders of their world. I wasn't sure what to think of them, or what they would think of me.

As Herne walked toward the group, I stood up straight. Herne was the son of a god, and as long as I was walking beside him, I would do my best to show the respect he deserved. The Elves stopped talking, and turned to greet us. One of the men stepped forward.

"Lord Herne, well met." He was tall and lithe, with golden hair tumbling down his back. His face was smooth and impassive, and even though he bowed deeply, he never lost the sense of regality that seemed to be second nature. He was altogether beautiful, shining with an inner light.

"Trospos, well met, my man." Herne inclined his head. "Is my father in his chamber?" He didn't bother introducing me, which was fine. I wasn't sure what to say, anyway.

Trospos gave him a brief nod. "Yes, he is. He said he was expecting you and to send you right up. Are you here for long?"

Herne shook his head. "Unfortunately, no. We're just here for a brief chat with my father, and then we must head back. If you'd prepare a key for Ember, I'd appreciate it. No doubt, she'll be coming over off and on, and I'd like her to be able to make the transfer without my help. Ember Kearney, please bid greetings to Trospos. He's one of my father's oldest assistants."

I started to stick out my hand, then stopped. I wasn't sure what the proper greeting was.

"Very good, my lord. My lady Ember, well met and hello." There was nothing in Trospos's eyes to indicate that he recognized my mixed blood, or that he felt I was anything but a welcome guest.

I smiled, grateful and eager to make a good impression. "How do you do? I'm afraid I don't know the customs here." I stopped, suddenly realizing that Trospos was speaking English. I blinked, glancing at Herne with a question in my eyes.

"My father's assistants know almost every language. Before we go, he'll fit you with the key for the portal." With that, Herne took my hand and once more, we were headed toward the base of the gigantic oak.

As we drew near, I saw that the entire stand of trees had calved off of one massive trunk, joined together at the base, but weaving in and out to form what looked like an entire latticework of trees. A labyrinth of staircases winding up the different trunks looked like a jumbled maze, but Herne knew exactly where we were going. He led me to the center of the trunk, where branches wove together to form a staircase. Clinging to each branch was a globe of light—some were flickering white, some were green, others purple and blue, still others pink. A railing was attached to the center of the trunk. I grabbed hold of it, not sure of my footing, and began to follow him up the steps.

I wasn't sure how tall the tree was. It seemed far taller than any oak I had ever seen, and by the time we were halfway up, I was dizzy. I glanced over the edge, quickly pulling back when I saw how far we were from the ground. I wondered what they did in case of emergency. You wouldn't just jump off the edge of the tree, would you? But then again, we were in the realm of the gods. Or rather, Annwn, to be precise. And here, everything seemed different.

"How far do we have to go?" I asked, feeling a little sheepish.

"About six more yards. There's an exit there into the palace."

And sure enough, not quite twenty feet ahead, we were standing on the landing, in front of a double door that led into the trunk. The stairs continued up the trunk, but Herne placed his hand on the door and whispered something. The opening shuddered and slid to the side, allowing us entrance.

He led me into a hall, illuminated by lanterns on the sides of the walls. It forked off in several different directions as we went along, and it occurred to me that the inside of the palace seemed far bigger than the outside. The floor was highly polished stone, black as obsidian, and it gleamed with our reflection under the lights guiding our way. The walls were smooth. I couldn't tell they were the inside of a tree trunk. Instead, they looked like polished ivory tiles with flecks of gold and silver sprinkled throughout.

"The palace seems like it's in yet another dimension. This seems far bigger than the tree outside." It felt like reality kept bending in and around, twisting when it needed to change.

"It is. Most homes belonging to the gods are. Try not to analyze it."

I realized we hadn't seen anybody so far, and that in itself seemed odd.

"Where is everybody? I would think we'd pass some servants or court members." I wasn't exactly sure just how Cernunnos ran things. The Fae Courts were packed with nobility, and even though they were spread out, they were crowded.

"They're around. But they're usually busy, doing my father's bidding. This isn't a court like a kingdom with people living within the castle walls. Only his assistants live here, and Morgana when she chooses to visit. I lived here most of the time when I was young. I stayed with my mother at times, but mostly, I lived with my father."

The winding labyrinth of hallways reminded me of underground tunnels. It was hard to believe we were high above the floor of the forest, crossing through the arboreal canopy. We passed several doorways, some of them open, and inside I saw what looked like various bedrooms and sitting rooms. The entire complex seemed so empty that when we did come across a couple serving girls, it startled me. They came around the corner as we were rounding a bend in the hallway. They suddenly stopped giggling, staring at Herne as if they had just seen a ghost. They backed up quickly, and dropped into a deep curtsey. I realize they, too, were Elves.

"Pardon, Your Lordship. We didn't realize you were here," one of them said, her gaze downcast at the floor. She was petite, with long dark hair wrapped up in a chignon. She wore a rather plain dress, but it was clean and neat.

Herne gave them a quick once-over, nodding with a faint smile.

"Not a problem. Carry on." He skirted around them, and I followed, not sure if I should say anything. As we passed by, I saw one of them giving me a glance, but she lowered her gaze the moment she saw me looking at her. There was no expression on her face that I could read. The Elves were even more impassive than Herne.

We came to a set of stairs at the end of the hallway, and Herne began to climb them.

"Surely this isn't all in that one copse we entered? It feels like we walked for a mile." I wasn't complaining, just curious.

Herne glanced back at me. "We're still within the thicket. As you said, this is a realm within a realm. Just like a Barrow mound. Most abodes of the gods exist in an interdimensional space. You should visit Caer Arianrhod at some point. Talk about labyrinths!" He laughed. "I remember when I was young, Morgana took me to visit. I got lost for three days by going down the wrong hallway. Finally somebody found me and returned me to my mother."

"Weren't you afraid? If I'd gotten lost for three days when I was a little girl, I would have been terrified."

"No. I knew eventually they'd come looking for me. And the gods can go without food or water far longer than mortals. Oh, we get grumpy and hungry, but we're not going to die."

I thought about what he said, and then asked, "Do you even *need* to eat?"

"Not particularly. I get hungry, as I said, but it's not going to hurt me. I suppose if I didn't have food for a thousand years it might make me grow gaunt and I'd be hella bitchy. Most of the gods I know enjoy eating."

That brought another thought to mind. "Can you get drunk?"

"Depends what I'm drinking. But yes, a number of the gods can get drunk, including me. I don't think you want to see that, though. It's not a pretty sight. Especially with gods like Thor or Dionysus. It can be amusing, but dangerous for mortals to be around at that point. Even...around me, it would be dicey." He laughed. "I remember once..." He paused, then shook his head. "No, I'll save that story for another time." He pointed ahead to the top of the stairs. "We're almost to my father's chambers."

"Tell me how I should address him, please. Should I curtsey or bow or fall on my face?" The last thing I wanted to do was make a bad impression on my boyfriend's father, especially since he happened to be the Lord of the Hunt.

"My father doesn't require groveling, unless you've pissed him off. A curtsey will do, or even a short bow. And address him as 'Your Lordship.' He'll tell you what he wants you to call him after that." He must have seen the consternation in my face because he paused, leaning down to give me a kiss. "Everything will be fine. Trust me, if I thought my father was going to do anything to you—anything nasty, that is—I wouldn't bring you here."

He sounded so genuine that I believed him. Herne struck me as the type who would defy his parents to protect those he cared about. I stared into his eyes, deciding to trust him.

"All right, but that doesn't make me any less

nervous. I don't know why, but meeting your father seems like such a huge deal. So was meeting Morgana. I know you're a god as well, but somehow you don't seem quite so intimidating."

"It's gotta be the leather jacket and jeans," he said with a laugh. "Someday I'll let you see me in my natural form, but we'll leave that for later."

We were at the top of the stairs now, and he put his hand on the doorknob. I took a deep breath and gave him a nod.

He opened the door. "We're off to see the wizard," he said, then entered the chamber.

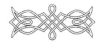

THE ROOM WAS vast that it was hard to even *see* the ceiling. The walls were a maze of tree trunks and roots and branches, all entwined around one other, fossilized to the point of looking like stone. Perhaps they *were* stone, carved to look like giant root balls. I wasn't sure, and for some reason, I felt hesitant to reach out and touch them.

The room was larger than a football field. Here and there, benches lined the walls, hewn from a lustrous white marble, run through with veins of black. Matching tables sat near the benches, but there was no one sitting at them, and the chamber felt cavernous.

I glanced up. Stalactites dripped down from the ceiling, sparkling with crystals of quartz. They flickered, illuminated from within. As we fully entered the chamber, the entire ceiling blazed to life, a brilliant light spreading throughout the network of crystals.

I blinked, momentarily blinded. As my eyesight adjusted, I found myself staring at a giant throne in the center of the room. It too appeared to be formed of roots and branches, twigs and limbs all knotting together in a woven tangle to create a giant chair. It, too, had sparkling crystals peeking out from crevices and nooks that hid between the branches.

Seated on the massive throne was an equally massive man.

His muscles rippled, his olive skin gleaming, showing every shadow and highlight of his muscles. His biceps and chest were bare, a topographical map chiseled in flesh. His hair was long, hanging in multiple braids that draped over his thighs. He wore a bearskin cloak and his face was illuminated by the crystals shining from both throne and ceiling.

Cernunnos's eyes were wide set, tilted like a cat's, and they flickered with gold and green lights, reminding me of faceted gems. His lips were full, and I saw where Herne got his good looks, but the Hunt Master's smile held the slightest hint of cruelty, although I didn't feel any sense of malice coming from him. But I knew that to cross him would be dangerous—deadly, no doubt. He stood as we approached.

I stared at him, stopping in my tracks when I realized he was wearing a pair of camo pants. I blinked, trying to take in the juxtaposition in his dress.

Herne led me up to the throne, where he went down on one knee, bowing his head. Since I wasn't wearing a dress, I felt odd curtseying, so I followed suit, lowering myself to one knee beside Herne.

Cernunnos towered over us, he was at least seven feet tall. He stared down at us for a moment and, as I snuck a peek, he caught my gaze and the haughty smile widened into a grin.

"Well met, Ms. Ember Kearney. So, I finally get to speak to the woman who has stolen my son's heart."

And that stopped me cold.

Chapter 10

BESIDES ME, HERNE snorted. But he didn't contradict his father.

Cernunnos leaned down, inches from my face as he held my gaze. I was afraid to look away. I didn't want to appear rude, or anything like that. After a moment, he held out his hand. I stared at the massive fingers for a moment, then took them, allowing him to help me to my feet.

"Welcome, Ember, to my home. Herne, mind your manners and bring over a bench so she'll have a place to sit."

Herne jumped up and, without a word, carried back one of the marble benches as though it were light as a feather. He sat it down in front of the throne and I obediently took a seat, still staring at the god that Herne called "Papa."

"Thank you," I finally got up the courage to say. "Your Lordship," I added hastily.

He leaned back in his seat, his elbows resting on the arms of the throne, as he contemplated both of us. "You may call me Lord Cernunnos. I don't stand on ceremony."

"Yes, sir," I started to say, then scrambled to add, "Yes, Lord Cernunnos." I felt all the world as though I was in the principal's office again, only this time the principal could probably strike me dead with a lightning bolt.

"You are enjoying my son's company?"

I blinked. What the hell was I going to say? *No*? But grateful I could tell him the truth, I nodded. "Yes, I truly am. Herne has been wonderful to Angel and me."

"Ah. Your best friend. So, you like working for the Wild Hunt?"

Again, I nodded. "It beats what I was doing before, to be honest. And it's fascinating work. It also... You know my heritage, I assume?"

He inclined his head. "Yes, but I never let my prejudices interfere with individual relationships. I have to admit, the Fae have the potential to be an incredible people, but with the petty warring that goes on between the two factions, they push my patience to the very edge. However, my personal feelings beside the point, Morgana speaks highly of you. And your father was a faithful acolyte to me."

"I never even knew he was pledged in your service."

"Your parents were fairly close-mouthed. Pity about their deaths." He seemed to muse over his words for a moment. "Ah, well. It's good to finally meet you. And I'm glad that my son and you are happy. But I didn't call you here just for social banter. I actually have something serious to discuss with you both."

He snapped his fingers, and a moment later a servant rushed in, though how she heard him, I wasn't sure. She gave him a deep curtsey, then stood back, waiting for orders.

"Bring us mead. And bread." As she ran off, he turned back to me with a big smile. "I have developed a taste for what you call French bread. I had one of my servants go over to your realm in order to learn how to bake it. I could eat it day and night."

I couldn't help it. I dissolved into slightly hysterical laughter.

Cernunnos stared at me for a moment, looking puzzled. "I said something funny?"

I shook my head, trying to stop laughing. "No—no. It's just that... I'm standing here in front of the Lord of the Hunt and we're talking about baking bread. It seems like such an odd juxtaposition." I wiped my eyes, trying to compose myself.

"Ah," he said, still looking bewildered. "Well then, onto more serious subjects. You are working on a case now for the Foam Born hippocampi, aren't you? Up on Whidbey Island?"

Herne nodded. "Yes. Is that a problem?"

Cernunnos paused as the servant returned with a tray heaped with freshly toasted baguettes slathered in butter, along with three goblets and a huge bottle of mead. She poured our drinks, handed them around, and then handed us plates filled with a crunchy, yeasty bread. It smelled incredibly good and I realized I was hungry. With a curtsey, she left.

The Lord of the Hunt bade us eat, and we spent a moment or two tearing into the bread. The mead was also good, though it went to my head immediately and I realized I needed to take very small sips or I'd end up drunk off my ass. Apparently, the gods made their booze stronger than humans did.

Herne noticed as I shakily sat down my drink. "I should have warned you. The mead here is probably comparable to 151-proof rum back at home. I suggest you drink it slowly."

"I kind of figured that out," I said. "I've probably had enough for now."

Herne glanced back at his father. "So, is there a problem? The case didn't seem like something to bring to your attention. I don't think it actually has anything to do with the Fae, except there seems to be attempted coverups for several murders over some time. Actually, what looks like twenty murders now that we've pried into it."

Cernunnos finished another chunk of the bread. "The Light Fae woman Astrana has approached me. You obviously know who she is, so I'm not going to reiterate her history. She has petitioned to have you removed from the case. I need to know more about it so I can make an informed decision. She said it has nothing to do with mitigating the Fae war, but I feel that she's hiding something and I don't like being led on a wild goose chase."

"We were approached by Rhiannon, the Matriarch of the Foam Born, to look into an unsolved murder case. Her cousin's death." Herne relayed everything that had happened since we arrived at Whidbey Island. "I'm getting extremely irritated with Astrana, given it looks like we have a serial killer on our hands. Twenty murders that went cold, buried under silence, and that doesn't even account for the forty-odd people who were reported missing and never heard from again. Most of the murders were attributed to random vampire kills, but I will tell you this, there's no way in hell that a vampire killed them."

"What do you think is happening?" Cernunnos asked.

Herne shrugged, frowning. "I'm not certain. However, Ember and I found a stand of blackthorn on the island, and those trees are sentient. They attacked us, and actually managed to do some serious damage to Ember here. Take off your bandage and show my father your puncture marks. Marks of the kind that have been found on every murder victim, as far as we can tell."

Cernunnos blinked. "*Blackthorn*? Blackthorn isn't supposed to grow around there."

"I know. And the doctor told Ember that she was imagining it. Not the wound, but that it was from a blackthorn. He categorically denied that there was any on the island."

The Lord of the Hunt shifted on his throne, frowning as I undid the bandage and showed him my wounds. They hadn't festered, but they were deep, and didn't look like they were healing as fast as I usually did. Once the open air hit them, they hurt like hell and I winced.

"Oh dear. That makes me—hold on a moment."

Cernunnos reached down and rang a bell by the side of his throne. Once again the servant returned.

"Bring me Ferosyn. And tell him to move his ass. This is important." As the servant ran out of the room, he turned to me. "Ferosyn is my chief healer. He's one of Brighid's grandsons. He's part human, so he's a demigod, somewhat like my son although not quite so powerful. But as a healer, there are none better."

I hadn't realized demigods existed before I met Herne. I had never thought about it.

Cernunnos gently took hold of my arm as I held it out. He could have crushed my wrist with his fingers, but his touch was light and comforting. He held my wounds up so that he could see better, then snapped his fingers and one of the flickering lights sailed down and hovered right over my wrist. It illuminated the punctured skin as brightly as an LED light bulb would.

"Ferosyn will know for sure, but this is more than just a blackthorn wound. They can be nasty, and the plant itself has a horrendous temper, but there is something...else here."

Herne crowded in, staring at the puncture marks. "The wound doesn't look like it's healing up as fast as it should."

"I know," I said, getting more worried by the moment. "I don't think it's infected—at least not yet. But I heal quickly. I'm not sure what's going on. I've been using the salve the doctor gave me."

At that moment, a tall, lithe Elf walked into the room. He looked young, but the aura of age surrounded him. He was probably at least a thousand years old, given how long the Elves lived. He bowed low before Cernunnos, then glanced at Herne and me.

"You know my son, Herne. Meet his consort, Ember."

Ferosyn murmured what seemed like an appropriate greeting, then turned back to Cernunnos. "What can I do for you, my lord?" Like many professionals, he was all business.

"Examine her wrist. A blackthorn bush attacked her. She didn't fall into it, the bush reached out and wrapped itself around her arm. What do you make of that? And why isn't she healing as fast as she should be?"

"I'll need to take her into the examination room, Your Lordship."

"Then do so. Return when you have your diagnosis. Herne, go with her." Cernunnos gave me a kind smile, and I realized that he understood how nervous I was. I was starting to really like Herne's father, even though he still scared the shit out of me.

We followed Ferosyn out of a door opposite the one we had come in, and down a long corridor that was filled with Elves. I realized that we were in the heart of the palace now. The passage we had entered through hadn't been one of the main thoroughfares. The Elves passing by all gave Herne respectful bows, but their eyes were locked on me, and I realized they probably wondered what the hell one of the Fae—especially a tralaeth—was doing here.

Ferosyn led us into a room off one of the main corridors. It looked remarkably like a regular doctor's room, with beakers and lab equipment on one side table, an examination table that seemed to have been pilfered from our realm, and enough of the flickering lights that the room was bright. He motioned for me to hop up on the exam table, and I grinned as I did so. Apparently the gods weren't above borrowing human know-how and technology.

"Are you allergic to anything that you know of?" he asked.

I shook my head. "I don't think so. I can't tell you for sure, but I've never encountered a problem yet."

Using an eye-dropper, he began to drip various substances on different puncture marks. Some of them stung and I grimaced, but forced myself to sit still. Others seem to have no effect. As I watched, a wisp of smoke came up from one of them and I wondered what the hell he was doing to me. Herne didn't seem concerned, though, so I tried not to worry. After a few moments, one of the puncture wounds turned a brilliant, vivid green around the edges.

"Bingo. We have an answer." But then, the joy in Ferosyn's voice vanished and a look of concern filled his eyes. *That* had me worried. When an *Elf* actually looked concerned, it made me nervous.

"What is it? I can tell you're disturbed." It wasn't that I wanted bad news, but it was better to know about it and start treatment, than wait till it became an even bigger problem later on.

"Oh, it's blackthorn, all right. But it's more than just the bush. We need to talk with His Lordship." He paused, looking through several vials. Finally, he found one and handed it to me. "This should heal you up faster. Use it twice a day. Rub the salve in carefully, making sure to get it inside the puncture wounds. It will sting, but it will definitely heal you up. You won't have to wear a bandage unless you want to, but try to keep the wound clean."

I gave Herne a curious look, and he returned it, shrugging. We followed Ferosyn back to the throne room, where Cernunnos was waiting. He motioned for Herne and me to sit down again.

"Well? Did you find out what's going on?"

"Yes, Your Lordship. She definitely was attacked by blackthorn bush, there's no question of it. However, there was more to the poison than just straight blackthorn. I detected Ante-Fae magic. I gave her some medication to heal the wounds. Otherwise, they would eventually fester."

Cernunnos blinked. "*Ante-Fae*? Are you certain?"

Ferosyn nodded. "Most definitely. I suggest you find out which of the Ante-Fae rule that area. One name in particular comes to mind, and I suspect you'll find out better than I can."

Cernunnos held his gaze. "You're talking about Blackthorn, aren't you?"

Ferosyn nodded. "It would make sense. But I don't know if any of the others use the blackthorn tree as a weapon. As I said, you'll know better than I would."

"Very well. Thank you, you may go." As Ferosyn

exited the room, Cernunnos turned back to Herne and me. "So, that answers one question. Several, perhaps."

"What are the Ante-Fae?" I had never heard of them.

"They're highly dangerous," Herne said. His smile vanished, and the look of puzzlement darkened into a scowl. "In fact, they can be as dangerous and as powerful as the gods."

"If you had been raised with your family, your parents might have told you about the Ante-Fae. If they knew about them, that is. Not many of the Fae actually know they exist. Astrana must have somehow stumbled onto one. Given what I suspect, she has a reason to want to keep those murders under wraps. Her life may depend on it." Cernunnos's expression was as dark as Herne's.

"Tell me what they are." I had a feeling I was about to find out something that I would regret knowing.

"Before the Fae traveled over the Great Sea to your realm, before the great cities of TirNaNog and Navane rose in Annwn, and before the Fae grew to become so powerful, there were the Ante-Fae. They were the forerunners of your race—both sides of it. Herne is correct in that some of them are as dangerous and as powerful as the gods. They are ancient and treacherous, and each one is unique with different powers. Most of them are rooted deep within the earth and water, although some are connected with the elements of sky and fire."

I sucked in a deep breath. I knew what he was talking about. There had been tales of such creatures—mythology was full of them. Each one was named, and each one seemed to have been the mother or father of a branch of Fae. A lot of the sub-Fae seemed to descend from them.

"You're talking about creatures like Jenny Greenteeth, or the Black Annis, aren't you?"

Cernunnos nodded. "Those are two of the more famous ones. There are hundreds of them, perhaps thousands. They inhabit wild areas, and ancient caves, but some of them live near civilization. They hide in plain sight. The one Ferosyn and I were talking about is named Blackthorn, the King of Thorns. He's a deadly, dangerous, and greedy soul. I need to find out where he was last located. Morgana and I keep track of the Ante-Fae as much as we can, because although they do not bother themselves with the Light and Dark courts, they sometimes stir things up and put humans in peril. We can't do much about them, but if this one—and I'll bet my boots it's Blackthorn—has enlisted Astrana to cover up murders, then we have a problem spilling into the mortal world. I assume not all of those who were killed were Fae?"

Herne shook his head. "No, a few were human. Then we can stay on the case?"

"Most assuredly. Especially now that I know the Ante-Fae are involved. I'll inform Astrana that there is call for you to investigate. Unfortunately, she will then, no doubt, relay the information to Blackthorn. Be on your guard. The covenant we have with the Light and the Dark Fae does not include the Ante-Fae."

"What's that mean?" I asked.

"It means if Blackthorn attacks you, I can't step in directly. All we can do is try to control the damage and keep the Light and the Dark from taking part in it. This is a delicate matter. Bluntly put, we have to put a stop to it, but Blackthorn is free to fight back." Cernunnos looked troubled.

"So, we can intervene, but unlike with the Light and Dark courts, he doesn't have to offer us protection," Herne said.

"That's about the size of it." Cernunnos stood. "I need to talk to Morgana and see if she has any ideas. Meanwhile, return to your realm. I'll contact you as soon as we can verify which of the Ante-Fae you are facing. Meanwhile, walk softly. One of the first things you need to do is locate where he's hiding."

"We were going to talk to the families. If we can ascertain where the victims disappeared, then we may be able to triangulate a common point. We also have forty missing people who vanished from the area over the past thirty years and no clue of what happened—the stories, again, were buried. As far as the dead, four of the families seemed to come into a spot of good fortune shortly afterward. Sixteen didn't, and they're the ones who moved. Marilyn said she was notified about some insurance payout that she assumed was a scam because she had already received a check, so that could be related." Herne stood, motioning for me to join him.

As I did, Trospos entered the room. "I have your key for the portal," he said. "Please hold out your hand—your healthy one."

I did as he asked, and he pressed his hand over mine. A warmth rippled through my fingers and as he pulled away, I could see a faint gold sigil under the skin. "How do I use this?"

"Just hold your hands up to the twin oaks, and they will register the energy within the sigil. When the portal opens fully, you'll feel a shock in your hand. I'm sure Lord Herne will teach you how to use it. This will open any portal to Lord Cernunnos's realm."

Cernunnos watched Trospos, then turned back to Herne. "If the murder victims' families were paid to keep their mouth shut, regardless of who handed out the coin, they're not likely to be very friendly to strangers." He gave me a quick bow. "Ember Kearney, I'm glad we met. I hope that you continue to enjoy working for the Wild Hunt. Your father's death saddened me. We will speak again, hopefully sooner than later."

And with that, he motioned us out of the throne room.

BY THE TIME we returned to John's yard, stepping through the scarlet oak portal, two hours had passed. It felt like far longer, but that's how interdimensional realms tended to work. Herne pulled out his cell phone, checking to see if he had any messages.

"Talia wants to know if we're back yet. I'll text her that we are on the way."

I glanced at my wrist, which Ferosyn had wrapped again. It wasn't hurting as much, and the jar of salve was comfortably tucked away in my bag.

"So what did you think of my father?" Herne held the car door open for me and I slid into the passenger seat, fastening my seatbelt.

I had expected the question and was prepared with an answer.

"He's intimidating. I sure as hell wouldn't want him angry at me. But he was really nice, and I wasn't as afraid of him as I thought I would be."

Herne's phone rang and he answered it before turning on the ignition.

"Cernunnos," he mouthed to me. "Yes? Uh-huh, really? So what does that mean for us?" He paused, frowning. "Can you send me the information? Email me the file, if you would. All right, thank you." Again, he paused. "Yeah, she is, isn't she? She said she liked you, too."

As he popped his phone back in his pocket and started the car, I waited for him to tell me what he had found out. I already knew he had been talking about me at the end.

"My father likes you a lot. He says you have spunk. That's a compliment. It looks like we are dealing with Blackthorn, the King of Thorns. My father is emailing me a file on him now. He warned me to be very careful. Blackthorn is highly dangerous. He's extremely old, which makes him even more cunning. He's going to hold off talking to Astrana for as long as he can."

"Then we've bought a little time before she figures out we're on to things. Once he gets back to her, she'll know we talked to Cernunnos and told him everything. Or will she? Is there any chance that she'll assume he made an arbitrary decision without finding out the facts?" It wasn't likely, but I could hope.

"I don't think so. She's not stupid. My father's right, we have to walk carefully on this one. Considering what those bushes did to your wrist, I think that being tangled up in an entire patch of them could very quickly lead to death."

"Do you think the murder victims found out something about Blackthorn and were going to cause trouble?"

Herne turned onto Oceanside Drive. "That seems like it would be a possibility, except for the timing. They died during two time periods per year. Near Beltane and near Samhain. When did all the missing people vanish?"

I thought for a moment. "It had to be during those time periods. They were the only ones we checked the papers for. April and May, and October and November."

"That's hard to ignore. Some of the Ante-Fae are drawn into the cyclical nature of the year. There's something ritualistic about these murders. Which means they'll continue until we put a stop to them." He paused. "Wait, why did we just look during those times?"

"Rosetta told us she looked into it and suggested we check those periods. Why? Do you think there might be others throughout the year?"

Herne paused, staring at the road as we drove. "I

don't know. My head says yes, we should go back and check every single month. My gut tells me no, that we're onto the right path."

"Then go with your gut. I know it's counter to logic, but there's a reason your father put you in charge of the agency. But we can always have Talia or Yutani go back over it, if you like." I paused. "How long has Blackthorn been in this area? If it's longer than thirty or so years, why weren't there unexplained murders before then? Or were they just never found or recorded? Has this been going on since he came to the area? And if not, why did it start now? Or rather, forty years ago? What set off the spree?"

"Maybe the file my father emailed us will answer some of those questions. They're good consider-ations, though." Herne parked the car. "It really does seem unlikely that, after thousands of years, one of the Ante-Fae would suddenly turn into a se-rial murderer. I don't know, Ember. I'm perplexed. Come on, the file's in my inbox so let's go inside and have a look."

As we headed into the hotel, my phone rang. I glanced at the Caller ID. It was Rachel Madison, the real estate agent. "Hello?"

"Well, if you still want it, the owner has accepted your offer. The house is yours, pending inspec-tion." She sounded almost giddy. I supposed I would, too, if I finally sold a house that had been on the market for well over a year.

"Yes, I do! I will set up an inspection as soon as I can. I'd like to be there, but I'm not sure how much longer this case is going to take."

"Just let me know by tomorrow if you've been able to reach anybody. We should get this going as soon as possible." Which was code for: *I really don't want this to fall through, can you please follow up on this.*

"I'll be in touch with you by tomorrow morning. Thank you!" As I hung up I couldn't help but feel a little gleeful. "I got the house! If the inspection goes through, that is."

Herne clapped his arm around my shoulders, pulling me close to him as he planted a kiss on my forehead.

"Congratulations! You and Angel need this. That condo of yours is nice, but it's far too small."

"It served its purpose, but you're right, it's time to move on. And Mr. Rumblebutt will like having a place to stretch out and a garden to play in."

We darted across the parking lot, dodging the rain that had suddenly broken loose. Herne must have texted for everyone to meet us because when we entered the Edgewater Coffee Shop, they were all there at one of the tables. I stopped at the counter to order a quint-shot mocha, and Herne asked for a triple-shot cappuccino. We carried our drinks over to the table and joined them.

"Well, you look like you survived," Angel said, giving me the once-over.

"I actually enjoyed my visit," I said, playing it blasé. "Cernunnos is intimidating, but he made me feel welcome. However, I think right now we have more important matters to discuss." I looked at Herne.

"Ember is correct. We have a major problem on

our hands. I'm going to email each of you a file that my father sent me. We need to discuss this, and we need to discuss it in private. Yutani, can you check my room again, just in case they figured it out and came back to plant another bug?" Herne took a sip of his cappuccino. "Text me if everything's all right." He handed his key card to Yutani, who nodded and took off toward the elevator.

Talia frowned. "We aren't dealing with a simple murder case, are we?"

"No," Herne said. "And we're into a delicate balancing act. A deadly one."

He said no more, and I turned my attention to my drink, welcoming the rush of caffeine into my system. A few moments later Yutani texted that everything was all right, so we gathered up our drinks and gear and headed upstairs to Herne's room, where he shut the door and locked it.

As we settled down around the room, he dove in.

"First, Astrana knows that we're on to this case. She's complained to Cernunnos. He's going to put off answering her as long as he can, but chances are, she's going to know—or at least think we know—her secrets. So she's absolutely no help and will interfere with us if she can. Now please, open the documents that I just forwarded to you."

I quickly brought up the document, startled that it was so detailed and well laid out. Apparently, the gods really did understand technology.

Morgana had emailed Herne several files on Blackthorn, and Herne directed us to the first one. With my help, he filled everybody else in on what had happened during our visit with his father.

"The Ante-Fae? Crap." Talia shook her head, and the look on her face told me she already knew what they were. "We really don't need to tangle with them."

"To make things worse, we're dealing with Blackthorn, the King of Thorns. Cernunnos seemed extremely unhappy about that. Let's see what my mother has to say about him."

Morgana's document contained what appeared to be an encyclopedia definition, although it wasn't from any encyclopedia I was aware of.

Blackthorn, the King of Thorns, is one of the most ancient of the Ante-Fae. Originating from the UK, he has control over almost every thorn-bearing plant, specializing in blackthorn trees. But he can also control bramble bushes, rose bushes, and any other bushes containing thorns. Like most of the Ante-Fae, the source-roots of the King of Thorns are unknown. However, he is linked to shadow magic, dream magic, and it is said he feeds off of pain and despair.

He has had a number of children with various other Ante-Fae, and not all of them are accounted for. Unlike a number of the Ante-Fae, the King of Thorns thrives in inhabited areas, and has an insatiable greed for power. He is, however, willing to make deals, and in fact, is always looking for a way to increase his network. He is said to have made alliances with some of the vampires over the eons, finding them useful allies. He tends to prefer coastlines, and at one time or another has lived all over the world. His most current known whereabouts is said to be somewhere in the Puget Sound area. Very little is known about his ultimate goals, and any further information would be welcomed by the Historians.

I stared at the information, trying to reconcile it to what we knew about the case.

"He doesn't *sound* like a serial killer to me. What about religious beliefs? Could he follow some ancient god who requires a sacrifice every few years?" I still wasn't clear on the Ante-Fae and how they related to the gods.

"That's one possibility," Herne said. "But I tend to agree. He doesn't sound like a serial killer. He may feed off of pain, and he probably has sadistic tendencies, but that alone does not a serial killer make. That doesn't even necessarily correlate to regular murderers. Sadists tend to get off on pain, not death."

"He likes deals, which accounts for his dealing with vampires. They're all about networking and grasping for power that way. Ten to one, he's made a deal with Astrana, in his favor, of course. So she's covering up these murders for a reason. If he's *not* the killer—and we don't know that yet—then why is he enlisting her to hide them?" Yutani tapped the other documents, opening them. "Most of these say approximately the same thing. Who's the historian mentioned?"

"I can tell you that," Talia said. "There are several agencies that watch over the Ante-Fae, as well as other ancient creatures and beings. The Ante-Fae are only one sector of bogeyman that we have to pay attention to. The historians belong to the society of record-keepers. They do their best to keep track these creatures and beings. They aren't always up to date, but they do what they can."

"What's the name of the society?" Angel asked. "Are we even supposed to know about it?"

"It can't hurt that you do—especially considering that we're part of the Wild Hunt. It's better off that most people don't know about it, though." Herne flipped through his wallet, then pulled out a business card and tossed it on the table. "You all might as well enter that information into your contacts. That's the local representative for LOCK—the Library of Cryptic Knowledge. It's the brainchild of Taliesin, one of the Force Majeure—and the less you ask about that, the better. He started it about two thousand years ago, and like the Wild Hunt, it's spread all over the world. There are branches of the library in every major country."

I picked up the card. The name on it read Gwydion Jones. I entered it into my contacts along with the phone number and address, both of which were in Redmond.

As Angel entered the information into her phone, she asked, "Just how many secret societies are out there? I think I've learned more about the world in the past few months than I ever have before in my life. It feels like everywhere I turn, there's some secret organization or group doing something or researching something."

Talia laughed, her eyes twinkling. The harpy had quite a sense of humor, I had to give it to her for that.

"You haven't even scratched the surface, child. You should feel privileged, though. Not many humans know much about this, and a lot of those who do stumble over this sort of information end up vanishing off the face of the earth."

At Angel's horrified look, Talia added, "I don't mean they're killed. It's just that sometimes information needs to be kept private in order to safeguard operations. Some of them end up being relocated with their families, or they have their memories wiped of whatever they learned. A few of the darker organizations, of course, resort to murder."

"Lovely. Let's just hope we can keep out of their way." Angel handed the card back to Herne.

"My father suggested we still interview those four families, but our goal is to find out where Blackthorn's located, and what his intentions are. We need to put a stop to these murders. That Cernunnos was firm on. The carnage is spilling out into the mortal world, and even though the Ante-Fae are not part of the Fae Courts, he still wants us to end this. So we have our marching orders. Angel, you might as well book our rooms for the next few days. I don't think we're going anywhere soon. But do so under my own account. I'm not charging Rhiannon for the rest of this investigation since my father ordered us to continue."

"It's going on four o'clock now. Should we interview the families today? We can probably get through all four in the next couple hours if we split up," Yutani said.

"I think so. Yutani, you're with me. Viktor and

Ember, you go together. Angel and Talia, stay here and do whatever research you can. Try to find out just where the blackthorn patches are on this island. The doctor said there weren't any, but we know that's a lie."

"That means he may be in on this, too," I said.

"He could well be. Somebody has to be examining those bodies and not making a peep over how they were killed."

"We'll comb the Net," Talia said.

"Right. Don't go driving around looking for them." Herne's hair fell forward. Before I could stop myself, I reached out and brushed it back behind his ear. He gave me a twinkling smile and winked.

Yutani's nose was still deep in the files. "If all the bodies were found in the state park, shouldn't we search the park as well?"

"Yes, we should. But for now let's interview those families. Then we can decide how to approach the park." Herne looked around, letting out a long sigh. "Are we ready?"

I suddenly remembered Rachel's call—with all the worry over Blackthorn, the good news had slipped my mind.

"Oh, I forgot! Angel, we got the house!"

Angel gave me a high five.

"Can you look into inspectors—you know, house inspectors—while I'm out?"

"Sure thing," she said.

And with that, we headed out.

Chapter 11

THE FIRST FAMILY that Viktor and I were headed to meet were the Douglases. The murder victim had been Rebecca Douglas, their daughter, and she had vanished sixteen years ago. They found her a week later. She was human. And they were one of the four families that had come across a sizable streak of good fortune, although exactly what that fortune was, nobody really knew.

I was driving, and Viktor was in the passenger seat, looking glum.

"What's the matter?" I asked.

"We're facing the Ante-Fae. I'm surprised you've never heard of them, given your heritage, but given your background, I guess it makes sense."

"What do you mean?"

"Let's just say that Fae Courts don't appreciate not being considered the top of their game. A lot of them don't want to acknowledge the Ante-Fae as their ancestors, because the Ante-Fae are so much more powerful."

I groaned. "I hate to admit it, because I bear their blood, but you're right. It seems a little ridiculous, kind of like humans denying their Neanderthal ancestors. Or something like that."

"Nobody ever said people have to make sense—regardless of race or species or whatever you want to call it. You know that most of the Fae are anything but sensible." He paused, then added, "How do we want to go about this? How do we introduce ourselves?"

"We could say that we're reporters investigating cold case files for a story." Even as I said it, another thought crossed my mind. "Wait. What if Astrana has gotten to them first? Do you think that she has the foresight to visit the families and warn them to keep their mouths shut?"

It made perfect sense to me that she would do that, given her nature. And if Blackthorn had something on her, then it was in her best interest to obey.

"I suppose."

It occurred to me we were looking at this the wrong way. "What if... Suppose that it's not Blackthorn dictating to Astrana? Could she be blackmailing him? That seems right in her nature."

Viktor flashed me a quick look. "You're right, that does seem right up her alley. However, I'll say this. The thought of blackmailing the Ante-Fae—that's playing a deadly game. Worse than Russian roulette. You'd have to have nerves of steel to do that and I don't know if she's capable of that."

"Nerves of steel, or a massive ego. What's her background? Can you dig up anything really quick? You guys may have worked a case she was involved in, but I wasn't around at that time."

Viktor scrolled through his files.

"Yeah, I remember it vaguely, but here's a record. Astrana was kicked out of Navane for overstepping her boundaries with Névé. She dared to speak for the Queen, without getting permission in advance, and nearly caused a serious incident with the town of Woodinville."

"Oops. That's not good. What did she do?"

"Hmm… Looks like she promised something like an appearance at a local festival. Névé had already refused. It ended up causing a rift that took a lot of smoothing over. Apparently it was the last in a long string of events where Astrana took it upon herself to speak for the throne without permission. She had already been reprimanded three or four times for pulling a similar stunt. She was on probation and dismissed from Névé's service after making a full apology to the mayor and explaining that she hadn't had the authority to make any such promise. She left in disgrace, and she was pissed as hell from what I can see here."

That Astrana was willing to speak for the Queen without permission indicated an egotistical personality. Either that, or she thought she'd manage to get away with something. *Or* she might have been deliberately trying to *cause* trouble.

"No matter what the reason, she's a risk taker." I thought for a moment. "Can you find any evidence that she's a gambler? I doubt if money would be the focus, but the addictive nature of raising the stakes might be. She could be an adrenaline junkie."

Viktor spent another couple minutes tapping away at his tablet. All of a sudden he stopped, staring at a page on the screen. "Well, lookie here."

"What did you find?"

"Just a notation that our fair sheriff took out an extensive loan for her house. And we're talking massive. As in the realm of four million dollars. She's living well above her means, therefore she has to find a way to pay that mortgage every month."

"Can we be sure she didn't pay cash for it? Remember, the Fae are very long-lived. She could have been saving for most of her lifetime."

"Not this time. There's a mortgage holder listed for her property. And her mortgage company is VN Worldwide Bank, Washington state branch." Viktor flashed me a smug smile. He nodded. "Mmm. As I thought."

"I don't think I've ever heard of them."

"VN—the Vampire Nation Worldwide Bank. The vampires own her to the tune of over three and a half million dollars."

I almost swerved into the other lane. Owing the vampires that much money felt like a death sentence. Or at least, it would throw her into the realm of indentured servitude.

"But *why* would they give her such an enormous loan? Especially on her salary?" It seemed ridiculous. Even if she had already paid over five hundred thousand dollars back to them, which it sounded like.

"Think. *The Fae are extremely long-lived.* So are vampires. What better than a long-term investment? If they had lent a human that amount, you can bet the interest would be sky high, or they probably figured that person might be coming into a massive fortune. But a loan to the Fae? Over the years, the interest makes it worth the chance. She'll be alive a long time, and by the time she pays the loan back, the interest will double, if not triple the amount. We know that the vamps are all about money."

I blinked. Viktor was right. "So she has to figure out some way to pay the vampires back if she doesn't want to be in their debt forever."

"You can bet Blackthorn has more money than she'll ever need. So if she can dig up some dirt on him and blackmail him, bingo. She'll probably have the vamps paid back in ten years and then be counting on the rest of the blackmail to set her up for life." Viktor shrugged. "It seems out there, but I can see it."

"So, you think that either Blackthorn—or someone he's connected with—started killing off people and Astrana found out about it. She blackmails him, looking the other way when the murders take place and making certain that the victims' families do, too. But why doesn't Blackthorn just kill her and be done with it?"

"Because the next sheriff might not be so willing to overlook a string of murders."

A few moments later, we pulled up in front of the Douglases' house. I tried to clear my thoughts.

We needed to be focused. As we headed up the walkway, I wasn't sure what to expect.

A MAID LET us in and told us to wait in the foyer. From the outside, the house looked modest and old, but once we were guided inside the foyer, it looked like the entire place had been updated and redone. The floor was travertine tile, the walls were creamy white, and the staircase leading upstairs was highly polished. Everything gleamed and looked new.

As she came sweeping down the hallway, Naomi Douglas also looked exceptionally poised and manicured. She was wearing a linen pantsuit. Her nails were perfectly manicured, and every hair on her hair cascaded gently into place in a long euro bob, slightly longer in front than it was in back. Her hair was that golden blond that you often see on children, but rarely on adults unless it was from a bottle. She carried a designer bag over her arm, and all in all, looked ready for an afternoon luncheon or a charity function or some other society affair.

"May I help you?" she asked, her gaze traveling over us with a puzzled air. "I was about to go out. Teresa said you wanted to talk to me?"

"I'm sorry, but we won't delay you long," I said with an apologetic tone. "We just need a few moments of your time."

"If you're looking for charity donations, I already

contribute to a variety of shelters." But by her tone, it was obvious she knew we weren't there to ask for donations.

"We'd like to ask you a couple questions about your daughter, Rebecca." Viktor lowered his voice, trying to be gentle. "It's rather important."

The blood drained from her face, and she leaned back against the wall.

"I'm afraid that I'm already late. *Who are you?*" The politeness vanished. I could feel the barricades going up even as we stood there.

"We're investigating a series of deaths, of which your daughter's was one. We hate to bring up old wounds, but it's really important." Viktor was firm, but insistent.

Mrs. Douglas tried to stare him down, but after a moment she looked away. "I don't have much time to answer questions." She gestured to a bench near the door. "If you'll have a seat."

We sat down with her, and I decided to let Viktor handle things, while I kept an eye on her for any telltale signs that she might be lying.

"We understand that the police never caught her killer. Can you tell us about her last night?"

"I want to see some identification first. I have no clue who you are, and I'm not going to discuss my daughter's death with strangers."

Viktor and I pulled out our identification badges, showing them to her. She took mine, looking it over carefully, before handing it back.

"I've never heard of the Wild Hunt Agency before. Are you aligned with the FBI?"

Viktor shook his head. "No, but we are licensed

to investigate. We stumbled onto the news of your daughter's murder while investigating a more recent homicide. We think that they might be connected."

Mrs. Douglas blinked, and I could feel her struggling. Her lips pursed, she stared at the entryway floor, the confidence sagging out of her.

"It's been sixteen years since Rebecca died," she whispered. "Can't we just let it be? Nothing's going to bring her back. I've finally accepted that."

"We're looking to catch a serial murderer," I said, leaning forward. "Mrs. Douglas, what did the police tell you about her death?"

After a moment, she looked up. "Call me Naomi. The police said she was killed by a vampire. They said it would be no use to look for whoever did it because they would be long gone."

After a moment, Viktor said, "You know that's not true, don't you? You are her mother—you have intuition."

Naomi's taciturn façade began to crack, and she squeezed her eyes shut, biting her lip.

"I know my little girl wasn't killed by a vampire. But..."

"But?" I prompted.

She paused for a moment, then whispered, "I have a son. He's twenty-four now, but he was only eight then. Someone called me, suggesting that I let Rebecca's death be. They implied that if I didn't, my son's life would be in danger. I told the sheriff, and she shrugged it off as a prank. She said that I should just accept the fact that a vampire had killed my daughter. I was frightened. My husband and I had recently broken up, and he had moved to Seattle. He came back for a short time when Rebecca died, but he didn't want to deal with it. He was an angry man, and Rebecca's death only made him angrier. So I decided to do what they said. To focus on my son and keep him safe."

"You seemed to have a stroke of good fortune shortly afterward. Can you tell us about that?" Viktor asked.

As reticent as Naomi had been when we first arrived, it was as if the dam had broken open.

"I don't know how it happened, but I received a letter a few weeks after that phone call. It was from an insurance company that I had never heard of, and it included a check for $300,000. It said Rebecca had been covered by a policy that she had purchased a few days after she turned eighteen, and the money was guaranteed if we didn't hold up the investigation."

"Meaning if you didn't push the cops?"

She nodded. "That's the way I understood it. I had never heard Rebecca talk about insurance. She was only nineteen when she died. But the check was certified, and the letter looked official. I called the number on the letter, and some woman reassured me that it was legitimate. So I called the cops. The sheriff advised me to just accept it as serendipity. So...finally...I cashed it."

"Did you ever hear from them again?"

"No," she said with a shake of her head. "And there's always been some part of me that felt like something was wrong, but what else was I going to do? The police didn't want to hear from me.

Every time I called them to see if they had made any progress, they told me that the case was cold and that they would call me if there were ever any leads. And after that phone call threatening my son, well, I finally decided that it was better just to keep my mouth shut."

"Do you still have that letter anywhere?" I asked.

Naomi shook her head. "No. It's odd, you know? I thought I had filed it away, but one day I went to look for it, and all I found was a blank piece of paper. I must have been mistaken."

"Is there anything else you can tell us about the day Rebecca disappeared? She was missing for a week, I gather." Viktor was jotting down notes as she spoke.

"Not much. Rebecca was on her way to meet a new beau. She told me he was charming, and she used the words 'almost princely.' She said he seemed rather old world, and she wanted me to meet him. She told me that the day before she disappeared. But she didn't tell me what his name was." Naomi stared at her hands, shaking her head. "I wish I'd had a chance to meet him. My daughter didn't make friends easily. She seldom dated."

I glanced over at Viktor, wondering if he was thinking the same thing I was. "Old world" could mean many things, one of them being someone who was old. Perhaps someone who was ancient. I wondered if Blackthorn was engaging and "charming"?

"That's all I can think of," Naomi said. "I'm not certain if whoever it was who warned me against talking about Rebecca's death is still around, but now that my son is grown and on his own, I don't really care. A part of my heart died when Rebecca was murdered. The fact that I wasn't allowed to talk about it made it worse. I've never gotten over the grief. I just buried it."

"I'm sorry," I said. "I'm sorry we had to bring this up."

She shook her head. "It helps, in a way. It helps to know that Rebecca isn't forgotten. That her existence hasn't just been wiped off the face of the earth. Do me a favor," she said. "If you find her killer, let me know. I'd like some sort of closure."

And with that, she picked up her purse, indicating the interview was over. As Viktor and I went back to the car, I glanced back and watched as she got into her midsize SUV. She looked very much alone. I had the feeling that Naomi Douglas had very few friends.

ONCE WE WERE back in the car, Viktor and I didn't say much for a moment.

"Naomi's pain is still so raw. I feel like a heel for intruding on her personal grief." I stared at the dashboard, trying to find some way of reconciling my guilt.

"We gave her the chance to talk. Something she hasn't had until now." Viktor gave me a bleak look. "Interviewing victims' families never gets any easier. You might as well accept that now. At least we know something about the 'stroke of good fortune.' There was never any insurance company mentioned in any of the articles."

"Ten to one, there isn't any such insurance company. I wish she could have found that piece of paper." I started the car.

"Oh, I wager she did. It just didn't have anything on it. There are vanishing inks, and spells that can make writing disappear. My guess is that whoever sent the letter and check to Naomi decided to make sure that she wouldn't have a record of it."

Viktor paused, chewing on his lip. After a moment he added, "I wonder if we can hack into her bank account. There has to be some record of who gave her that check. A check for that large would have been recorded on her account. I'm not sure how banks work."

"Given that it's been over ten years, there's a good chance the records are gone. But if anybody else we interview has received a similar payout, we might be in luck." I glanced at the name and address on the next line. In addition to Naomi Douglas, we were interviewing a man named Robert Chance. His wife had vanished eighteen years ago, and had been found a week later. Two years before Rebecca.

"Let's head over to see if he's home." Viktor took the tablet back from me, staring at the screen as I backed out of the driveway, heading to our second destination.

ROBERT CHANCE'S HOUSE was on the other side of Seacrest Cove, on South Seashore Avenue. Although it had private access to the beach, the house was small and weathered. If he had gotten some payout, it didn't look like he had used it to keep up his property.

"Do the notes indicate whether he received a financial windfall as well?" I asked, parking across the street, on the side of the road.

To our left was a strip of Puget Sound, and across the patch of water that filtered in from the sound were two long narrow fingers of land with boat moorings bordering the edges. It was as though someone had carved out channels for the water in order to provide boat access. Chance's house was on our right, across the road.

"He did, although like the others, there's no notation of where it came from. It just says that he received a sizable amount of money about five months after his wife's death." Viktor glanced at me. "Want to make a bet it's another insurance payment?"

"Maybe he'll remember the name of the insurance company."

We hopped out of the car. Given the road ended just behind us, it wasn't likely that anybody was going to come speeding along and rear-end us. As we walked across the road, I noticed that there was a pickup in the driveway. It too looked worn down.

Viktor rang the bell, but there was no resulting chime that we could tell, so he knocked on the door. A moment later, the door opened.

"Yeah, what do you want?" The man didn't even try for a false politeness. He clearly looked annoyed. He was wearing a stained undershirt and a pair of baggy jeans held up by a worn leather belt. His hair was thinning, and he had a five-o'clock shadow. He leaned against the door jamb, folding his arms across his chest.

"Are you Robert Chance?"

He stared at me for a moment. "Who wants to know?"

"We'd like to ask you some questions about your wife's death, if you have a moment."

He didn't move, but the muscles in his cheek twitched, and his eyes narrowed.

"I've got plenty of time, but I'm not interested in talking about that bitch." The anger behind his words slammed into me as strong as if he had reached out and punched me.

I blinked, instinctively taking a step back. I wasn't exactly sure how to proceed.

Viktor cleared his throat, drawing the man's attention to himself. "This won't take long, but it's important. If you cooperate, we will get out of here as soon as possible."

Robert's gaze traveled up Viktor's long torso, resting on his face. "You the cops? You finally figure out who killed her?"

"Not exactly," Viktor said, handing him his identification. "We're working on a case that may tie into your wife's death. If you could help us, we'd appreciate it."

Robert glanced over the ID, finally handing it back. Then he begrudgingly stood back, opening the door for us to enter. Viktor stepped across the threshold before he could change his mind, motioning for me to follow.

"I suppose you aren't offering a payout for my cooperation, huh?"

We ignored the question.

We were obviously in a living room, although it was difficult to tell given the number of boxes and stacks of paper sitting around. There was a mildewed scent to the air, as if the mold had settled in and was breeding. Overhead, the lamp was covered with cobwebs, and I wondered how hot it had to be before they caught fire.

The entire room was covered in dark, dingy paneling and the carpet had seen better days. The house felt bogged down under the weight of dirt and neglect. The only thing that looked even relatively new was a sofa, nestled in between some of the boxes. The TV was on, so he was obviously using the room.

Robert Chance crossed to the television and turned it down. There was a baseball game on, and he paused to watch the action before turning back to us.

"All right. You get ten minutes. Ask your questions and get on with it."

Since Viktor seemed to have better luck with him, I let him take the lead.

"Were you contacted by anyone after your wife was found, asking you to keep her murder under wraps?" Apparently, Viktor had decided to go straight for the jugular. "And did you receive a payout from an insurance company for her death?"

Half listening to Viktor, half watching the game, Robert Chance shrugged. "Yeah, somebody called suggesting I keep my mouth shut and get on with my life. I didn't have any problem with that, given the bitch was cheating on me."

I blinked, wondering if he had been this unfriendly while his wife was alive.

"Do you know who called you?" Viktor asked.

Chance shook his head. "No idea, and don't care. And yes, I received a check from some insurance company that she had taken out life insurance with. She hadn't told me about *that*, either, but at least it was a good surprise compared to the other crap she pulled on me. Too bad she hadn't bought a higher policy."

I blinked. "How much was the payout? Three hundred thousand dollars?"

At that, Chance's gaze narrowed. "No. Fifty grand. Why, did they stiff me?"

Viktor jumped in. "Do you remember the name of the insurance company?"

As one of the players hit a home run, Chance let out a loud shout, pumping the air with his fist. Then, as if aware that he had shown some sign of life, he froze, slowly lowering his arm.

"Yeah, actually I do. It was called the Spinosa Insurance Corporation. I remember it because I have a cousin named Vinny Spinosa." He shrugged. "I didn't even know the bitch had gotten herself insured, and I'm surprised that she named me as the beneficiary."

A thought kept poking me in the back of my mind. "Do you remember who she was having an affair with?" If Rebecca Douglas had been seeing a *charming old-world man*, perhaps Liza Chance had been fooling around with a *charming old-world man*.

Once again, the thunderclouds rolled into his voice.

"I don't know his name, but he was a foreigner. Or maybe he was a SubCult freak. I know they were having an affair because I happened to catch them fucking in the garage loft. She was bouncing up and down on his dick like she was on a pogo stick, her tits flopping around."

I swallowed a knot that rose in my throat. Robert Chance was an angry man.

"What happened?"

"I was about to bust his head open, but then I must have got dizzy and fell, or something. The next thing I knew, I opened my eyes and I was lying at the bottom of the ladder and he was gone. I was filing for divorce when she vanished. At least her getting knocked off saved me the cost of an attorney. Then I got the payout for the insurance after the phone call, and decided to take the advice and move on with my life. The money's gone, just in case you're looking for any of it."

"Could you identify the man? Can you give me a description of him?"

Chance's eyes narrowed. "Why? She have another insurance policy stashed around?"

I wondered if he had been this way when she was alive. "No. No more money. We're just investigating similar murders and trying to see if there's a common denominator."

He shrugged. "Too bad. I can't tell you anything else. We had a big row and she drove off that day. The day she vanished. I never saw her again. And don't you judge me," he added. "Liza knew better than to ruffle my feathers. She knew that I'd beat the crap out of her if she ever snuck out on me. The bitch told me she had a low sex drive, and I find out she was banging some stranger? You can bet your ass I was mad."

We beat a hasty retreat, neither one of us wanting to stay in that atmosphere any longer. The man was so angry and so bitter that it almost turned my stomach. We hurried back to the car, where I tried to shake off the residue energy that clung like cellophane wrap.

"Well, that was just lovely," Viktor said after we got back in the car.

"I don't blame her for cheating on him, but damn. Why not just leave him? At least we have a name for the insurance company." I wondered if the company was actually for real, but then shook my head. It didn't seem likely that Liza Chance would have taken out an insurance policy and named her husband as the beneficiary.

Viktor tapped away on his tablet. All of a sudden he froze. "Ember, the Latin name for blackthorn happens to be *prunus spinosa*."

"The *Spinosa* Insurance Corporation. That can't be coincidence. So what do we do next?"

"We head back to the hotel and fill in the others on what we've learned. At least we have something to report." And with that, Viktor fastened his seatbelt as I put the car into gear and we returned to the road.

Chapter 12

WE GOT BACK to the hotel just as Herne and Yutani pulled in. Herne wrapped his arm around my waist as the four of us headed to the dining room.

"Yutani, text Angel and Talia and have them meet us for dinner. It's almost seven." Herne brushed a stray strand of hair away from his face as the wind gusted past.

Clouds were starting to drift in, but the rain wouldn't start until later and the evening was a balmy sixty-five degrees. With the breeze, it felt cooler, but the weather was still comfortable, and we decided to eat out on the patio. The waitress brought our drinks as we gathered around the table, and began to piece together what we had learned.

"You fared better than we did, at least at our first meeting," Yutani said, after Viktor and I told them about Naomi Douglas and Robert Chance. He was already tapping away on the keyboard of his laptop. "Well, you're right. There's no such company as Spinosa Insurance. I can't find any reference to there ever having been one. However, as Viktor indicated, *prunus spinosa* is Latin for blackthorn. That tallies with what we found out from our second meeting."

I glanced over at Herne. "What happened?"

"Well, our first meeting, with the Roseland family, was a washout. They're Fae, and they flatly refused to discuss the case. They have a very big dog, and he made a convincing argument that we should get off the porch." Herne's eyes twinkled. "I'm not sure if he sensed Yutani's coyote nature or if he just didn't like us, but any hopes we had of finding out anything vanished the minute Leticia Roseland called him out onto the porch. We barely made it out of there with everything intact."

The thought of Herne and Yutani racing off the steps, followed by a very big dog, almost set me to laughing even though I knew it wasn't funny.

"What about your second interview?"

"It went marginally better. The Smiths—a human family—lost their uncle and their story was similar to the ones you heard. They received a phone call, warning them to quit looking into the homicide. Shortly after that, an insurance settlement check arrived for $500,000. Apparently their uncle had been well placed in society."

"Did they mention the insurance agency?"

"Yeah. Once again, Spinosa Insurance. Most of the family didn't care for their uncle, and they didn't question anything too deeply. The cops told them it had become a cold case a few months after the murder. None of them seemed interested when we explained why we were there. In fact, I doubt if we would have gotten *any* information out of them, except for one of the family members—Mike Smith. He actually cared about his uncle to some degree. He's thirty-five, and he was fourteen when the murder happened. Mike did tell us something else."

"What?" Viktor made room on the table for our appetizers when the waitress brought a massive platter of calamari and fried shrimp to the table. After she set it down and left, Herne answered.

"Mike saw his uncle's body. In fact, he's the one who discovered the corpse. Not only was his uncle covered with puncture wounds, but Mike happened to see a couple large thorns poking out of two of the puncture wounds. By his description, I would place them as blackthorn spikes." Herne glanced at the sky. "It looks like the rain's going to hold off until later this evening. I think after dinner we should take a look at the park."

"What do we do with Blackthorn if he turns out to be the murderer? How do you arrest one of the Ante-Fae? Can you even *do* that?" It occurred to me that an ancient being who was almost as powerful as the gods wouldn't respond well to being slapped in cuffs.

"I'm not sure. I'll need to discuss this with my father, I think. But I want to find out as much as we can, as quickly as we can, because I have the nasty feeling that we're going to be asked to leave the island. Probably sooner than later. If word gets out that we were inquiring about past homicides, you know that Astrana is going to be on our backs."

"Yeah, about that. Viktor, tell them what we found out about her."

Viktor told them about the loan from the vampires.

"Great. Well, this is getting thicker than shit, isn't it?" Herne said. "The park, then, tonight."

"Should we all go?" Yutani asked.

"No, I don't think so. The more of us out there thrashing around, the more attention we'll call to ourselves." Herne was about to say something else when Yutani held up his hand.

"Hold that thought. I've got to go take a piss." He headed away from the table, into the restaurant proper.

I loaded up my plate with calamari, which I preferred over the shrimp. Angel handed me the cocktail sauce. As we began to eat, my phone dinged. I glanced down at the text. It was from Ronnie. It was a picture of Mr. Rumblebutt, who was on his back playing with a toy. She had texted me: MR. RUMBLEBUTT LOVES THE FEATHERS, DOESN'T HE?

I texted back: EVERY SINGLE TIME. HOW IS HE DOING?

HE'S DOING FINE, she answered. I JUST THOUGHT YOU MIGHT LIKE TO SEE A PICTURE OF HIM PLAYING.

I thanked her, and feeling oddly at ease, set my phone back on the table. Angel glanced at me quizzically. I motioned to the phone, and she picked it up, glancing at the text and laughing.

"Thank you very much for introducing me to

Ronnie," I told Talia. "She's great, and Mr. Rumblebutt seems to like her a lot."

"She has a way with animals, I'll say that for her. And she prices her services reasonably. I trust her in my house, and I don't trust many people."

"It's good to have somebody to check up on him. Mr. Rumblebutt's been with me for several years now, and I can't imagine trusting him to just anybody." Mr. Rumblebutt was one of my closest friends, and even though we spoke entirely different languages, I had the feeling that we were meant for each other.

Yutani returned to the table, a worried look on his face. "I just had a vision."

Herne set down his fork, glancing up at the coyote shifter with a concerned look. "From Great Coyote?"

Yutani nodded. "Yeah, it was from Coyote, all right. I don't know what to think about it. It feels like it was a warning. I was standing on the shoreline, and the next moment I was being sucked under the water and I couldn't kick my way free from the waves. I heard his voice and he told me to go home. But I can't do that. We're on a case."

"What do you want to do?" Herne asked. He was taking Yutani's vision seriously, and I had the feeling that this had happened before.

"I can't just up and leave you guys here. I'm needed." Yutani frowned at the table.

"Remember last time you ignored one of his warnings," Talia said. "It wasn't pretty."

"I know, but I'm not sure if this was an actual warning or...what. Maybe I'm just not supposed to go down by the water."

"You're splitting hairs and you know it." Talia sounded grumpy now. "Don't come crying to us when something happens."

I wanted to know what they were arguing about, but it really wasn't my business.

"I'll think about it. Meanwhile, can we just go on with the discussion?" Yutani set his lips, looking like he was spoiling for an argument.

Herne rubbed his forehead. "Fine. Don't say we didn't give you the chance. Now, I think that you and Ember and I should go prowling around the park." He paused as his phone rang, and he pulled it out, frowning as he looked at the screen. He answered, stepping away from the table.

Angel didn't seem to have my reticence, because she leaned forward, her elbows on the table, and asked, "So what happened last time you ignored Coyote's warning?"

"I don't want to talk about it," Yutani said.

"That's because you know we're right," Talia said. "You know what happens when you ignore Coyote. *Bad things.* Bad things happen to you *and* the people around you. It's like a spillover effect. You know we're all in this together, and if Coyote comes dogging your heels, chances are one or more of us are going to be in the direct line of fire."

"Just let it be for now," Yutani said. "You act like I don't know what I'm doing. Coyote has been dogging my heels for over two hundred years. Give me some credit, won't you?"

"Children, quiet." Herne looked exasperated as he came back. "We can't make you listen, Yutani, but please be careful. Meanwhile, I've decided that Viktor, Ember, and I will go explore the park. I have an unsettled feeling that we need to go as soon as possible. So finish dinner and let's get moving."

Yutani sulked all the way through the meal, although we let it drop. When we finished, he, Talia, and Angel headed up to their rooms, while Herne, Viktor, and I headed out to Herne's car. I rode shotgun, and Viktor slipped into the back.

As we steered out of the parking lot, I asked, "How often does Yutani get warnings from Coyote?"

Herne didn't say anything, but Viktor answered.

"Too often," the half-ogre said. "Actually, he seems overdue, given the timing of the last few visions he's had."

"What is it with Yutani and Coyote? How are they bonded?" I still hadn't figured that one out.

Herne let out a long sigh. "It's complicated. I have my suspicions, but even Yutani doesn't know what I'm thinking and I'd rather he not know."

"Okay, I won't say anything," I said slowly, thinking that there were so many hidden secrets in the agency that even the *secrets* had secrets.

"Yutani's father vanished shortly before he was born. All that Yutani seems to know about him is that the man had been new to the village and had taken up with Yutani's mother shortly before she got pregnant. He vanished before Yutani's birth. When he got older, Yutani looked for him but in those days, well...it would have been futile if the man had been an ordinary human. The only name he had for his father was the one his mother gave him. But my guess is that Yutani bears Coyote's energy directly."

I blinked. "You think Yutani is Coyote's *son*?"

"I don't know." Herne turned on the windshield wipers to sweep away the gentle rain that had begun to fall. "Sometimes the gods mate with the mortals. My father did—he's the one who raised Morgana to goddesshood. It also keeps the divine spark moving throughout humans. I don't know if we'll ever know about Yutani. I don't even know if he suspects anything. I think he believes that Coyote cursed him, and a part of him seems to hate Coyote as much as he reveres him. In some ways, Yutani is still very young. And if Coyote is his father, I don't think Yutani is ready to face it. So don't mention this to him. He has to come to the conclusion himself."

Herne took a right turn off of Smugglers Cove Road onto Park Road.

"We're going to have to walk down to the beach. There isn't a drivable road that leads to the water. At least, not that I know of." He pulled into a parking lot and stopped at the northern end. "Over there," he pointed to an opening in the trees. "The trail starts there."

Viktor and I tumbled out of the car, stretching as we looked around in the evening air. The rain had already backed off again, and while we were still a ways from sunset, in the crowded growth of the forest the light had already started to wane. Herne led us to the trailhead and then, with him out in front, we plunged into the forest.

The trail down to the beach was narrow, winding through the forest proper. The birds were singing their evening songs, calling back to their nests that they would be home soon. Overhead, an owl glided by, fresh on the hunt. And from here, we could hear the gulls at the edge of the water, their haunting cries echoing through the forest.

Herne paused, turning back to Viktor and me. "You know, I think I'll have a look through the woods while you head down to the shore. I can go faster in my stag form."

Viktor and I stepped back, giving him room. I had never actually seen Herne turn into his stag form, and I wondered if he transformed like other shifters.

As we watched, he held out his arms, stretched wide, and arched back, as a silver light began to emanate from his chest.

Nope, not like other shifters.

The light grew so bright it was hard to look at, and I blinked. In a brief, brilliant flash that echoed on the inside of my eyelids, he shifted. I could feel the transformation even with my eyes shut. It was as though the air rippled around us. When I opened my eyes, there he stood, luminous and shining.

Herne looked like a red deer, large and imposing, with a magnificent rack. And yet his hair was a brilliant silver, illuminated against the darkening forest around us. Regal and haughty, he turned to stare at us, a puff of steam spiraling up from his nostrils. Without another sound, he raced off into the forest, a blur of movement.

I caught my breath. That was how I had first met Herne, when I was searching for Angel's brother. I hadn't known who he was at the time, but even then I knew there was something godlike about the stag, otherworldly and divine.

"He really does take your breath away," Viktor said softly.

"Don't I know it." I tore my eyes away from the vanishing trail of the stag. "Let's get down to the beach before it gets much darker."

Viktor took the lead, following the trail as I kept close behind him. Somehow, everything seemed a little more nerve-wracking without Herne beside us.

The trail led north, passing by several ravines until we hit a bend where it abruptly turned south, curving back around the other side of the ravine. Here and there, Viktor pointed out roots and stones that were jutting out of the trail, waiting to trip us up. I was grateful. His eyesight was better than mine in the deepening dusk.

Finally, fifteen minutes later, the trail branched off toward the beach.

"If we continue straight, the trail will loop around. It also leads directly to the beach, but this is a shorter, if steeper, route." Viktor looked back at me. "Which would you rather take? The longer loop, or the quicker path?"

"Let's go for steep and quick."

Viktor hadn't been kidding. The trail bent into an abrupt decline. While it wasn't straight up and down, I found myself wondering if we had made a mistake. The slope was rough going, even for someone who was as in shape as I was.

Viktor paused for a moment, bracing himself against a tree. He reached back for my hand, and steadied me over a five-foot drop from one part of the trail to the next. Another hundred yards and we broke through the tree line, finding ourselves at the edge of the beach.

Scattered driftwood littered the shore, the massive logs coming in on the tides. They were big enough to be dangerous while floating in the water, and made incredibly comfortable benches once they were beached. Once again, the power of the tides around here amazed me. They could toss hundred-foot logs around like toothpicks. The sun was hovering a hand's width above the horizon. We would see sunset before we left the beach.

I looked around, watching the gulls that were hunting a last-minute meal before bedtime.

"Where were the bodies found? Did Herne tell you?"

Viktor nodded. He pointed over toward a large boulder that sat near the water. "There. They were all found by hikers."

"What a lovely way to get back to nature. Finding mutilated bodies." I headed over toward the rock. I could sense the water elementals were playing, but several of them seemed agitated. As I neared the water's edge, I found an area next to a small log. I could sit on the log and yet reach down to touch the water.

"I'm going to see if I can find out anything from the water spirits."

Viktor was hunting around the boulder, searching through the sparse vegetation and dunes next to it. The beach wasn't large, but it was big enough that we couldn't just take it all in with one glance.

I realized that my feet were starting to get wet, so I swung my legs over the log and knelt in the sand behind it, leaning over the driftwood to place my fingers in the water. The shock of the icy waves ran through me. No matter what time of year, the water was almost always cold, except during the middle of the day on hot summer days. As I closed my eyes, I reached out. The water elementals suddenly froze as they noticed me.

I was pledged to Morgana, Herne's mother. My own mother had been a member of the Water Fae, and her blood ran through me. I could work with some aspects of water magic, although I wasn't terribly proficient, but my ability to contact the water spirits was growing. Now and then, they initiated the connection.

I brought up the image of the boulder, and superimposed it with images of dead bodies near it, inserting a question into the image.

Water elementals didn't think in terms of words, not like we did. Instead, I received impressions and emotions from them. Sometimes I received warnings—either images or simply the feeling of danger.

The elementals here were cautious, but one of them seemed braver than the others. Or perhaps, it was simply more curious. As it moved forward, rolling in on a wave that splashed over my hand, I could feel the edge of its thoughts touch my own.

The image of Jona's body sprang up in my mind,

along with sorrow and a brief shudder. I waited, forming a question in my mind, seeking information.

And then, it came tumbling in. Visions of a dark shadow, of someone carrying a dead body and dropping it near the boulder. The shadow emerged from the edge of the embankment, like a spider creeping out of a trapdoor. Only this was humanoid—a man, although I couldn't get a good look at him. He felt gnarled and tangled, like yarn that had been knotted up so tightly that you couldn't unwind it. I could feel tension surrounding him, a sick sense of satiety as though a void had been filled. It was dark and ugly, bloated with blood and pain and joy. The energy was dragging me down and I began to fight it.

Abruptly, the elemental broke off the image, washing it away with a wave that splashed over me, breaking any cords that had formed. I almost fell backward on my butt, but I managed to hold onto the log, to keep my hand in the water.

Almost immediately, a wave of remorse came out, a hesitant apology from the elemental for immersing me into that energy. I reached out with gratitude, reassuring it that I had needed to see what it had shown me. And then, slowly, the elemental began to withdraw, with one last splash against my hands that felt like a graceful good-bye.

I opened my eyes, realizing that the sun had set while I was communing with the water. I turned around to find Viktor watching me, sitting on a nearby log.

"Well," I said, still trying to unwind the puzzle in

my mind. "There's an entrance along the embankment somewhere here. I got a brief look at it, but I can't pinpoint where it is now that I'm looking at the actual bank. But whoever the murderer is, that's how he's getting the bodies down here. He doesn't carry them through the forest."

"That would make sense," Viktor said. He glanced up at the forest behind us. "I wish Herne would return. I don't feel safe here."

"Neither do I," I said. "There's something tainted in the forest around this area, and my guess is that it's Blackthorn."

"I think one thing we have to remember is that most of the great Fae—and I'm assuming this applies to the Ante-Fae as well—have courts surrounding them. It would behoove us not to assume we're dealing with just a single individual."

Viktor paused when a figure appeared out in the water. He stood, slowly drawing his blade. I followed suit. As we watched, it churned up a wave around it. I shaded my eyes, following its movements. And then, in the middle of the waves, I saw the brilliant head of a horse emerge. It was frolicking with the waves, playing with them. Then, as the sun was creeping toward the horizon, it turned toward shore and made a beeline toward us.

"A hippocampus," I said softly.

"They are beautiful," Viktor said, his gaze fastened on the stallion that rode the waves toward our little area of the cove. Within minutes, the horse emerged from the water, racing ashore, a brilliant white stallion with mane and feathers the color of sea foam. It was a male—that we could see—and his eyes were the color of coals with diamonds inset where pupils would normally be. He reared, his hooves slashing at the air, then settled down, eyeing us with curiosity.

"We're not here to harm you," I said, holding up my hands. "We're investigators. We were hired by Rhiannon, the Matriarch of your encampment."

That seemed to do the trick. There was a blur as the horse moved faster than we could follow, and the next moment, a tall man stepped out of the swirl of mist, naked as the day he was born. I averted my eyes, trying to maintain some decorum, though he was as magnificent in human form as he was in horse form. My mind went to clichés, namely, being hung like a horse, but I wisely kept that to myself.

"Well met, good people. What are your names?" He gave us a stately bow as though he didn't even notice he was naked.

I cleared my throat. "I'm Ember Kearney and this is Viktor. We're with the Wild Hunt Agency."

"Ah yes. Rhiannon mentioned hiring you to look into Jona's death. I'm Madrigal. I'm a music teacher at our encampment." He positioned himself on the log, crossing his legs, which did nothing to hide his considerable assets.

I glanced at Viktor, who was blushing like a lobster. "Tell me, do you come to this area of the beach often?"

He tilted his head, looking around, then nodded. "I used to. I still do, on occasion, because it's the easiest way to access the water around here. But...I'm cautious." A wary look crept over his face.

"You'd do well to watch yourselves in these wood-lands. There are dangers here."

Hmm, so he was aware of a problem. "What kind of dangers?"

"None that I know of by name. But...things... prowl the woods, and there have been unexplained deaths over the past years. I'm not blind. I know why Rhiannon called you in. She is thinking of Jona, of course, but there have been others. I'm strong. Very few would tangle with me and come out on the winning side. But others haven't been so lucky. Just watch your footing in the forest. I'm not certain what lurks here, but whatever it is, it's not conducive to good health." Madrigal stood. "I've said more than I probably should, but I'm not one for keeping my mouth shut and watching oth-ers get hurt because I didn't think to warn them. I must go now—it's not safe to be here after dark. If you have any sense, you'll follow me out."

"We're waiting on a friend," I murmured. "But we'll take your warning to heart." I wanted to ask him more questions, but I had the feeling that Madrigal had told us everything he was going to for the moment.

"Then be safe, and may Poseidon watch over you." With that, Madrigal darted into the forest, still naked, and vanished in the tangle of under-growth.

"Cripes. If he's braving the forest naked, then he must have a tough hide," I said, watching the bushes shake in his wake.

"The hippocampi are a hardy people. They don't injure easily. I think it would take one of the Ante-

Fae to take down Jona," Viktor said. He froze, his hand going to his weapon. "Shush."

I drew my own dagger, waiting. A brilliant silver light flashed in the bushes, and then, a beautiful silver stag leapt down onto the sand. In another flash, Herne was standing there. I let out a sigh of relief.

"Dude, you scared the hell out of us." I sheathed my dagger. "You just missed meeting one of the hippocampi—he came out of the water."

"I found something in the forest," he said. "I think it has to do with Blackthorn." He paused, glancing over at the boulder. "One of the hippo-campi was here? Who?"

"His name is Madrigal," Viktor said.

I told Herne what the water elemental had shown me, and then about Madrigal's visit. "I can't figure out exactly where against the embankment the trapdoor is. But it's somewhere around here. I think that's what Madrigal was feeling."

"Well, I think I found the touchstone leading to Blackthorn's lair. I took a picture of it, and charted the location so we can come back to it. I don't think it's a good idea to infiltrate at this time of night." Herne glanced around at the forest. "We'd better get back to the car. Madrigal was right. The forest isn't safe after dark. Or in the daylight, I imagine."

"Viktor and I were just talking about that. There's a lot of unsettled energy here, and it feels like it's growing as we close in on night."

With Herne in the lead, and Viktor behind me, we headed back up the trail, Viktor giving me a boost up over the steepest areas. Oddly enough, the route back to the car felt much quicker than the way down to the beach. Perhaps it was that we had already traversed this route, but somehow it felt like time had shifted. I suspected Herne had some ability in that, but I decided to save my questions.

Once we were back at the car, we slid inside, and I locked my door, finally feeling more secure. I didn't like feeling uneasy, especially when I didn't know what was causing the sensation. But I had a feeling that it was because of Blackthorn.

"Yutani should be able to figure out the markings on the touchstone," Herne started to say as his phone rang. He pulled it out, frowning as he looked at the Caller ID. "It's Rhiannon," he said as he answered. "Hey, Rhiannon—what's up?" He paused, a somber look crossing his face. "Are you all right?" Another pause. And then, "We'll see you at the hospital. Yes, we *are* going to come to the hospital. I don't care, we'll see you in a little while."

As he pocketed his phone and started the car, Viktor and I waited. Edging out of the parking lot, we returned to Park Road, and then to Smugglers Cove Road before Herne spoke again.

"Rhiannon's in the hospital. Someone ran her off the road."

"Is she all right?" Viktor leaned forward.

"No, she's pretty bruised up and has a broken leg. If someone hadn't been coming in the opposite direction and stopped, I'm not sure what would have happened. Whoever it was that ran her off the road took off as soon as the other car slowed down. She told us not to come, but I think we should head out there right now. She'll be in the hospital till at least tomorrow, that's for sure." He glanced at me. "Can you let the others know?"

"Sure," I said. "Do you want them to meet us there?"

"That might be overwhelming." He paused as his phone rang again. "Can you answer that?"

I reached over and slipped the phone out of his jacket pocket. The Caller ID read "Talia."

"This is Ember. We're on the road headed back to the hotel."

"Well, turn around and get your asses up to the hospital."

"Oh, did Rhiannon call you, too?" I asked.

"What are you talking about?" Talia said.

"Rhiannon—she got run off the road and she's in the hospital right now."

"Well, hell. I guess we'll have a nice big reunion when we get there. No, she didn't call. Yutani is hurt. He went out for a run, and damned if he didn't land in a trap. Luckily it was his front paw, not one of his back ones. But he's hurting pretty bad and I suspect there may be a broken bone, as well as some nasty cuts and gashes. We haven't been able to get the trap off, and I'm afraid to wait for the paramedics, given the situation with Astrana. We have no clue if she has her fingers in the emergency services around here. Yutani had to shift back into his human form so he could dig out the peg holding the trap in the ground."

I close my eyes, trying to calm myself. This was

the last thing we needed. I glanced over at Herne.

"What the hell's going on?" he asked. "I can feel something's wrong—it's emanating off you like garlic off of spaghetti."

"Yutani's hurt. He went for a run and got caught in a trap. It's on his arm."

"Fucking hell. And he wouldn't listen to Coyote... Where are they?"

"On the way to the hospital. I guess Angel's driving because Talia is on the phone. What should I tell her?"

"We're headed there now. Tell them we'll meet them there."

"Herne says we're on the way, we'll meet you there. Be careful, the night feels dangerous and it would be really good if we could avoid any more accidents."

As I hung up, putting Herne's phone in the cubbyhole by the gearshift, I realized I was craving caffeine. But now was not the time to stop at a coffee shop. I'd get a cup of coffee when we got to the hospital.

"This is not shaping up to be an ideal day, is it?" He paused, then punched the button on the dashboard. "How far to the nearest hospital?"

The GPS answered. "The Whidbey Island Medical Center is approximately fourteen miles away."

"Lovely. At least it's not on a different island." Herne glanced over at me. "I need some coffee. There's a drive-thru right up ahead."

I nodded, grateful. We took our place in line at the drive-thru to get triple-shot mochas. We were back on the road in under five minutes. We didn't speak much on the way to the hospital, mostly so that Herne could focus on driving. He sped along, going as fast as he dared. The road wound along, and while it was well paved, it was still a two-lane highway and we were traveling in the dark. Most of the way, the road was forested on both sides until we reached Coupeville.

Coupeville was a small town that had once been a farming community and was now an artist's retreat. While there were still farms on Whidbey Island, the town had turned into something of a tourist town, and here the ferry traveled across the sound to Port Townsend. Unfortunately, it was one of the few runs where reservations were necessary as a matter of course. To the north lay another state park and Oak Harbor. And farther north, at the end of the island, was Deception Pass, with the bridge that led over to Anacortes.

As we pulled into Coupeville, it was obvious that most of the town had rolled up for the night and gone to sleep. Although, to be fair, we weren't near the waterfront. Maybe downtown Coupeville was more active. We pulled into the parking lot of the medical center and headed for the ER. While fairly small compared to big-city hospitals, it was a full-scale health care unit.

I wondered whether Talia and the others had already made it here. Herne had driven like a bat out of hell, but I knew Angel could give him a run for his money. I paused, seeing my car parked in the unloading zone.

"They made it." I made a beeline for the car, where I saw Angel starting to pull away from the curb. She paused, unrolling the window.

"Talia and Yutani are inside. I was just about to go park."

Viktor glanced around at the darkened lot. "I'll walk you back to the building. There have been too many things going on tonight to take any chances." He slid inside the passenger side of the car and, relieved, I slapped the hood and rejoined Herne. As they headed over toward the main parking lot, we hurried into the building.

There, filling out forms, was Talia. Yutani was nowhere in sight. We hustled over to her side and she looked up as we approached.

"They took him right back. The trap is a nasty one. He's lucky he had the forethought to pry it open enough to take a little of the pressure off, though he couldn't get it all the way open. He's going to be hurting like a son of a bitch."

"Fucking hell." Herne sat down beside her, and I sat next to him.

"What happened?" I asked, leaning around him so that I could see her.

"Yutani decided he needed a run in his coyote form. I was worried, given we aren't near the Shifter-Run, but he was pretty jarred up by that vision. I guess he needed some time alone. About twenty-five minutes later, he dragged himself back into the hotel, that damned trap caught on his arm. He was almost passing out from the pain. All he could tell me that he had landed in the trap somewhere in a nearby patch of woods."

"Did you call the paramedics?" Herne asked.

Talia shook her head. "No. Angel called the

hospital and they told her it would be better if we headed straight here, rather than wait for the paramedics. They asked if he was losing blood, and while he was, it wasn't like he was bleeding out. Given the state of the authorities around the area, I made the decision that we should bring him here. I don't trust any of the emergency services down near Seacrest Cove. Not with Astrana watching over the area so tightly."

"I would have made the same decision," Herne said, reassuring her.

As Viktor and Angel entered the building, a doctor hustled out, looking around until he saw us. He hurried over.

"You're Yutani's friends?"

Herne nodded. "We are. How is he? Can we see him?"

"He'll live. But he's got a nasty break in his arm, and he's going to need at least seventy-five stitches to close all of the gashes made by the trap. He's a coyote shifter?"

Herne nodded. "Yeah. Do you have a specialist for SubCult injuries?"

"Actually, it's one of *my* specialties. We always have a doctor on duty here at the hospital who can handle SubCult medical issues. At least the break is clean, so we'll just have to splint it up and then he'll need a cast as soon as the swelling goes down. The nurse is prepping him for stitches now. I'll have her come get you when we're done." And with that, he turned and hustled off again.

Talia finished filling out the forms and took them up to the desk, handing them to the receptionist along with Yutani's insurance card. That was one of the great perks we got with the Wild Hunt—fantastic insurance and a retirement savings plan.

We moved over to one of the corner seating areas, where we couldn't be overheard.

"We need to go see Rhiannon while we're here," Herne said. "It'll probably take a little time to sew up Yutani's arm, so the rest of you wait here while Ember and I go visit her. Viktor, please fill in Angel and Talia on what happened at the park."

As we headed over to the reception desk, I wondered at the timing. Had the trap been set deliberately? It seemed odd to have both Yutani and Rhiannon end up in the hospital at the same time. But then, if whoever had run Rhiannon off the road had their way, they probably would have killed her. As far as the trap went, nobody could know that Yutani was going out for a run. We swept our rooms every night now for listening devices, so they couldn't have overheard him tell Talia that he wanted to go out, or have time to set the trap, even if they had followed him to find out where he was going. It had to be a coincidence, albeit a nasty one.

"We're here to see Rhiannon of the Foam Born," Herne said, giving the receptionist with a bedazzling smile.

She glanced at her roster, then at the clock. "It's a little late for visiting hours."

"We just found out she was in an accident."

"All right, wait for a moment and I'll call someone to take you back to her."

Sure enough, a moment later a nurse appeared and motioned for us to follow her. As we headed down the hall, through a pair of swinging doors, I wondered if Blackthorn had orchestrated the attack. Had he seen us down on the shore talking to Madrigal? If so, we were all in danger. With that thought, we entered the room where Rhiannon was confined to a bed, her leg in traction. When she saw us, she didn't look happy.

Chapter 13

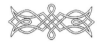

RHIANNON WAS BANGED up pretty bad. She had bruises over her left eye, which was a purplish black—the color of deep bruising that hadn't begun to heal yet. One side of her jaw was swollen. Her left leg was elevated, in a splint, and she looked both scared and angry.

The nurse turned to her. "You have company," she said. "Are you up to having a few visitors?"

Rhiannon frowned, then winced. "For just a moment. I'm not feeling very well."

The nurse left the room, and I crossed to Rhiannon's side. I wanted to take her hand, but decided to let her take the lead.

"Can we get you anything?" I genuinely liked the woman, and I was really pissed at whoever had chased her down. "Do you need us to bring you some things from your home?"

"No," she said. "A friend's doing that." She

paused, then said, "Listen, I want you to stop the investigation. Just drop it." A note of fear clung to her words.

"I can't do that," Herne said, approaching the bed. "My father has made this investigation mandatory now. We've identified twenty potential murder victims, and over forty missing people, Rhiannon. And since the murderer is targeting more than just Fae, we're stepping in. Tell us what happened tonight."

Even though his voice was soft, it was also firm.

Rhiannon seemed to hear the determination in it as well. "I can't risk my people. I just can't. Don't you understand?"

"*You already have.* We're dealing with one of the Ante-Fae."

She froze, staring at him. "Oh great gods. The *Ante-Fae*?"

"Yes, and we're all on his radar now. So tell me, what happened?" Herne was still speaking gently, but the command was there.

Rhiannon glanced at the door. I moved to it, peeking out to make sure nobody was listening in. I shut it softly, leaning against it so that nobody could intrude on us unexpectedly. She let out a long sigh, wincing as she twisted her lip. Finally, she looked up at Herne.

"I'll tell you, but you have to promise me to make sure Marilyn and her son Ryan are safe."

"We'll do our best to ensure their safety. Maybe my mother can help transport them back to their pod." Herne paused, then he leaned forward, his elbows resting on the bed rails. "Rhiannon, you have to help us. It's the only way for us to help you and the others, now that this thing seems to be blowing open."

"I was heading toward a friend's house. She lives over in Greenbank, on the other side of the island. I was on Bakken Road, and I was almost to the highway when a car pulled up behind me. Let me think for a moment," she said, closing her eyes.

A few seconds later, she opened them again. "The car came off of Day Road—I remember now. It swung in behind me, really fast, and sped up until it was tailgating me. I tried to put some distance between us, but the car lurched forward and smashed into the back of my car, forcing me off the road. It hit me so hard that I spun into a tree. Another car was coming along the other side and they immediately slowed down. That's when the car behind me roared past and took off."

"Did the other car stop?"

"Yes, thank the gods. When I hit the tree, it crunched in the driver's door and my leg was stuck. I didn't get a chance to look at the license plate or anything. The people who stopped called the cops and an ambulance. Astrana sent a deputy out. I told him what happened, and even though the driver who was helping me had seen that my attacker was driving a blue sedan, the deputy said they probably would have a hard time finding it. If the other car hadn't stopped to help, I'd be dead. Whoever hit me wasn't playing any games. He meant business."

She seemed exhausted by the effort of telling us what it happened. She leaned back against the upraised head of the bed, closing her eyes again and breathing softly.

"Do you happen to have the name of man who helped you?"

She shook her head. "I asked the deputy as I was being put into the ambulance and he said that he'd get me that information when he could. I haven't heard one peep out of the police since I got here."

"It might be time to pay a visit to Astrana's office," Herne said. "Except that's probably going to blow up in our face. First we have to check on Yutani."

"I'm frightened. I told the deputy I was afraid whoever hit me might try to finish the job, but he laughed and told me it was probably some rowdy teenagers. I can tell you this: *It was no teenager out on a joy ride.*" Rhiannon was getting upset again. "I asked him if he would post a guard on my door, and he said there wasn't any need. So I have a couple guards from the Encampment coming in."

"Until they get here, Viktor can watch over you." Herne looked pissed. "My father's right. We have to take care of this, and the sooner the better."

"I'll go get Viktor. You stay with her until I come back." The truth was, I didn't want to listen to her plead with Herne to back off. I felt bad for her, but Cernunnos was right. I slipped out of the hospital room, back to the waiting room. The others looked up expectantly.

"She's pretty banged up. And of course, Astrana's writing it off as a joke. Viktor, Herne wants you to stay on guard for Rhiannon until her own bodyguards get here." I gave him the room number, and he took off. I was about follow him when the doctor came out.

"You can see your friend now," he said.

Talia, Angel, and I followed him back through the labyrinth of corridors until we came to a set of double doors leading into an examination room. Yutani was on the bed, his head elevated, his arm swathed in bandages and a splint. His eyes were glassy from the pain. Most shifters didn't handle drugs very well, so they usually opted out of pain medication.

"Hey, I'd ask how you're feeling, but you'd probably hit me." I crossed over to the bed.

"I've been better," he said. He struggled to sit up. The doctor helped him. "I did *not* expect a trap in the woods."

"Traps are illegal," the doctor said. "There are too many shifters around. We have an ordinance against them. I had to report it."

I groaned. Another run-in with Astrana seemed likely, although *this,* she would probably take some sort of action on.

"Any idea of who would set up something like that?"

The doctor gave me a little shrug. "A few of the humans around here don't appreciate the SubCult community. Rather than just being vocal about it, they tend to take action. A lot of crap like this."

He nodded toward the bloody trap that was sitting on one of the trays. It was a nasty piece of work, with sharp jagged teeth. It almost looked homemade, which would give credence to what the doctor had just said. If it was some wingnut hate group, they probably sat around on Saturday afternoons crafting their weapons.

"You'd think they'd be weeded out and ostracized by now. But then again, you never know what's lurking beneath the surface of any community." Talia moved over to Yutani's side, resting her hand on his knee. "You really should sleep for a while. This is the best place for you."

He shook his head. "I'd feel safer back at the hotel. Besides, the doctor gave me meds to keep it from getting infected, and I won't be able to have the arm cast until we get back to Seattle. The swelling has to come down first, and the stitches have to come out."

"True," the doctor said. "However, when that splint comes off to change the dressings, you need someone trained to keep the arm from spontaneously shifting. I have to insist that if you leave the hospital tonight, when you need the dressings changed, you consult a doctor. I'm writing that up in your instructions, because if you don't and something happens to your arm, I don't want to be held liable."

"Fair enough," Yutani said, gritting his teeth as he moved his shoulder. "I can do that. When should I have them changed?"

"I'd say tomorrow afternoon. Don't overwork yourself, and don't bump that arm. You have seventy-five stitches in your arm, and a broken bone. Coyote shifter or not, you're not in any shape to go bouncing around poking into dangerous cases."

He gave Yutani a long look. "I saw on your registration form that you work for the Wild Hunt. I have an inkling of what that entails, so the rest of you need to keep him quiet." He turned to look at Talia, Angel, and me. "I am writing him a prescription limiting him to indoor activity only. And no shifting until the bone heals up. And a lot of bed rest for the first forty-eight hours."

Yutani groaned, but Talia shook the doctor's hand.

"We'll make certain he behaves." By her tone of voice, I believed every word of it.

At that point, Herne entered the room. He took one look at Yutani, then turned to the doctor.

I suppose he's insisting on leaving tonight?"

"Yes, but I just had a long conversation with your friends here about keeping him quiet and confined to indoor activity. I'm writing it up in my discharge notes. You're free to wait in the waiting room until I'm done. I'll have the nurse bring him out in a wheelchair when he's ready."

He pointed toward the trap. "You're a very lucky man. That could have severed your arm if it had closed just right. Or a foot. I'll turn this over to the sheriff, and we'll see if we can find who built it. If we do, I'll have the authorities notify you in case you want to sue the pants off of them for your medical bills." Again, the doctor paused. "And if I were you, I'd take every opportunity to do so. People need to realize they can't just run around targeting anybody they don't like."

With that, he chased the rest of us out, back to the waiting room.

"I ASSUME VIKTOR is still with Rhiannon?" I asked.

Herne nodded. "I contacted the Second Lieutenant of the Foam Born Encampment. He said there are four men on their way to stand watch over Rhiannon. They'll be here within half an hour. We'll wait until they get here. Rhiannon's not at all happy with us. She wants us to stop the investigation, but it's too late for that. If anything, this makes it more pressing. I should talk to my father. I'm going to go call the intermediary, to contact him."

I suddenly understood. "You have someone you call who contacts him, so he can get in touch with you?"

"Yeah. Since cell phones won't work in his realm, he has to pop out into ours to give me a call. As a matter of fact, John—with the portal in his yard? He's one of my intermediaries. There are others in case he's busy." He moved away from us, pulling out his phone.

I turned to Talia. "Will we have any trouble keeping Yutani quiet?"

She cracked a faint grin. "I can keep him under control. Even when Herne can't, I'm able to get through to that fur-brained skull of his. He's stubborn, but I'm a harpy. And even if I don't have my powers, I still have my nature." She winked at me. "Sometimes I think Yutani thinks of me as a substitute mother."

Remembering what Herne had told me about Yutani, I wondered just how much the others knew.

"Is his mother still alive?"

"I don't know. He never talks about her." Talia gave me a speculative look, and I returned it with a slow smile. She gave me a nod, but I knew that she wouldn't say anymore until she knew exactly what I had been told. She was a cagey old bird, that was for sure, but she was smart and observant.

"Cernunnos will call me back as soon as he gets the chance. Or rather, as soon as John is able to go through the portal. It shouldn't be long. I told him it was a code yellow situation. Which, technically, it is."

At my look, he explained. "A *code red* situation is emergency, we have to take care of something before all out war breaks out. *Code orange* indicates an escalating situation that can endanger a lot of people, and a *code yellow* situation indicates that we are running into serious trouble and need advice."

"Here comes the nurse," Angel said, nodding toward the doors by the reception desk. A nurse was wheeling out Yutani. The doctor followed behind, handing a chart to the receptionist. She made some sort of notation on it, then gave the sheath of papers to the nurse pushing the wheelchair. We walked over to meet them.

"Here are his discharge papers," the nurse said, giving them to Talia. "Is someone bringing the car around?"

Talia glanced at Herne. "Do you want to drive

Yutani back to the hotel, or should we?"

"Why don't you take him? Ember, Viktor, and I will follow once Rhiannon's guards arrive. If you take off now, you should get back to the hotel in about half an hour. Drive carefully, and watch yourselves on the road."

Talia nodded. "Will do. Angel and I will go get the car now. I think it's better if we go in pairs."

I spoke up. "I'll walk out with them. I've got my dagger, and it's just safer."

We headed out into the chill night air. The wind had picked up, and the faint smell of saltwater wafted through the air. None of us had much to say. It had been a long day for everybody, all the way around. As we drove back up to the loading zone, I wanted nothing more than to go back to the hotel, go to sleep, and leave this island as soon as we woke up.

The nurse helped transfer Yutani into the backseat of the car, where he leaned back and closed his eyes, working on pain control. With Angel and Talia in the front and buckled in, I made sure their doors were locked and waved them off. As I headed back into the hospital, I saw four members of the hippocampus encampment heading across the parking lot, and I waited for them to join me. Madrigal was among them. He nodded at me, and we all went into the hospital, to Rhiannon's room.

BY THE TIME we filled the guards in on what

had happened and left them watching Rhiannon, it was well past one A.M. As we headed out for the car, Herne's phone rang. Cernunnos was calling him back. He answered, sliding into the driver seat. As Viktor and I got ourselves adjusted, Herne ran down what had happened. A few minutes later he hung up.

"He says to check out the touchstone I found in the forest and use it in order to find Blackthorn. If we have to, we're to apprehend Astrana for complicity. That's going to be a barrel of laughs, because you know she's working with the King of Thorns. I'm not looking forward to that little altercation."

"Can we contact Névé about this? After all, Astrana is Light Fae. Doesn't that give Névé some control over her?"

"I suppose that's a possibility, but given she was exiled from the court, she's probably no longer subject to its rulings. Once you are excommunicated, I don't believe you owe fealty, though I could be mistaken." Herne hit the steering wheel with his fist. "Let's get back to the hotel and check out that touchstone." He glanced at me as I yawned. "Take a nap on the way home. It's not much, but it will help."

I let out a little groan. "I suppose we have to pull an all-nighter."

"Welcome to the world of the Wild Hunt. Take a nap, but we have to get back out in that forest to track down Blackthorn. Now that he's targeting Rhiannon and her people, we can't let the situation get any worse."

I let out a sigh, leaning back as I stared out the window at the dark night as it passed by. Soon, the movement and warmth of the car rocked me into a dreamless sleep.

BACK AT THE hotel parking lot, I groggily let Viktor pull me out of the car into the chill night air. It braced me, waking me enough to make it back into the hotel. We met up in Herne's room, where Talia had made a fresh pot of coffee. Yutani was asleep in his room, safely locked in. Herne had called ahead, apparently, and Talia had the laptop open and ready to go. Angel had ordered room service, which luckily ran all night. Three pizzas sat on the dresser.

I realized I was hungry as well as tired, and accepted a paper plate with a couple slices of pepperoni pizza on it. After I sat down beside the desk and took a sip of the astringent caffeine, which tasted double strength, I bit into the pizza. The warm flavors exploded in my mouth, and I murmured appreciatively as I chewed.

"I've been comparing the photo you texted me with symbols and signs online. I think I found something." Talia turned the laptop around. "This is the picture Herne texted me as you guys were on the way home. Note the markings on top of the rock?"

I blinked, leaning in to see what she was talking about. The picture was of a standing stone, and there was an indentation on the top, which held what looked like a crystal wheel. The wheel looked movable, and had several glyphs scattered around the edges, much like the numbers on a clock face. The lines looked squiggly to me, making no sense, but I realized they were deliberate markings.

"Are those runes?" I leaned in even closer.

"Of a sort, yes. They aren't Norse runes, nor are they the Celtic Ogham. But they appear to be glyphs of some sort, or pictographs. I've run them through a comparison program that Yutani has on his laptop. While they aren't from any of the arcane Fae languages, they resemble one of the most ancient—the Tuanadeth tongue. This one here—the one that looks like a loop with a tail—is very close to the glyph for 'open door.' And this one over here? It looks like three lines with bars through it? That resembles a glyph meaning 'hidden.' I can't tell with the others yet."

Angel cupped her mug, which had a teabag in it. "What exactly is a touchstone?"

Herne studied the picture, and the comparison chart.

"A touchstone can be several things. It can be a locking mechanism, in which case if you turn it just right, it will open a door or unlock a chest or something like that. There are more complicated ones that are almost...think *magical computer system*, if you will. Each glyph would then act as a different program. Or a touchstone can simply be a landmark."

"Touchstones can also be portals," Viktor said. "The reason it's called a touchstone is because it's usually aligned to one place or person. If the touchstone is aligned to a person, nobody else can use it without permission. If it's aligned to a place, then it will only connect to that particular location."

"In this case, my guess is that it's aligned to a place and is probably a portal or a key lock. The fact that it has a glyph similar to the open-door glyph makes it more likely to be the latter." Herne glanced at the clock. "We need to test it."

I paused mid-chew, praying he wouldn't say we were heading out now. It was two A.M., and the nap in the car had only made me more tired. Viktor glanced at me.

"We should wait till morning. It's been a rough night. We can all use a little sleep. A few hours aren't going to matter, one way or another. Rhiannon's being protected in the hospital, and Yutani's asleep in his room." The half-ogre gave me a gentle grin.

I smiled back gratefully. I knew he wasn't as tired as I was, and Herne could probably run all night without a problem, but there was no way I had the stamina or energy to get through the rest of the night.

Herne frowned, but reluctantly agreed. "All right. We'll head out at first light. Let's meet in the dining hall at seven o'clock."

I groaned. "Can we make it seven-thirty? Or eight? An extra hour of sleep would do me a world of good." I hated admitting that I wasn't up to the task, but every part of my body ached. I hadn't felt this tired in a long time. And my wrist still hurt like hell. "I need to change the dressing on my wrist tomorrow morning."

Talia patted my hand. "I'll help you."

"All right. Eight A.M. sharp, in the dining room. Be there." Herne shooed us out of his room, and I realized I was too tired for even a good-night kiss. I blew him a quick peck, darting out with Angel.

As Angel locked our door, I began to strip off my clothes, wincing as my wrist throbbed. "That damned bush really got me."

Angel pulled back my covers for me. "Climb into bed, and go to sleep. You need all the rest you can get. Why don't you use the extra pillow to prop up your hand?"

Doing as she suggested, I snuggled underneath the blankets. I was out in no time.

MORNING CAME FAR too early, and five and half hours of sleep didn't seem like enough, but it was better than nothing. I staggered to the bathroom, brushing my teeth and washing my face before hopping in the shower for a quick rinse.

"Are you ready for breakfast?" Angel asked, tapping on the door.

"If I was ready I'd be out there and dressed. Give me five." I quickly toweled off and wrapped my hair in a high ponytail so that it would dry naturally. I pulled on a pair of jeans and, since we were headed out to the woods, I decided on a long-sleeve microfiber shirt that wouldn't catch on the foliage. I tucked it into my jeans and then threaded a black leather belt through the belt loops, buckling the silver clasp that had Celtic knotwork on it.

The shower had revived me some—I was finding that the more I worked with water magic, the more showers and baths perked me up.

As I returned to the bedroom, Angel was waiting for me, my boots in hand. As I thrust them on, she gathered our purses and unplugged our tablets from the charging bay. She slid mine into my purse and hers into her own purse, then handed me my phone. I tucked it into the pocket of my jean jacket. Finally, we were ready. Heading out the door, we locked it firmly behind us.

We decided to take the stairs since it was quicker than waiting for the elevator, and by the time we reached the bottom, the lift car opened and Herne and Viktor emerged. Talia was already in the dining room, waiting for us. She had secured a table. As I pulled out my chair, I glanced around. The hotel seemed to have more guests than it had the day before. Tourist season must be starting.

"I ordered for you," Talia said. "Herne asked me to. I hope you don't mind waffles and sausage."

"Sounds good to me," I said, unfurling my napkin and draping it over my lap. "Has anybody heard from Yutani this morning?"

At that moment, Angel poked me in the arm and pointed through the glass doors, across the lobby to the elevator. Yutani was walking out of the lift even as I asked the question. As he entered the dining room, I restrained a gasp. He looked pretty beat up, even more so than the night before. He had a black eye, and purplish bruises on his face. They were already turning color, which meant he was healing fairly quickly.

Herne pulled out the chair next to him, and Yutani dropped into it, letting out an *oomph*.

"I feel like I was hit by a truck." He glanced around at us, a sheepish look on his face. "All right, before any of you say it. I *promise* next time Coyote gives me a warning, I'll listen."

"Don't say I didn't tell you so," Talia said, a rueful smile on her face.

Yutani stuck out his tongue at her. "I'm going to pretend I didn't hear that. What's for breakfast?"

"Apparently, waffles. Talia ordered for us."

"As soon as breakfast is over, Ember and Viktor and I are headed out to the woods. We want to check out that touchstone." Herne unfurled his napkin, laying it across his lap.

"What touchstone?" Yutani asked.

"You were already on your way to the hospital when we left the woods." As Herne told him about it and showed him the pictures, I darted over to the counter and ordered a quad-shot mocha, asking the waitress to hurry it if she would.

"I should go with you," Yutani was saying as I returned. "You know that I've got magic that can help in those situations. As well as a good technical eye."

"When are you going to learn?" Herne asked. "You'd think what happened to that arm of yours would teach you something. We're not dragging you out in the woods, especially after one of the Ante-Fae."

They were still arguing when breakfast arrived, along with my mocha. I ignored the debate, focusing instead on the sugar and caffeine as a source of energy. I noticed that neither Talia nor Viktor were getting involved, and Angel was reading her email. It didn't take long before Herne won, and Yutani turned to his breakfast, sulking a little.

"If the touchstone is a portal, then what do we do?"

Herne glanced at me. "Then, we take a little trip."

"Without knowing where we're going?"

Viktor laughed. "You'd be surprised at some of the places we've ended up over the years by jumping through strange portals. And we're still alive."

"Oh, joy—what a comfort," I said, diving into my breakfast.

Chapter 14

AT TEN O'CLOCK, after Talia changed my dressing—which hurt, though the wounds were healing up faster now—we headed toward the park. Not far from the hotel, the sound of a siren whirred twice behind us. I let out a disgruntled grunt as Herne pulled the side of the road. A moment later, a haughty-looking woman in a khaki uniform came ambling over to the driver's side, looking rather disgruntled. Herne let out an "Oh, shit" and rolled down his window.

When she peeked in and saw me, the snotty look intensified. I realized exactly who we were facing.

"So, where are you going?" She was asking Herne, but her gaze was glued on my face.

"Did we do anything wrong, Sheriff? Did I make an illegal turn, or is my brake light out, or was I going over the speed limit?" Herne's snide reply surprised me. It also made me nervous, given what he was capable of.

Astrana seemed to feel the same way I did, because she stepped back, her look turning from patronizing to wary. "May I see your identification?

Herne pulled out his wallet, and his identification badge. "You know who I am, Astrana. And you know I have the authority to investigate this case. Don't try to interfere or I'll notify my father and mother that you're putting up resistance." His voice was flat, with no inflection, and it was far more chilling than if he had yelled at her. He didn't even look at her, just stared directly ahead at the road.

Astrana glanced at his wallet and badge and then handed them back as if they had bitten her. "I make it my business to know what's going on around here—"

"You don't make it your business to know what's going on with the various murders that happen around here, do you? Especially ones that might have dicey consequences for you, should you actually do your job." This time, Herne turned to face her directly. He held her gaze until she looked away.

Her voice flat, she said, "Just wrap up your business as soon as you can." And with that, she returned to her car and sped off down the road.

"I think you just made an enemy, boss," Viktor said.

"Do you think I care?" Herne said. "She has to know we're on to her. She'll be lucky to still have her job after we're done with this."

He rolled up his window again, and pulled back

on the road. A few moments later, we were back in the parking lot of the state park.

"Getting to the touchstone isn't easy. I'm pretty sure that Viktor can manage it, but you should probably ride on my back, Ember. I know you're physically fit, but with that wrist, it's going to be hard for you to balance yourself against the steep slope."

By now, I had learned to recognize when Herne was in a bad mood, and Astrana had plummeted him into one. It was just best to accept his offer, rather than argue that I could make it on my own. Besides, if the slope was as steep as he seemed to think, he was probably right given the state of my throbbing wrist.

"Not a problem," I said. "I'd appreciate the ride." And I didn't even put any innuendo into it.

A LITTLE WAYS off the road, Herne turned into his stag self and knelt so that I could crawl on to his back. I had ridden on him a couple times before, and it still took my breath away as to how fast he could go and how nimble he was. Oh, I knew that the cervidae family was quick footed, but Herne could out-run any deer or elk out there. And he was massive, at least shoulder height next to me. He lowered himself to the ground, and I climbed on his back. Slowly, he stood, waiting for me to get a good hold on him. I held tight, leaning forward to rest my arms against the sides of his neck. Then, picking up speed, he led the way, holding himself back so that Viktor could follow.

We wound our way through the forest, startling the odd bird here and there, and a fox, who scampered off to the right. I yawned, still tired, but grateful that Viktor had bought us some downtime. Herne had been right, the slope of the ravine was extremely steep, and while I would have been able to make it, it would have been a struggle and I would have worn myself out by the time I reached the top. As it was, Herne made quick work of it, and Viktor wasn't far behind.

At the top of the ravine was a narrow plateau, about three feet wide before the ravine started down the other side. Herne let out a little huff, one that I recognized as "Hold on tight," and I pressed myself harder against his neck. He began to descend, picking up speed until we were racing between the trees in a blur. I didn't look back to see how Viktor was doing—that would have required letting go of Herne's neck and I wasn't about to do that.

As we darted between the trees, I held my breath, wincing every time we came to a log or boulder. Yet Herne always managed to jump without hesitation, sailing over the obstacles as though they didn't exist. We arrived at the bottom and he slowed, finally coming to a halt beside a streambed that trickled along through the ravine.

The entire network of Western Washington geology was made up of forests like these, thick fir and cedar, overzealous ferns that covered the forest floor, along with vining plants and huckleberry bushes, all filling the ever-present ravines that had been caused by the retreat of the massive glaciers during the last Ice Age. The glaciers had withdrawn, leaving only the ravines and bluffs and alluvial deposits to mark that they had ruled over the land at one time. The massive rockslides covered white slopes, a stark reminder of the strength of the planet.

Herne knelt for me to jump off of his back. As I turned around, Viktor was descending the last few feet of the ravine. He was surefooted, but even he was using the closely spaced trees for balance. As he joined us, Herne turned back into himself.

"Are we near the touchstone?" I asked, looking around. The bottom of the ravine was dry, covered with forest debris.

Herne pointed ahead of us, toward a small clearing where the sun was pouring in. At least it wasn't raining. He led us through the knee-deep undergrowth until we reached a large boulder that was flat enough to sit on. Atop the boulder was the inset crystal wheel that we had seen in the photograph. Around us, the cliffs were almost glowing. There was magic in the area, and it crackled in the air around us. I caught my breath, holding out my hands as I tried to pinpoint the source.

"You can feel it too, can't you?" Herne asked.

I nodded. "Whatever it is, it's very powerful and very old. It has to be Blackthorn. I can't imagine that he would settle near any other forces as strong as he is, given what little I know of the Ante-Fae."

"You're right. The Ante-Fae tend to be solitary beings, with their own courts and their own rules.

Weapons ready?"

Viktor patted the dagger by his side. "I also have an iron blade tucked in my boot." He glanced at me. "Be sure not to touch it, because it's specifically designed to harm the Fae. I'm not sure if the Ante-Fae also have the same weakness, but it occurred to me they might."

"Oh, they do," Herne said. He turned to me. "How's your wrist?"

"I'm left-handed, which means my writing sucks, but I wield my dagger with my right hand. So I should be okay." My wrist was still throbbing, but the salve Ferosyn had given me was definitely helping it mend. I would end up with an interesting array of scars, though.

"I'm not certain how this particular touchstone works, so take hold of me in case it only affects the person touching it." Herne reached out toward the knob in the center of the wheel.

I took hold of his right arm, and Viktor took hold of his left. Herne turned the knob to the glyph we thought represented the word "open."

I held breath, slowly exhaling as a shimmer formed around us. The circle of dancing lights grew brighter. The next moment, a loud rumble split the air as a crack in the side of the ravine began to open, pushing back, exposing a dark and pungent maw. The tang of fresh earth hung heavy in the air. I shivered as a tremor ran through the ravine. This was heavy magic, dark and ancient, permeating every single drop of moisture in the soil, and every breath of air in the breeze that raced past. As the circle of lights faded, we faced the passage into the earth.

Herne let go of our arms as he slowly stepped forward. Viktor and I followed close behind. As we approached the opening in the side of the ravine, the sensation of magic grew stronger, and my knees felt weaker.

I had seldom encountered the ancient beings of the world. In fact, the only one I had run across who felt this old and dangerous had been the inter-dimensional assassin Kuveo, whom we had stumbled across on my first case with the Wild Hunt. It unsettled me to know just how many creatures out there could wield the kind of powers we were facing.

The entrance to the cavern was as black as pitch, black as night. We couldn't even see the floor. There could be a dropoff, or spikes along the floor, or even a polished marble dance floor, for all we knew. Herne motioned for Viktor and me to take hold of his hands.

"In case this is a portal or a vortex, we don't want to get separated. On the count of three, we step through. The moment we hit solid ground, ready your weapons." He took a deep breath, and I steeled myself.

Herne counted. *One, two*...on the third beat, we stepped through.

The world shifted. There was no other way to describe it. It was as though we were standing in one reality for one second, and then we stepped over a line, and everything changed.

It wasn't the same sort of portal like the one at John Shelton's house, but it was definitely some type of vortex.

I caught my breath as my foot hit the floor, and I let go of Herne, reaching for my dagger. The next second, everything blazed to light, and we found ourselves standing in a circular meadow, a lea of vibrant grass dotted with wildflowers and surrounded by a grove of oak and blackthorn. The sun felt hot against my skin, yet I could smell the sea on the wind, and my senses told me that the water was near. I looked around quickly, searching for the entrance to the cave behind us, but it was nowhere in sight.

"Be cautious," Herne said. "We're in Blackthorn's territory. Where that is, I'm not sure. I know we're not in the UK, even though this reminds me of it."

The magic was so thick, I could practically taste it on my tongue. It swirled around us, like the wake left by some wandering dragon. Hell, I didn't even know if dragons *existed*, but the energy was so stifling that I could believe just about anything.

Viktor looked around, shaking his head. "Toto..."

"We're not in Kansas anymore," I finished for him.

"Not even close," he said, flashing me a ghost of a smile.

Herne knelt, examining the grass. He let out a shout and shook his hand, standing abruptly. "Damn it."

"What?"

"Something bit me. There," he added, pointing.

Fluttering nearby was what looked like a tiny figure. She was winged, about six inches tall. While the creature was pretty, with petite breasts and a narrow waist, her face was far from human. Two narrow eyes sat above a large oval mouth that was ringed with sharp teeth.

"What is it?" I asked as the figure hovered near. Then she let out a sharp whistle.

"I don't know, but I'm not sure I want to stick around to find out." Viktor was edging away.

I was inclined to agree with him. Especially when, in response to its—her—whistle, at least two dozen others just like her rose out of the grass and began to head our way.

"I don't think they're the welcome wagon," I said, backing up.

"*Knucklebones!* Run!" Herne shouted, bolting toward a particularly large oak.

Viktor and I followed, as the swarm of knuckle-bones made a beeline for us. Their teeth chattered as they zipped this way and that, darting to try to catch up to us.

Unfortunately, they were good at flying and before we could dive into the thicket of trees, they were on us. One of them managed to catch hold of my upper arm and bit me. His teeth were sharp and scissor-like, and I dove for the ground, roll-ing over onto him, hoping he would let go. He did, looking dazed, and I wasted no time. I sliced through the air with my blade, bringing it down to stab him through his torso. He let out a shriek as I pinned him to the ground, convulsing once and then, he was still. The next moment, his body van-ished as if he had never been there.

Herne turned around, and with a deep breath,

shouted, *"Stad! Is mise mac Cernunnos!"*

The knucklebones froze, slowly lowering them-selves to the ground where they knelt in front of him. Herne turned to us. "That should put a stop to their antics."

"What are they?" I asked. I had never seen any-thing quite like them, not even among the sub-Fae.

"Knucklebones. They're also known as nixien-acks. When there's only one or two around, they're just a nuisance. But in a swarm? They can take down a giant. They're carnivorous, and they'll eat their victims alive. Think of them like piranha. One can bite off your finger, a swarm can eat you from the outside in."

I shuddered. I was discovering all too many delights like this and more, working for the Wild Hunt. "They don't exist back in our world—*my* world—do they?"

Herne shook his head. "Not usually. Sometimes they manage to slip over, but most often you find them in other realms, like Annwn."

"Are they Fae? Or sub-Fae?"

Herne nodded. "Sub-Fae. They tend to gather in forested areas, and they breed in colonies." He glanced back at the group of them. They were starting to inch away, backing off. He turned and jumped at them, racing forward and yelling. The whole group swirled into the air, like deadly but beautiful butterflies, and then hightailed it back toward the thicket, vanishing before I could blink.

"Well, that takes care of that." Viktor let out a sigh, shaking his head. "There's a reason I don't come over into these realms very often. So, which way should we go?"

Herne eyed the tree line suspiciously. He was watching the blackthorn trees in particular. "It seems like a dangerous proposition to go wading into the middle of the blackthorn bushes, don't you think?"

I nodded, holding up my wrist. "I'm the proof in the pudding for that. But we can't just stay *here*. We don't even know how to get back to Whidbey Island."

"Let's have a look around. There should be another touchstone nearby, and it should have the same glyphs on it." Herne began to nose around, poking through the grass.

"Will it be on a boulder just like the other?"

"No," he said. He pointed over toward a large oak. "Why don't you check over there, Ember? Viktor, skirt the edge of the blackthorn trees if you would. I'll start hunting around here."

We poked around, probing through the grass and searching through the undergrowth. After about ten minutes, Viktor gave a little shout.

"I think I found it!"

We hurried over to his side, keeping an eye on the row of trees nearest to us. There was no way in hell we weren't being watched, that much I knew.

Viktor was standing next to a tree stump, surrounded by tall ferns. Unless you were looking directly at it, the stump would be easy to miss. The top had been hollowed out, and inside sat the exact duplicate of the crystal wheel on the stone back in the forest.

"So, we know where to find the doorway out."

Herne looked around, then cautiously placed his hand on the wheel turning it to the glyphs that symbolized the word "open." Sure enough, there was a noise behind us, and when we turned, we saw an opening into darkness. "I assume that's the way back into that cave."

"All right. We know the way out. Now what?"

"Now, we look for Blackthorn. I'm assuming he keeps a network of spies, so we might as well announce ourselves." Herne strode away from the tree stump. "I am Herne, son of Cernunnos! I'm here on official business to see the King of Thorns. I demand an audience."

I looked around, nervous. What kind of response would that would provoke?

We didn't have to wait long for the answer. A moment later there was a stirring among a group of the blackthorn trees. I placed my hand on my dagger, waiting, and noticed that Herne and Viktor were doing the same.

As we watched, the branches parted. Seven creatures emerged, looking for all the world like a combination of praying mantises and very thin, angular men. Their heads were oval, almost triangular, and their eyes were wide-set and bulbous. Their skin was a pale green, and their limbs were wispy thin. Their legs bent forward, reminding me of goat legs. They didn't walk on hooves, however, but on what appeared to be feet enclosed within leather boots. Their uniforms were militaristic, in shades of purple and black with gold trim, and they carried long, razor-sharp blades that glinted in the sunlight.

One stepped forward. "Do not draw your weapons. Follow."

They turned as a unit and headed back into the thicket without looking back to see if we obeyed. Herne gave us a nod, and we fell in behind. I eyed the trees suspiciously as we approached. My arm ached where the knucklebones had bit me, and my wrist was still stinging. The last thing I wanted to do was face another renegade tree that had it in for me.

But as the odd creatures marched in formation—and they *did* march—straight toward the patch of thorny trees, the trees gave way, pulling back to create a corridor for us. They behaved themselves, although they creaked and groaned as we passed by, whispering in some ancient language that predated the creatures of the earth. They were aware in a way that I had never before seen. There was an intelligence, a sentience lurking behind those ancient trunks, their thoughts so active that they electrified the air.

The path seemed unending, but eventually the guards in front of us slowed, stepping to the side to form two lines. The one who had spoken to us before gestured toward the corridor formed between their lines.

"Go forward."

Herne gave them a quick nod, then set forward, with Viktor and me following.

Beyond the guards, the trees thinned out, revealing a clearing. In the middle was a giant mound, formed of woven branches bearing thorns, reminding me of the tale of Sleeping Beauty and how her castle had been overcome by a wall of thorns. Only we weren't planning on rescuing the person within. Centered against the side of the mound was a large silver door.

"This reminds me of a Faerie Barrow," Viktor whispered under his breath.

"It is, of a sort." Herne paused, glancing from side to side. All around the Barrow were vast thickets of brambles and blackthorn trees. They were all in flower, beautiful and brilliant, filling the air with their musky scent.

"Where are the leaves?" There weren't any leaves on the trees yet, despite the flowers.

"Those will come later after the flowers set and the fruit begins to grow."

"Is the fruit safe to eat?" I asked.

"Sloe berries are generally used for jam and gin." Herne coughed and rubbed his nose. The pollen was thick, and the smell was overwhelming. "Let's get this over with."

He headed toward the door, and Viktor and I scrambled to keep up. As we neared the edge of the Barrow, I could feel a resonant energy racing through the ground below our feet. It was almost a heartbeat, a slow murmur, that sounded like some ancient giant slumbering deep beneath the ground.

Herne paused as he grabbed hold of the giant silver door handle. He turned back to us, a warning look on his face. "Remember, Blackthorn is crafty, and he's smart. We are in *his* realm now, and if you displease him there's not much I can do to intervene. I could call upon my father, but even that would take some time. I suggest you let me do the talking unless he asks you something specific. And if he does, watch what you say. Think before you speak. And whatever happens, don't let him rile you. We draw no blades within his palace or we'll be dead. *All of us.*" He sounded so somber that I found myself hoping I wouldn't have to speak up at all.

As he opened the door, I could hear the murmured rush of voices filtering past, as though they had been caught up in a bottle and were now set free.

I leaned close to Herne. "Did you hear that?"

He nodded, tilting his head to the side. "Yes, I don't know what it is. Be very careful. There's ancient magic here. Older than me."

There was no one to greet us, so Herne stepped through the door. Viktor and I followed. It was difficult to see in the darkness, but then a silver light the size of a pebble appeared on the ground in front of us. It bounced a couple times, then flew into the air where it hung for a moment before taking off at a decent pace.

Herne started after it, and I realized that this was our guide. Whether it was a creature or simply some strange form of magic, I could not tell. I tried to keep my senses open, searching for any water elementals or spirits that might be near, but everything felt knotted and twisted. Just when I thought I had pinned the energy down, it would twist again, like a cat playing with a ball of yarn.

I reached out and my hand met a wall. There was a tingle, almost like a snap, and I pulled my fingers away quickly, not wanting to set off any traps.

"I think we're in a passage," I said.

"We are, but the way it twists makes me think we're in some sort of labyrinth." Herne's voice echoed back. It was so dark I could barely see him. Only the brilliant silver pebble ahead of us seemed to shine through the darkness, still hovering above us.

It felt like we had been walking forever, but I knew it couldn't have been more than a few minutes when the pebble stopped. A beam of light radiated from it, illuminating a door straight ahead of us. In that thin beam, I could see the edges of the walls left and right. It seemed we were at the end of the road. I couldn't see any other passages. Whether we had passed by a side-passage in the darkness, I couldn't tell.

The door—or rather, doors, as there were two of them—were silver, ornately engraved.

Herne reached out and gripped the handle, pulling the massive door open. From inside, a pale light emanated, blinding us even with its weakness.

A deep voice echoed out. "Enter, son of Cernunnos. And bring your friends with you." The voice was throaty and strong.

Herne strode in as if he owned the place. The door behind us slammed shut the moment we were through, and I jumped at the noise.

Inside the chamber, the light was weak, but it grew brighter as we stood there. I blinked, trying to shade my eyes while they adjusted.

"Well met, Herne, son of the Hunt. What do you

want in my territory? Why did you come to my kingdom?"

The voice was coming from behind the light, and I stepped to the side, trying to see around the brilliant glow. But it began to fade, lowering its intensity even as we stood there.

"Whom do I address? Are you Blackthorn, the King of Thorns?" Herne sounded more belligerent than I'd ever heard him. I wondered if this was some sort of power play.

At that point, the light dimmed enough for us to see, and there, in front of us, stood the King of Thorns. He was taller than I had expected. Tall and muscled, and yet, looking almost as gnarled as some of the trees. He was mesmerizing. He was wearing what reminded me of a Hawaiian *malo*. The cloth was a deep purple, trimmed with silver. His chest, arms, and legs were bare, his olive skin covered with a network of black work vines that had been tattooed over every inch of his body, including his face. He was carrying a spear that looked to have a silver tip, with long, sharp barbs surrounding the spearhead.

"I am Blackthorn, the King of Thorns. What do you want in my world?"

He squared his shoulders, and I found myself wanting to back away, to put distance between the Ante-Fae and myself. There was something terrifying about him. Perhaps it was the dark green that tinted his eyes, or perhaps it was the way every inch of his body seemed to glow with an inner light that felt fetid and dank. He didn't feel evil per se, but dangerous and chaotic.

As if he had sensed what I was thinking, he turned to me. I tried to look away, but couldn't untangle myself from the mesmerizing snare of his gaze.

"And *what* do we have here? An unholy mixture, perhaps? Do both of your peoples deny you? Do they whisper that you should have never been born? That you are *tainted*, that you should never have been allowed to live? *Tralaeth*?" His voice wove over the words like a magical cord, tying them up with tension and pain.

"What they think of me is none of my concern." I trembled, trying to block out the wash of energy flowing around me.

"You just keep telling yourself that when you're lying in the dark, trying to blot out the images of your parents dead on the floor." Blackthorn slowly rose from his throne, every move deliberate. He held out his hand, tipping his spear toward Viktor, his fingers wrapped around the hilt.

"And you... Yet another mixed blood. I wonder. Do the humans accept you into their world? Do the ogres allow you free access in their world? Or do they turn you away, a joke to your father, and an abomination to your mother?"

Viktor mumbled, staring at the King of Thorns with smoldering eyes. I reached out to take hold of his arm. Shaking my head, I gave him a warning look and he nodded, taking a deep breath and letting it out slowly.

"No answer? Ah well, we *all* know the answers to my questions," Blackthorn said, returning his gaze to Herne. "And so we come to Herne, the son of Cernunnos. The lord of all things wild and free. You keep strange bedfellows for the son of a god. Is it because you, too, have diluted blood? Your mother was once human, before your father gifted her with immortality. Do you, perhaps, bear all of the weaknesses that she once bore? Or do you hearken after your father, running wild with the hunt? I wonder, how diluted can the world become before it falls apart? Is nothing *pure* anymore?"

His voice was hypnotic, reeling me in even though I resisted. I found myself leaning toward him and abruptly pulled away as I tried to snap out of it. Before I could move, Blackthorn was by my side.

"The girl feels my magic." Blackthorn reached out to stroke my cheek with one finger. His nails were spikes, like the spikes of the blackthorn bush, and he trailed one along my skin, not quite breaking the surface. His touch hurt, like a thin burn against my skin, and I shivered as his magic rippled through me. It felt like a snake was slithering around my feet, looking to catch hold of me and trip me up.

"You *know* me, don't you?" He bent down to whisper in my ear. "Would you stay in my kingdom if I asked? Would you take your place as one of my toys? I can drench you in magic like you've never tasted. I can feel my pulse within you— you've tasted pain and you understand the freedom it brings. A river of blood has crested through your life and you long to dive in, to let it sweep you under. You're one of the waterborne, aren't you? You smell like lilacs and spring rain."

His words spun a web around me, making me dizzy. I swayed, my breath coming in short, ragged pants. My body was responding to him and it made me angry. I didn't *want* to feel this way. I didn't want the presence of this creature to affect me. I moaned, afraid, and Blackthorn laughed. I tried to move away but found that I couldn't. I let out a soft whimper as he licked my throat, his tongue raspy.

"Tasty, very tasty," he said. "You even taste of magic."

Herne stepped forward, his hand on his dagger. "Leave her alone. She's mine. I claim her." His voice contained a threat even I couldn't ignore.

Blackthorn gave him a long look, then slowly pulled away. "*So protective*, son of Cernunnos. You *claim* her? The dog keeps a tight chain on his bone." With a shrug, Blackthorn swept back to his throne, the hypnotic pull of his voice fading as he went into an all-business mode. "Not to worry. She isn't worth my time. She would break at my first blow...perhaps." He watched us with a cunning gaze. "What do you want?"

"You know why we're here," Herne said, glaring at him. "Admit it."

"No, I don't know why you're here." Blackthorn shifted in his seat. "I'm not at all sure what this meeting is about, other than wasting my time."

It was the first lie I'd heard from him. I could feel it, the hesitation. He believed everything he had said to us, except this. I steeled my shoulders. Blackthorn terrified me, but I turned to Herne. "He's lying. I can hear it in his voice."

Herne nodded. "So can I. Blackthorn, you cannot tell me that you aren't aware of what's been going on."

"If you're so certain I know, then it won't hurt to inform me of what you think," the King of Thorns said. "Why don't you acquaint me with the reasons your father sent you into my world?"

"You know full well we're here because of the murders you've committed. Your mark is on the bodies. And that's not even touching on forty missing people over the past few decades. My father has ordered me to put an end to it, since this affects the humans."

Herne was doing his best to remain calm, but his jaw muscles tightened. His hand moved toward his blade, but then he stopped. "If you promise by sacred oath to stop, we'll leave you be. But you must break the pact you made with the sheriff, asking her to keep your dirty little secret. She's complicit in these deaths."

Blackthorn eyed Herne with an impassive look. "For the life of me, I cannot figure out what you're talking about." And then he stopped, a slow smile stealing across his face. "So the pup has gone and made himself a nuisance. Well, that doesn't surprise me."

"What the hell are you talking about?" Herne asked.

"You're not looking for me," Blackthorn said. "The person you're looking for is my *son*." And then, he began to laugh.

Chapter 15

"YOUR *SON*?" HERNE stared at him, his anger draining out of his face, replaced by shock. "I'm not sure I follow."

"Then listen well, Herne, son of Cernunnos. You're not looking for me. You're looking for my *son*. I will admit, I've been out of my realm off and on, but I have no keep with the mortals on this island. And I know my son." He frowned. "The whelp is incapable of restraint."

"Why do you think your son is capable of committing murder?" I meant to keep quiet, but the words came pouring out.

Blackthorn turned back to me and I immediately regretted speaking. He regarded me carefully, his lips stretching into a crooked smile.

"*All* of the Ante-Fae are capable of committing murder, as you call it. To us, it's nothing more than removing an irritant or stepping on an ant. But as to why I think my son is capable of murdering humans? It's a simple matter. I caught him the first time. That's when I ejected him from the realm."

"Forty years ago?" Herne asked.

Blackthorn nodded. "Thereabouts, give or take a few years. I don't care what happens to mortals, but I *do* know that your father has a persnickety bone about it. And while I am not bound by the Fae covenant, neither am I looking for trouble. I have chosen to settle in this area, and I choose to stay here for now. I have very little interaction with those in the outer world, by choice. My son is another matter. Or should I say, my *youngest* son. So I kicked him out in hopes of forcing him to grow up. Apparently, it's taking longer than I hoped."

He sounded so blasé that it made me want to slap him, but I wasn't stupid.

"There are people whose lives have been ruined because of him."

Blackthorn glanced at me, even as Herne gave me a sharp shake of the head.

"She speaks again. Really, this is a feisty little wench you have, Lord Herne. If you ever want me to take her off your hands, just whistle. She'd be good for some amusement. At least, as long as she'd last."

"I told you, leave her alone." Herne turned to me. "And you, *be quiet.*"

I noticed he hadn't introduced either Viktor or me, but I had no qualms about it. We were better off if Blackthorn didn't know our names, though I didn't put it past him to already know all about us. He knew we were mixed blood, and that wasn't always an easy thing to peg. I nodded, closing my mouth and scooting back to stand beside Viktor.

"I take it your son can control the blackthorn trees, like you?" Herne asked.

Blackthorn gave him a long look, then shrugged. "What can I say? He's my son."

"You do know he doesn't just kill his victims? He's torturing them."

"I have some idea. Straff, my son, had a very peculiar mother. I can't remember her name, she's dead now. But she had a particular disease that made her waste away. The only treatment was to draw life force and blood off others. I kept her alive as long as I could, but in the end, she asked me to let her go and so I did. Straff inherited her disease. To survive, he must feed off both energy and blood. Luckily, the disease hasn't taken full hold of him yet, so his needs are sporadic."

"The murders started forty years ago. Twenty victims we feel are his work, and forty missing that we think are connected." Herne crossed his arms, waiting for Blackthorn to answer.

"While he was in my realm, I could attend to him here. But he decided to visit outside the realm. I overheard him talking to a friend about murdering a human. He reveled in it. I enjoy the pain of others as well, but I cannot allow him to involve the mortal world in my business. So I gave him a choice. Stay and remain my son, or be disowned and go out on his own."

"Where can we find him? I'm going to have to take him to my father."

Blackthorn snorted. "Do you really think that

I keep tabs on him? I told you, I kicked him out. You'll likely find him near the water. He loved it."

"If I do catch him..." Herne paused.

"If you find him, do what you will. I want nothing more to do with him." He motioned toward the door of the Barrow. "Our interview is done, although I have little doubt we'll meet again." He was staring at me when he said that. I wanted to crawl into the shadows.

"No doubt. Shall I notify you when we find your son?"

"Why would you? He's dead to me." Blackthorn glanced back at Herne, his voice as cold as the grave. "Please leave before I have my guards evict you."

"How can we find him? What should we look for?" Herne looked angry, but again, he forced himself to remain as calm as he could. I could feel the struggle raging within him.

Blackthorn, who had turned to walk away, glanced over his shoulder. "You suspect him of bribing the sheriff? Ask her." And with that, he vanished into the darkness.

There was a noise at the door, and we turned to see the lead guard waiting for us. Herne silently motioned for Viktor and me to follow him, and we left the Barrow, following the guards back to the meadow. We didn't speak until we reached the touchstone again. Herne thanked the lead guard, but they just withdrew without a word, leaving us alone.

"Let's get out of here." Herne turned the knob, and the portal appeared again. We joined hands and, without a word, walked through the gate back into the forest.

AS SOON AS we saw the familiar trees and undergrowth around us, I let out a sigh of relief and dropped to the ground, feeling like a million pounds had just sloughed off my shoulders. I glanced at my watch. It was a few minutes before noon. We had been with Blackthorn less than an hour but it had felt far longer.

"That was an experience I never want to have again. What kind of freakshow creatures are the Ante-Fae?" I lowered my head between my knees, breathing deeply.

"I told you, they're cunning and deadly. I don't care how pleasant they seem on the surface, and some can seem very charming. Whatever you do, do not make an enemy of the Ante-Fae." Herne reached down, offering me his hand. I let him pull me back to my feet. He paused, looking deep into my eyes. "Ember, be cautious," he murmured. "You caught Blackthorn's attention, and that's never a good thing."

As I was digesting his words, Viktor spoke up.

"Do you think Blackthorn will blow up if we take out his son?"

Herne shook his head. "Are you kidding? He as good as handed over the keys to the dungeon. What happened back there was that Blackthorn gave us permission to do what we needed to stop

Straff. "

"Why won't he do it?" I paused, then shook my head. "Never mind. I know. He doesn't care about the mortals here. Human or SubCult."

"*Ding*! You win. Thank you for playing," Herne said. "Seriously, the Ante-Fae don't care whether mortals live or die. Blackthorn simply doesn't want to be tied to this mess. So he severed ties with his son and sent him out into this realm for somebody else to deal with."

"I assume our next move is to pay a visit to Astrana and force the information out of her. She must be protecting him." Viktor glanced at the side of the ravine. "It's a long hike. Herne, you should turn into the stag again to take Ember to the top."

"Let's save the rest of this discussion until we get back to the hotel. We need to check in with the others before we head over to the sheriff's office." Herne stood back, and once again, he shimmered as a great light surrounded him.

As the stag appeared in his place, I felt the same sense of awe that I had the first time I'd seen him. He was so beautiful, so luminescent and shining. He knelt once again, waiting for me to take my place on his back, and as I did so, grabbing hold. Then we were away, racing toward the top of the ravine. I closed my eyes, trying not to think about the fact that I had caught Blackthorn's attention. A moment later, we were through the ravines and back to the car. As Herne let me off his back and transformed back into himself, Viktor came panting behind.

"You can sure put on the speed when you want

to," I said.

"Being half-ogre doesn't hurt." He grinned, opening the door for me to climb in the car. As he took his place in the back, Herne slid into the driver's seat.

I leaned my head against the headrest, closing my eyes, trying not to think of Straff. If he was anything like his father, we had our work cut out for us. And right now, I had no doubt that he was walking among the people of Whidbey Island, planning his next kill.

WHEN WE REACHED the hotel, Angel pulled me aside.

"I wanted to get your opinion on the inspector I found." She showed me the email. He had twenty years' experience and a great rating on Lisa's Listings—a referral site for professionals from all aspects of home repair and upkeep. An inspection business called Joseph's Inspections had forty-five reviews, with all but one stellar. The one negative review sounded like a disgruntled rival and I discounted it for what it was.

"Sounds good. Can you make an appointment? If he needs a retainer, have him call me for my credit card info." I grinned at her. "I hope that everything checks out. I really want that house."

"I want to live there too, even with the...history. If he needs payment up front, I'll do it. Let me put something into the house. I know I'm just renting from you, but I want to feel like I'm pulling my weight." She emailed him back as I took a quick shower. We were all meeting up in twenty minutes to discuss our next move.

"I feel like I'm covered in Blackthorn's cobwebs. Seriously, his energy clings like static electricity and it's creepy as fuck." I was soaping myself in the shower as Angel sat on the toilet, talking to me. "Can you hand me the shampoo? I forgot to bring it in with me."

She thrust the bottle behind the shower curtain and I grabbed it, lathering my hair liberally. "Thanks."

"So let me get this straight. He's not our murderer? His son is?"

"Yeah, that seems to be the case. And if his son—Straff—is anything like his father, he's going to be a piece of work. I wouldn't put anything past Blackthorn, but he seems to have the sense to avoid tangling with mortals. I actually think he feels we're all beneath his consideration. He seemed almost offended that his son was involved."

I wasn't sure if that was true or not, but I had gotten the impression that Blackthorn was more offended by his son interacting with mortals than he was by the murders.

I toweled off and accepted the clean jeans and top that Angel had pulled out for me. As I slid into my underwear and bra, I bumped my wrist against the side of the counter. "Damn it, that still hurts, even though I'm using the salve as Ferosyn told me. It's healing up, but it aches."

"Are we meeting for lunch?" Angel asked, heading back into the bedroom.

"I don't think so, so why don't you run down and grab us something to eat? Unless you happen to have any protein bars on you, or candy." I wasn't picky.

She laughed. "I have a couple of breakfast bars, but that won't hold your appetite. I'll meet you in the lobby—that's where we're gathering, isn't it?"

"Yeah. Herne wants to take this discussion outside to make certain that nobody overhears us. What...well, I'll wait till then. I know Yutani checked our rooms again for bugs, but..." I trailed off. Just because he had the latest-greatest gadget didn't mean something better hadn't just been built to thwart it.

Angel headed out of the room as I finished dressing. I zipped up my jeans and pulled on my top—it was a corset top, lacing in the front instead of the back, and I quickly cinched it and tied off the bow. As I stopped to fix my makeup—most of which had washed away in the shower—my personal cell phone rang. I was careful to strictly follow company guidelines and not use my work phone for any personal business. Frowning, I glanced at the Caller ID. The only people I usually got calls from were Angel and Herne, and I didn't recognize the number on the screen.

"Hello?" I asked, holding the phone to my shoulder as I sat on the bed and zipped up my ankle boots.

"Is this Ember Kearney?" The voice was male, low and gruff.

"This is she. Who's this?" I didn't have the patience to play guessing games.

"You've never met me, but my name is Farthing. I'm calling you because...I'm your grandfather—your father's father. Your grandmother and I want to meet you."

MY GRANDPARENTS?

As the words reverberated through me, I almost dropped the phone. Slowly, I lowered my foot to the floor and cleared my throat. I found myself at a loss for words, unable to form a coherent answer.

"I realize you're probably in shock, but I assure you, this is no joke." He paused, waiting. As I still remained silent, he added, "Ember? Are you there?"

Scrambling to say something—anything—I nodded. Then I realized he couldn't see my head bobbing. "Yes. Yeah, I'm here."

"I know you never thought you'd hear from us, given the situation, but I expect you to give us the courtesy of a meeting." My grandfather's voice took on a tone that reminded me all too much of Blackthorn—he expected respect, and he expected obedience. I decided to be bluntly honest.

"I have no clue how I feel about this. And right now, I'm late for a meeting. Is this your number that you called me from? If so, I'll call you back when I've got more time, and when I've had time to think about this. And when I do call, I'd like to know...*why*? Why do you want to meet me, and why now?"

He was silent for a moment, and I realized he hadn't expected my response.

"I've got to go," I pressed.

"We'll expect your call. Don't wait too long. We have a great deal to discuss." And with that, he hung up.

I let out a long breath, thinking that the day couldn't get any weirder. As I grabbed my jacket and slung my purse over my shoulder, I tried to push thoughts of my grandparents out of my head.

ANGEL WAS WAITING in the lobby with Talia. She handed me a quad-shot mocha and I gratefully accepted it, along with the sandwich she had picked up at the coffee shop.

"You look like you've seen a ghost. What could possibly have happened in the past ten minutes?" She scooted over, making room for me on the ottoman as she pulled one of the side tables closer for me to rest my drink on.

"I think I would have rather seen a ghost." The call had shaken me more than I thought it had. I realized that my voice was trembling and I took a sip of the drink to steady my nerves. "I got a call from somebody claiming to be my paternal grandfather."

"What?" Talia swung around, staring at me. "You're kidding."

"What the hell? They call you *now*? After all this time?" Angel sounded as outraged as I felt.

"No shit, Sherlock. I'm more shocked than you are. He called me to ask if I would meet with him and my grandmother. No, he didn't *ask* me. He *informed* me that they expect me to meet with them. Just like that. I've never met either side of my family. I'm not even sure if they weren't in on my parents' deaths. And now, all of a sudden, they want to meet me?" The more I thought about it, the more agitated I became. "Cripes on a shingle, why the hell would they assume I'd even *want* to hear from them?"

At that moment, Herne, Viktor, and Yutani appeared.

"Them who?" Herne asked as he leaned down to give me a kiss. "Somebody bothering you?"

I shook my head, feeling near tears. "While I was changing, I got a phone call. My grandfather—on my father's side—called me. He and my grandmother want to meet me. No, strike that—they *expect* to meet me." I gazed up at him. Besides Angel, he was the one person who knew how I felt about the Fae that had cast out my parents.

The smile slipped from his face and he crowded onto the sofa next to me, taking my hands. "Ember, are you all right? What did they say?"

I realized I was shaking. I took a deep breath and let it out slowly. Then, as calmly as I could, I told them what Farthing had said. "How do I know it's even him?" But even as I said that, I knew. In my gut, I knew that it had been my grandfather.

"I can ask my father to check up on it for you."

"Or your mother. Morgana might be the better one to ask." I paused, then with a tight shake of the head, decided to change the subject. "I don't want to think about it right now. Let's discuss Straff. Where did you want to go for the conversation?"

"Away from here. Outside will do. It's not raining. There's a corner park near here—we can sit there and talk." Herne gently took my elbow, helping me up. I gathered up my sandwich and coffee, and we all headed outside. Yutani was still bruised up, but he seemed to have stabilized the pain and he allowed Viktor to carry his backpack without any protests.

We headed into the open air, which helped revive me. The sun was bright, and it was a balmy seventy-two degrees. The sky was filled with wispy clouds, but they were high and drifting past at a rapid rate, driven by the wind. We weren't due for rain again for another couple of days, and I welcomed the warmth, letting it slide over me like a golden shroud.

We walked the two blocks to the park—it was called the Seacrest Cove Memorial Park, apparently named in honor of some local naval officers who had died on a mission—and there, we found a picnic table that was unoccupied. The park was filled with mothers and their small children, and I caught sight of one of the women from the Foam Born Encampment. She didn't see us, though, as she chased after twins who were rampaging around the park, having a blast keeping their mother on the run.

We settled at the table. Yutani set up his laptop,

as did Talia, while Angel and I sat cross-legged on the ground. Viktor joined us, and Herne sat opposite Yutani, stretching out his legs as he leaned back against the edge of the table, his elbows propped on the wooden slats. Nobody said anything for a moment as we just let the sun beat down on us, listening to the birdsong and the droning of bumblebees that passed by, darting from clover to clover.

Finally, Herne cleared his throat and turned around, swinging his feet over the bench. He motioned for Angel, Viktor, and me to join them at the table. We slid in—I sat beside Herne, Viktor on his other side, and Angel sat beside Yutani, offering her help with the keyboard if he should need it.

"So here's what happened with Blackthorn," Herne finally said. He ran down our meeting.

"You mean Blackthorn's *son* is the murderer?" Angel asked. "And he gave us permission to do what we needed?"

"I think Blackthorn isn't worried about what happens to Straff. He's disowned him, and when the Ante-Fae put a mark on you like that, it sticks. He's probably got children all over the place that he's forgotten about or cast aside." Herne frowned. "That brings to mind a thought. If Straff has been wining and dining women—like, for example, Chance's wife—could he have children running around the island? Offshoots of the Ante-Fae mixed with human or SubCult blood?"

I shuddered. "That thought's not a pleasant one, given Blackthorn's nature, and what we can ascertain about Straff's nature."

"No, it isn't. But there wouldn't be much we can do about it. It's something to keep an eye out for over the coming years, however. Regarding Astrana...when she stopped us this morning, I wonder if she had an inkling of where we were going." Herne glanced at Viktor. "I wonder if she tailed us."

"I doubt if she could have followed us through the park—not at your speed. And I move pretty quickly too." The half-ogre frowned. "However, we have to assume that she's warned Straff we're onto something. She may not know how much we actually know about the issue, but that doesn't matter. If they think we're close to figuring out it's him, then he might disappear."

"What about her? She might try to vanish, too. What if we apprehend her?" I asked. "Make her tell us where he is?"

"That's an idea, but I'd like to leave that as a last resort. If Straff is watching her and he sees us go after her, chances are he'll vanish, leaving her to take the fall. But we can give it a try. Yutani, do you have any tracking devices with you? Something we could attach to her car?"

Yutani shrugged. "I do. But we should really track her personal car. She probably isn't using the sheriff's car for her personal errands. No doubt, she's smart enough not to draw attention to herself when she goes visiting him."

"Where's she live? Where is this four-million-dollar estate?" I asked.

Talia brought up the address. "Not far from here, actually. It's waterfront property, which makes it no wonder it's so expensive."

Herne's phone rang and he glanced at it, looking surprised. "A moment." He walked away from the table.

"So, who's going to take care of bugging her car?" Talia asked. "You usually take care of this sort of thing and there's no way you can right now."

"It's not rocket science. Ember can do it," Yutani said. "She's quick and she's used to sneaking up on critters from her freelance days."

My freelance days. I hadn't ever really thought about them in those terms, but now I blinked. He was right. I had a lot of experience going solo, and while Herne was good at many things, I was far more adept at creeping around, sneaking up on goblins and the like.

"Yeah, I guess you're right." I heaved out a sigh.

"Well, better you than Viktor. No offense, dude," Yutani said, as the half-ogre snorted. "You're just not quite the stealth-machine Ember is."

"So I'm a stealth-machine now? When did you decide that?" I stuck my tongue out at him.

He laughed. "Since the past few weeks when you've taken on all the legwork Herne assigned to you. I admit it, I wasn't sure when you joined the agency, but you've more than proven yourself and I stand corrected in my opinion of you."

I stopped laughing, uncertain whether I should feel offended or applauded. I hadn't realized that Yutani didn't feel I was up to the job, at least at first. I decided that, for now, I'd ignore the back-handed compliment. At least until we were home and done with this case. Then we'd have a little talk and get things out in the open.

"Okay, then. I know where I stand," I said. My words came out sharper than I intended, because Yutani winced.

"I didn't mean anything by it, Ember. I just... When Viktor came into the agency, I wasn't sure about him, either."

"Right. Well, let's get on with it." I was probably overreacting, but I felt like I had been slapped. Herne returned just then and I welcomed the interruption.

"That was my father on the phone. I gave him the rundown on what we found out. He says we must catch Straff—if possible, alive—and bring him in. We're to take him directly to Cernunnos for judgment." Herne looked troubled. "He specified... alive. If we kill him, the Ante-Fae in general will be on our case about it."

"*Alive*? Pffft." Viktor let out a disgusted sound. "Okay, I knew taking him down would be hard, but catching him? How on earth are we going to do that?"

"That's our job to figure out. Also, Cernunnos congratulated us for meeting with Blackthorn and coming out unscathed." He shrugged. "I gather that doesn't happen all that often."

"We just were talking about having Ember sneak a tracker onto Astrana's vehicle."

Herne nodded. "I wish we could just go ask her about this. Demand answers."

"That's not going to happen and you know it." I was still irritated—first at my grandfather and then at Yutani—but pushed aside my feelings. "However, another thing occurred to me. Would Rayne know where to find Straff? The vampire who talked to Rhiannon? The vamps always seem to have their fingers on the pulse of what's going down."

"Good idea. We need to address all avenues. If Astrana's at work, maybe we can sneak the bug onto her personal car without her knowing. Let's head over to the sheriff's office and see what we can do. I imagine she drives her own car to work." Herne stood. "Where's the device, Yutani?"

"In my room."

"Let's get it while Ember and Viktor head over to the parking lot. Talia, you and Angel stay at the hotel with Yutani. Do what you can to dig up any info on Straff—any mention of him that you can find. Blackthorn wasn't about to tell us much about his son."

We split up. Viktor and I headed toward the parking lot while the others walked back to the hotel. As we leaned against Herne's car, waiting, I decided to broach the subject.

"Was Yutani telling me the truth? You guys didn't trust I was up to the job when I came to work for the Wild Hunt?" It felt like I was picking a scab, but I had to know.

He ducked his head. "I thought you could do it, but yeah, Yutani wasn't all that sure. But you have to understand, Yutani doesn't trust anybody, not until he's had a chance to see them in action. You and I've been betrayed, but he...think about it. He's been pushed away from everybody who's ever been connected to him. He was run out of his village, and the moment anybody finds out that Coyote dogs his heels, they shy away from him if they have a choice. People are afraid of—not him, but what he can unwittingly bring into their lives."

I hadn't thought about it that way. If everybody looked at me with distrust, I'd probably return the favor. "He's very close-mouthed, isn't he? I don't know much about him, even now. Does he have a girlfriend? Does he have a pet? Hell, I didn't even know Talia had dogs until this trip." It occurred to me that Angel and I needed to get to know our coworkers better. "I'm not used to letting people in my life, either. So I guess I just make it my business not to pry into theirs."

Viktor gave me a gentle laugh and clapped me on the shoulder. "Don't sweat it, Ember. Trusting people—friendships—all of these take time to build. As for your questions, no, Yutani doesn't date. He's afraid of getting involved with anyone just in case they feel the backlash of his connection with Coyote. Pets? He has an iguana named Dodo whom he pretends not to care about. But when that lizard got sick, he was at the vet's before they opened. And to fill you in on a few other things, Talia dates around but she never lets herself get serious. I don't think she wants the responsibility. I have a girlfriend and one of these days, I'll introduce you. She's a witch. Human, to a degree, but born of one of the magical families."

As he finished speaking, Herne came jogging our way. I cleared my throat.

"Thanks, Viktor. You've been straight with me from the beginning. I appreciate it."

"No problem," he said. "I think you're an asset to the company. And you make Herne happy. And a happy boss is so much more pleasant than a grumpy one. Trust me, you are so much better for him than Reilly was. None of us liked her."

With that, we fell silent as Herne approached.

"Ready to get this show on the road?" he said.

"Ready and able." I called shotgun and we headed out for the sheriff's office.

Chapter 16

THE SHERIFF'S DEPARTMENT in Seacrest Cove was about as big as you'd expect it to be. That said: the size of a rat's nest. It was tucked in next to the city hall, which was equally small. I wasn't even sure if it was a proper city hall, since Seacrest Cove wasn't really an incorporated community. As we parked in the lot across the street, it occurred to me that I had no clue what kind of car Astrana drove.

The lot itself was laid out with one row cordoned off for the sheriff and her deputies. There, I could see a line of cars, and a couple patrol cars. They were empty, though. The rest of the lot was given over to a mixture of reserved parking and pay-by-the-hour slots. We managed to find an open parking slip, but for the most part, the lot was filled to capacity. I figured a lot of the Seacrest downtown business owners reserved parking here.

"Hey, what are we looking for? And shouldn't I be doing this at night, when there's nobody around to watch?"

Herne shook his head. "She drives a red Jeep. Personalized license plate of ASTRAFAE. As for doing it at night? Well, the parking lot is packed and that alone provides cover. And I don't see anybody here now except us."

I glanced around. He was right, the lot looked to be empty as far as people went, but the cars provided plenty of cover. It wouldn't take me but a couple of minutes to find her Jeep and slap the tracker up underneath the back bumper.

"All right, guard my back, guys."

Before they could speak, I was out of the car and sprinting—trying to keep as low a profile as I ran. I darted around the "Reserved" sign and glanced along the row of cars. Sure enough, there was a red Jeep with a personalized plate. I didn't see a car alarm anywhere, so I darted over to it, rolling to the ground as I went, poked my head beneath the back bumper and slapped the magnetized tracker to the metal beneath the car. It took, and I glanced at the app on my phone as the signal took hold and began to blip out a light on the map. Before anybody could spot me, I slipped back to Herne's side.

"Done. And it's working. What next?"

"Next, we head back to the hotel. Viktor, you'll download the app for the tracker, then take Yutani's car and station yourself to follow Astrana in case she heads out. Ember and I will dig up Rayne and talk to him tonight."

We slipped back into Herne's car before Astrana

could catch sight of us. I texted Viktor the information and he downloaded the surveillance app on his phone. By the time we got back to the hotel, he was ready to grab Yutani's keys and take off. Angel and Talia were scouring the Net for anything they could find on Straff. Yutani was taking a nap. Herne and I took the chance to step outside and talk.

The courtyard of the hotel had rose gardens out back of the coffee shop, with benches and tables for their customers. We stopped to get coffee and then walked out into the warming afternoon, settling down on a bench near a particularly prolific hydrangea whose brilliant blue flower heads were scenting the air.

I leaned back in the chair, closing my eyes as the sun beat down on my face. "Do you think we'll be able to find Straff?"

Herne thought for a moment, then shrugged. "I hope so. I can't say for sure, but we'll do what we can. I put in a call to Rhiannon, asking her where I could find Rayne. She's supposed to call me back in a few minutes. She was on her way home from the hospital today. Madrigal is sticking close to her side. He seems a good sort."

"He is. Just from meeting him once, I'd trust him." As I said the words, I knew they were true. Madrigal had struck me as upright and trustworthy. He'd take care of Rhiannon. "I wonder why the hippocampi would come ashore at all. There are so many issues here, so much that I'd love to escape from."

"I assume they have just as many problems

below the surface. Think about it—life under the waves can get pretty rough. Not all of the water-borne are friendly—in fact, it seems like a lot of them are just waiting to lure victims to a watery grave. The kelpie and the sirens, just to name a couple. They're dangerous and unpredictable."

"Like Blackthorn." I paused, then decided to ask him what was on my mind. "Back there, in his realm... You told him you claimed me. That I'm yours. Was that for show? To make him back off?" I wasn't sure how I felt about the thought, now that we were out of immediate danger.

"Ember, I consider you my girlfriend. My consort at this point. But I don't own you. However, had I not stepped up and put a claim on you, Blackthorn might have pressed his luck in trying to knuckle you under. He was trying to break you, to feed off your worry and insecurities."

"I thought as much. Well, thank you for stopping him. I like being your girlfriend. Consort's an un-usual word for me, but it doesn't make me uneasy. I just... I don't belong to anybody." I smiled at him, reaching out. He took my hand and entwined his fingers through mine. We sat there, in silence, for a few minutes, basking in the warmth.

"Do you really believe Yutani is Coyote's son?"

Herne cleared his throat and folded his hands across his chest as he lounged back in his chair. "I do. But I can't be certain."

"Why would Coyote endanger him? That trap was no laughing matter. It could have dismem-bered him." It didn't make sense to me that Coyote would put his own son in danger.

"Remember, Coyote warned him to be careful. He didn't drive Yutani into the trap. He seems to appear in Yutani's visions whenever there's a crossroads coming that could shift his life into a bad direction. The last time it happened, Yutani almost died. Talia and I jokingly remind him, but behind all the camaraderie, we're deadly serious. He needs to pay attention to the warnings, but I think he takes them as interference." Herne leaned forward, frowning. "I have a feeling one of these days, Coyote's going to show up for real and then Yutani's going to have a lot of reckoning to do."

At that moment, the door to the coffee shop opened and Angel and Talia came back out, Angel carrying two cups and Talia carrying the laptop. They joined us, settling in at the table. Angel handed Talia one of the cups as the harpy logged in and brought up a document of notes.

"You have something for us?" Herne leaned forward, peeking at the screen.

"We do. We found out the location of the vampire." Talia brought up a map of Seacrest Cove. "You see the downtown area? Five blocks from the sheriff's office is a restaurant. The bottom story of the building is Club Majewel. That's Rayne's nightclub. It will be open tonight at 9 P.M. From what I gather, he's almost always there for at least a few hours."

"I guess we get to go clubbing tonight," Herne said, grinning at me. "Did you pack your disco dress and leg warmers?"

I snorted. "Somehow, I have the feeling the vamps aren't into sparkly balls and repeat showings of *Saturday Night Fever*."

"I don't know about their *balls*," Talia cackled. "I've never seen a naked vampire, but they passed the 'alive' stage a long time ago."

"What's the scuttlebutt on the nightclub?" Herne drained the last of his coffee and carried his cup and mine over to the recycling bin.

"The Club Majewel is primarily a vampire club, but a lot of goth-geeks flock there. It's off-limits to werewolves—to most shifters in general, but the Wulfine especially. We all know how well those two groups get along." Talia frowned. "A little bit of background on Rayne. He's an old vamp—relatively old. He was turned in 1888, in New York, and eventually made his way west to the Seattle area. He's established a tidy territory for himself here—he's the Regent claims holder for the San Juan Islands, as well as Whidbey Island. He doesn't hold the keys for Camano Island, though."

"What's his background? Born in America?" I wanted to know as much as I could about who we were getting involved with.

Talia consulted her notes. "Born in New York in 1862, so he was twenty-six when he was turned. Born to an upper-class family. The father was a banker, the mother an heiress. Even though he was turned, it seems his parents accepted the fact that he was now a vampire and they gave him a sizable chunk of the family fortune. My guess is he used his glamour to effect that. They didn't care for Rayne's brother, who decided to make his fortune by helping the poor. Apparently they weren't exactly an altruistic family. So brother George ended up with a small payout before his parents died and was excised from the will. The majority of the money was put into trust for 'Rayne'...a long-lost *cousin*."

"Let me guess. Since they couldn't will the money to a dead man..."

She nodded. "Precisely. Rayne's original name was Winthrop. After he was turned, he changed it to Rayne, and his father set him up with a bank account. He never had to go in to the actual bank because he made arrangements for his personal servant to do so. One of his enthralled victims—a Johan Bates—was his toady for years until the man died. By then, Rayne had established a business and hired accountants. They knew he was a vampire and were very careful never to do anything to make him angry. Apparently he paid well as long as you did the job right."

"So Winthrop got the bulk of his parents' fortune while they were still alive. What happened to the rest?" Herne leaned over Talia's shoulder.

"His parents left it to a small company, which in turn cashed it all in and dissolved the business. There's no proof, but speculation is that Rayne owned that company as well. So he was well-set when he came to this area. He was able to buy his way into the Blood Brothers Elite, which is supposedly a secret vampire society. Not so secret, not anymore. They became the frontrunners as the Vampire Nation emerged from the shadows."

Talia clicked through her files till she came to one shadowy image. "Here's a copy of the daguerreotype taken of him in 1884 when he was twenty-two. It was right when the process became easier and his parents insisted on having photographs of Winthrop—aka Rayne—although I notice they didn't bother paying for one of his brother."

The faded photograph showed a stately-looking young man with longish-black hair, down past his ears, and glittering eyes. Even that young, through the veil of years, he looked like a force to be reckoned with. He had a slight build, but looked anything but fragile.

"So, we have an idea of who we're looking for, at least." I stared at the image. "What's he like?"

"Smart. Ruthless. Over the years his love for money has translated into a desire for power. He runs the nightclub, but he has his investments in a number of places, of course. He's a silent partner in at least twenty different companies, including a weapons company, an organic baby food company, three different restaurants, and several other assorted businesses."

"A baby food company?" I blinked. That seemed odd for a vampire.

"As long as people keep breeding, there will be a need for baby food." Talia shrugged. "Good business sense."

Herne frowned. "He's had a long time to grow financially savvy. What's it take to get into the club? Is it for members only?"

"Nope, though there's a dress code. No jeans. No casual clothing. Ties are optional for men, but sports coat is the least you can get away with." Talia glanced up. "I think you and Ember should do a little shopping if you want to talk to him. Showing up at the door and asking to be let in looking like *that*? Not going to fly. Unless you brought some fancy duds, you'd better get out to the mall right now."

"You're kidding. I don't want to go visit a vampire club." I held up my hands. "I don't like vampires, I don't want to know vampires."

"You're going to meet them tonight. Yutani can't go in, he's a shifter. Viktor probably wouldn't stand a chance in hell in getting in. Angel's human and I don't want her in danger. And Talia..." He paused, blushing.

"I look older, I know. I'd possibly be able to get in if I draped myself in a fur coat and diamonds, but that's not going to happen." She leaned back, shaking her head. "I chose an older form to be anchored into for a reason. People take me more seriously, and frankly, I wanted to be a little invisible in society. And older women are invisible. Nobody notices a grandma—she's not young enough to be fuckable to a lot of guys, and she's not a threat to wives or girlfriends." With a shrug, she added, "It was deliberate on my part."

"You look lovely, Talia. Seriously. But do you ever regret it?"

At that, she laughed. "No. Luckily for me, I don't have the aches and pains associated with age, at least not for humans. I go about my life relatively unnoticed. It works for me, especially after my past and the heartache I went through."

Herne slapped the table, pushing himself to his feet. "All right. Let's get a move on. Come on, Ember, I'm going to buy you a pretty dress." He was grinning. "Whether you like it or not."

Grumbling under my breath, I stood and, slinging my purse over my shoulder, followed him toward the parking lot.

AN HOUR LATER, we were arguing in the closest department store we could find. Herne had found a nice black suit, and a pale green button-down shirt. We were in the women's department now, and I was staring at the racks of dresses. There were a lot of pretty clothes, but not many fit my style.

"What do you want to wear?" he asked.

"Jeans. I guess, though...I have a corset with me—it's black. I can wear that with a nice skirt."

"Or short shorts," he suggested playfully.

I gave him my best *are you kidding me* look. "I'm dressing for this club, not for you."

"I'm sure they wouldn't mind looking at your legs. Though I imagine your neck would be of more interest." The smile vanished as he turned to me. "How much have you had in the way of interaction with the bloodsucker group?"

"Vampires? Not much. The most I've ever talked to them is when Viktor and I met that pair beneath Viaduct Market when we were hunting for Kuveo."

"A nightclub run by a vamp will be far different than a chance encounter. There are certain tells that indicate you're willing to be a blood donor. Wearing a certain type of necklace, for one thing, certain phrases. Anybody walking into a vampire club is usually looking for either an adrenaline rush—kind of like slumming, only more danger-ous—or they're looking to hook up with a vamp. A lot of wannabes searching for a potential sire hang out there."

I cringed. The thought of willingly subjecting myself to being turned into a vampire made me queasy. Very few of the Fae ever went that route, and almost no shifters. It was mainly a human thing—a desire to become more than mortal, to become stronger, more powerful. Although the ro-mance of the vampire still existed, now it was more about longevity and freedom from illness, as well as the ability to accrue a fortune over the years.

"I can't imagine offering myself up for that."

Herne held up an iridescent red skirt with an asymmetrical hem. "This would be pretty with a corset."

I didn't hate it, though I wasn't much into wear-ing red. I held it to my body. It fell to the right length. "All right, I'll try it on."

"As far as offering oneself up to be turned, con-sider—you're Fae. You're at the beginnings of your life. You're what, thirty? That means you have a long, long lifespan ahead of you. If you were thirty and human? Not so much." He hesitated, then added, "It's something you need to think about, especially with your friendship with Angel."

I froze. "What?"

"Remember, you're going to outlive her by po-tentially thousands of years. You have to remem-ber that." His words were soft, but they hit me like a sledgehammer.

I blinked furiously, trying to keep back a sudden wave of tears. "I can't even think about that. I don't want to think about losing her."

"You may not want to think about it, but one day it will happen. And you'll still look like you... while she will be older and tired. Ember, I didn't want to hurt you, but to understand the impetus some of the vampire wannabes face—think of that. Humans have a fragile timeline in this world, and they're usually well aware of that." He handed me the skirt. "Try this on, see how it fits."

As I silently carried it into a fitting room, my heart was racing. I hadn't really thought about it before. Mama J. had died, but she had been killed by a drunk driver. My parents had been murdered. I had lost two boyfriends to the creatures I hunted down before I worked for the Wild Hunt. But losing people to age—that hadn't happened in my world yet.

I tried to shake it off, tried to push it away as I tried on the skirt. It fit perfectly, draping at just the right length. I hated it—oh, it was pretty, but it made me think of blood, which made me think of the vampires, death, and that brought my thoughts back around to Angel.

"She can't die on me," I whispered to my reflection. "I need her in my life." And then it occurred to me that Morgana hadn't always been a goddess, though I wasn't sure just what she had been. She had been turned into a goddess. If it could happen once, it could happen again. There *had* to be some way to extend Angel's life.

But for now, I pushed away the thought. We had business to take care of. Angel and I were young—well, youngish. And since there wasn't anything I could do about the situation now, I decided to re-visit it later. Resolutely steering my thoughts away from the subject, I slipped back into my jeans and carried the skirt out.

"This will work," I said, turning toward the shoe department. But I knew that as soon as the evening was over, I was donating the skirt to a thrift shop. I'd never wear it again.

CLUB MAJEWEL WAS an underground club, literally, beneath a SubCult restaurant that catered to all varieties of shifters, Fae, and other Cryptos. The club had an outside entrance, around to the side, and was very low-key in terms of advertising. From the outside, it could have been a basement entrance to any apartment or private residence. There was an old saying about how old money didn't need to advertise—it was only the nouveau riche who went all out for gaudy representation. In this case, it held true.

The club and restaurant were found on Pirate Cove Road, a side street off the main boulevard that ran through the town. Here, the shops were boutiques, mostly, including a few tourist souve-nir shops. There was quite a lot of foot traffic, but most of the pedestrians seemed headed to one of the cinema complexes across the street. I wished I was over there, about to see *Bad Bitch 3* instead of headed down into the heart of bloodsucker territory.

Herne and I were decked out in our new clothing, and I had done my makeup to match. We parked a block away in the nearest parking lot, and walked to the club. Along the way, heads turned as we passed by—and it didn't take a genius to notice that most of them were appreciative glances. I caught sight of our reflections in a shop window and had to admit, we made a striking couple. Herne was hot to trot in his designer knockoff, and I looked pretty damned good, even if I still thought I'd be giving the skirt away.

"Have you thought about whether you're going to see your grandparents?" he asked as we turned the corner and we came to the Saltwater Cuisine, the restaurant atop the Club Majewel.

I groaned. "Lovely. Yet another subject I really don't want to think about. Can we have one outing where we're not discussing something I really don't want to think about?" I loved hanging with Herne, but today his choice of conversation was sorely lacking.

He coughed. "I guess I'm batting a thousand on the helpful-boyfriend scale today?"

"No, it's not that." I didn't want him to think I was pissed at him. "But right now, we're about to subject ourselves to an evening with a group of people I really don't trust, don't want to know, and am pretty much afraid of. I'd rather focus on the job and save tackling my social quandaries like my friends dying before I'll even remotely hit middle age, and dealing with family I don't want in my life, later."

"Got it. Sticky subjects off the table for now," he said, taking my hand as we approached the entrance. He squeezed my fingers and I flashed him a grateful smile.

The entrance to the club was at the bottom of a wide staircase that led down by the side of the restaurant. At the top, guarding a red velvet rope that was strung across the steps, was a tall black man. He was wearing a designer suit—it was no knock-off, that much we could tell by its cut—and a black hat. He reminded me of one of the Rat Pack members from the old movies of Frank Sinatra, looking suave and yet burly enough to take apart anybody causing trouble.

A line of people stretched around back of the restaurant. Some caught my eye immediately, and I could feel a strong pull coming from them— glamour. They were vamps, no doubt. Others were waiting nervously, whispering together in groups of three or four, and I realized they were fans, hoping to get in.

We took our place in line, waiting quietly behind a woman who was wearing a red dress so tight I could see every curve—and she had plenty of them and they were in the right places. Her shoes were black platform pumps, and her hair was piled high in a blond chignon. Her eyes were dark, glittering and bright, and her lips seemed super-plump, rouged with a bright red lipstick. She gave us the once-over, and smiled slowly, revealing the tips of her fangs.

"Well, what a handsome couple. You're new here?" Her voice was husky, sounding like she had smoked for too many years, but it still drew me in.

Herne gave her a slow nod. "Yes, we are. We're just visiting."

"How lovely. And I love your skirt," she said to me, holding my gaze.

I felt like I wanted to move toward her, to be her friend, and then I realized she was using her glamour on me. The Fae weren't immune to it, even though we had our own brand of glamour, but vamps were very, very good at mesmerizing people. It was innate to their nature.

I shook my head slightly, trying to clear my thoughts. "Thank you," I said, unsure of what to add. I decided to play it safe and leave it at that.

She waited for a moment, then, her eyes lingering on Herne, she turned around to face the front of the line again.

The line was moving, as the bouncer allowed some of the people in. A few groups he turned away, and they stood opposite the club, looking forlorn. I wanted to tell them to go to the movies, go do anything but wait here with wounded egos, but again, decided silence truly was golden.

When the woman in front of us came to the bouncer, she whispered something to him, and I saw her give us a short nod. He nodded back, and—after checking our identification for age—let us through without a word.

We followed her down the steps and into the club.

The inside of the club in no way matched the

dreariness of the outside. Inside, the main room was a swirl of color. They weren't disco balls, but illuminating globes swirled from the ceiling, creating a lightshow as good as any I had seen at a concert. The bar was long and gleaming—chrome and glass and sparkling clean. Behind the bar, three bartenders were fielding a steady flow of drinks. I wrinkled my nose when I realized that a lot of the drinks going out were bottled blood—which again was carded for. They carded for age for alcohol, and to see if the customer was a vampire in order to buy blood.

The noise level was high, with music was playing in the background, and every corner of the room was filled. I spotted one corner booth where two girls—I assumed they were human—were practically hanging on the arms of a vampire. He was dressed to the hilt, but they were barely clothed in sparkling dresses so low cut that the V-necks reached their bellybuttons. I glanced away when I spotted the bloody marks on their necks.

We spotted a small table near the bar and I sat down to claim it as Herne went up to order our drinks. I glanced around, looking for Rayne. The sooner we got this over with, the sooner we could leave.

Herne returned with our drinks. He had ordered a Sazerac for me—cognac, sugar, bitters, and absinthe, and a drink for himself that I didn't recognize.

"What's that? It looks like straight cognac."

"It's a Blood & Sand. Scotch, OJ, cherry brandy." He settled in beside me, sipping the drink.

"May I join you?" The vampire blonde was back, standing beside our table, a bottle of blood in hand. She stared at me, but I felt like she was asking Herne.

I glanced at Herne, uncertain. He motioned for her to take the empty chair next to me.

"Of course. Please, have a seat."

She gracefully slid into the chair, resting her bottle on the table. Bottled blood was mass-produced, usually from animal blood, for vampires to drink when they were mingling with the outer world. The bottles ranged from simple to ornate, but were all colored so that you couldn't see the contents. It sold briskly and new brands were coming out every week, it seemed like.

"Thank you. I'm Christa." She held out her hand to me.

I reluctantly accepted it, her fingers chill to the touch in my hand. I shook her hand, and then she offered her hand to Herne, who also accepted the gesture.

"I'm Herne, and this is Ember, *my girlfriend*." Herne emphasized the "girlfriend" part.

"Nice to meet you both. You're such a striking couple." She paused, then, tilting her head to the side, added, "You said you're new in town? Visiting?"

"Yes, we're here on business, actually." Herne paused, then added, "Do you happen to know Rayne, the owner of this club?"

She bobbed her head, taking a long, slow sip from her drink as she stared at me over the top of the bottle. I felt like she was analyzing every aspect to my appearance.

"Rayne? Yes. He and I go back a ways." She paused. "Did you need to meet him?"

"Yes, actually. I have a few questions I need to ask him."

She let out a soft laugh. "I'm sure you do. You're definitely not tourists. I can tell that just by looking at you, but you're pleasing to the eye, which I also appreciate." Pausing, she glanced around the room. "Rayne will be here shortly. He always puts in a short appearance around ten P.M. or so. Some nights he'll tarry here, others not. I'll make sure to introduce you. Meanwhile, tell me about yourselves. And your...business."

I wasn't sure what was up—she seemed to know more about us than we knew about her, but I decided to let Herne take the lead. He had more experience with vampires than I did, and I didn't want to mess this up.

Herne let out a soft breath and I suddenly realized that Christa hadn't taken a single breath since she sat down. It brought home to me the fact that she really was a vampire. My stomach knotted again as I glanced up to once more find her staring at me. She winked, and I froze.

"I own the Wild Hunt Agency over in Seattle. We...investigate cases and act as a liaison between the Dark and Light Fae, in a manner of speaking." He was choosing his words carefully. I suppose blurting out that he was a demigod wouldn't be considered polite, though I wasn't sure of the actual decorum.

She leaned forward, placing her hand lightly

over mine. "And you, Ember? Are you an investigator, as well?"

I nodded, trying not to yank my hand away. "Yes, actually. I work for Herne."

"Fraternizing with management," she said with a laugh. "Then I hope it works out for the both of you." Suddenly, she craned her neck as she looked out into the crowd. "Rayne's here. I'll go ask him to come over." And without another word, she was off, into the throng of people now populating the club.

I shivered. "She scares me."

Herne nodded. "She's close to Rayne, I'll bet you. Probably his eyes and ears here. Watch what you say in front of her. I think she's attracted to you."

"I think she's attracted to both of us," I said, shutting up as she headed back with a tall, slender man in tow. Even in the dim light, I could tell it was Rayne from the daguerreotype we had seen.

"Herne, Ember, I'd like to you meet Rayne," Christa said, introducing us as he joined us at the table.

As he reached out his hand, I stared at his fingers. They were pale, almost translucent in this light, and I didn't want to touch him. But I gently placed my hand in his. As we shook hands, a stab of fear raced through me.

Rayne stared at me, his eyes glittering with an icy light, and I found myself falling into his gaze. He was ruthless, and cold, and graveyard dust clung to his aura. The night had suddenly been blotted out except for his gaze on my face.

"How do you do, Ember Kearney, and Herne the Hunter. I've been waiting to meet you. I knew you'd find your way to my club. I'm surprised it took you this long."

And with that, I felt totally exposed, and all I could think about was how I wished I had worn a turtleneck, and I hoped to hell Rayne was in a pleasant mood.

Chapter 17

I AVERTED MY eyes, waiting for Herne to speak. The noise from the rest of the room seemed to fade as though it was disappearing into a tunnel as I focused my attention on our table and the two vampires sitting opposite us.

Herne held Rayne's gaze, not showing any sign of nervousness. I knew he was cautious, but he was—after all—a demigod. And demigods didn't have much to fear from vampires.

"We aren't here to interfere with your business. We're seeking information about a case that we are investigating. My father has entrusted us with a task, a vital case, and we need your help, if you can provide it."

"Need my help? What can *I* do for *you*?"

"We know you spoke to a member of the Foam Born Encampment about a murder. You assured her that it was not a vampire kill. I believe you may know more about this than you told her."

"And if we do?"

"I'm looking for the whereabouts of a certain individual belonging to the Ante-Fae."

Rayne didn't answer for a moment. Finally, he crossed his hands on his lap.

"What makes you think that I have any knowledge of the Ante-Fae? They certainly don't have anything to do with me."

Herne shook his head. "I don't believe that you have dealings with this man. Actually, it seems hard to imagine, on either side. But you have lived in Seacrest Cove for quite some time, haven't you? You've watched a lot of people come and go. I don't think it's escaped your notice that there have been a number of murders over the past three or four decades attributed to your kind. Murders that, bluntly put, are in no way associated with the vampire population."

Herne was dancing delicately around the subject. I wondered if he thought that Astrana had her own connections with the vampire community, other than the loan she had taken out from them. But when I thought about it, she wouldn't be in any position to ask favors from them. If anything, it would be the other way around.

"That might be true. Do I take it that you're interested in putting an end to this string of so-called vampire kills?" Rayne looked interested now.

"That seems to be my task at hand," Herne said. "I'll get to the point. I know *who* is behind the murders, and I'm pretty sure you do as well. But finding him is a problem. The one person who has

his ear has a vested interest in protecting him. I'm
not sure what that interest is, but we really don't
want her involved in our plans."

Rayne motioned for a waitress and ordered a
bottle of blood. After she left, he looked directly at
me. "You're awfully quiet over there in your corner, Ember Kearney. Do you have any opinions on
the subject?"

I cleared my throat, stalling for time. Finally,
after glancing at Herne and getting an abrupt nod,
I turned back to Rayne.

"I just work for the Wild Hunt. But...I'd hate
to see these murders continue. I don't like seeing
crimes swept under the rug and attributed to the
wrong people."

Rayne leaned forward, staring at me. "It must be
difficult, given the unsolved murders in your own
history." He didn't wait for me to react before he
continued. "Oh, yes, I know who you are. I keep
tabs on everybody who makes waves in this region.
It's part of my job as Regent. And trust me, you
have made waves here. Your entire team."

"No doubt," I said, my throat dry.

A faint smile fluttered across his face. "I know
that none of you are well loved by the sheriff.
You're treading on thin ice, at least as far as our
beloved law enforcement is concerned. However,
given the backgrounds involved, I doubt if Névé
would entertain any complaints, even if her court
doesn't take kindly to those whose very existence
insults their senses."

The words began to spin around my head. It felt
as though we were talking all around the edges of

the situation. Which, I supposed, we were. I admired Herne's ability to approach matters like this. I was never very diplomatic, and as much as I was trying to learn, I had a long ways to go. If I had been Herne, I would have slapped my cards down on the table. And *that* would have probably gotten us nowhere.

"I see you understand the situation," Herne said. "So, again, I'm looking for the presence of one of the Ante-Fae. And I'm not talking about the King of Thorns."

Rayne waved a hand in his direction. "That much I know. I've had a few conversations with his thorny lordship. Let's just say that I keep to my lane, and I leave his lane alone. Not much frightens a vampire, but I can guarantee you, I do my best to keep away from the King of Thorns and his...pleasures." He paused, accepting the bottle of blood from the waitress when she returned. Herne and I shook our heads when she asked if we wanted refills.

After another moment, Rayne seem to have made up his mind.

"Very well. Now, mind you, I'm not certain if he still lives there, but the last known whereabouts of the man you seek...look for a now-closed boat shop near the state park."

"Whitaker's Old-Time Boat Rides," Christa said, recoiling as Rayne gave her a sharp look.

"When I need your tongue, I'll ask for it."

"Yes, sire." Christa sat back meekly, staring at her hands in her lap. The glamour around her vanished in a wash of fear.

"Christa spoke out of turn, but she's correct. The shop is closed, but it's still there, boarded up. I believe you may find who you're looking for there. I've been tracking these murders through the years. But I have kept quiet because our fair sheriff thought to warn me that, if I brought them to anyone's attention, she would make certain I was implicated. Given her resources, I decided to remain silent."

Herne let out a long breath, sitting back. "Thank you. If we can put this to rest then you will be free from any suspicion. We owe you a debt for this information."

I caught my breath. Herne didn't indebt himself easily. It was more than just lip service in the world we ran in.

Rayne let out a soft laugh. "Herne, son of Cernunnos, if you can put this to rest, *we* will owe *you* a debt. And the Vampire Nation always pays its bills."

With that, he stood and threaded his way back through the crowd.

Christa slowly stood, regaining her poise. "I assume that you're leaving now?"

Herne nodded.

She leaned across the table, her low-cut dress leaving nothing to the imagination. "Then, please remember. If you ever want to return for entertainment, I would be delighted to play your hostess. Either one of you, or both of you together." And with that, she wiggled her way across the floor, catching every eye as she vanished into the throng.

Herne gave me a long look, then shrugged, laughing. He reached out his hand. "Come on, let's get back to the hotel. Somehow, I don't think this is our scene."

Grateful to be leaving, I took his hand and we maneuvered our way toward the door, then back to the car. I leaned against the seat, breathing deeply, relieved to be out of the Club Majewel.

ON THE WAY back to the hotel, Viktor texted us. SHE'S ON THE MOVE. I'M FOLLOWING.

I texted back: IS SHE IN HER JEEP?

YES. SHE LEFT THE SHERIFF'S OFFICE AN HOUR AGO. I FOLLOWED HER HOME. SHE APPEARS TO BE HEADING TOWARD THE STATE PARK.

I glanced at Herne. "Ten to one she's headed toward that boat shop."

"You're probably right. Tell Viktor what we learned at the club. We don't want him stumbling in there without knowing what he's getting himself into. He may be half-ogre, but alone, he's still no match for one of the Ante-Fae."

I started to text Viktor, but realized there was too much to text. Instead, I called his cell phone.

"You're on speaker. I'm alone in the car. What have you got for me?"

I ran down everything that had happened at the club, including the location of Whitaker's Old-Time Boat Rides.

"Rayne was pretty sure that that is the last known location for Straff. So if you get there first, don't just barge in." I glanced at Herne. "Are we on the way?"

He nodded. "I'd like to go back and get some weapons, but we can't spare the time. There's a good chance Astrana is out to warn Straff to get out of town."

I returned to the phone. "We're on the way. When you get there, keep a close eye out. We think Astrana may be warning Straff that we're on to him. My guess is she had someone watching us in the woods and saw us vanish into Blackthorn's realm."

I hung up as Herne sped up. We were zipping along, and I was grateful that it wasn't raining. The night was about sixty-one degrees, and the stars wheeled overhead in a dizzying array, unclouded by light pollution. I stared out the window as the car ate up the asphalt. A streak through the heavens caught my attention. I watched as a shooting star flamed across the sky, then faded toward the horizon.

"Rayne didn't seem like a bad sort," I said.

"For a vampire, he was pretty cordial. Actually, vampires are far more charming than people give them credit for. It's much easier to get what you want when you set out a little honey. What did you think of Christa?" There was a hint of laughter in Herne's voice.

"I think Christa takes her social life seriously. And by social life, I mean sex life. Though I'm not certain whether she was asking us to donate blood, or join her for an orgy."

"Oh, I'm pretty certain it was both. She was ready to jump our bones in a ménage à trois." He glanced at me, quickly returning his eyes to the road. "Interested?"

A lump rose in the pit of my stomach. Christa was a hell of a lot more polished than I was. In fact, she reminded me a lot of Herne's last girl-friend—Reilly.

"Not really. She's not exactly my type." I paused, then, not really wanting to hear the answer, asked, "What about *you*? Do you want to take her up on her offer?"

I knew some of the gods were horndogs, but I wasn't certain about Herne. So far, he had seemed fairly happy being in an exclusive relationship.

As for myself, I had never had the opportunity to experience an open relationship and I wasn't certain I wanted to try even if it was offered. It was hard enough dealing with one partner, let alone two or more. I loved sex, and when I thought about it, I wasn't averse to the idea of taking a female lover, but it wasn't something I was going to do just for the hell of it. For me, taking *any* lover meant I wanted to feel some sort of connection with them.

"Are you joking?" He laughed, then suddenly sobered. "You aren't, are you? You didn't think I was *serious*, did you?"

I wanted to laugh it off, but decided to be honest.

"I'm not really sure, to tell you the truth. *I don't know.* I mean, look at your last girlfriend. Reilly's gorgeous. She could be a sex goddess if she was deified. And I'm not saying I'm ugly, either. I know I can be hot if I try. But... I'm not exactly..." I drifted off, uncertain of where I was going with this conversation, and wishing I had never started it.

Herne shifted gears, taking a left on Shoreline Drive, which led to the abandoned boat shop. He didn't speak for a moment before he finally let out a long sigh.

"Reilly is absolutely stunning. But you do know why I ended the relationship, right?"

"I think so," I said, not wanting to admit I'd pried the info out of Talia and the others.

"I like my women grounded and smart. I prefer one-on-one relationships. I'm not exactly a monogamist, but I like getting to know my partners and it's difficult to do when your attention is divided between several lovers."

"Oh," I said, still not clear on what he meant.

"Damn it, Ember. You're smart, and you're sexy as hell. I love that you don't hold back, either in life or in work. Whereas toying with someone like Christa might be fun for a night, but that's about it." He was starting to talk circles around himself now, and I realized he was just as nervous as I was.

"In other words, she's good for a quick fuck but you wouldn't want to hang out with her?" Sometimes being blunt helped to clarify matters.

"Yeah, you could put it that way." He paused, then added, "Damn it, I just like you, Ember. A lot." He cleared his throat. "We have to talk about Straff. If he's there, Astrana's probably going to be with him. She may not be one of the Ante-Fae, but she's dangerous and she has a gun. Bullets won't affect me much, but they can damage you. We have to decide how to tackle this."

I switched gears. "Did your father give you *any* idea of how to take Straff down without killing him? And what if we can't manage it? What if we have to kill him?"

"Then all hell will break loose. Oh, we could stumble our way through it, but it would be a lot of damage control. Sometimes it's just so much easier when you can take out your opponent without worrying about fallout. But there are so many political ramifications involved in this situation."

I watched the houses pass by in a blur as we were approaching the state park. We'd be to Whitaker's Old-Time Boat Rides in no time.

"Do the Ante-Fae have a court like the Light and Dark Fae courts? I mean, suppose we do kill Straff? Would we then face his father? Or is there some council of Ante-Fae that we have to worry about? There's so much I don't know."

"To answer your questions: the Ante-Fae do *not* have a cohesive legal or social system like the Light and Dark do. However, if we kill Straff, even if his father doesn't care, other Ante-Fae will hear about it and will be far less likely to help us in the future. Some of them may even come after us, feeling we are a threat to them. It's much harder when you're dealing with rogue elements than when you're dealing with an organized agency. That's one thing I've learned over the years."

"So how do we take him into custody?"

"We have to subdue him. Be cautious. I have the

feeling he's inherited some of his father's abilities. Those puncture wounds on all of the bodies? Did you notice Blackthorn's fingernails? They look like the spikes on a blackthorn tree. My guess is that Straff has the same trait. I'm speculating here, but I have a feeling that he can transfer energy to himself through those thorns, while injecting poison into his victims."

That set me to shivering. "All right then, make a note of that: Watch Straff's fingernails. Anything else that you think you might have?"

Herne shrugged. "Nope. While we have tabs on a number of the ancient Ante-Fae, we don't have a lot of information on all of their children. And I believe that Straff is a relative newborn. If his mother had a wasting disease that required her to feed off of others, then Straff has probably had this his whole life. His father seemed clear that Straff was a youngster and rebellious."

Herne stopped as he nodded up ahead. "There, to the left."

I looked at where he was nodding. Across the road, and a turnout away from the shore, there was an old building. A large sign read Whitaker's Old-Time Boat Rides. The building was covered in boards, but I could see lights flickering from within, and sure enough, Astrana's Jeep was parked right beside it. I wondered that nobody had ever reported squatters to Astrana. But what if they had? She knew who was there. She would probably have reassured any tattletales that nothing was wrong, and to go on their way.

Herne parked along the shoulder of the road.

Up ahead, I spied Yutani's car. I texted Viktor that we were there. He slipped out of the driver's seat, shutting the door and walking back to where we were parked.

"I see you finally got here. So you think that Straff is in there?" He leaned down, resting his elbows on the driver's side window.

Herne nodded. "Did she make any stops along the way?"

"No. Everything was quiet at the sheriff's office until she came racing out of there, and I do mean racing. She beat a path straight to her Jeep and almost took out another car in her haste to get out of that parking lot. It's a good thing I got there when I did or I would have missed her. By the way, the tracker on her Jeep works like a charm." Viktor glanced up the road at the boarded-up building. "I wonder what tipped her off?"

"Could Rayne have called her? Why would he have a reason to?" The thought that we had been double-crossed played through my mind.

"He wouldn't have done so in order to help her. I wonder...she owes the Vampire Nation World-wide Bank a large debt. What if he mentioned to someone on the bank's board that she had become a security risk? Could they have called her loan so quickly?" Herne furrowed his brow.

"I doubt if they would have acted quite so quickly. It's in the Vampire Nation's best interests for us to catch Straff and expose him for what he is. I'm pretty sure that, even though she still owes them three and a half million dollars, that's a drop in the bucket to the likes of their kind." I shook my head.

"No, something else set her off. I'd like to know what, but we can leave that for later. We'd better get in there if we want to stand a chance in hell of catching Straff before he vanishes."

We slipped out of the car. Herne paused to arm himself with a handheld crossbow as well as his sword. Weapons ready, we skirted the side of the road, trying to keep in the shadows of the trees. Ahead the building loomed, backed up against an embankment. Across the road, there was a faded sign that I imagined had, at one time, pointed the way down to the cove for the patrons seeking an "old-time boat ride." Briefly, a thought flickered through my head as to exactly how an old-time boat ride differed from a modern one, but I shook it away. This wasn't the time to let myself get distracted. I wished we had Yutani with us—the coyote shifter was handy in altercations and he had a bit of magic tucked away that proved itself useful.

As we neared the building, I squinted. In the light of the waning crescent overhead, I could tell only that the siding was weathered and peeling, and the boards that had been tacked over the windows and doors were nailed haphazardly, as though someone had just wanted to get the job done and it didn't matter to them how it looked. From the front, it was hard to see if there was any other entrance.

Herne motioned for us to follow him and we skirted around the back. There, we found the answer. There had to be a basement—because we saw a stairwell leading down to what I assumed was a door. There was also an exit on the ground

level, but that too was shuttered by long planks
and nails. Herne edged toward the stairs. He
held out a small flashlight, then covered it with a
handkerchief before turning it on. The light was
muted. If anybody was watching us, they would
have noticed, but he trained it on the ground so it
didn't flicker across any of the openings between
the planks.

Slowly, we descended the steps, Herne first. I
went second, and Viktor brought up the rear. The
staircase was made of concrete, the steps broken and crumbling in places. Grass was growing
through the cracks, and moss, and the railing was
iron. I found that out the hard way. I reached out
to steady myself and as I touched the railing, a jolt
of bone-deep pain raced through me and my stomach lurched. I reeled back, yanking my hand away.

"Fuck," I blurted out before I could stop myself
as Viktor steadied me.

Herne swung around, aiming the light at my
hands. My left hand now matched my left wrist in
terms of damage—my palm had blistered up and
now I guessed it had turned bright red. I averted
my eyes. I wasn't squeamish, but if I couldn't see
how bad it looked, then I might be able to ignore
the pain.

Viktor fumbled in his pocket and brought out
his own handkerchief, which he tied around my
palm. I hoped to hell he hadn't blown his nose on
it. Then, clasping Herne's shoulder for balance, I
nodded that I was ready and once again, we headed down the steps.

As we approached the bottom, the flashlight

showed the faint outline of a door. No boards, so this was probably where Straff was gaining entrance. We paused long enough to draw our weapons before Herne tried the door and the knob turned. He eased the door open, then peeked inside. A second later, he motioned for Viktor and me to follow him in.

The room was dimly lit by what appeared to be battery-operated candles. Of course, the electricity would be turned off, I thought. The shop had been closed for some time.

It appeared to be a storeroom, with old boxes and crates sitting around, and a desk and chair against one wall. Then we saw a bed against another wall, and a bottle of wine on the desk, along with a glass. A piece of rope hung over a nail on the wall, and Herne grabbed it. Here and there, tendrils of ivy and brambles had encroached from the basement windows, and they were busy growing into a tangle to cover the walls.

Herne nodded to the opposite side of the room. Another staircase led up, into the building proper, and we could hear voices echoing down. I recognized Astrana's voice from when she had stopped Herne and me, while the other voice was male. They appeared to be arguing, judging by the tone and pitch of their words.

"You have to get out of here. It isn't safe for you, and because of you, my position has become tenuous. That damned godlet is determined to put a stop to your feeding." Astrana sounded frantic. "I can't hide you any longer."

"You aren't going to betray me." The voice was

smooth like silk, but threatening in a way that I couldn't pinpoint. But I could hear the deliberation behind it, and it jarred my nerves.

"I don't have any intention of it, but you can't expect to continue on, business as usual, now that they know what's happening." Astrana paused. "If that damned Rhiannon hadn't set them on track, everything would be fine. But they're onto you, and I don't want to have to turn you over to them just to save my own skin."

There was a tense pause, and it occurred to me that she could have just signed her death warrant. Astrana might be smart, but her panic had clouded her judgment.

Herne readied his crossbow and began to creep up the stairs, motioning for us to follow. Grateful that, although I was left handed, I could use my blade with my right, I checked the railing before touching it this time. It was wood. I used my fingers to steady myself—gripping anything with my blistered hand would hurt like a son of a bitch—and followed him. Viktor brought up the rear, amazing me once again by how quiet such a large man could be.

As we neared the top, the growing illumination made it easier to see. The door to the basement was open, and whatever lights Straff was using were bright enough to show us up the minute we hit the top of the stairs. We'd be visible in seconds. Herne seemed to realize this as well. He paused, then gave us a nod, and ran up the last three stairs, charging out into the main room. I didn't think, just followed suit. Viktor was hot on my heels.

We burst into the room and froze. Brambles and ivy twined through the room like some monstrous plant creature, covering walls and part of the floor. In the center of the room was a long narrow table covered with dried blood, and I had the sudden feeling of being inside a thorny bird's nest. A serial-killer bird's nest.

As Herne took aim at Straff, Astrana turned to stare at us. Sitting on the counter beside her, with an expression that bordered on murderous, was a tall man who reminded me of a young version of Blackthorn. Straff had the same markings as his father on his body. He was dressed in a pair of dark jeans and what looked like an expensive sports coat, and his hair tumbled down his shoulders in a cloud of raven black.

When he saw us, the markings vanished and he suddenly looked nothing more than a tall, elegant human with fingernails that looked like spikes. I blinked, but then shook off the surprise.

Before we could approach him, he grabbed Astrana, pulling her to him with his arm around her waist. With his other hand, he toyed with her throat, stroking the flesh with those long, sharp thorns.

"One step closer and she dies." Straff's eyes glittered, as though he were almost enjoying the scene. "Shoot me, and you shoot her."

Still holding his bow aimed at Straff, Herne held up his other hand. Viktor and I skidded to a halt. We stood there, in a standoff.

"Let her go. Come with us and we won't hurt you. In the name of Cernunnos, Lord of the Hunt,

I'm here to apprehend you, Straff, son of Black-thorn."

"Call me the 'Prince of Thorns,' " Straff said, scraping Astrana's throat with one of his nails.

She gasped. "What are you doing? Let me go. I'm on your side." She sounded almost offended and I almost snorted.

"Do you really believe you mean anything to me, Astrana? You're a means to an end, my dear," Straff said. "And your usefulness is obviously over and done with." He glanced up at Herne. "Why should I come with you? Your father holds no covenant with the Ante-Fae. When my father hears about this—"

"*Your* father gave us permission to kill you, if need be." Herne stiffened. "And quite frankly, given the nature of her crimes, if you want to use Astrana as a pincushion, be my guest. I'm not going to stop you, but your threats won't buy you an escape."

Astrana let out a hiss and, without warning, jabbed Straff in the stomach. She must have put muscle into it, because he abruptly let go of her, and she darted out of reach. She pulled out a gun, which she trained on me.

"It appears we're at an impasse," she said. "You can shoot Straff, but you come at me and the trala-eth eats it."

I froze, staring at the handgun. Bullets might not do a lot to Herne, but they could damage me, and probably Viktor as well.

Herne gave her a slow nod. "Make no sudden decisions, Astrana. I'm not after you." His voice was gentle, but I noticed that he was eyeing the walls. Then, I saw one of the brambles behind her rising up. I quickly looked away, not wanting to give her any hint of what Herne was planning—at least, I thought it was Herne, because it could have been Straff as well.

Straff's expression flickered from murderous to amused, but he just leaned against the counter, waiting.

"Now," Herne said with a slow breath, and the bramble whipped around Astrana. I leapt to the side as she squeezed the trigger. The bullet sailed past where I had been standing, but she dropped the gun as the thorn-covered vine dug into her skin, wrapping her tight. She began to swear in what I assumed was a dialect of Light Fae.

Straff cleared his throat. "Now that *that* little matter is taken care of, you do realize that we are evenly matched. Your arrow might hit me, but you must be aware that I can command these vines as well as you. The fight would be a standoff."

Herne shook his head, still holding his aim. "I can't let you go."

"Then you'll have to kill me. Because I'm not turning myself over to you. I enjoy my freedom far too much." Straff jumped up on the counter as a large cane from the thicket of brambles lashed out, aiming for me. I saw it coming, and leaped to the side again, swearing as I rolled hard on my blade, cutting my leg a little in the process.

Viktor lunged forward, aiming for Straff. He swung his sword toward Straff's leg, aiming to disable him, but Straff was lithe and quick, and he leaped atop the counter, out of the way. Herne held up one arm and his voice thundered as he shouted, "Rise!"

The ivy vines shot forward, aiming toward Straff, and as they wrapped around his left arm and leg, they took on a dark green glow, looking for all the world like rope instead of vegetation. They stiffened, holding him tight. He barked something at them, but they didn't budge. I suddenly realized that, while Straff could control the thorns, he couldn't control plants that were thornless.

Astrana struggled, screaming epitaphs at...well... everybody.

Straff let out a bellow, then another command and the entire nest of brambles began to move and twine around us, edging in.

"Silence him!" Herne held out a hand, aiming for the writhing mass of canes that twisted and writhed. "He can still control the brambles and I can hold him off, but he's strong."

"How about you just shoot him?" Viktor lunged toward the counter where Straff was standing captive, but one of the nearby brambles shot out and wrapped around his leg, digging in. Viktor shouted, bringing his sword down as he hacked against the canes. The room was covered with them. They slithered like massive snakes to fill every surface of the empty floor.

I gauged the distance between Viktor and Straff. Viktor was close enough that, if I used him for leverage, I could leap the distance between the two.

"Hold still," I shouted at Viktor. He glanced at me, puzzled, but froze. I made a running jump

toward him, landing on his back. He seemed to understand what I was doing, because he let go of his
blade, reaching up to steady me as I rose to stand
on his shoulders.

Straff started to say something, but Herne
shouted "Gag" and a large tendril of ivy wrapped
around Straff's mouth, thrusting itself down his
throat.

As the Ante-Fae struggled, trying to tear the
vines out of his mouth with his free hand, I sucked
in a deep breath and leaped to the counter. Landing precariously atop the old cash register, I tried
to balance.

Straff ripped at the ivy that Herne was trying to
shove down his throat.

As I steadied myself, a flicker in the back of my
mind took hold. I had learned a few odd spells
here and there over the past few months of working with Morgana, and now, one stood out in my
mind. I didn't know if it would work, but I began
to whisper the conjuration.

Rise, mist, I conjure thee.
Every drop from every tree,
From every bramble, save ivy vine,
Collect and rise, mist of mine.

A mist began to rise from the floor as some of
the canes lost their color. They were drying out,
the moisture sucked out of them, as the mist col-
lected it. The fog filtered over the brambles, leaving the ivy alone, pulling the moisture from the
canes and leaving them dry and lifeless as I fo-

cused my will on it.

I was getting ready to bind up Straff when laughter echoed from the corner of the room.

The brambles holding Astrana had fallen to the side.

Shit. I hadn't thought of that.

She was free and had pulled out a dagger, and now, she sent it flying through the air. I realized it was coming toward me too late. The blade bit deep into my leg and I stumbled, losing my concentration as I fell into a pile of brambles. The mist evaporated and they took life once more, trussing me up like a turkey, their jagged thorns coming dangerously close to my face.

Chapter 18

I LET OUT a scream as the canes whipped dangerously close to my face, and I shut my eyes although I knew that wouldn't stop them from blinding me. As the thorns bit deep, I focused on how to get free. Struggling only made it worse, so I forced myself to stop moving. The canes held me fast, but they stopped digging into my skin.

I chanced opening my eyes. From where I was lying, I could see Herne. His eyes were glowing with a dangerously brilliant light—a yellowish green that mirrored the sparkle of peridot. The next moment, he let out a roar.

"Wrong move." He raised his bow and pulled the trigger. The arrow sang straight and true, lodging deep in Astrana's chest. She froze for a second, then toppled into the writhing canes. Then, turning to Straff, Herne called out, "Fire!"

A blaze started, burning along the ivy as it traveled toward Straff's face. He screeched around the vines that were filling his mouth, and the canes holding me suddenly loosened. Viktor was freed as well and he lunged toward the counter.

Straff was frantically trying to beat out the flames traveling up the wick of vegetation. Viktor reached his side and roughly yanked him down, throwing him onto the floor, where he promptly knelt on Straff's back. The fire died away as Viktor bound Straff's arms behind his back with the piece of rope that Herne threw to him, hog-tying the Ante-Fae.

Herne gently lifted me out of the pile of canes, setting me atop the counter. Then he pulled out a small vial from his pocket and squeezed Straff's nose until the Ante-Fae gasped for air. The moment Straff opened his mouth, Herne poured the contents of the vial down his throat and Straff immediately slumped to the side, unconscious.

"That will hold him till we get him back to my father," Herne said.

Viktor crossed to Astrana, kneeling. "She's dead."

"Of course. My aim almost always hits true." Herne sounded so casual that it made me wince, but then I remembered that the woman had not only shot at me, but tried to stab me as well. She had been ruthless and the world was better off without her in it.

I glanced around. "What next?"

"We take this freak back to Cernunnos. And then, damage control." Herne paused, stopping to pat down Straff. He pulled a wallet out of his pocket. "Hmm, didn't Rosetta say a man named 'Roland' called her editor?"

I nodded. "Yeah."

He tossed the wallet to me, There was a driver's license inside that read "Roland Straff."

"That answers that. Any bets that the man Chance's wife was fucking went by the same name?" Herne laughed roughly. "I'll bet she never saw the inside of *this* place."

"What's with his stripes? The markings?" I asked, watching as the markings slowly reappeared on the unconscious Ante-Fae.

"My bets are that Blackthorn can do the same. Many of the Ante-Fae have ways of altering their appearance. It's part of their glamour, though I imagine some aspects are almost involuntary. You have Fae glamour, though you don't know how to use it. *Yet*." Herne looked at me. "The Ante-Fae have far stronger abilities in altering their appearances. Viktor, will you carry Astrana's body? We need to take her with us. I'm going to call John and ask him to get the portal ready. You'll both need to come with me. I can't manage Straff and a corpse."

Viktor obligingly slung Astrana's body over his shoulder.

I glanced around the room. "Is there anything we need to take?"

"No. I'm going to call Talia and have her and Angel come out here to search the place before the clean-up crew comes in. I'll tell all of the vines to retreat." He closed his eyes, holding out his hands toward the mass of canes and ivy. The next moment, the vegetation began beating a hasty retreat. I turned to head back downstairs, but Viktor yanked open the front door and busted through the boards on the front of the building. We exited into the night, bruised, scratched up from the thorns, and more than a little battered, but with our quarry.

THE TRIP THROUGH the portal went smooth-ly, and on the other side, Trospos was waiting for us with specially made handcuffs, ankle-cuffs, and a ball-gag. Straff was just beginning to wake as we bound and gagged him. He struggled briefly, but gave up as the shackles seemed to drain his en-ergy. He shot a vicious look toward us, but the gag prevented him from speaking as two of the Elves carried him ahead of us.

This time, the journey went quicker. We went through a different route that was lined by mem-bers of Cernunnos's court. They bowed deeply as Herne passed through their ranks, but he took no notice as he strode along in front of Viktor and me, all business. There was now something autocratic about him, reminding me of his father. He was Cernunnos's son, all right.

We passed through the brightly lit hallways, with everyone making way as we passed through. The polished wooden floors of the tree palace gleamed so brightly I could see our reflections in them as we marched along, and I focused on that, feeling awkward and all-too conspicuous.

In the throne room, Cernunnos waited. He was sitting atop his throne, leaning forward as Trospos motioned for the Elves to place the prisoner before him. Another Elf, who had taken Astrana's body from Viktor, laid her out beside Straff. Cernunnos motioned for everyone else to back away as we neared the throne.

"Well met, Ember and Viktor. I see you've managed the capture, my son?" Cernunnos rose, descending the steps of the throne to peer into Straff's face. He towered over the lanky Ante-Fae, and as he stared at Straff, he let out a derisive laugh. "I've spoken to your father. He gives me leave to do with you as I will." He motioned for one of the Elves to remove Straff's gag. "Do you have anything to say for yourself?"

"*Hypocrite.* You can't tell me you've never toyed with humans for your own pleasure. I did so for my life, rather than out of fun." Straff spit out the words, his eyes narrowing. "But you have me, and you have my father's permission. Be done with it. What is your will?"

"I toy with humans as I will, but not for perverted amusement. You fed on their pain and torture, as well as their life force and blood. That I will *never* do," Cernunnos said, wrinkling his nose as though he smelled something disgusting. He let out a sigh. "Is there *any* hope you might reform yourself? I do not wish to be at odds with the Ante-Fae."

I blinked. Could Straff simply say yes and get away with everything? But I should have known it wasn't that simple.

The Ante-Fae was sweating now, and he blinked furiously. "You know I cannot lie to you, Lord of the Hunt. Not with the spells you've woven so heavily around yourself. Reform? Why should I? I take my pleasure with my need. I must feed and I let myself enjoy the process. I won't lie about my nature. I inherited it from my father, you know."

I stepped back. The energy was growing heavier as it spun a vortex, a mire of anger and hatred and delight in all things savage and painful.

Straff laughed. "I expect no better from *him*, though. The King of Thorns is the king of treachery. If he were weak enough to plead my case to you, I would lose all respect for him. Do as you will. I will bathe in your fires and emerge stronger and brighter. Unless you kill me, you will never triumph over me."

Cernunnos returned to his throne and took up his oaken spear. He pointed it at Straff. The tip glittered wickedly, sharpened to a keen point.

"Hear my decree. Straff, Prince of Thorns, son of Blackthorn, King of Thorns. My command is that you be incarcerated in the deepest lair of my dungeons until such time that I deem you worthy of being set free. By the power of Oak and Ash and Thorn, so I do ordain." As Cernunnos spoke, the air in the room grew even thicker. It felt like sparks were arcing along my arms. A thunderclap rippled through the air, echoing around the chamber.

As the reverberation faded, Cernunnos motioned to Trospos, who hurriedly set three of the Elves to take away Straff. The Ante-Fae slumped as they affixed a collar of iron around his neck. He let out a moan as they dragged him off.

"*Iron*? How long will he wear the collar?" I couldn't imagine someone draping an iron collar around my neck. The pain and discomfort would be constant.

"As long as he stays in my dungeons," Cernunnos said, and I heard the warning in his voice.

Never question a god when his mind is made up.

"As to the dead Fae...I will speak with Névé. Leave the body here." Cernunnos's gaze flickered over the three of us, but today there was none of the gracious manner that had greeted me the last time. The god seemed impatient for us to leave.

Herne read his father better than anybody, I thought.

He bowed low. "We will return home, if you give us leave."

"Yes, you must leave. I've much on my mind and need peace in order to think. Go home, and make no mention of this to anyone until I've thought through matters. There will be ramifications from imprisoning Straff, but they shouldn't be as great as if you had killed him."

"What about the victims' families? Should we..." My words trailed off as Cernunnos turned back to me, his expression so stern that I bit my tongue in an attempt to turn invisible.

"Did you not hear what I just said? *Say nothing.* You may go." And with the wave of his hand, he dismissed us.

Herne grabbed my elbow and quickly turned me around. Viktor was right on our heels as we exited the throne room. We said nothing until we were back at the portal, and crossing back into John's yard.

"CRAP. I BLEW it, didn't I? Will he forgive me for speaking out of turn?" I turned to Herne as we stumbled back through the scarlet oaks.

"No worries." Herne let out a long sigh. "He'll forget all about it. Probably. He has something on his mind, but I can tell that he's not ready to talk about it. But next time you meet him and he's in one of his moods, just keep quiet. It just makes matters so much simpler." He kissed me on the forehead. "How are you both feeling?"

"It's nearly four in the morning, we just got the crap beat out of us by a bunch of bloodthirsty blackberry bushes, and I don't know about Viktor, but *I* feel like a pincushion. That good enough?" My tone was sharper than I meant it to be, but I was feeling unnerved.

Herne stared at me for a moment, then shook his head. "I guess I deserve that. Come on, let's get back to the hotel." He put in a quick call to Talia, then motioned to his car. We had driven together so that Viktor could hold Straff down in the back-seat, should the Ante-Fae have woken up. "We need to stop by the building to pick up Yutani's car, but after that, back to our rooms and some much-needed rest."

Rest we got. The moment we reached the hotel,

Talia and Angel took over, helping Viktor and me doctor our wounds from the bramble canes. They also had sandwiches and hot cocoa for us, and as soon as we ate, we all staggered to our rooms and passed out. Everything else could wait for morning to sort out.

HERNE LET US sleep in. But promptly at nine, he knocked on our door. Angel had woken me up fifteen minutes earlier and I was brushing my wet hair back into a ponytail to dry. I had dressed in a pair of shorts, which showed off all the nifty bruises and cuts on my legs, and a tank top, hoping for an easier day.

"Breakfast awaits in the dining room, ladies. Talia's ordering for all of us. And my father called me this morning." He stopped, staring at me. "You're so beautiful."

"I'll meet you downstairs," Angel said, leaving us alone as she closed the door behind her.

I ducked my head. "I'm covered with scratches and cuts from thorny plants and bruises. And I don't have my makeup on yet."

"Do you really think that makes you any less beautiful to me? *Any of that*?" He sauntered over, wearing a pair of black leather pants and a muscle shirt that showed every lovely curve of his biceps. His ass looked pretty good, too. He leaned against me, taking me in his arms as he nuzzled my neck.

"You know it's wrong when your boyfriend looks

prettier than you do," I whispered, pressing one hand on his chest.

He brushed my hair back from my face, kissing my forehead, then my nose, then brought his lips down to meet mine. His tongue darted into my mouth and he pulled me tighter, the kiss intensifying as it set off sparks throughout my body, ricocheting through my stomach to stoke the fire building between my legs.

"Don't we have to go down to breakfast?" I whispered, catching his lips again, nipping at them.

"So we're a little late. Who's going to care?" His hand slid under my tank top, stroking upward to cup my breast. He fingered my bra, his fingers spiraling against the material as my nipples grew hard against his touch.

I let out a gasp, reaching down to stroke against the front of his pants. He hardened behind the leather, pressing against the supple material. And then, the heat of the rut exploded between us. As the wave of desire crashed over me, I stripped off my tank and shorts. Herne shed his pants and shirt, and we dove onto the bed. Leisurely foreplay went out the window as he shoved me back, holding my arms against the bed.

"I need you." His voice was throaty, low with lust.

I let out a grunt, freeing my arms. As I dragged him between my legs, his chest pressed against my naked breasts. He drove himself into me, his shaft spreading me wide as he filled every inch of my waiting pussy. The hunger grew more demanding.

"Ride me, damn it." I wanted him in every

corner, every niche I had. I wanted him so deep within me that nothing would separate us. "*Fuck me, hard.*"

And he did.

Hard and quick, his breath was heavy in my ear as he rode me on the crest of our passion. I clasped his ass with my hands, holding him firm as his thrusts came harder, making me so wet that all I could focus on was his presence inside of me.

I was crying then, and I didn't know why. But with the tears came release, hard and quick, and then once again. As the orgasms rippled through me, Herne dropped his head back, letting out a shout as he came. He thrust again, then once more, before he collapsed on my chest.

We lay there in a sweaty embrace for a moment until he gently rolled to the side.

"I needed you." He paused, looking down at me, then kissed me gently. "Are you good?"

I nodded. Something had shifted with our fucking. We hadn't been making love, it had been too carnal and driven for that, but it had bound us together with a magic that I couldn't even explain to myself.

"I'm good." I slowly pushed myself up to a sitting position, wondering if we should talk about it. Herne was looking at me differently, but it was a good look. A loving look. A look that told me he truly saw who I was and he accepted everything he saw.

Finally, I whispered, "We're holding up breakfast." Whatever we had to say would come in its own time. For now, we had our passion. And we had each other.

With a laugh, he swatted my ass as I crawled out of bed. We took a quick shower to rinse off the sweat, then dressed and headed down to the dining room. I felt as though I was glowing.

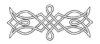

EVERYBODY WAS THERE, but conspicuously avoided asking why we were late, although Talia snorted as we took our chairs. There was a brunch buffet set out, and I loaded my plate with eggs and bacon, toast and fruit, and sausage. When we were all set with drinks and food, we went over what had happened with the others, letting Herne take the lead.

"My father said that we can tell Rhiannon we caught the killer, but we can't say anything about who he is, or what happened with him. But I hope she'll be comforted to know that he's been taken into custody."

"What about the Douglas woman? She was hoping for some closure," I said, waving a piece of bacon at him.

Herne laughed. "Eat that or I'll take it away from you. Yes, we can tell her the same thing. But that's all. As to Astrana, that's a trickier subject. We're not to say a word. Morgana is going to take care of cleanup on that."

"You mean we don't even mention it when we talk to Rhiannon?" I wondered how we could avoid that subject, but Herne simply nodded.

"Yes, that's what I mean. *Or anybody else.* This case remains under lock and key for now."

"What about Blackthorn?" Yutani asked. "We just...leave him be?"

Herne bit into a muffin, chewing silently for a moment. "Yeah. But we're on his radar now. *Ember's* definitely on his radar. In the way of the Ante-Fae, we owe him a favor. He allowed us to go after his son without disputing it, so we're in his debt. And being in debt to one of the Ante-Fae? Never a good thing."

"On that note, Angel and I found several interesting things when we went through Straff's hideout," Talia said. "One was a tunnel in the basement that leads out to the shore—right to where they found the bodies." She shrugged. "So now we know more about how he was operating."

"That explains what the elementals showed me about how he got the bodies down to the water. What else did you find?"

Talia glanced around the room to make certain no one was eavesdropping, then pulled out a small satin bag. She set it on the table and opened it. Out spilled a gorgeous amethyst necklace, a ruby ring, and several other assorted jewels.

"These aren't made by any human jeweler," Herne said after a glance.

Talia nodded. "Right. They're old—very old, and they reek with magic. We'll have to analyze them to figure out just what they are, so don't go trying them on. Otherwise, we didn't find much except for one major find. Down in the basement we found a trapdoor that leads to a bone pit. I'm pretty sure that the remains are those of a number of the missing victims. The bones looked gnawed on. Why Straff ate some of them and just dumped some of the bodies, I don't know, but it was gruesome."

Angel shuddered, nodding. "Even though the bones were old and nearly picked clean, I don't think I'll forget about it anytime soon."

"A team from my father's realm will be here shortly. They'll make certain that everything telling vanishes. There won't be anything left to tip off anybody," Herne said. "We can't chance this getting out to the human population. Father says that the Oracle told him in no uncertain terms to keep it all squashed. Danu herself contacted him this morning."

"Oracle?" Angel asked.

Herne shook his head. "It's too early to talk about the nature of the Oracle. Leave it to say, when she speaks, we listen."

"You were up bright and early," I said to him.

"Oh, I haven't slept at all. I'm afraid this case isn't over yet. But for now, it will be marked closed and we can lay it to rest, just like Jona. But don't forget what's happened here. I have no doubt we'll be revisiting a few of the particulars later on, once Cernunnos gives us the go-ahead."

I wondered what else was bubbling under the surface, but knew better than to ask. I had learned my lesson. When the gods were ready to talk, they would. Until then? Leave well enough alone.

Herne gathered up the jewels and tucked them away as we finished our breakfast in silence.

LATE THAT EVENING, we met Rhiannon, Marilyn, and Ryan down by the beach. Rhiannon had brought a bouquet of white lilies, and she set them against the boulder where Jona's body had been discovered. Marilyn watched silently, then carried Ryan down to the edge of the water and began stripping the both of them.

"What are you doing?" Angel asked.

"I'm going home. It's time. Now that Jona's murderer has been caught, I just...I'm ready to let go of this place. I'm taking Ryan and leaving." She turned to the rest of us. "Thank you. I'd like to know who killed him, but just knowing that he's been caught is enough for me."

"Where will you go?" Herne asked.

She gazed out at the water, smiling. "We'll swim up through the sound, then out into the open water. I contacted my family. There will be an escort waiting for us at the edge where the ocean pours into the straits."

Rhiannon was crying. "I don't want you to go."

"I know, but Ryan needs to meet his family. I want him to know the ocean, like Jona and I knew it. I want him to listen to the waves and feel them in the very marrow of his bones. I'm not happy on land. I came here because Jona wanted to. Now that he's gone, I'm ready to go home."

Rhiannon knelt beside Ryan and gathered him in her arms. "Don't you forget me. Don't ever for-

get Auntie Rhiannon." The little boy looked perplexed but gave her a long hug.

I walked down to the water's edge and knelt,
dangling my hand into the waves that crested on
the shore. I closed my eyes and immediately found
myself staring at the same elemental I had seen
before. I summoned up an image of Marilyn and
Ryan, then shrouded them in a cloak of protective energy, sending a question to the elemental. It
caught my meaning and agreed. The water spirits
would guard them on their journey.

Herne was standing a little ways up the shore,
staring at the forest behind him. Viktor had carried Yutani down the trail, carefully, and they were
sitting on one of the driftwood logs, talking quietly.
Angel moved over to me, taking my arm as she
leaned against my shoulder.

"I can't help but think how much I would miss
if I didn't have this job," she said. After a pause,
she added, "I feel sorry for Rhiannon. She lost the
love of her life, twice. First to Marilyn and then to
Straff. Now, she's losing the last bit of him. When
Marilyn leaves with Ryan, Jona will be gone forever."

"Jona's already gone," I said. "Ryan isn't his father. Children may carry the genes of their ancestors, but they aren't the same. Not always."

"True." Angel gave me a brief hug. "You're a
good testament to that."

"I certainly hope so."

"So, what about *your* grandparents?" She shaded her eyes, watching as Marilyn began to wade
into the water, holding her son. "What are you go-

ing to do about them?"

The hippocampus sat her child down into the water, and whispered something to him. As we watched, the boy slowly transformed into a small white foal and dove under the water. Marilyn changed shape, turning into a glorious white horse. Her mane fluttered in the breeze. Under the waning sunset, she forged her way into the water, right behind Ryan. The waves rose up around them and, with a sudden kick, Marilyn galloped into the cresting foam, diving below the surface. A flash of white fins appeared in place of her back feet, and she vanished below the waves. Then, they were gone. As Rhiannon broke into tears, Talia walked her back to one of the driftwood logs and sat with her, talking in soothing tones.

I turned back to Angel. Rhiannon was shedding her past, even as Marilyn was headed toward her future. I thought about closure and the peace that it brought. Maybe it was time to face *my* past. Maybe I had to get to know it before I could ever hope to leave it behind.

"I'll call them. I'll see what they have to say." But I didn't want to think about my grandparents right now. Instead, I inhaled a long breath filled with the scents of brine and seaweed and the salt sea air. "Let's hope the inspector has good news for us when we get back."

"He does." Angel grinned. "I got an email from him this morning. He found a few things that need to be addressed, but the house checks out."

And just like that, we had a new home.

HERNE AND I sat on one of the driftwood logs, staring at the water. We had stayed behind while the others went back to the hotel to pack. We were all ready to go home.

"Ember, I have something to say to you, and I don't want you to answer me until you've thought about it." He sounded so serious that I was worried.

"What is it?"

"I'm going to turn into my stag form and let you ride me back."

I snorted. "Is that all? Fine."

"No, twit-brain." He playfully bopped me on the nose. "It's just that... I don't make a lot of hasty decisions. I'd rather think things through. But here's the thing." Taking hold of my hands, he stared down into my eyes. "I think I'm falling in love with you."

Before I could say a word, he jumped up and transformed into his stag form. As he knelt for me to get on his back, I stared at him, trying to decide what to say.

But then I decided that words could wait. Because in my heart, I could tell that the fears of getting closer and of letting down my guard were melting. And it was because of Herne. And while he didn't expect me to make a snap decision, I realized I had already decided.

Feeling oddly at peace, I climbed aboard the silver stag and hung on as we began to lope back through the forest.

If you enjoyed this book and haven't read the first, check out THE SILVER STAG for the beginning of Ember's story. Preorder Book 3—IRON BONES—now! And more to come after that.

Meanwhile, I invite you to visit Fury's world. Bound to Hecate, Fury is a minor goddess, taking care of the Abominations who come off the World Tree. The first story arc of the Fury Unbound Series is complete with: FURY RISING, FURY'S MAGIC, FURY AWAKENED, and FURY CALLING. There will be more Fury books coming.

If you prefer a lighter-hearted paranormal romance, meet the wild and magical residents of Bedlam in my Bewitching Bedlam Series. Fun-loving witch Maddy Gallowglass, her smoking-hot vampire lover Aegis, and their crazed cjinn Bubba (part djinn, all cat) rock it out in Bedlam, a magical town on a magical island. BLOOD MUSIC, BEWITCHING BEDLAM, MAUDLIN'S MAYHEM, SIREN'S SONG, WITCHES WILD, BLOOD VENGEANCE and TIGER TAILS are available. And more are on the way!

If you like cozies with an edge, try my Chintz 'n China paranormal mysteries. The series is complete with: GHOST OF A CHANCE, LEGEND OF THE JADE DRAGON, MURDER UNDER A MYSTIC MOON, A HARVEST OF BONES, ONE HEX OF A WEDDING, and a wrap-up novella: HOLIDAY SPIRITS.

The newest Otherworld book—HARVEST SONG—is available now, and the next, BLOOD BONDS, will be available in May 2019.

For all of my work, both published and upcoming releases, see the Bibliography at the end of this book, or check out my website at Galenorn.com and be sure and sign up for my newsletter to receive news about all my new releases.

Cast of Characters

The Wild Hunt:

Ember Kearney: Caught between the world of Light and Dark Fae, and pledged to Morgana, goddess of the Fae and the Sea, Ember Kearney was born with the mark of the Silver Stag. Rejected by both her bloodlines, she now works for the Wild Hunt as an investigator.

Herne the Hunter: Herne is the son of the Lord of the Hunt, Cernunnos, and Morgana, goddess of the Fae and the Sea. A demigod—given his mother's mortal beginnings—he's a lusty, protective god and one hell of a good boss. Owner of the Wild Hunt Agency, he helps keep the squabbles between the world of Light and Dark Fae from spilling over into the mortal realms.

Angel Jackson: Ember's best friend, a human empath, Angel is the newest member of the Wild Hunt. A whiz in both the office and the kitchen, and loyal to the core, Angel is an integral part of Ember's life, and a vital member of the team.

Viktor: Viktor is half-ogre, half-human. Rejected by his father's people (the ogres), he came to work for Herne some decades back.

Yutani: A coyote shifter who is dogged by the Great Coyote, Yutani was driven out of his village over two hundred years before. He walks in the shadow of the trickster, and is the IT specialist for the company.

Talia: A harpy who long ago lost her powers, Talia is a top-notch researcher for the agency, and a longtime friend of Herne's.

DJ Jackson: Angel's little half-brother, DJ is half Wulfine—wolf shifter. He now lives with a foster family for his own protection.

The Gods:

Cernunnos: Lord of the Hunt, god of the Forest and King Stag of the Woods. Together with Morgana, Cernunnos originated the Wild Hunt and negotiated the covenant treaty with both the Light and the Dark Fae. Herne's father.

Morgana: Goddess of the Fae and the Sea, she was originally not divine, but Cernunnos elevated her to deityhood. She agreed to watch over the Fae who did not return across the Great Sea. Torn by her loyalty to her people, and her loyalty to Cernunnos, she at times finds herself conflicted about the Wild Hunt. Herne's mother. The daughter of Merlin.

Danu: Mother of the Pantheon. Leader of the Tuatha de Dannan.

The Fae Courts:

Navane: The court of the Light Fae, both across the Great Sea and on the east side of Seattle, the latter ruled by Névé.

TirNaNog: The court of the Dark Fae, both across the Great Sea and on the east side of Seattle, the latter ruled by Saílle.

The Ante-Fae:

Creatures predating the Fae. The wellspring from which all Fae descended. Unique beings who rule their own realms. All Ante-Fae are dangerous, but some are more deadly than others.

Blackthorn, the King of Thorns: Ruler of the blackthorn trees and all thorn-bearing plants. Cunning and wily, he feeds on pain and desire.

Straff: Blackthorn's son, who suffers from a wasting disease requiring him to feed off others' life energies and blood.

Playlist

I often write to music, and OAK & THORNS was no exception. Here's the playlist I used for this book. I consider two songs to be 'theme songs' for Oak & Thorns: *King in the Tree* by Shriekback, and *Hymn to Herne*, by S.J. Tucker.

Alice in Chains: Man in the Box; Sunshine
AWOLNATION: Sail
Band of Skulls: I Know What I Am
The Black Angels: The Return; Evil Things Don't Play with Guns; Holland; Love Me Forever; Always Maybe; Black Isn't Black; Young Men Dead; The First Vietnamese War; Manipulation; The Sniper
Black Mountain: Queens Will Play
Black Rebel Motorcycle Club: Feel It Now
Boom! Bap! Pow!: Suit
Broken Bells: The Ghost Inside
Camouflage Nights: (It Could Be) Love
Cobra Verde: Play with Fire
Colin Foulke: Emergence, Caravella
Corvus Corax: Filii Neidhardi; Ballade de Mercy
Crazy Town: Butterfly
Damh the Bard: Obsession; Cloak of Feathers; The Wicker Man; Spirit of Albion
David & Steve Gordon: Shaman's Drum Dance
Death Cab For Cutie: I Will Possess Your Heart
Donovan: Sunshine Superman; Season of the

Witch

Eastern Sun: Beautiful Being (Original Edit)

Everlast: Black Jesus; I Can't Move; What It's Like

Fatboy Slim: Praise You

FC Kahuna: Hayling

The Feeling: Sewn

Fluke: Absurd

Foster The People: Pumped Up Kicks

Garbage: Queer; #1 Crush; Push It; I Think I'm Paranoid

Gary Numan: Ghost Nation; My Name Is Ruin; Broken; I Am Dust; Here in the Black; Love Hurt Bleed; Petals; Cars (Remix)

Gorillaz: Kids with Guns; Hongkongaton; Rockit; Clint Eastwood; Dare

The Gospel Whiskey Runners: Muddy Waters

Gypsy Soul: Who

In Strict Confidence: Forbidden Fruit; Silver Bullets; Snow White; Tiefer

Julian Cope: Charlotte Anne

Justin Timberlake: SexyBack

The Kills: Future Starts Slow; Nail in My Coffin; DNA; You Don't Own the Road; Sour Cherry; No Wow; Dead Road 7

Korn: Freak on a Leash

Lorde: Yellow Flicker Beat; Royals

Low with Tom and Andy: Half Light

Marilyn Manson: Personal Jesus; Tainted Love

Mark Lanegan: The Gravedigger's Song; Riot in My House; Phantasmagoria Blues; Wedding Dress; Methamphetamine Blues

Matt Corby: Breathe

MIA: Bad Girls

Motherdrum: Big Stomp

Nirvana: You Know You're Right; Come as You Are; Lake of Fire; Lithium; Heart Shaped Box

Orgy: Social Enemies; Blue Monday

A Pale Horse Named Death: meet the wolf

Pearl Jam: Even Flow; Jeremy

People in Planes: Vampire

Puddle of Mudd: Famous; Psycho

Rob Zombie: Living Dead Girl; Never Gonna Stop

Roisin Murphy: Ramalama (Bang Bang)

S. J. Tucker: Hymn to Herne

Scorpions: The Zoo

Screaming Trees: Where the Twain Shall Meet; Dime Western

Shriekback: The Shining Path; Underwaterboys; This Big Hush; Now These Days Are Gone; The King in the Tree

Tamaryn: While You're Sleeping, I'm Dreaming; Violet's in a Pool

Toadies: Possum Kingdom

Tom Petty: Mary Jane's Last Dance

Wendy Rule: Let the Wind Blow

Wild Cherry: Play that Funky Music

Zero 7: In the Waiting Line

Biography

New York Times, Publishers Weekly, and *USA Today* bestselling author Yasmine Galenorn writes urban fantasy and paranormal romance, and is the author of over sixty books, including the Wild Hunt Series, the Fury Unbound Series, the Bewitching Bedlam Series, and the Otherworld Series, among others. She's also written nonfiction metaphysical books. She is the 2011 Career Achievement Award Winner in Urban Fantasy, given by RT Magazine. Yasmine has been in the Craft since 1980, is a shamanic witch and High Priestess. She describes her life as a blend of teacups and tattoos. She lives in Kirkland, WA, with her husband Samwise and their cats. Yasmine can be reached via her website at Galenorn.com.

Indie Releases Currently Available:

Wild Hunt Series:
The Silver Stag
Oak & Thorns
Iron Bones

Bewitching Bedlam Series:
Bewitching Bedlam
Maudlin's Mayhem
Siren's Song
Witches Wild
Blood Music
Blood Vengeance

Tiger Tails

Fury Unbound Series:
Fury Rising
Fury's Magic
Fury Awakened
Fury Calling

Indigo Court Series:
Night Myst
Night Veil
Night Seeker
Night Vision
Night's End
Night Shivers

Otherworld Series:
Moon Shimmers
Harvest Song
Earthbound
Knight Magic
Otherworld Tales: Volume One
Tales From Otherworld: Collection One
Men of Otherworld: Collection One
Men of Otherworld: Collection Two
Moon Swept: Otherworld Tales of First Love
For the rest of the Otherworld Series, see Website

Chintz 'n China Series:
Ghost of a Chance
Legend of the Jade Dragon
Murder Under a Mystic Moon
A Harvest of Bones
One Hex of a Wedding

Holiday Spirits

Bath and Body Series (originally under the name India Ink):
Scent to Her Grave
A Blush With Death
Glossed and Found

Misc. Short Stories/Anthologies:
Mist and Shadows: Short Tales From Dark Haunts
Once Upon a Kiss (short story: Princess Charming)
Silver Belles (short story: The Longest Night)
Once Upon a Curse (short story: Bones)

Magickal Nonfiction:
Embracing the Moon
Tarot Journeys

For all other series, as well as upcoming work, see Galenorn.com

71575985R00234

Made in the
USA
Middletown, DE